# Praise for
# Robin Talley

'The main characters are terrific in what is **a moving YA novel**. And an important one.' – *The Telegraph*

'This is so **thought-provoking** it almost hurts to read it, yet every word is needed, is necessary and consequently this is a novel that **lingers long after you've finished it**' – *Lovereading*

'This is an **emotional and compelling** read that I did not want to put down. It is [...]**beautifully written** and the tension just simmers on the pages.' – *Bookbabblers*

'This book **packs a very powerful punch**' – *Historical Novel Society*

'With great characterisation, tough issues covered, and a plot which had me guessing right up until the last pages, this is a must-read. **Massively recommended!**' – *The Bookbag*

'This **exceptional novel** of first love and sexual awakenings is set against a backdrop of shocking racism and prejudice. It is **incredibly well written** as the tense, riveting story seamlessly combines fiction with historical fact.' – *Booktrust*

'Every now and then a Young Adult book comes along that **I want to push into every readers hands both young and old** and *Lies We Tell Ourselves* is that book for 2014' – *Jess Hearts Books*

'Talley has mixed two controversial topics together to create a firecracker of a story' – *Cheryl M-M's Book Blog*

**\*A Goodreads Choice Awards semi-finalist 2014\***

*Also by Robin Talley*
LIES WE TELL OURSELVES

# WHAT WE LEFT BEHIND

## ROBIN TALLEY

MIRA Ink is a registered trademark of Harlequin Enterprises Limited, used under licence.

Published in Great Britain 2015
by MIRA Ink, an imprint of Harlequin (UK) Limited,
Eton House, 18-24 Paradise Road,
Richmond, Surrey, TW9 1SR

*What We Left Behind* © 2015 Robin Talley

ISBN: 978-1-848-45391-3
eISBN: 978-1-474-03099-1
47-1015

Harlequin (UK) Limited's policy is to use papers that are natural, renewable and recyclable products and made from wood grown in sustainable forests. The logging and manufacturing processes conform to the legal environmental regulations of the country of origin.

Printed and bound by
CPI Group (UK) Ltd, Croydon, CR0 4YY

**Robin Talley** grew up in Roanoke, Virginia, writing terrible teen poetry and riding a desegregation bus to the school across town. A Lambda Literary Fellow, Robin lives in Washington, D.C., with her fiancée, plus an antisocial cat and a goofy dog. When Robin's not writing, she's often planning communication strategies at organisations fighting for equal rights and social justice. You can find her on the web at www.robintalley.com or on Twitter @robin_talley

# BEFORE

## TONI

Even before I saw her, it was the best night of my life.

It was Homecoming. I was about to walk into a ballroom full of people. A girl in a flouncy dress was clinging to my elbow, her photo-ready smile firmly in place, her left hand already raised in a preparatory wave.

I didn't smile with her. I didn't know if I could even remember how to smile.

I was happy, yeah—I was so, so, *so* happy that night—but I was terrified, too. Any second now I was bound to throw up.

Everyone in that ballroom would be looking at us. Everyone in there would be looking at *me*.

I'd known them all since we were kids. To them, I was Toni Fasseau, substantively unchanged since kindergarten. Short red hair and black-rimmed glasses. Pompous vocabulary and a pompous grade point average to match. And most of all, gay. Extremely, incredibly gay.

Tonight, though, when they looked at me, they'd see something else. This morning, a story had come out that had temporarily made me the most famous student at Martha Jefferson Academy for Young Women in Washington, DC. It would probably only last until the next senator's daughter got caught shoplifting at Neiman Marcus, but still.

It took all my concentration just to breathe as I walked through the ballroom doors. My date, Renee, beamed out at the rapt crowd, still hanging on my arm.

For her, the attention was fun. For her, tonight was nothing.

For me, tonight was everything.

It was too much. My stomach clenched, unclenched and clenched again as my brain whirred with a thousand thoughts at once.

I'd won. I'd actually *won*.

We turned the corner and saw the crowd. A few hundred of our classmates and their dates, dressed up in their finest finery.

All I saw was their eyes. Hundreds—no, thousands, it felt like thousands—of eyes fixed right on me.

I looked down, took a breath and tried to focus on something else.

My outfit. That was something.

Tonight was one of the first times in my entire life when

I actually liked what I was wearing. Spiffy new gray-and-black-striped pants, a bright blue shirt, shiny black shoes, black-and-white-striped suspenders, and a black top hat.

Granted, the top hat might've been a little much, but the suspenders rocked. Before we'd even made it through the parking lot, a dozen different people had come up to high-five me about the lawsuit. Half of them complimented me on the suspenders, too.

There's something about looking exactly how you want to look—finally—*finally*—that feels like you're being set free.

Like most of the girls at our school, my date, Renee, had gone the fancy-designer-dress-and-matching-high-heels route. She'd worn bright blue to match my shirt, which was awesome of her. She kept her arm tucked through mine and beamed at the crowd as we entered the cheesy hotel ballroom through the balloon arch we'd spent hours making at yesterday's Student Council meeting.

"You go, T!" a guy I vaguely knew yelled from across the room, giving me a thumbs-up. "Lesbians rock!"

I gave him a thumbs-up back. Even more heads had turned in my direction at the guy's shout. People grinned and held their punch cups out to me.

"You're popular tonight." Renee grinned and waved at the crowd again.

"Oh, that guy was just expressing appreciation for how my suspenders show off my übertoned physique," I said. Renee laughed and fake-punched me in the arm. I made a face like it hurt, and she laughed again. Renee was just a friend, being straight and all, but I was so, so glad to have her there with me that night.

My hands shook as I exchanged smiles and nods and more high fives. I made a big show of escorting Renee around the room, holding her elbow and using my free hand to make swooping motions with my arms like a guy in an old movie might do. That made her laugh.

I laughed, too. I couldn't believe tonight was really happening.

I never thought I'd win. For so long it had seemed impossible. Then, last night, the school administration had finally backed down.

For years, I'd begged. I'd written strongly worded letters that were just as strongly ignored. I'd given impassioned speeches to my classmates. I'd gone to administration meetings and made presentations full of graphs and statistics and quotes from important court cases.

It hadn't mattered what I said. I spoke at meeting after meeting, but at each one, the administrators just thumbed their phones until I'd stopped talking.

Then last week our school's Gay-Straight Alliance decided that since we'd already tried everything else, we might as well go the old-fashioned route and have a rally. We made posters and sent out an invitation telling people to gather on the front lawn of the main building after eighth-period bell. We figured we might get a dozen people there.

Instead, almost the whole school showed up.

I couldn't believe it. I didn't think anyone besides my closest friends even cared, much less agreed with me, but those speeches I'd been making had paid off. The photos in the news reports that day showed hundreds of my classmates waving homemade posters and burning old school uniforms with the gleaming glass Martha Jefferson Academy sign in the background. You could hear the chants on the video clips.

*"What do we want? Equal rights! When do we want them? Now!"*

*"Gay rights are everybody's rights!"*

And, embarrassingly, *"We stand with Toni! We stand with Toni!"*

The news coverage woke the school administration up. So did the letter my newly acquired ACLU lawyer sent over. She called me last night with the news. I could hear the glee in my lawyer's voice as she told me they'd caved.

Starting immediately, I was allowed to wear pants to school.

It was like being let out of prison. Except my prison was the entire world. I would never, ever have to wear that stupid blue-plaid uniform skirt again for the rest of my life.

The *Washington Post* called to ask me a bunch of questions. My lawyer drove me to two different TV stations to do incredibly scary on-camera interviews, and a profile of me went up on a website that was so big even my grandparents read it.

And now I was at the Homecoming dance, and everyone was looking at me.

I'd been buzzing and giddy for hours, but as I stared around at the crowd, another feeling climbed in. The one that comes when you know people are talking about you but you don't know what they're saying. It's like bugs crawling over your skin. It was nearly as bad as it was before, with my mother, when she... No. I wasn't going to think about my mother right now.

It was all too much. My mind was skittery, unsteady, unfocused. I couldn't deal with this rapidly growing ache.

I needed to get out.

The idea bloomed fast inside me. I'd feel so much better if I'd just turn around and walk off the polished wooden dance floor. Go hide in the parking lot until everyone found someone else to stare at.

Then I saw her.

She was dancing. Her head was thrown back with laughter. Her eyes sparkled. Her smile radiated light.

Everything else that had been spinning through my head floated away like air.

## GRETCHEN

The last thing I wanted to do was go to the Homecoming dance.

We'd only moved down to Maryland the day before. I hadn't even unpacked. I wouldn't start my new school until Monday, and going to a dance where I didn't know a single person was guaranteed to be the most awkward experience of my life, basically.

But my parents thought it was the best idea ever. They even found me a date. My dad knew someone who knew someone who had a nephew who went to the University of Maryland who wasn't doing anything that night. A recipe for true love if ever there was one.

So I opened my suitcases and tore through my boxes

until I found the green-and-silver lace dress I'd worn to my brother's wedding last year. It was a little tight, but I could dance in it. Mom lent me a pair of heels that pinched my toes so much I wound up leaving them in the car and going into the dance barefoot. At least my toenails were still polished from when my friends and I gave each other mani-pedis at my goodbye party back in Brooklyn.

The nephew, whose name was Mark or Mike or one of those, turned out to be a pretty nice guy. He told jokes that made me laugh. He poured my punch for me, which was cute. And since neither of us knew anyone else and we didn't have anything to talk about, after just a couple of minutes of us standing around self-consciously he asked if I wanted to dance. I said sure, because I will pretty much never turn down an opportunity to dance.

Mike/Matt/whatever wasn't a half-bad dancer, and soon we were in the middle of the floor, shaking our booties to the Top 40 the DJ was playing. (Were all DJs in Maryland this boring, I wondered?)

No one else was dancing that early, and before long a bunch of people had gathered in a circle to watch Matt/ Marc/etc. and me. So I hammed it up, because what else was I going to do? I started doing this Charleston-type thing I'd seen on TV once, where you bend at the waist and move your knees in and out. It was a blast. Mike/Matt tried to do it, too, but we could barely keep up with each other. He started laughing, then I started laughing, then he started going faster, then I started going faster, and then he grabbed me and swung me around into a dip. I was laughing so hard I nearly fell over.

I was upside-down when I saw the girl in the top hat and suspenders smiling at me.

The blood was rushing to my head. When Mark set me back on my feet, I could barely stay upright.

I smiled back anyway.

## TONI

I couldn't believe I'd never seen her before.

She must have gone to a different school. There was no way I could've just not noticed her.

She had long blond hair, almost to her waist, brilliant blue eyes and the warmest, widest smile I'd ever seen. Even upside down.

She was in the middle of the floor with a guy I'd never seen before, either, dancing like a maniac in a punk-looking green dress. Her feet were bare and her toenails were blue.

*No one* came barefoot to Homecoming. In fact, every other girl in the room—except me, of course—was wearing shoes that must've cost at least a hundred dollars. Maybe two hundred. Come to think of it, I had no idea how much shoes were supposed to cost.

"Who's that?" Renee asked. I shrugged, helpless.

The song ended. The blond girl climbed back up, clinging to the guy she was with.

Her face was mesmerizing even though she was probably the only girl in the room who wasn't wearing any makeup. Except me, again.

She was probably straight. God, though, she was beautiful.

It wasn't just her model-perfect face, either. It was her smile. It was the light in her eyes.

Lord. I'd thought all that love-at-first-sight stuff was supposed to be a load of bull.

I could feel my face turning pink. Crap. I'm pale with red hair, so my face will turn pink pretty much anytime the wind blows, but it's never stopped being embarrassing.

A new song came on.

"Want to dance?" Renee asked.

No one else was dancing except the blond goddess and her equally blond boyfriend. That was probably why Renee wanted to go out on the floor. She was never happier than when everyone was looking at her.

"Sure," I said.

I couldn't actually dance, but I figured Renee would take care of the hard parts. Plus, people at our school always gave extra leeway when they saw gay people being noticeably gay. They liked to coo about how cute we were.

Renee grabbed my hand and pulled me behind her onto the dance floor, leaving maybe ten feet of space between us and the blond couple. This close, I could get a better look at the girl's face. She and the guy were still dancing like maniacs, with the guy's back to us. The girl looked so happy. So light. For a second I thought I saw her look at me, but I probably imagined it.

Renee started doing this dance I'd seen some boy band do on TV once. I tried to imitate it. I felt ridiculous, but I laughed so it would seem like I *meant* to look ridiculous. Renee laughed, too. I took her hand and tried to spin her around, except I didn't know how to do that, so we both stumbled, but we kept laughing. I pumped my fist in the air in one of those crazy '70s dances, and Renee laughed again and started doing the same thing opposite me. The people watching us started to clap.

I could've sworn I saw the blond girl look at me again.

## GRETCHEN

Crap. I was being too obvious. The girl in the top hat saw me looking.

I mean, she had to be gay. She was dancing with a girl and she was wearing a top hat. Right?

Not like it mattered, since apparently she had a girlfriend.

Of course she did. I'd always had awful luck with girls. Besides, I could tell this one was popular, what with the way everyone kept smiling at her and reaching out to high-five her. The popular ones never stayed single for long.

Everyone was gathered in a circle around her and her girl-friend, clapping while they danced. Mitch/Max and I stopped to watch them, too. The girl in the blue dress was being kind of show-offy, but the girl in the top hat looked like she was having the time of her life, dancing like John Travolta in one of those old movies where he wears those gorgeous suits.

I couldn't help it. I wanted to dance like that, too.

I wanted to dance like that with *her.*

So I did.

I walked over to the two of them, tapped the girl with the top hat on the elbow and smiled at her.

She stopped dancing and blinked at me. Then she smiled, too.

Max/Miles/Mark figured out what I was doing, and he went with it. He strode right up to the girl in the blue dress, grabbed her hand and started twirling her. She laughed and followed him.

The girl in the top hat bit her lip, but she looked right at me as we started to dance. She was still smiling.

I kept my shoulders even and my smile in place so she couldn't tell, but I was pretty sure that was the most nervous I'd ever been in my whole life.

## TONI

I was pretty sure I was hallucinating.

Beautiful blond straight girls you've never seen before don't just come up to you at your Homecoming dance and start disco dancing with you out of nowhere. Not in normal life.

Of all the things that had happened to me lately, this was by far the strangest. And maybe the best.

It took me a second to realize the girl was mirroring me, doing the same weird feet-shuffling and arm-waving moves I was doing. I dialed it up and added in some swaying from side to side. The blond girl grinned and did the same.

The song changed again, but we didn't stop moving. It was the first time I'd ever had fun dancing.

The girl leaned in toward me. I have a thing about personal space, so normally that would've made me back away. But I didn't want to back away from this girl. She moved her lips toward my ear so I could hear her over the music. The proximity made my face flush again.

"I'm Gretchen," the girl said.

Gretchen. It was such a gorgeous name.

"Toni," I said.

Gretchen shook her head. She couldn't hear me. I had to lean in to her ear, too. I blushed to the roots of my hair.

"I'm Toni." I tried desperately to think of something to say that would make me sound cool. "Nice shoes."

Gretchen laughed. Her whole face opened up when she laughed. Dear lord.

My heart was racing. I did not have the mental or emotional capacity to deal with this.

Gretchen pushed a strand of hair behind her ear, looked down at me and smiled again.

Yeeeeaaahhhhh. I was going to be dead before the song was over.

## GRETCHEN

Did she like me?

It seemed like maybe she liked me.

That was a flirty thing to say, wasn't it? "Nice shoes," all casual like that? When I wasn't wearing shoes at all? Ha ha.

Also, she kept, like, staring at me. In a cute way, not a creepy way.

It didn't matter, though. She already had a girlfriend. The little ninny in the poufy blue dress. A pox on the poufy ninny, I wanted to say.

Still, I felt like touching Toni. Nothing dramatic, I mean. Maybe I could just accidentally brush up against her shoulder. Or maybe a piece of her spiky red hair would fall down into her eyes and I could brush it away. Yeah, that would be perfect.

I waited, but none of her hair fell down. It was packed

pretty solid with gel. Plus, most of her hair was tucked under her top hat.

Maybe the music would switch to a slow song, and I could put my hand on her waist. Or loop my arms around her neck. Yeah, that. The neck thing.

Except you weren't supposed to do that to someone else's girlfriend. Darn it all to heck.

Maybe Toni and I could be friends. I needed friends at my new school.

Except I didn't want to be friends with her. Not just friends anyway.

She leaned into my ear again. I got the same thrill I'd gotten when she'd done that before. "Are you new here?" she asked.

I nodded. "I'm from New York."

She opened her eyes wide, like she was impressed, and smiled. I smiled back.

She moved in again. "So. Would you rather run for president or go to Mars?"

I laughed. It was such a random question. "Mars."

"How come?"

"Because then at least you get to do something no one's ever done before. Go exploring. Learn new things. Being president just means you have to try to fix a bunch of stuff no one's been able to figure out how to fix yet."

I had to lean close to her for a long time to say all that. By the time I pulled back, I was blushing as hard as she was.

"What about you?" I asked.

"President," she said. "Just because no one's figured out how to fix it yet doesn't mean no one ever can."

I nodded. If anyone could fix the world's problems, it just might be this girl with the red hair and the top hat.

I smiled at her.

The music switched to a slow song.

## TONI

I put my hand on her waist.

So she was probably straight. Whatever. Screw it. She could take my hand off her waist if she wanted to.

She didn't take my hand off her waist.

## GRETCHEN

My heart was pounding so fast.

I had exchanged, like, three sentences with this girl, but somehow, I felt like I'd known her forever.

My hands were trembling, but I linked them behind her neck and stepped in closer. I was a couple of inches taller, so I looked down into her eyes and smiled again.

God, she had the most amazing eyes.

## TONI

I wanted to ask Gretchen something else. I wanted to know everything there was to know about her.

It was just—

There was something about the way she was looking at me.

I love to talk. I talk constantly. When you're talking, people always know you're there.

But I didn't have any words just then.

Not with her looking at me like that. Like she could see all the way inside me.

## GRETCHEN

I leaned in to her ear again, even though we were close enough now that I didn't need to. I swallowed my nervousness and asked, "Is that your girlfriend in the blue dress?"

Toni didn't pull back. She didn't answer, either. For an anxious second I thought she hadn't heard me.

Finally she shook her head. "Just a friend."

## TONI

"Oh," Gretchen said.

She was blushing.

God, she was adorable.

I nodded toward the blond guy who was now leading Renee around the room in a dramatic-looking tango. Everyone was watching them. Which meant they weren't looking at Gretchen and me anymore. "What about you? What's up with that guy?"

"Oh, right." Gretchen glanced over, then turned back to me with a cute little quirk in her eyebrow. "I don't know. My dad's friend knows him or something? He's all right. Not for me, though."

She scrunched up her face adorably. God, everything this girl did was adorable.

"Not for you 'cause...why?" I asked.

She blushed again.

I seriously could not deal with how this felt.

Oh, my lord.

I was really, truly, genuinely about to melt into a puddle of utter uselessness.

Oh, my *lord*.

## GRETCHEN

I was still nervous.

So nervous I didn't know how I was even going to stay standing, let alone move.

So nervous I could hear my heart beating in my ears. Louder than the music. Louder than the people talking and clapping.

So nervous it was like I was floating outside my body, watching this whole thing play out from the ceiling of the hotel ballroom, somewhere near that carefully crafted balloon arch.

I was so nervous I could barely breathe.

But I kissed her anyway.

## TONI

I melted.

1

## TONI

I still melt every time I kiss Gretchen, but it's different now.

That first night, back at a high school dance, we barely even knew each other's name. Now we're about to leave for college, and we know each other inside and out.

Before I met Gretchen, I wondered if I'd ever even have a real girlfriend. It seemed impossible, once. I'd gone out with other girls, sure, but nothing had ever lasted. I didn't think I'd actually find anyone willing to put up with me for more than a month or two.

But I still daydreamed. I'd sit there in health class, my eyes soft-focused on the whiteboard while I pictured some pretty girl and me skipping hand in hand through daisy-strewn meadows, gazing into each other's eyes, laughing at our little inside jokes and never, ever getting tired of each other. I used to think no real relationship could be as exciting as my health-class fantasy.

What blew me away was that the reality turned out to be so much more. I never imagined that being one half of a whole could make you feel more whole all by yourself. I never dreamed I'd want to tell someone all my secrets and know their secrets, too.

But now everything's changing. I don't know what our lives are going to be like after tomorrow, but at least I know that no matter what happens next, we'll always have each other.

Knowing I can count on that is the only thing holding me in one piece while I count down our last few hours together. I'm trying to act like it's not a big deal, but as the minutes tick by it's getting harder and harder to pretend.

"Pass me the shampoo?" Gretchen asks. I find the Target bag with four bottles of Sun-Kissed Shiny Grapefruit and hand it over.

"You know, they do have stores in Boston," I say as Gretchen loads the bag into a suitcase. I'm sitting in Gretchen's desk chair, one of the only surfaces in the room that's not covered in open boxes, suitcases and laundry baskets. "You don't have to turn your dorm room into your own personal CVS."

"You are *so* funny, T." Gretchen kisses me on the cheek and grabs a stack of socks from the dresser. "You must teach me your ways. How much shampoo are *you* going to pack?"

"I already packed, but I'm not bringing any shampoo. I'll get some when I'm up there. How are you going to take all these suitcases on the plane anyway? Are your parents going to pretend your bags are theirs or something?"

Gretchen laughs. "Do you think I should bring all my shoes or just some of them? I can probably leave my cowboy boots here, right? They'll take up so much space."

I eye Gretchen's closet door, still covered in photos from two years' worth of debate tournaments. "You only own, like, two pairs of shoes. I think you should bring them all unless you want to go around barefoot."

Gretchen sighs fake-dramatically. "I own more than two pairs of shoes."

"Well, yeah, I guess there's three if you count your sneakers *and* your Birkenstocks."

Gretchen laughs again, even though it's the oldest joke there is. For the last two years of high school Gretchen wore Birks every day unless it was raining or snowing. On those days, the sneakers came out. Gretchen always looked totally out of place in hallways filled with girls in designer ballet flats or chic dress code–friendly one-inch heels.

Not that any of it ever stopped Gretchen from becoming absurdly popular. That part was pretty much guaranteed from the first fateful Homecoming dance on. When you make that much of a stir before it's even your first day of school, you're going to amass a sizeable crew of devotees.

Which I guess meant I wound up being kind of popular, too. Walking down the hall holding hands with Gretchen every day was enough to make anyone feel like a celebrity. Winning that fight with the school administration junior year didn't hurt, either. The blue plaid pants I finally got to wear looked ridiculous, like old-man golf pants, but it was such a relief to be out of those stupid skirts I'd been wearing since kindergarten.

Every time I walked down the hall wearing my old-man golf pants with my gorgeous girlfriend by my side—every single day felt like that night at the dance. Ever since Gretchen came here, it felt like I could finally be—well—me.

Now it's all over. High school. Everything about the life I've had here. The bad parts and the good.

I watch Gretchen pack, dressed in an old pair of cutoff shorts and a tank top, blond hair hanging loose and messy, perpetual smile firmly in place.

Gretchen is definitely one of the good parts. Gretchen's *the* good part.

I can't keep pretending.

"I'm going to miss you." I don't mean to say it. The truth just sort of spills out of me. "So much."

Gretchen turns around, face falling. Right away I feel bad. I hate making Gretchen look like that.

It's been happening more and more lately. All summer we've been making plans, looking up our roommates online and studying the Boston T map and talking about what it's going to be like to be on our own, but over the past week or so, Gretchen's gotten a lot quieter. I think it's only just started hitting home for both of us how big a change this is going to be.

"I mean," I go on, trying to act nonchalant, "I know we aren't going to be that far apart in the geographical sense, but it just feels like I *need* to see you every day, you know? This

is going to be so hard. I actually kind of can't deal when I
think about how hard it's going to be."

"I know." Gretchen puts down the socks and draws me
into a hug. "I'm so sorry."

"Don't be sorry." I squeeze tighter. I love the way Gretchen
feels in my arms.

I can't wait any longer.

"Hey," I say, still trying to make my voice sound breezy.
"You know how I snuck off at Target while you were in the
toothpaste aisle?"

"Yeah." Gretchen pulls back. "I figured you were buying
something embarrassing. I saw you checking out that box
set of *Pretty Little Liars*."

"Well, yeah. You know I always had that thing for Emily.
That wasn't why I snuck off, though."

"So why did you?"

Gretchen's leaning against the hand-me-down dresser, the
sad expression from before replaced by the smile we both
get whenever we play this game. The I-have-a-secret-and-
I-can't-wait-to-tell-you game.

"Close your eyes," I order.

Gretchen obeys.

"Now promise not to laugh," I say.

"T! You know I can't promise that. I always laugh, even
when it's not funny. I'm already laughing now just standing here!"

"Okay, but you have to promise not to laugh with malicious intent."

"I swear I won't laugh with malicious intent! Can I please
open my eyes?"

I stand up and pull the tiny bag out of my pocket. "Okay."

Eyes open, Gretchen looks inside the bag, then claps and laughs. "This is perfect! You really got this while I was picking out my Aquafresh?"

"Yep." I grin and pull out another bag. When Gretchen gets happy like this, especially when it's because of something I did, I always turn into a giant, embarrassing, grinning goof. "I got one for me, too."

"Aww. You are such a sap! I love it!" Gretchen hugs me again. "That was such a fantastic night, remember?"

"Yeah, I remember."

The Target has a kiosk where you can get jewelry engraved. I got us each a silver disk on a leather cord. Gretchen's disk has a top hat in the center. Mine has a bare footprint.

When we leave tomorrow, Gretchen and I will be apart for the first time. We'll be in the same city, but at different schools—Gretchen at Boston University, me at Harvard. We'll only be able to see each other on weekends. Maybe the occasional weekday if we're up for trekking across the city.

I wanted us to have something solid we could look at. Something to hold in our hands when we couldn't hold each other. Something to remind us both of where we started out. Not that there's any way we could forget.

"This is so insanely sweet," Gretchen says. "I should've gotten you a present, too."

"No, you shouldn't. Don't be crazy. It only occurred to me when I saw the kiosk."

"Toni. Tell the truth."

"Okay, I've been thinking about it for months." We both

laugh. "If you want, you can always pay my mom back for the twelve ninety-five I put on the credit card."

"Your mom can afford it." We laugh again, and Gretchen's arms link behind my neck. I'm still freaked about tomorrow, but touching Gretchen helps. Touching Gretchen always helps.

"Thank you," Gretchen says. "Really."

"You're welcome, really."

We kiss.

Have you ever wanted to breathe someone in until they become part of you and never let them go? That's what kissing Gretchen is like.

Maybe that's how it is for everyone when they kiss someone they really love. I don't know.

We break away and Gretchen goes over to the closet, where most of the clothes are still hanging.

"Hey, so, there was something I wanted to talk to you about," Gretchen says, grabbing a bunch of pants still on their hangers and tossing them into an open suitcase. I wince at the thought of the wrinkles. "It's kind of, um, a thing."

"What's up?" I sit on the edge of the bed to watch Gretchen pack.

"Well, it's just that—"

Gretchen's phone buzzes. That's the third time in the past five minutes.

"Who keeps texting you?" I ask.

"Uh." Gretchen glances down at the screen. "Well. If I tell you something, will you promise not to get mad?"

I laugh. "You know that's never a good way to start, babe."

Gretchen puts on a mock-innocent expression I've seen many times before. There's no way not to smile at it.

"It's *possible*," Gretchen says, "that I told Chris and Audrey they could come over and help us pack tonight."

"Why?" I can hear the whine in my voice. It's our last night together.

"They were asking when they could say goodbye," Gretchen tells me. "This was the last chance. I said they can't stay long. Chris tried to make a stink about it, but I told him he'd just have to deal."

I roll my eyes, but I can't really complain. Chris is my best friend, and Audrey is my little sister. I'll see Gretchen every week once we leave for school, but I'm not going to see Chris or Audrey until Thanksgiving. If I come home for Thanksgiving.

"It'll be fun," Gretchen says. "We can hang out on our own after. Don't worry."

I cross the room, loop my arms around Gretchen's waist and kiss the back of Gretchen's neck, provoking a round of giggles.

"I never worry about anything when you're around," I say. "How long until they get here?"

"Half an hour, maybe?"

We both smile. Then we start making out.

It'll be a while before we get another chance, after all. At least a week. The last time I went a week without seeing Gretchen was when my family went to a resort in the Dominican Republic. I was so lonely. Plus I kept feeling guilty about the exploited workers who handed me fresh towels every morning. For the first two days I texted Gretchen every other minute. Then my sister told me to put the phone down already because I was embarrassingly whipped.

I guess we lose track of time, because we're still kissing when the front door slams.

"Crap." Gretchen scampers off the bed. I go over to the mirror to check my hair. It's all mussed. I try to smooth it back, but it's a lost cause.

Gretchen's mom opens the bedroom door without knocking, coming in with a bright smile and a long glance around the room. The rule in Gretchen's house, which we tend to break a lot, is that we can hang out as much as we want but we're supposed to leave the door open. Gretchen's parents are keeping up the pretense that all we do is hold hands. It's kind of cute, actually. My parents prefer to believe Gretchen and I don't even do that much.

"How's the packing going, girls?" Gretchen's mom asks. I bristle at the "girls" thing, but I try not to let them see.

"It's going great!" Gretchen smiles.

My annoyance slides away. Gretchen's smile beams out so much happiness, so much warmth, that sometimes I can barely stand it. I gaze at Gretchen's bright, open face and wonder for the trillionth time how I ever got this lucky.

Gretchen's mom steps aside, and Audrey and Chris poke their heads into the room. Chris is grinning big, but my sister looks pouty. Audrey just turned sixteen and doesn't have a driver's license yet, so Chris must've stopped by our house to play chauffeur.

"Hiiii!" Gretchen sweeps forward and grabs them both into a three-way hug. I'm not a hugger, so I stay where I am.

I'm going to miss them, though. My friends. My sister.

Even Gretchen's parents, who have always been really nice to me.

It's not that I won't ever see any of them again. They'll be around when I come back for breaks. Except that coming home for breaks also means seeing my mother again.

My mother, who still calls me Antonia, no matter how many times I say I hate that stupid girlie name.

My mother, who hasn't allowed me to get a yearbook photo taken since I turned twelve and finally cut my hair supershort, the way I'd always wanted to.

My mother, who'd pretended the whole threatening-to-sue-the-school thing wasn't happening junior year, except to walk around the house muttering about how no daughter of hers should want to go to school looking like a freak show.

Maybe I should find some excuse to stay on campus for every break over the next four years. After all, it's not like I need to come back to Maryland to see Gretchen.

Audrey, though… I'd hate to leave my sister in that house alone for good.

"Hey, T." Chris fist-bumps me. Chris has gotten really muscly over the past couple of soccer and basketball seasons. Whenever we fist-bump now, I'm afraid this is going to be the time Chris forgets to exercise self-restraint and I wind up with a dislocated shoulder. "You ready? Starting tomorrow we're mortal enemies."

"I'm so ready," I say. "When's the game?"

"Right before Thanksgiving. Remember, we have to hate each other on game day. It's the rules."

"Are you guys seriously going to the Harvard-Yale football game?" Audrey asks. "That's got to be the nerdiest event of all time."

"Actually I think it's less about nerdiness and more about drinking cheap alcohol in a field with your buddies," Chris says.

"Gross," Audrey says.

"Oh, because you've never done that," Gretchen says. Audrey laughs.

"How are you holding out after yesterday?" I ask Chris.

"Oh, I'm great. We got back together this morning, actually." Chris grins big. I sigh.

Last night I got an epic series of texts about Chris's latest breakup with Steven. They were on and off for pretty much our whole senior year. They kept saying they were going to break up for good before the end of the summer—they still believe that old wives' tale about how you shouldn't start college in a long-distance relationship—but they could never stay apart for long.

Chris says it's because their love is pure and true. I say it's because they're hormonal teenagers who don't know how to keep it in their pants. Not that I'm one to talk.

My friends are always fighting with their boyfriends or girlfriends about the littlest things. My friend Renee, who was my date for Homecoming junior year, realized she was bi and got together with this girl named Liz soon after the dance. Then they spent the entire year fighting about what movie to see that weekend, or whose music to plug into the car stereo, or which of the guys on the lacrosse team was the most obnoxious. Then they broke up. Now Renee's going out with the lacrosse guy they rated third on their list.

Gretchen and I, though—we never fight. We take turns listening to each other's music. We only like dramas or high-brow comedies that don't have any *Saturday Night Live* stars in them. I think all the guys on the lacrosse team are ob-noxious, but Gretchen thinks that's only because I never took the time to get to know them. I think Gretchen only thinks that because Gretchen's too nice to think anything bad about anyone.

The thing is, who cares what music you listen to on a random Tuesday afternoon? The stuff that really matters runs way deeper than any of that.

And when it comes to the deep stuff—the *really* deep stuff, the things we can only tell each other, the things no one else could understand—Gretchen and I are golden.

"Well, good luck," I tell Chris with a shrug.

Audrey pokes me in the side. "Chris, please ignore my sister's indifferent tone. She's still learning how to function in our normal human society."

"Hey." I flick Audrey on the shoulder. "Don't call me an abnormal human."

"I call them like I see them," Audrey says, flicking me back.

"Whatever. We'll be fine," Chris says. "I leave tomor-row and he leaves the day after. I'll be in Connecticut and he'll be in California. This is why they invented texting and video chat."

"I know you two will make it work," Gretchen says, smil-ing as big as ever.

"Thank you, Gretchen," Chris says. I'm not nearly as sure,

and I'm about to say so when Chris adds, "I mean, you guys are doing it, right?"

"Well, it's not like that for us," I say. "We'll be in the same city. It'll be a pain to go across town, but we'll deal."

Chris makes a weird face. "You are? I thought—"

"Actually, hang on." Gretchen bounds over to where I'm sitting on the bed and grabs my hand. "Let's go talk outside for a sec."

"What?" There's something going on that I don't know about. I hate not knowing things. "Why?"

"Just for a second." Gretchen pulls me up and through the door. I get a quick glimpse of my sister's face as we leave the room. Audrey won't meet my eyes.

I have a really bad feeling about this.

We wave to Gretchen's mom in the kitchen, go out the front door and walk down to the grassy strip on the corner of the block. Someone tied a plastic swing set to a tree root there with a bike lock years ago. The swings are too small for us, but we climb on anyway, dragging our feet on the ground and leaning back so our hair doesn't get tangled in the plastic chains.

"What's going on?" I hate the antsy feeling in my stomach. The idea that Gretchen's been keeping a secret from me. On our first date, we said we'd always be honest with each other. Since then we've always told each other our secrets. *I* have, at least.

"I was trying to tell you today," Gretchen says. "Actually, I've been trying for a while. It keeps not being the right time."

"I think it's the right time now," I say.

Gretchen's wide blue eyes are locked on mine. "I'm scared you'll be upset."

"I'm upset already. Just tell me."

Gretchen's chin quivers. I hate seeing that. I take Gretchen's hand and that seems to help. Gretchen smiles, a small smile.

"So you know how I applied to a bunch of different schools," Gretchen says. "Tufts would've been my first choice if I'd gotten in."

"Yeah, I know. Their admissions office is made up of complete idiots. Your application essay was amazing."

"Thanks." Gretchen takes a long breath. "My second choice was NYU, but they wait-listed me."

"NYU?" I shake my head. "No, you only applied to Boston schools. That was our whole plan. We love Boston."

"You love Boston, sweetie." Gretchen's voice is soft. "You love Harvard. It's always been your dream."

Oh.

I love Harvard. Gretchen loves New York.

New York was where Gretchen lived before the Daniels family moved down here. They had a brownstone in Brooklyn. It sounds like paradise whenever Gretchen talks about it.

"You got in off the wait list," I say.

Gretchen nods and rubs my palm gently. I have to struggle not to pull my hand away. "I found out last week."

I close my eyes. "Last *week*?"

"I'm sorry."

"You didn't tell me."

"I didn't know how."

Gretchen isn't coming with me.

We can't just hop on the subway and see each other whenever we want to.

Gretchen's leaving me. This is only the first step.

"Oh my gosh, no, don't cry, T!" Gretchen squeezes my hand tight. I blink fast against the tears, trying to focus on the orange light of the sunset that's pouring in through the trees. "I'm so sorry I didn't tell you sooner! Look, it's only for a semester, just to try it out. I can always transfer back to BU after that. I talked to them on the phone, and they said that would be really easy. I only thought—you know, maybe it wouldn't be so bad. Maybe we could just sort of see what it's like. New York and Boston are superclose. We can take the train and be there in, like, seconds."

I pull my hand out of Gretchen's grip and turn to stare at the cheap red plastic leg of the swing set. It's covered in grime from yesterday's rain. I didn't notice that before we sat down.

I can't believe Gretchen didn't even tell me. Applications were due in January. That means Gretchen has been keeping this secret for eight *months*, maybe longer.

Did I do something wrong?

I must've done something wrong, or else Gretchen would've stuck to the plan, right?

Gretchen doesn't really want to be with me. There's no other explanation for this.

"Toni." Gretchen's hand is on my shoulder, gentle. I want to wrench away, but instead I lean into the touch. I always lean into Gretchen's touch. "We'll still see each other. It'll be all right. We can do this."

I turn and stare into those blue eyes. I'm looking for anger, but I don't see it there. I see guilt and something else. Hope, maybe. Hope that I'll go along with this new plan.

Well, it's not as if I have a choice.

Gretchen's plans are already made. So are mine. No wonder Gretchen laughed off my question about fitting all that luggage on the plane. They wouldn't fly to New York. They'd drive. It's only a few hours north of here.

Wait. Chris. Chris said something before about us doing the long-distance thing. *Chris* knew about this before I did. So did Audrey.

How many others knew about my girlfriend's not-so-secret plan before me?

It's getting hard to breathe. I lurch to my feet, the swing set creaking as my weight leaves it. Behind me I hear Gretchen suck in a breath, but I don't turn around.

I'm not used to feeling like this around Gretchen. I *love* Gretchen. Anger is reserved exclusively for my mother.

I close my eyes. I can't let Gretchen see what I'm feeling.

We never fight. We aren't like that. Anger and love don't go together.

"Fine," I say. "Fine. It's fine."

Gretchen's fingers are light on my arm. "Are you sure?"

"Can we take the train and see each other every weekend?" I ask. "Because I thought I was going to see you every weekend."

"Yes, sure, totally, every weekend." Gretchen lays a soft hand on my cheek. I turn, and our eyes meet. I hate seeing Gretchen look so sad. "I love you."

"I love you, too." I sniff. I'm such a wuss, crying out here on the street.

"Oh, crap," a familiar voice says.

I look up. Audrey's standing right in front of us, wavy brown hair streaming over awkwardly folded arms.

Christ. Now my kid sister is seeing me cry.

"Are you guys fighting?" Audrey asks. "You guys never fight."

I answer quickly. "No."

"No," Gretchen says at the same time.

Audrey looks back and forth between us. "Chris wanted me to say he was sorry. He's a total idiot who can't keep his mouth shut."

I don't react, even though I want to flinch. I can't believe Gretchen told them and not me. My fingers curl and uncurl, the nails digging into my palm, but I hold my hand down low where they can't see.

"Relax," Audrey says. "It's just college. Whatever. Afterward you can get married and have your little picket fence and adopt a hundred Chinese babies and be the most boring, stable couple on the planet, like you've always been."

I try to smile. Coming from my sister, that's a compliment.

When we were kids, Audrey and I used to say we were BFFs. The truth is, though, for a long time, I've felt much closer to Gretchen than I ever felt to Audrey or even Chris. Gretchen knows me better than anyone ever has or ever could.

Like with the gender stuff. I've never been able to talk to anyone but Gretchen about that.

Gretchen's always listened and never, ever judged. When I first said I was genderqueer, Gretchen was so cool with everything, I couldn't believe it. When I said I wanted to stop using gendered pronouns, Gretchen didn't laugh once. It was never an issue between us at all.

I couldn't imagine telling anyone else about that. Audrey was out of the question, because what if Mom overheard? I couldn't tell Chris, either, because Chris was the ultimate joiner—a member of every sports team at the guys' high school and half the clubs, too. Chris would've founded an interschool Transgender-Cisgender Alliance and ordered trans and nontrans folks to hold gender-neutral-themed softball tournaments and car-wash fund-raisers. And *that* would've been the final straw that made my mother officially disinherit me.

Back in ninth grade, when I first came out about liking girls, my mother told me I was in a "rebellious phase." As far as Mom was concerned, this was yet another attempt on my part to torment my family. It got so bad I had to leave home and stay at a friend's house for a week. I can only imagine what my mother would consider my real motive if I announced that I wasn't even a girl in the first place.

So when I needed to talk about that stuff, I needed Gretchen.

I still need Gretchen now. It'll take a lot more than a couple hundred miles between us to change that.

It'll take more than a couple of lies, too.

Gretchen's chin is still quivering. I put my finger in the dimple there, and Gretchen laughs. Only a small laugh, but it's something.

*This will be okay.* If I just keep telling myself that, it'll have to be the truth.

"Hey, this way we get to prove that the urban legend about long-distance college relationships is dead wrong," I say.

Gretchen's smile is almost too bright this time. "That has always been my number-one goal in life!"

I laugh, but now I'm actually thinking about it kind of seriously.

I'm pretty sure that rule—the don't-go-to-college-with-a-girlfriend-back-home-unless-you-want-to-get-cheated-on-and-break-up-immediately rule—is just about casual relationships. Once they're in different places, people in relationships like that probably get distracted as soon as someone new and shiny shows up in their dining hall. None of that has anything to do with Gretchen and me.

Plus, we'll only be apart for a semester. After that, Gretchen can transfer back up to Boston, and college will be just like we always pictured it.

I squeeze Gretchen's hand. The quiver in Gretchen's chin has been replaced by that smile I love so much.

I lead us back toward the house, trying to think of a nice way to tell Chris and Audrey it's time for them to go.

Gretchen and I still have tonight.

A few more hours until our world is scheduled to turn upside down.

*2*

AUGUST
FRESHMAN YEAR OF COLLEGE
1 DAY APART

## GRETCHEN

I'm in New York now. So I have to do New York things.

There's no point thinking about other stuff. Especially not about the car ride up here. About crying quietly in the back-seat while Mom and Dad droned on about meal plans and registration. About how I wouldn't let them help me unpack and basically shoved them out of my dorm room as soon as we got here. About how now I'm sitting on a bare mattress surrounded by boxes and laundry baskets full of towels and a suitcase full of jeans and old stuffed animals, waiting for the tears to start again.

There's no point thinking about Toni up at Harvard. Being

all smart and wearing wool scarves and doing whatever else it is people do up there.

Being mad at me.

Because, yeah, Toni's mad. I've never seen Toni as mad as I did last night.

It's all my fault. I lied. I spent a week acting like I was going up to Boston even when I'd already made up my mind. I spent months not mentioning I'd even applied here.

I just couldn't do it. Tell the truth. I tried and tried, but I could never say the words.

Toni was *so* excited about college. About finally getting away from all the crap back home and living the life T had always dreamed of. I didn't want to ruin that.

Instead I made it a thousand times worse.

I've got to find a way to make this up to Toni.

It seemed so important before. Coming here. Coming *home*.

Now it just seems stupid. How am I going to make it through a whole semester until I transfer? I can barely make it through a single day without Toni.

No. Thinking about that won't help. I need to focus on fixing this. Making Toni forgive me.

I looked up the bus schedules from New York to Boston in the car, and I sent Toni a long email with a list of times I could go up there this weekend. Today's Thursday, so I figure I could go up on Saturday morning. That way we'll have had only two days apart, which seems like a good way to start. I figure for the first few weeks I can go up there instead of Toni coming down here. It's the least I can do. The *very* least.

I haven't heard back from my email yet, but Toni's texted me twelve times since I got here anyway. Mostly funny stories about stuff the flight attendants said or jokes about how scary Boston cabdrivers are.

Maybe things will start to be all right. Maybe.

God, though. I've never seen Toni look the way T did last night. Like I'd just destroyed everything that was good in our world.

A random guy sticks his head inside the door of my dorm room. I jump up off the mattress, alarmed.

Then I remember my door is propped open. Everyone else's doors were propped open and I figured it was the thing to do.

The guy grins at me. I try to smile back.

"Hey," he says. "They told me there was a blond girl in this room."

"They told you right," I say.

"A bunch of us are going to a comedy club. Floor trip. We're meeting downstairs in five."

"Okay, cool."

The guy leaves.

Perfect. A distraction!

Wait. Can I really just…leave? What about Toni? What about what I did?

I should really just sit here for the rest of the night. I don't deserve distractions.

My phone buzzes. Another text from Toni.

My roommate and I are going to some burger place. What r u doing tonight?

Oh. Well, I guess if Toni's going out, it's OK for me to go out, too. I text back about the comedy show. Toni writes back right away.

Don't forget ur pepper spray!

I smile and respond,

You too!

That's a joke. Toni's maid Consuela is awesome but also kind of scary. She makes Toni and Audrey carry pepper spray around with them whenever they go outside after dark. She stands in the door and yells after them, "Don't forget your pepper spray!" It gives the muggers an unfair advantage, really. They can all probably hear her from miles around. They'll know to be prepared.

I stare down at my phone screen and breathe in and out until I'm sure I'm not going to cry. Then I go to the mirror and brush the fattest tangles out of my hair. I look around the room one more time—at my side, with the bare twin bed and plain wood desk and half-empty boxes everywhere, and the other side, where my roommate's neatly made-up bed sits under black lace tapestry hangings and the desk is decorated with pretty purple candles. I decide it isn't worth trying to clean up my side. I don't want to miss the group leaving, and it will take me hours just to make a dent in this mess. I head out into the hall, locking the door behind me, and take the elevator down fourteen floors to the lobby.

When I get outside the dorm, a dozen people are standing

around the sidewalk, waiting to go. We're all freshmen, so no one knows each other yet, and everyone's checking out everyone else. You can tell what they're all thinking:

*This is it. This is the only chance I will ever have to establish my college social status. If I do not immediately bond with the coolest people here, I will be friendless and pathetic until graduation, and I will whimper alone in my dorm room every night.*

I sit down on a bench to text Toni again.

A guy standing a few feet away lights a cigarette. Smoke gets in my face. I wave my hand around to blow it away. The guy doesn't notice. He's cute, but it's the scruffy kind of cute, with messy hair, a bored expression and a pair of bowling shoes poking out from under his khaki pants.

A girl across from me is looking at the guy, too. She's rocking on her heels, about to pounce.

*It's now or never,* I imagine the girl thinking. *I will be the first girl here to approach the mysterious cute boy. He will think I am bold and intriguing, and will immediately want to make out with me.*

She walks toward him, smile in place. I try to catch her eye and signal her to stop—this guy is very obviously gay—but she's too fast.

"Hi," she says to the guy. "Excuse me. I was wondering. I couldn't help but notice. Those shoes, with the stripe, that you're wearing. Are those bowling shoes?"

She's doing that thing where you're nervous, so you use more words than you need to. I feel bad for her.

"Yes," the guy says.

"Because I've been wanting to get bowling shoes," the girl says. "Where'd you find them?"

The guy exhales a long puff of cigarette smoke. I cough.

"I slept with the little old man," the guy says.

The girl blinks at him. "Uh. What?"

I feel even worse for the girl, but it's hard to keep from laughing.

"Who?" she asks.

"The old man," the guy says. "At the bowling alley. With the foot spray. His name was Gerald. Charming fellow."

"Oh," the girl says.

The guy looks at her.

"Um, okay," she says. "Well, I guess I'll see you around."

The girl walks away. Probably to give up on the whole comedy-club idea and slink back to her room for the next four years.

When she's far enough away, I laugh out loud.

The bowling shoes guy turns around. His lips twitch.

"What's funny?" he asks.

"That was so mean, what you did to that girl!" I say, still smiling.

He frowns. "It was just a joke."

"Oh, come on. How was she supposed to come back from that?"

He frowns some more. "I don't know. I didn't think about that."

"Where *did* you get those shoes?" I ask him.

"A vintage shop down on Canal. Are you into vintage clothes?" He looks down at my Martha Jefferson Academy for Young Women Tennis Team T-shirt. "By that I mean *real* vintage, not some ancient crap you dug out of the bottom of your girlfriend's closet."

I clutch at my heart. "Your wit, it burns me."

The guy sits down next to me. "Hi. I'm Carroll."

I laugh some more. I can't believe how good laughing feels after everything that's happened. "No way."

"Yes way." He pulls out his wallet and shows me his New Jersey driver's license. It says Carroll Ostrowski next to a photo of him looking twelve years old and even scruffier than he does now.

"Little-known fact," he says. "In 1932, Carroll was the hundred and seventy-third most popular name for boy babies in the United States."

"What happened after that?"

"It fell off the chart thirty years later." Carroll smiles, showing off extremely prominent dimples. "My folks fancied themselves eccentrics."

I laugh again. I can't wait to tell Toni this story later. Toni's parents are into old-fashioned names, too, so they named their daughters Antonia and Audrey. Bad, but not as bad as Carroll.

"You don't have a nickname?" I ask Carroll.

"In high school I tried to have people call me Carrey, 'cause at least that sounded kind of like a guy's name. Then I got beat up anyway, and I figured now that I'm out of that hell town, I should embrace the real me."

"Okay, Carroll." I smile. He's clearly rehearsed this speech, but it's funny anyway.

"So?" he asks. "I showed you mine. You show me yours."

"Oh. Okay." I dig in my bag and pull out my Maryland driver's license.

"Gretchen Daniels," he reads. "Also somewhat old-fashioned, and yet not the sort of name that prompts disbelief. I like it."

"I'm glad you approve."

The other guy, the one who stuck his head through my doorway earlier, motions for us to come with him. We get up and follow him down the street. I don't know if he's our orientation guide or our RA or just a very outgoing freshman, but whoever he is, he doesn't know the city at all. He has us looping all the way around Washington Square Park.

It's fine, though. I'm busy with Carroll. It's distraction city over here.

"That's my roommate," Carroll says, pointing to a tall guy in a sports jersey. "Juan, from LA. He already hates me, but he's hot, so I'm okay with it. Who's your roommate?"

"I still haven't seen her. I know her name's Samantha and she's from South Carolina. Oh, and she's a goth. I know because there's black lace and purple candles spread out all over her side of the room."

"Is she in Tisch?" Carroll asks. Tisch is the arts school, where all the wannabe dancers and filmmakers go.

"No," I tell him. "She's Arts and Sciences, same as me."

Carroll snorts. "Why'd you pay all that money to come here for that? You can take English and math anywhere."

"Hey." I give him a shove. "*Anywhere* isn't New York. I guess you're an artsy fartsy Tisch kid, then, since you have such an attitude about it?"

"Absolutely! I'm a drama queen all the way, baby." He strikes a pose like he's about to burst into song. I laugh.

We make fun of each other for the rest of the walk to the comedy club. Once we get inside, it turns out the comedians aren't that great, so we spend most of the show whispering to each other and writing funny notes on our drink napkins. We annoy the heck out of everyone else in our group, but that's probably because we're having a way better time than they are. Carroll's not as much fun to talk to as Toni, but then, no one I meet here is going to be as much fun as T. That's the thing about soul mates, I guess.

It's late when we get back to the dorm after the show, but my roommate still isn't there.

"Maybe she had a séance to go to?" Carroll says when he sees all the candles.

"What if she's been kidnapped?" I ask. "She *is* from South Carolina. A stranger in the big city. Some weirdo could totally have lured her into a van."

"Yeah, you always hear about that happening to goth country bumpkins."

"Should we go ask the homeless people outside if they've seen her?"

"Nah. Let the vampire fend for herself." Carroll shoves some boxes out of his way and sits down on the floor. "Sit with me."

I join him on the floor. For the first time all night, it's awkward.

Suddenly I don't know what to say. I don't know what you're supposed to talk about when you're sitting on dirty industrial carpet in a dorm room surrounded by cardboard boxes full of books and shampoo and tampons and all the other junk you made your parents haul up from DC.

"So tell me about your girlfriend," Carroll says, and just like that, the awkwardness is gone.

"What makes you so sure I have a girlfriend?" I finger my top hat charm and smile. Carroll's certainty that I'm taken is making me feel a lot better about what happened yesterday. Things between me and Toni can't be too terrible if I'm radiating coupledom.

"You've got that hippie granola Indigo Girls vibe." Carroll points to my Birkenstocks, which aren't so much hippie as they are superbly comfortable, but whatever. "So I figure that makes you a lesbo, and all lesbos have girlfriends. It's, like, a law. I mean, not that I've ever met a lesbo before you, but trust me, I am wise in the ways of lesbos."

I laugh. Toni would point out the lack of logic in his arguments, but that sort of thing doesn't bother me.

"We've been together for almost two years," I say. "T left for college today, too, in Boston."

He asks to see a picture. I pull up our Queer Prom photo on my phone.

"Wow," he says. "A redhead. She's really butch, huh? With the short hair and the suit and all that?"

I shrug.

"You clean up good, though," he says, pointing to the dress I was wearing in the photo. I'd borrowed it from my friend Jess. It was long and black with pink dinosaurs printed all over the fabric. "You should try combing your hair more often."

I elbow him. "Some of us have better things to do than hang out in front of the mirror for hours every morning."

"Touché," he says, but he smiles like I complimented him. "What did you say your girlfriend's name was?"

"Toni. T for short."

He gives me back my phone and starts rooting around in the nearest open box. It's full of high school stuff. I'd wanted to have it with me up here, but this afternoon, as I watched my dad sweat while he hauled boxes out of the car, across the jam-packed New York sidewalk, through the lobby and up the fourteen floors to my room, I wondered if maybe I should've just left a couple of those things back home.

Carroll pulls my yearbook out of the box and flips through it. He laughs. "You went to an all-girl school?"

"Yeah." I wonder if everyone in college always goes through everyone else's stuff without asking or if this is a New Jersey thing.

"So you and your girlfriend are trying to stay together?" he asks. "Even with the long distance?"

"Toni and I aren't *trying* to do anything," I explain. "It's not, like, an effort. Toni and I have always wanted to stay together, and we still want to."

"Come on. Everyone knows you're supposed to be single when you get to college. How else are you supposed to have any fun?"

"Being with Toni *is* fun."

"But you don't even know what other girls you're going to meet."

"Doesn't matter. I don't want to be with other girls. I want to be with Toni."

"What's up with how you keep saying her name over and over? It sounds weird."

Yeah, I know it's weird. I sigh.

"I don't use gendered pronouns when I talk about Toni," I say.

My life would be a lot easier if he let it go at that, but I already know he won't.

"'Gendered'?" he asks. "What, you mean like *she*?"

"Yeah." He's giving me the strangest look. Maybe I shouldn't have tried to explain.

"That's so weird," he says.

"It's what we do." I shrug. "Toni doesn't use gendered pronouns at all anymore. For anyone."

"That's impossible." He sits back on his elbows like the point is now settled.

"No, it's not," I say. "I thought it would be, too, when Toni first told me about it, but I've been listening to Toni talk without saying *he* or *she* even once for the past year."

"So she used to use pronouns, but she doesn't anymore?" he asks. I nod. "So you're saying when she talks about you she says *Gretchen* over and over?"

"Basically."

"So weird!"

I sigh. "Look, this is a big deal to Toni, and I love Toni, so that means it's a big deal to me, too, okay?"

He grins and cocks an eyebrow. "Love, eh? *Twoo* love?"

He pronounces it like the priest in that old movie *The Princess Bride*. I can't help laughing.

"Yes," I say. "It's totally *twoo*."

"Come on, though. You've got to admit this thing with the pronouns is crazy."

"No, it's not. We should all do it, really. Our language patterns are totally sexist."

He laughs. "Do you say *ovester* instead of *semester*, too?"

"No," I say. "That's dumb."

"Hey, look, it's funny. What, is your girlfriend one of those hard-core bra-burning lesbo feminazis? 'Cause you don't seem like that type at all."

Should I tell him?

Toni isn't out to many people back home. Just me and some online friends. No one ever asks, and Toni doesn't volunteer it.

No one's ever asked me before, either. When I moved to DC I joined Toni's group of friends right away, so all my friends there were Toni's friends first. I never talked to them about Toni, since they knew T better than they knew me.

But I can already tell Carroll's going to be a good friend, and it's not as if Toni ever asked me to keep it a secret. Besides, Toni doesn't even know Carroll. I want to text and ask if it's okay for me to tell him, but Toni's probably asleep by now.

Well, if it turns out Toni minds, I won't tell anyone else after him.

"Toni's genderqueer," I say.

Carroll looks at me blankly.

"You know," I say. "It's like being transgender."

He pulls back, an ugly look on his face. "Your girlfriend's a *man*?"

I grimace. "No. God, come on."

"So, what? Your girlfriend's an *it*?"

"No!" This conversation isn't going how I thought it would. I wish I'd never told him. I stand up and pace to the other end of the room.

I don't know how to say this so he'll understand. I've never had to explain this to anyone. I've barely even talked about it with Toni besides the really basic stuff. Toni and I talk a lot about how *male* and *female* are such restrictive, limiting terms, and how our society is so rigid about labels and it's so damaging and…to be honest, mostly it was Toni who said all that. I nodded like I understood it all because I wanted to be supportive, but there was an awful lot I didn't follow.

"Sorry." Carroll shakes his head. "Look, I'm from this tiny town way out in Jersey, okay? We don't have this stuff out there."

I sigh. I can tell Carroll really doesn't know any better.

"It's okay," I say. "I didn't mean to freak out on you."

"Seriously, I'm just trying to understand," he says. "I didn't mean to say the wrong thing. But what does this all mean? Did she, like, get a sex change operation?"

I lean my head against the base of my roommate's bed. Carroll's flicking through my yearbook again.

"No," I say.

"So, what, she's just a butch lesbian?"

The truth is, I'm not really clear on where the lines are between all these things. I was always afraid I'd say the wrong thing if I asked Toni too much about the details.

"No," I say. "Toni hates the word *lesbian*."

"So, what is she?"

"It's complicated." I'm getting tired now. "You should look it up sometime. *Genderqueer*. It's, like, a really well-known word."

"Right. Okay. I'll look it up."

I should look it up again, too. I read some stuff online back when Toni first told me about it, but I got kind of anxious reading all that, because it seemed really complicated, and

I couldn't figure out where Toni and I fit in. So I stopped reading. That was more than a year ago.

This whole conversation is making me feel really guilty. Not just because I outed Toni to Carroll, though I'm kind of wishing now that I hadn't done that, either. But talking about Toni at all just reminds me of what I did. Of how Toni looked at me last night.

I need more distractions.

So I show Carroll yearbook pictures and tell him more about my friends back home. He's shocked by how many gay people went to our high school.

"I think it was partly because it was an all-girl school," I say. "Going across the street to the guys' school was so much effort. People got lazy."

"At my school, I was the only one," he says.

"That you know of."

"No. I'm positive. It was a small school. Everybody knew everybody's business."

He's got to be totally wrong, but I let it go. "Were you out?"

"No, but everyone knew anyway. It sucked." He sticks his lip out in a fake pout. "Do your parents know?"

"Yeah. I told them the summer before ninth grade."

"Wow." He shakes his head. "Do your girlfriend's parents know, too?"

"Yeah. Well, not totally. Toni's out to them as gay, but not as genderqueer."

"Is she going to tell them?"

This one I do know the answer to.

"Not at least until college is over," I say. "Toni's mother is awful. She's this total rich bitch. She practically kicked Toni out of the house just for being gay."

For some reason, Carroll smiles.

"Hey, are you hungry?" He stands up. "I'm starving."

"Yeah." Now that he's mentioned it, I'm starving, too. "Is there a vending machine?"

"Who cares? We're in New York! They have twenty-four-hour delis here."

I laugh. I can't help it. He's like a little kid.

We take the elevator down fourteen floors again and go outside. I've forgotten how much I missed New York at night. Even the stores that have their shutters pulled down for the night still have their signs lit. People are walking down the sidewalk in groups, laughing. I'm going to miss this next semester.

There's a deli at the end of the block. We pick out ice cream and crackers and peanut M&Ms. At the counter, Carroll asks the clerk for a box of condoms.

I laugh. "What, you think you're getting lucky tonight?"

"You never know who you'll meet at breakfast," he says, all mysterious.

We stop by Carroll's room so he can drop off his stuff. Juan's honking snores are so loud we can hear him from the hallway. This sends me into a giggle fit.

"Shh," Carroll whispers. "I don't need to give him any more reasons to hate me."

"Why do you think he hates you?" I ask on the walk back to my room.

"He's a jock. Jocks always hate me."

"That doesn't even make sense."

"It's in the jock DNA. It's like, jocks are born with a fear of falling, a taste for Pabst Blue Ribbon and a powerful hatred of Carroll Ostrowski."

I laugh and push open my door. The light is out. Strange—it was on when we left.

Then I see a dark shape on one of the beds.

"Crap! She's alive!" Carroll stage-whispers behind me. "Shh!"

Wow. I'd forgotten I even had a roommate.

"Mom? Is that you?" the lump on the bed mutters.

Carroll loses it.

I shove him back out the door before his echoing laughs can wake up Samantha. I grab a blanket out of the nearest open laundry basket, dart out into the hall and lock the door behind us.

"Sorry about that," Carroll says, but we're both cracking up now.

We go to the lounge at the end of the hall. It's not much bigger than my room, but it has a microwave and a TV and a couple of unsanitary-looking couches. I find spoons for our ice cream and Carroll turns on the Food Network. It's a show about waffles. We sit on the least gross couch and eat ice cream out of the cartons with my blanket spread over our laps.

"It's like a sleepover," I say. "We should've gotten popcorn."

"Should we go wake up your roommate and invite her?" he says.

"Only if we get your roommate, too," I say. "Except then he'd just be honking in here."

"Yeah, it's better with just us," he says.

We watch the waffles bake in silence for a while. Then Carroll asks, "So, what do you do for fun when you're not eating ice cream and watching the Food Network with your new best friend?"

I laugh. "Back home, you know, the usual. Hanging out, parties. I played volleyball and did debate all through high school."

"Oh, no, you're a jock, too," he says. "Are you playing here?"

"No way. College volleyball is crazy intense. Besides, I was never really a jock. I liked playing, and I guess I was pretty good at it, but it was never my absolute favorite thing. Not like with you and theater."

"Why do you assume I'm obsessed with theater? Just because I could sing you the entire score of *Wicked* right now?"

I smack his arm and bounce in my seat. "I used to love that show! I've seen it, like, thirty times at the Gershwin. What's your favorite song? Mine used to be 'Popular' but it's so overdone. I think now I like 'For Good' more."

"What?" Carroll isn't bouncing with me. "You saw it here in New York? I thought you were from Maryland?"

"I am. Well, my family lives in the DC suburbs now, but I lived in Brooklyn until two years ago."

He looks pissed. "Wait, you're *from* New York? Have you been secretly laughing at me this whole time for being such a tourist?"

"No!" Then I remember. "Okay, yeah, I did a little bit when you got so excited about the deli, but only in the nicest possible way." I smile and tilt my head on his shoulder.

"Come on, you can't be mad at me. You're my only friend here!"

"That's true." He settles back. I guess everything's okay now.

We watch the waffle show for a while longer. I'm getting tired. I sink down lower on the couch and pull the blanket up to my chin.

Carroll is quiet for another minute. Then he slides down next to me and pulls the blanket up over our heads. I laugh sleepily. It's so dark under here, all I can see of his face is his nose and his eyebrows. The reek of cigarette smoke is strong.

Now that it's quiet, I can't help thinking about Toni again. About what I did. God. I'm a truly horrible person. I don't see how I can ever make this right.

"Look," Carroll says, as if he can hear my thoughts. "We're in college now. It's going to be amazing. This'll be a totally different universe from high school. We'll have nonstop fun from tomorrow through May. I guarantee you."

I nod against his shoulder. I think about seeing Toni the day after tomorrow, and how maybe college doesn't need to be *completely* different from high school.

"Besides, you know what the most important thing is?" he asks. "The key reason college is going to be so amazing, for you in particular?"

"What?" I say, already smiling because I think I know his answer.

"You have me," he says, kissing me on the cheek with a loud smack.

3

## TONI

I dodge an unusually aggressive squirrel as I cross Cambridge Street and take out my phone to text my roommate. I'm going to be late for lunch. Ebony will probably already have eaten and be long gone by the time I get there. Ebony's on the varsity tennis team and inhales food by the shovelful.

I played tennis in high school, too. I even thought I was good. Until I saw Ebony play.

Ebony is cool, though. Vastly superior to our other roommates. We all moved in a week ago, and right away Ebony and I decided we should share the smaller of the two bedrooms in our suite, and let Felicia and Joanna have the bigger one. We avoid running into them in our shared common room as much as we can. In return, Joanna and Felicia use their alone time to complain about Ebony and me. (We know. You can hear everything through the walls in this place.)

Sure enough, when I get to our usual table near the front of the dining hall, there's already an empty food tray in front of Ebony, who's wearing gym clothes and munching on a protein bar.

"Sorry." Ebony sweeps a manicured hand over the tray, indicating the plates full of crumbs and salsa splotches. "I was about to starve to death. I'll sit with you while you eat, though."

"You don't have to," I say. "I should be reading Race and Politics."

"Classes have barely started," Ebony says. "Stop being such a psycho overachiever and go get some food. The only thing you need to know about race and politics is that white people suck."

"Totally." I stand up. "Want anything?"

"A banana, maybe? Actually, make that two bananas."

My phone buzzes with a text while I'm in the food line. Gretchen.

Hey remember I told u about Briana from debate?? Crazy Texas chick w big hair?? Guess what she's here!!! In my nat sci lab.

Yeah. I remember Briana.
Briana was the star of the national high school debate cir-

cuit. Gretchen ran into Briana at tournament after tournament over the past couple of years. They started out as rivals but they got to be friends, sort of.

Here's what Gretchen told me about Briana: One, Briana was a cheerleader during the off-season. Two, Briana was hot. Three, Briana was brilliant. Four, and best of all, Briana was gay.

Now Briana's at NYU.

Not that it matters. Sure, Briana gets to see Gretchen every day, but that doesn't mean anything will happen. Obviously. I trust Gretchen. Mostly.

No, not mostly. I *do* trust Gretchen. Gretchen only kept the NYU thing a secret to avoid hurting me.

I understand. For real, I do.

I just wish I could force my brain to stop obsessing about it so much.

Gretchen sent me an email the day we left with a list of bus times, but I said I thought we should wait a week before our first visit. I said it was because we needed time to settle in, but the truth was, I also wanted time to figure out what all this meant. How we'd wound up hundreds of miles apart instead of across the river from each other like we'd planned.

I mean, I'm not one of those people who would insist my girlfriend go to a certain school just to be closer to me. I'm not some Neanderthal.

But, damn, this sucks.

What if Gretchen meets someone in New York? What if stupid Briana from Texas screws up everything we have?

Why couldn't Gretchen just leave well enough alone?

I text Gretchen about how funny it is that Briana's at

NYU. Then I pick up my burger and fries, and trudge back to where Ebony's drinking from an enormous water bottle. I manage not to slam my tray down on the table, but it's hard.

I *hate* being mad.

"You're lucky you can eat that crap." Ebony takes the bananas and gestures to my tray, stealing a french fry at the same time. "You're so skinny. What do you weigh, ninety pounds?"

"More than that," I say. Five pounds more than that.

Ebony whistles. "I know girls that would kill to look like you."

Yeah.

Except for the part where I don't want to look like a girl. At least, not most of the time.

Like, for example, I have this enormously complicated relationship with my chest.

I'm told most people have complicated relationships with their chests. My sister reads *Cosmo* and *Marie Claire*, so I've absorbed via osmosis the insecurities you're supposed to have about different body parts. If you have breasts, they're either too big or too small. They stick up too much or they hang down too far. Your nipples can be too pointy or not pointy enough. There are so many ways your breasts can be weird that I doubt anyone thinks they have normal, acceptable breasts.

I can't relate to any of those problems, though. My problems are more like...sometimes, I wish my breasts weren't there.

It isn't as if I hate them. Sometimes I almost like them. I usually don't want anyone else to notice them, though. Most days I wear loose-fitting tops and sports bras and try not to think about it.

It's worst in the summer, when there are pool parties and water parks and trips to the beach and all those other torturous hot-weather activities. I'll do whatever it takes to avoid wearing a bathing suit in front of other people. It's creepy, when you think about it, that people will strip down in front of complete strangers just because it's warm out. I've always found air conditioning vastly preferable.

There are things that can be done about breasts. There's chest-binding. And then there's top surgery.

Surgery just seems so…extreme. So permanent. My chest is part of me. It's bizarre to think about getting rid of a part of myself, forever.

Except—people get rid of parts of themselves all the time. Isn't that what shaving is? Cutting your hair? Getting your ears pierced? It's all costume. Fitting in to what society expects. Gender's no different.

It's exhausting, thinking about all this. It's easier to talk it through. But Gretchen is the only person I've really talked to about this stuff so far, and even Gretchen can't totally relate. My girlfriend's great at listening, but I can never tell how much Gretchen really understands.

"T? T, are you there?" Ebony's been calling me T lately. It makes me homesick. "Are you listening?"

"Oh, sorry."

"You always get that look on your face when you're missing the honey," Ebony says. "Is it that bad?"

I shake my head. "I can handle it," I say, though I'm not actually sure that's true.

We didn't get to talk last night. Chris and Steven are having issues again, so I spent hours online with Chris instead.
I resisted the urge to say I told you so. Instead I read over
drafts of the long email Chris was planning to send explaining why open relationships weren't a good idea. I also listened patiently and tried to offer helpful tips while Chris
ranted about some hot freshman interloper at Stanford who
had the audacity to be named Elvis. (Seriously, only Steven
would find a guy named Elvis attractive.)

It's been a week since Gretchen and I last saw each other,
though, and I hadn't realized how lonely it would feel. Even
with how complicated everything's gotten, I still wish I could
see Gretchen. I wish we could touch. I need someone I can
be honest with. Someone I don't have to act around.

I thought talking on video chat would help. We were
used to that since we talked online every night back home.
But it's completely different, talking from my dorm room
to Gretchen's dorm room instead of talking from one house
to another.

Back home, I knew Gretchen's room almost as well as my
own. When we talked I could see Gretchen stretched out
on the bed, ankles crossed, lips twitching into the camera. I
could pretend I was right there, my arm around Gretchen's
shoulders, my lips moving in for a kiss.

When we talk now, Gretchen's dorm room looks wrong.
Alien. White painted cinder block walls and brand-new Target sheets on the bed, still showing the wrinkles from their
cellophane wrapper. I've never leaned back against those
walls or felt those sheets against my skin.

I can't imagine being in that room. I can't imagine seeing Gretchen in my tiny bedroom, either, with the ancient bunk beds and the obnoxious roommates cackling on the other side of the door.

I don't know. Maybe it's not about our dorm rooms at all. But I don't want to think about what else it might be.

"Well, you're way better than me," Ebony says. "I was online with Zach for six hours last night. Almost slept through class."

"Crap, that sucks." Long-distance relationships. Hatred of our roommates. Tennis. This is what people bond over in college, I'm finding.

I like Ebony, but we're not exactly BFFs. I'm pretty sure Ebony's just nice to me because I don't have any other friends here. I just haven't figured out how to meet people yet. At least, not people I actually want to hang out with.

Everything will be easier if Gretchen transfers to BU. I can't imagine making it even one semester on my own here.

"So, do you know what groups you're signing up for?" Ebony asks.

I shrug. "Mostly."

The campus activities fair is this afternoon. Ebony and I spent breakfast going through the list of student organizations. Now we're about to come face-to-face with the upperclassmen who run all the clubs, and I'm getting nervous.

"What'll you do if you get hit on at the UBA table?" Ebony asks. "Tell them you're already taken or play it cool?"

"That," I say, "is the least of my worries."

Before I'd even gotten accepted to Harvard I already knew I wanted to join the Undergraduate BGLTQIA Association. (It stands for Undergraduate Bisexual, Gay, Lesbian, Transgender, Queer, Intersex and Asexual Association. I think. Actually, I get confused about what some of the letters stand for. They seem to change a lot.)

I started the Gay-Straight Alliance at my high school in ninth grade. It was awesome, but Harvard's UBA is in another league altogether. Last year, they held the first Intra-Ivy Queer Asian Weekend. People from all the other Ivy League schools came down and held panel discussions and led a Queer Asian Equality March. Then they had a dance party and played Margaret Cho routines on the big screen.

The UBA is one of the most important student groups at Harvard. Visiting their table at the activities fair will be putting my first foot in the door.

Sure, odds are, no one will even notice me there. Two hundred freshmen will probably sign up today. There isn't much I can do this year anyway—freshmen can't hold leadership roles in the big organizations. But I have to make a good impression, or at least avoid making a bad one, if I want to get a decent spot as a sophomore.

"You don't need to stress," Ebony says, stealing the rest of the fries off my tray as we get up. "You're going to comp that political blog, right? So you've already got your big activity."

"I might not make it onto the staff, though. Not everybody who comps their first semester gets invited." We turn in our trays and push through the doors into the open air. Everyone is already streaming toward the Yard. I shift on my feet. It's stupid to be nervous.

"Oh, no, I heard everyone makes it on those things unless they're seriously lame," Ebony says as we join the flow of people. Even in gym clothes, my roommate's tall, muscled form and long, swinging braids stand out as we walk through the crowd. People always turn to look when we're out together. Probably thinking I look like a little person next to Ebony.

It's weird being surrounded by classmates and not recognizing anyone. In high school I'd known everyone since we were kids. Sure, I hadn't liked a lot of them, but at least I'd known what I was dealing with.

"Anyway," Ebony says, "if you don't like the UBA you can always join one of the other gay groups instead."

"None of the other groups has as much clout as the UBA," I say. "You're not planning to settle for one of the lesser engineering groups, are you?"

"Well, no, but that's because the geeks in FES can kick the geeks in ESH's asses."

"Hell yeah, we can! FES has got it going on!" a guy on the sidewalk next to us yells, making the "Live Long and Prosper" sign from *Star Trek* at Ebony. Ebony laughs and signs back. I roll my eyes, but I laugh, too.

The truth is, I already love Harvard. I knew I would before I got here, but the real thing is even better. I may not know many people yet, but the way it *feels* is exactly what I always hoped it would be.

The Yard is packed—more crowded than it was on move-in day. I try to take deep breaths as I scan the booths for the groups I'm signing up for: the UBA, the PolitiWonk blog and the Model Congress. All I see in every direction is people jumping up and down, hugging, and eating the free candy the groups have set out on their tables. Am I the only lost freshman here?

Someone to my left yells, "Eb!" Ebony grins and waves at a girl in tennis gear.

"I'm going to go say hi," Ebony says. "You'll be okay on your own, right?"

What am I, a toddler?

"Of course," I say, but Ebony's already gone. All right, then. I push past a group of guys high-fiving each other by the Ukrainian-American Brotherhood table and find a spot blessedly free of people so I can collect myself.

A girl rushes up to me and presses a mini Snickers bar into my hand. "Hi! I'm so glad you're interested in the HSWMS! Let me tell you about what we've got planned for this year!"

I blink at the girl. Then I realize this spot was only free because I'm in front of the Harvard Students Waiting for Marriage Society table.

"Oh, sorry," I say. "I'm not interested."

I put the Snickers back on the table in case it has abstinence cooties.

I back away from the HSWMS table and allow the throng to carry me from booth to booth. There must be hundreds of them.

Hmm. Maybe I should sign up for some other groups, too, just in case. It probably wouldn't be a bad idea to join the College Democrats. And the Japanese fencing-club people look like they're having a great time waving swords around.

Then I see the giant rainbow flag pinned high on a brick wall. I've found the UBA.

The crowd in front is bigger than for any other table in the row. Behind the booth and wading out into the sea of

ROBIN TALLEY                71

students are upperclassmen wearing bright purple T-shirts that say, "We're so gay! Harvard UBA!"

Cute. Maybe too cute.

The sign-up sheet is front and center in the middle of the table. All around me, freshmen are elbowing their way toward it, but I linger at the back of the crowd.

*Just go up there and sign the list. You don't have to talk to anyone. Just put your name down and get out of there.*

"Hi!" someone perks at me before I've unfrozen. It's an alarmingly cheerful blond in one of the purple shirts. "Are you a *freshman*?"

"Uh, yeah," I say.

"That's *fantastic*!" the girl says as if we aren't surrounded by freshmen on every side. "We have special cupcakes for freshmen!"

The girl points to one end of the table. Eight neat rows of cupcakes are laid out, each with the pink letters *QF* carefully written on chocolate frosting.

"It stands for Queer Freshmen," the girl says.

"Uh-huh," I say.

Maybe Ebony was on the right track. There are at least four other LGBT groups on campus. Surely one of them is less focused on T-shirts and cake decoration.

"Don't worry about her," a short black guy with a buzz cut says as the blond wanders away to pounce on someone else. The guy is wearing a matching T-shirt, too. "Shari was the bake-sale queen four years running back in Kansas City. It's safest to humor her. Her bite is way worse than her bark."

I smile at the guy. "Thanks for the tip."

We shake hands. It isn't easy in the press of moving bodies.

"I'm Derek," the guy says.

"I'm Toni."

"Tony with a *Y*?"

"No, *I.*"

"Ah." Derek nods, as if this explains everything, and points to my wrist. "Great tattoo."

"Thanks."

"Queer history buff?"

I blink in surprise. On my eighteenth birthday I got a blue star tattooed on my wrist. Back in the thirties and forties, blue stars were one of those secret signals closeted people used to aid their gaydar. I'd thought that was cool. I'd also wanted to piss off my mother by getting a tattoo. No one has ever known its back story until I explained it, though.

"Sort of, yeah," I say.

Derek nods. "Are you trans?"

I blink again. No one's ever come straight out and asked me before.

No one I've met online. No one in the LGBT youth center where I volunteered in DC. None of my high school friends.

Not even Gretchen.

So it's strange acting all casual about it here, with someone I don't even know. For a second I want to look around to make sure no one's listening. Then I decide I don't care. I've been worrying about that stuff my whole life. I'm in college now. It's time to get over it.

What am I supposed to say, though? That I'm definitely somewhere on the transgender spectrum, and that even though I've spent hours upon hours upon hours reading websites and thinking about every possible angle of this stuff, I still haven't found a label that feels exactly right for me?

There are tons of options I've read about. I usually describe myself as *genderqueer* just because it's the word the most people seem to understand, but sometimes I think *gender nonconforming* would be better. Sometimes I think I'd rather go with *gender fluid*, and a lot of the time I want to pick *nonbinary*, because that one sounds the least committal. *Gender bender* sounds cool, but I'm afraid people will think it's a joke.

Should I try to tell Derek about how sometimes I think just *trans* by itself is the best word? It's just that I'm not sure I really consider myself a *guy*, necessarily, or at least not every day. I just don't consider myself a *girl*. If I call myself *trans* I'm afraid people will think I'm a dude when the truth is, I'm really not there. Maybe someday I will be, but it also seems entirely possible that I could stay exactly the way I am right now for the rest of my life.

I don't think I should say all that, though. Probably best not to scare Derek off with an ideological rant about the evils of labels thirty seconds after we've met.

"I'm genderqueer," I say.

"That's cool," Derek smiles. Like this is a totally normal conversation. Like those weren't the two most nerve-racking words I've ever spoken out loud. "There are a bunch of other GQs on campus."

"There are?" I haven't noticed any. Unless Derek is, but I doubt that. From the amount of stubble poking out of Derek's chin, Derek's probably been on testosterone for a while. As far as I know, guys taking hormones don't usually identify as genderqueer. They identify as guys.

Wait. Is that right? How do I know that for sure? Maybe there are hundreds of genderqueer people at Harvard giving themselves testosterone injections as we speak.

Shouldn't I know how all of this works, just instinctively?

Derek lets out a deep laugh, oblivious to my angst. "Yeah, believe it or not. I'm trying to get more of you guys to join the UBA. I'm the trans outreach cochair this year."

"Who's the other cochair?" I don't see anyone else in a purple shirt who looks trans.

"My roommate, Nance. She couldn't be here. Had an ultimate Frisbee game." Derek points to a tall guy with an expensive-looking haircut wearing a jacket, tie and suit pants with a purple UBA T-shirt despite the ninety-degree heat. "That's Brad, by the way. He's the UBA president."

"Why's Brad wearing a suit?"

"Oh, he's probably planning to change shirts and go to an informational interview this afternoon. Every time I've seen Brad in the past two years he's been on his way to an informational interview."

I laugh. My anxiety—about Gretchen, about labels, about meeting new people—is starting to fade into the background just a little.

Derek points out the rest of the UBA board members at the table. Shari, the perky blonde, is the social chair. All the other board members are guys.

"So, are you going to sign up or what?" Derek smiles at me again.

"Oh, right." I smile back. I can't believe how nervous I was about this.

While I wait my turn at the sign-up form, Shari notices

me again. "Oh, hi there! I'm so glad you're signing up! I see you already met Derek!"

"Yeah," I say, surprised to see that Derek is still standing next to me. I thought the UBA people were all supposed to run back into the crowd, seeking out more converts.

"Did you meet Brad yet?" Shari asks. I look up, but Brad has retreated back behind the table and is furiously poking at a tablet.

Shari and Derek roll their eyes at each other. I'm getting the sense that Brad is president of the UBA because it means Brad gets to go on informational interviews and talk about being president of the UBA.

"Well anyway," Shari says just as I reach the front of the line. "Ahem!"

Suddenly Shari's voice is projecting past the table and out to the gathered crowd. The freshmen stop talking and push toward the front of the table to hear. A hush has fallen at the booths around us, too. I have to admit, Shari's got some serious crowd-control prowess.

"You guys," Shari says, beaming out at the rapt group, "I'm so excited to tell you what the UBA board's decided to do this year! I know you'll all want to be part of it. You all know that awesome new show *The Flighted Ones*?"

Lots of people nod. I've never watched *The Flighted Ones*, but my sister Audrey is obsessed with it. It's about a group of twentysomethings who turn into winged superheroes at night and fly around fighting crime. Two of the characters are gay and are considered hot by the people who have opinions about such things.

"We've decided to have official UBA-sponsored *Flighted*

parties every Tuesday night!" Shari says. "We'll watch the show and have snacks! Everyone will want to come because everyone's watching the show anyway!"

Next to me, the other freshmen murmur assent.

"Well, but that's not all you're doing this year, is it?" I ask.

The murmurs stop. I can feel the other freshmen looking at me. Shari and Derek are, too. Even Brad has lowered the tablet and is peering in my direction.

Crap. I didn't mean to say that out loud. Now, though, with all those eyes on me, I have no choice but to keep going.

"I mean, it's not that I don't like cupcakes and cheesy TV shows, because I do, sometimes," I say. "But there's also going to be advocacy work, right? We're going to do stuff to address the key issues affecting the queer community?"

I stop talking when I realize Shari's glaring at me. I shouldn't have mentioned the cupcakes.

Great. I haven't even joined yet and I've already pissed off the UBA's queen bee. I should probably slink off and join the Queer Youth of America, Inc., Harvard-Radcliffe Chapter. I can see their table in the distance. A giant poster of Neil Patrick Harris is hanging from it.

"We need more members," Shari says to me, not project-ing anymore. "If you know a better way to recruit members than fun social gatherings then *you* can run for the board next year."

"Now, Shari," Brad says, chuckling, even though every-one else behind the table looks uncomfortable. "I'm sure she didn't mean to imply that—"

Derek interrupts Brad in a voice loud enough to match Shari's. "Hey, Toni has a point. We have a lot of other goals for this semester. Maybe the officers should each give our prospective new members some of the bullet points?"

Shari groans.

"Derek, that's an excellent idea," Brad says, turning back to the tablet screen. "Why don't you kick us off?"

"Okay," Derek says. "So, hi, everyone. I'm Derek Richmond, and I'm the cochair for transgender outreach. Now that we've got gender-neutral housing campus-wide, my fellow cochair and I thought this would be a good year to work on an official guide to transitioning at Harvard."

Wow. I'd love to read that. I've seen stuff on the internet about transitioning, but it's mostly about why binding your chest with ACE bandages is bad for you. It isn't about the scary, big-picture stuff that keeps me up at night, like having to ask my professors to call me by some other name. Or having to tell my mother.

I catch Derek's eye and nod. Derek smiles.

"So, I'm seeing a few confused faces," Derek goes on, looking around the table at the other freshmen. "What that means is, we need a guide for transgender students who are transitioning. They could be starting to live openly as women, or as men, or as a nonbinary gender, or making some other change related to their gender presentation. The transition guide will have sections on how to tell your roommates and professors you're transgender, how to get your name changed on your ID, where to find gender-neutral bathrooms, how to get legal hormone injections, safe places around town to shop for clothes and makeup, whatever. We'll post the guide on the web and try to get some stories in the *Crimson*, too."

The space around the table is getting even more crowded as the freshmen lean in to hear what Derek's saying, but there are still a lot of blank expressions. I'm so busy watching the crowd I almost miss what Derek says next, but I snap back to attention when I hear my name.

"We could use some help writing the guide from someone who's new to the Harvard community," Derek says. "Toni, are you up for it?"

Now everyone's staring at me again. The other freshmen in particular.

I shift from one foot to the other, but Derek looks perfectly at ease, waiting for me to answer.

It would be stupid to say no. This is as involved in the group as I can get freshman year unless I want to help with cupcake-baking duty. Besides, it sounds interesting.

I wish everyone would stop staring at me, though.

"Sure," I say.

"Cool," Derek says. "Why don't you come back with me after the activities fair? You can meet Nance and we can brainstorm."

"Excellent idea, Derek," Brad says without looking up. "I'm sure he'll have a lot to contribute. Kartik, your turn."

Kartik, the treasurer, takes over and starts talking about fund-raisers, but half the people gathered on both sides of the table are still looking at me.

I push my way toward the sign-up form and write my name, fast, then back away.

As soon as I'm safely anonymous in the crowd again, my heart starts to slow down. That was terrifying.

Also…kind of awesome.

Now that I'm not nervous anymore, it's easy to find the other clubs I liked and put my name down on their lists. I sign up for a couple of others, too. Why not? Maybe I should start being more spontaneous now that I'm in college. Maybe that's how you meet the people who are actually worth meeting.

As the fair winds down, I make my way back to the UBA table. I dodge Shari, who's sweeping the table clear of cupcake crumbs, just in time to see Derek look over and wave for me to follow.

Whew. I'd been half-worried Derek would forget about me.

We walk across the Yard onto a road I don't recognize. I've never been to any of the houses where the upperclassmen live.

"Will Nance be home when we get there?" I ask as we climb the steps to Derek's floor. "What about Frisbee?"

"Yeah, she'll be there," Derek says. "To be honest, Frisbee was an excuse. Nance hates hanging out with big groups at UBA events. She prefers to handle things behind the scenes."

That seems odd for someone whose position title has the word *outreach* in it.

Derek's house looks a lot like my freshman dorm—old and grand. Loud voices echo toward us as we climb the stairs to Derek's room.

"Er," Derek says before turning the key in the lock. "I should probably apologize in advance for anything my roommates might say over the course of the afternoon. Sometimes they get kind of…well. You'll see."

With that I'm nervous again.

Derek's room has a huge common area that's a lot nicer than mine. It has a bar on one side, a big-screen TV and two leather couches. As the door swings open, I see two people sitting hunched over on a couch in front of the unlit fireplace, arguing about what sounds like the plot of a video game involving toy ponies. When they see me, they stop talking right away.

"Toni," Derek says, "this is Nance and Eli."

Nance and Eli wave. Then in unison, as if they rehearsed it, they say, "Yo."

Then both of them, and Derek, too, start laughing and talking about how funny it is that they both said "Yo" at the same time.

I wave back.

Derek goes over to sit on the couch, perching on the arm and gesturing for me to come join them.

I do. All three of them smile back at me.

They look almost like a family, hanging out here. They remind me of my group of friends back home. Except that in my group of friends back home, I was the only one who was trans.

"Hey," I say. I try to smile at them as coolly as possible. In this moment, my greatest wish in the world is for the people in this room to like me.

"Toni and I met at the UBA table at the activities fair," Derek tells the others.

An extremely short Asian person with extremely tall pants stands and slaps my hand. "Hey, man. I'm Eli." Eli's voice is very high.

"This is Nance," Derek says, pointing to the girl who's

still sitting down. "Nance, Toni's helping us with the transition guide."

Nance squints at me through a pair of glasses that are almost identical to my own.

"You're a freshman?" Nance asks in a Southern accent that sounds fake.

"Yep," I say. "Sorry."

Eli and Derek laugh.

"S'okay, man. You can't help it," Derek says.

I sit down on the couch next to Eli, determined to act as if I fit in here. "What, are you all sophomores?" I ask.

"No way! We look like sophomores to you?" Eli asks.

Eli's the only one whose gender presentation I can't figure out. I'm pretty sure Derek's a trans guy, and I'm pretty sure Nance, whose haircut is almost identical to mine, is a butch lesbian. I can't tell about Eli, though.

"Sorry, no, you all look really old," I say, even though Eli looks about nine. All three of them laugh. "Grad students?"

"Juniors," Nance says, then turns to Derek. "Was tabling as vile as usual?"

Derek shrugs. "Will you guys please at least show up at the next meeting? Don't make me and Toni fend for ourselves all year."

I try not to smile, but I'm positively giddy that Derek's including me this way. As if I'm already part of the group.

"No way," Nance says. "I put up with those bitches enough as it is. I'm sick of hearing Brad go on and on about how he's one of the first out gay guys in his final club. It's like, way to be a groundbreaker. You're a rich white guy who got a bunch of other rich white guys to let you pay them to be their friend. Five points to Brad."

Eli laughs. "I might go to a meeting or two. I like free cupcakes."

"Does Shari make those for all the meetings?" I ask.

"Usually," Derek says. "She's gotten good at the food coloring. Every meeting has a different theme. Maybe she won't make them next time, though, now that you called her out on it."

"No way!" Nance says. "Did he really?"

It takes me a second to realize Nance is talking about me.

"Yeah, and you should've seen it," Derek says. "Toni opens his mouth once, and Shari's all over him."

Okay, now Derek's doing it, too.

No one's ever called me by male pronouns before.

It's strange. Not necessarily bad. It's...I don't know what it is, actually.

"So, Toni, what's your story?" Nance asks. "You got some-body back home?"

"Back home?" Was Nance asking about my parents? I don't usually rant about my mom to people until I know them better.

"You know, like a girlfriend?" Eli blushes. "I mean, or a boyfriend, or whatever?"

"Oh. Yeah." A boyfriend? How weird. First the pronouns, now this. It's been years since anyone thought I was into guys. "My girlfriend goes to NYU."

"Cool," Derek says. "Do you have a picture?"

"Yeah." I try to ignore the familiar twinge of anxiety that's flared back up in my stomach now that we're talking about Gretchen and flip through the photos on my phone until I find a good one. "This is us at Queer Prom last year."

"You had a Queer Prom at your high school?" Nance asks. "Where are you from?"

"DC," I say.

"Oh," Nance says. "Figures."

I want to ask what Nance means by that, but then Eli peers at my phone and whistles like a trucker. Except with Eli's high-pitched voice it sounds more like a teakettle.

"Nice," Eli says. "*Very* nice."

"Yeah, you've got a definite hottie there," Nance says.

"Uh. Thanks." I'm not sure whether to be proud or offended. I'm leaning toward proud.

"Yo, guys, don't be crass," Derek says, squeezing onto the couch with the rest of us and leaning over to look at the picture. "Show some respect."

"Hey, man, I have the utmost respect for hotties!" Nance says. Everyone's laughing, so I do, too. "Ask anyone!"

"That's not what I heard." Derek smiles and takes the phone out of Eli's hand. As Eli reaches over to give it to Derek, I catch a glimpse of a chest binder through Eli's T-shirt. I guess that means Eli presents as male, too. I wonder if Eli's definitely trans, like Derek, or still figuring it out, like me.

Nance turns back to me. "Are you going to try to stay with your girlfriend all year? You didn't want to take a break or anything, what with starting college?"

"'Taking a break' is juvenile," I say, making air quotes. "You're either with someone or you're not."

"Yeah, but freshman year is hard," Derek says. "Long distance is tough when you haven't done it before."

"I know. I've heard all the clichés," I say. "How everyone always breaks up freshman year. I'm just saying they couldn't have been that committed in the first place if all it takes is some distance to split them up. Besides, Gretchen and I are barely even long distance. New York to Boston is a couple of hours on a train. We can see each other every weekend if we want to."

"Methinks the gentleman doth protest too much," Nance mutters. I decide to ignore this.

"Every weekend?" Eli asks. "Are you really going to do that?"

"That's the plan." I don't mention that we skipped last weekend.

"Our friend Andy used to have a girl like that," Nance says. "She was gorgeous, too. She dumped him, though. She had issues with the trans stuff. You know how it goes with some girls."

"Is your girlfriend cool with it, Toni?" Eli asks in a soft voice. "Or are you not out to her?"

I can't imagine keeping such a big secret from someone I care about as much as Gretchen. Is that really normal?

Well, I guess Gretchen kept a pretty big secret from me.

"Gretchen's very much cool with it," I say. "We're completely honest with each other about everything."

"Hey, you should get her to come up for the Halloween dance so we can meet her," Derek says. "Since you'll be visiting back and forth all the time anyway."

"There's a Halloween dance?" I ask.

Nance snorts. "*Dance* isn't the right word. It's more of an excuse to dress up in slutwear and drink a ton of alcohol."

"That works for me," I say, and the others laugh. Not that Gretchen or I usually drink very much. Gretchen is such a lightweight, and I'm always the one stuck driving.

But I don't have to drive up here. Everyone walks everywhere at Harvard. I can do what I want here.

I can be who I want.

"Some of the straight guys come in drag," Derek says. "Mostly it's respectful, though. It's supposed to be just for the people in our house, but we can get you guys in."

"Cool, thanks. I'll tell Gretchen."

Nance launches into a story about last year's Halloween dance and Derek joins in. Soon all of them are rushing to tell me all the best stories from last year, and the details on everyone I met at the UBA table, and all the reasons we shouldn't be hanging out and talking right now (all four of us have reading we should be doing instead).

Derek and Nance and I don't do any work on the transition guide, but that's okay. We have plenty of time.

And I have plenty of time to think about this transitioning stuff on my own, too.

# 4

SEPTEMBER
FRESHMAN YEAR OF COLLEGE
2 WEEKS APART

## GRETCHEN

"I looked up your girlfriend online," Carroll tells me.

It's a Friday night, and we're in the lounge carbing up on microwave pasta before we go out. There's a club Carroll's been bugging me to try since our first day of classes. Plus my bus to Boston leaves crazy early tomorrow morning, so we figured it would be easier to just stay up all night. It'll be my first time seeing Toni since school started.

"Oh, yeah?" I say. "Are you and T officially best buds now?"

He laughs. "No. I mean I looked up that genderqueer thing you told me about."

Crap. I still haven't mentioned that conversation to Toni. I'll come clean first thing after I get to Harvard. No, wait, I should do it before I get there. Toni might be upset, and I don't want to ruin our first visit with this.

"So what did you find out?" I ask Carroll.

"The site said a lot of genderqueer people are just kids who haven't made up their minds yet whether they want to be a guy or a girl," Carroll says, turning the faucet on full blast. "It said in the end, most of them either get over it or wind up full-on trannies."

I sigh. "Don't say 'tranny.' It's offensive."

Carroll holds up his hands in surrender. He drops the bowl he was supposed to be rinsing out. It clatters into the sink.

"See?" Carroll says, pointing to it. "Another casualty of political correctness."

I roll my eyes. "Ha, ha."

"So, is it true?" He wipes off the bowl. "About gender-queers?"

I'm pretty sure adding an *s* to *genderqueer* is offensive, too— it's offensive to just say *queers*, I think, and the principle would be the same, right?—but I don't know that for sure, so I don't say anything about it.

"I think that's just a stereotype," I say, though I'm uncertain. What Carroll read sounds like the kind of thing people say about bi people—that bisexuality isn't real, and they're really all either gay or straight and are just being indecisive. Since I have lots of bi friends, and I used to think of myself as kinda-sorta bi, I know that whole thing is bull. Being bi isn't any less real than being gay or straight is.

The problem is, I *know* stuff about being bi. I don't know

enough about being genderqueer to argue with whatever Carroll's been reading. Toni and I talked about this stuff some back when T first told me about it, but it's all so complicated and it's hard to remember all the details. I really need to go online and read some websites that are better than the one Carroll found. How will I know which websites are the good ones, though?

I guess I could ask Toni, but—well, I don't want T to know I'm still kind of confused. A good girlfriend would remember all the details. Actually, a good girlfriend would just instinctively understand all of this.

Of course, a good girlfriend probably wouldn't have lied about where she was going to college, either.

Okay. Enough. We're going out. I can berate myself later.

A half-drunk girl wanders into the lounge and says hi to Carroll. He says hi back. She lives on a different floor, but she's in Tisch with him, I learn.

"Hey, have you met my girl Gretchen?" Carroll asks. "Gretch, this is Tracy."

The girl looks at me. "Oh, right. I heard there was a lesbian on this floor."

I laugh. "Yeah, two of us, even."

The first week of classes, I ran into this girl I knew from debate, Briana. After we stopped laughing about how funny it was that we'd both wound up at NYU, she recruited me to join this volunteer project she's doing with a middle school in Inwood. She also introduced me to her friends. One of her friends, Heidi, turned out to live on my floor.

It's nice to have some gay friends at school who are girls.

They aren't nearly as much fun to hang out with as Carroll, though.

"I need to call Toni before we go out," I tell Carroll.

"Take your time," he says. "Suck up to the ball and chain. I'm nowhere near finalizing my outfit anyway."

"Whatever. You'll wind up in that new shirt you got on Tuesday."

"Not necessarily! There's also the faux-vintage one you made me buy at Urban. I have to do a compare and contrast."

Tracy laughs.

"Don't encourage him," I tell her.

I take my pasta back to my empty room. My roommate, Samantha, is already out at a party with her goth friends. She wandered out earlier wearing a black dress, red fishnets and knee-high boots. I'm not sure exactly what look she was going for, but I don't think it quite worked out the way she was hoping.

Toni isn't available on video chat, but when I call, T answers the phone on the first ring. I can hear voices in the background.

"Hey, Gretch!" I can hear the smile in Toni's voice, and I automatically smile back. It's so weird thinking it's been more than two weeks since we were last in the same place. I thought that much time apart would be unbearable, but getting to hear Toni's voice helps a lot. "I was about to call you! Are you going out?"

"Yeah, to a club with Carroll. How about you?"

"I'm out now, actually. Derek and the guys are having a party in their room."

"For real? Do people at Harvard have really huge rooms?"

"Some do." Someone says something in the background, and Toni laughs. "Hey, I meant to ask you, do you want to come up here for Halloween weekend? There's a dance. It's supposed to be cool."

My face breaks into a full-on grin.

Two weeks ago, I'd emailed Toni a list of potential bus times for me to come visit. Toni had replied with a one-sentence note about being too busy.

When I first read that email, I thought that was it for us. I thought Toni was so mad about what I'd done that T had decided never to see me again. I'd gotten embarrassingly hysterical about it, actually. Then Samantha came in from the bathroom and I had to pretend I was all emotional from watching a sappy video about cats.

Then Toni sent me a totally normal text about dining hall food, and we'd gotten on video chat that night and gushed about how much we missed each other, and it seemed like things were back to usual between us. I guess Toni really was just overwhelmed in those first few days of school. I was so relieved I started crying as soon as we signed off the chat.

Now I'm going up tomorrow, and we're planning another trip for after that. I guess things really are back to how they're supposed to be.

"Sure!" I tell Toni. "I was thinking about going to the Village Halloween parade, but that's okay. I've been before. Should I get a costume for the dance?"

"Yeah. Get something sexy, all right? I want to show you off."

I laugh. Toni doesn't usually say stuff like that. "Okay.

Carroll can help me find something. Listen, do you have a
sec to talk? It's kind of serious."

"Yeah, sure. Hang on." A door closes on Toni's end of the
phone. "What's up?"

I tell Toni about what I said to Carroll that first night. I
don't mention what Carroll said back, or how I didn't know
the answers to his questions. I'll set him straight once I've
read the websites and know the details.

Toni doesn't react the way I expected.

"Oh, everyone knows now," Toni says. "Even my roommates. Joanna's in a class with someone who's in the UBA,
so they found out last week. It's not a big deal."

"Wow." I sit down on the bed. I can't believe Toni didn't
mention this before. I keep my voice normal, though, because Toni's acting like it's nothing special. "Really? Are
they being cool?"

"Felicia's being a bitch, but Felicia was a bitch already. Everyone else is acting extremely normal. Like they're making
a point of it. Ebony even asked me what pronouns to use."

"What did you tell her?"

"That I didn't care, yet." I can hear Toni fidgeting. "Derek
and Nance and those guys use male pronouns for me."

Oh.

Toni's never used male pronouns before. What does this
mean? Is Toni, like—becoming a guy?

Will Toni still like me as a guy?

I slide down from the bed onto the floor. I shake my head
even though Toni can't see me. "Why?"

"They assumed."

"Oh." I nod. That's good. That means Toni didn't tell them to do it. "Did you tell them to stop?"

"No. Actually, I kind of like it."

"Oh."

"It's kind of making me wonder if maybe someday I'll start asking other people to do that, too."

"Oh. Oh."

I shake my head again. I don't understand what's happening here. I don't like this.

Wait. No. That's wrong of me. It isn't up to me to like or not like this. This is Toni's decision.

Wait, but—*is* it a decision? Being genderqueer is like being gay, right? Being gay isn't a choice, obviously. My parents gave me a book about that in elementary school when my brother first came out. Being gay or trans is no more a choice than being Australian.

There's silence on the other end of the phone. Toni's waiting for me to talk.

"Oh," I say. "Really? When?"

"I don't know. I need to think more. I've talked to Derek about it. He's cool. Easy to talk to."

I can't tell if that was an accidental pronoun slip or if it was on purpose. I can't remember the last time I heard Toni use a gendered pronoun. Well, if they're already out at a party, they've probably been drinking, so...

"Derek sounds great." I swallow, still trying to sound normal. It's not like I'm freaking out or anything. I'm just kind of...confused? Lost? "I'll get to meet him when I come up tomorrow, right?"

"Yeah! Of course. They all can't wait to meet you. I showed them your picture. Nance called you a hottie."

I laugh. A little bit of the tension goes out of me. I can't wait to actually *see* Toni again. Everything would be so much better if we could just touch each other. Just occupy the same space.

Someone bangs on my door. "Gretchen! Let me in! I need your help with this shirt dilemma!"

I laugh again.

"Did you hear that?" I ask Toni.

"Yeah. Have fun tonight. It's a gay club, right?"

"Yeah."

"Don't do any drugs, okay? You would be so embarrassing high."

I laugh. "Will do. Have fun hanging out in somebody's room."

We laugh some more.

"I love you," Toni says in a low voice that brings a whole new smile to my face, because I know that voice is meant for only me to hear.

"I love you, too. I can't wait to see you tomorrow."

"I know. Me, too."

We get off the phone. Carroll, who's kept up a steady beat on the door, acts all annoyed when I let him in. He's topless, holding a stack of T-shirts.

"Finally." He plops down on my bed and holds the first shirt up to his chest. "Thoughts?"

"Red works for you," I say. "But isn't it a bit much?"

"'A bit much' isn't necessarily a bad thing." He holds up another. "Too boring?"

"No, but won't every other guy in the club be wearing that exact same shirt?"

"Maybe not. I heard straight people go to this place on Friday nights, too." He tries the one he bought at American Apparel last week. "This is the safest choice."

"I agree. It's hot, though."

"Yeah, it is." Carroll pulls on the T-shirt and saunters over to Samantha's mirror to play with his hair. "I must say, for someone who dresses herself like a slacker hippie, you have decent taste in guys' clothes. Maybe you're really a gay man trapped in a lesbian's body."

"No way," I say. "I have a really strong gag reflex."

He laughs. "So it's another boring T-shirt and jeans ensemble for you tonight?"

"All I have is T-shirts and jeans. Oh, and that reminds me, I need you to come shopping with me soon. I'm going to a Halloween dance up at Harvard."

Carroll's looking through my closet. He nudges aside the backpack I've already filled with clothes and books for the bus tomorrow. "You don't need to go shopping for that. No one at Harvard has any clue how to dress. Here, wear this tonight."

He hands me a blue silk top I borrowed from someone last year and never gave back. I go in the bathroom to put it on.

I've got to stop stressing out. I want to be normal tonight.

Is it normal to have a girlfriend who doesn't use the word *girl*, though? Wait, if Toni starts using male pronouns, would that make Toni my *boyfriend*?

No. Not thinking about this now. Tonight I will be Fun

Gretchen. Then tomorrow I'll go see Toni and everything will work itself out.

"Apparently this dance thing is a big event," I say through the open door. "Toni told me to get something sexy."

Carroll laughs. "Okay, whatever the missus commands. For now, though, could you please hurry up and do your makeup so we can get out of here?"

I slide on my Chapstick. "All set."

The club is enormous. I've been to clubs in DC but nothing anywhere near this massive. Carroll's never been to a club at all. I try to tell him this place is crazy huge, but as soon as our under-twenty-one hand stamps are in place and the doors have closed behind us, there's no point talking. All we can hear is the pulsing music.

But it's fun. It's so, so amazingly fun.

We did a couple of shots before we came out, in Tracy's room. (Tracy turned out to be awesome, actually.) Between the alcohol buzzing in my brain, the music pounding in my ears and the sight of hundreds of half-dressed guys grinding up against each other, I feel like I'm in a whole other fabulous universe. I stop thinking about everything that happened before this moment. I close my eyes and let the beat of the music flow up into my chest until it takes over my entire body.

And I dance. I never, ever want to stop dancing.

Carroll, for his part, starts grinning the second we walk through the doors and never stops. He's entered his own personal heaven.

We dance to Beyoncé. We dance to Britney. We dance

to Taylor Swift. Carroll makes the sign of the cross when
"Like a Prayer" comes on, and I laugh because Toni's sort
of Catholic, too, and apparently I am destined to spend my
life surrounded by sort-of Catholics, and right now that's
hilarious. Right now everything's hilarious.

Carroll and I dance together for what feels like hours because each song is about twenty minutes long. Carroll's an
okay dancer, but he needs to loosen up. He gets a drink from
somewhere, and that seems to help.

Suddenly there's a sketchy guy dancing next to us. He
has a mustache and a gold necklace that says Mama's Boy.
His bare chest is superhairy and soaking with sweat. I turn
around so I won't have to look at him while I dance.

I close my eyes again and sing along at the top of my lungs
to the chorus of "Born This Way." When I open my eyes,
Carroll has his tongue down the sketchy guy's throat.

Oh. Okay.

I dance by myself for a while. Then a guy with brown hair
comes over and dances next to me. He shouts something that
sounds like, "You're full of snot!"

"What?" I shout back.

"YOU'RE REALLY HOT!" he shouts.

Oh. This must be one of the straight guys Carroll said
might be here. I shout back, "I'm gay!"

"WHAT?"

"I'M GAY!"

"OH." The guy pauses. "THAT'S OK. GAY CHICKS
CAN STILL BE HOT."

I laugh.

The guy takes both my hands and we start dancing the

way you do in middle school—step-together, step-together, one-two-three. I'm laughing even harder now. We dance like that through all of "Hips Don't Lie." Then the guy leans in and yells, "IS YOUR FRIEND OK?"

"WHY?" I look where he's pointing. Carroll and the sketchy guy have broken their lip-lock, and the sketchy guy is talking really emphatically to Carroll. Carroll's trying to back away, but he can't get through the wall of bodies behind him.

I wave goodbye to the brown-haired guy and push my way through the crowd.

"IT'S TIME TO LEAVE!" I shout at Carroll. I grab his hand and tug him toward the door.

He tugs back, not moving. "IT'S EARLY!" he yells.

I look at Chest Hair Man. He's grinning at me. It's creepy.

"HEY, SORRY, WE GOTTA GO," I tell the guy. Then I have a brilliant idea. "HIS MOM WILL KILL US IF HE MISSES CURFEW."

I expect Chest Hair Man to be horrified at the implication of underage debauchery. Instead he licks his lips.

Okay, *ewww*. I stop smiling and turn back to Carroll.

"THIS GUY IS A DOUCHEBAG," I say. "WE'RE LEAVING RIGHT NOW."

This time I tug on both of Carroll's hands. After a second of resistance, he lets me pull him across the floor.

I look behind us a few times as we fight our way through the crowd, but Chest Hair Man has upgraded (downgraded?) to a kid with bleached hair who doesn't appear to have entered puberty.

We have to wait ten minutes for a cab. Carroll's annoyed with me at first. I'm irritated, too. I was having fun before.

It all fades fast, though. We're both too exhausted to be mad now that the high of the club music is gone. And suddenly we're both starving.

We get the cabdriver to let us off at the pizza place down the block from our dorm and eat our slices as we walk home, the grease dripping down our chins and onto our sweaty clothes.

"Can I tell you something superembarrassing?" Carroll asks me in the elevator after he's shoved the last chunk of crust into his mouth.

"Course." I wipe grease off his cheekbone and reach for my phone. I haven't looked at it since we got to the club. I have twelve new texts.

"That—" Carroll grins up at the ceiling, but he doesn't look amused. "That was my first kiss."

I gape.

"Don't laugh," he says.

"I'm not!" I sort of am, though, so I bite my lip. "But— seriously?"

"Yeah." We're at our floor, so I follow Carroll to his room. It's empty. Juan is always out all night on Fridays. Some sort of track team hazing thing I don't want to know the details of. "I told you before. I wasn't lying. There were no other gay people in Arneyville."

"I didn't think you were lying." I lie down on Carroll's bed while he changes. "Anyway, congratulations."

"Thanks. At least it's over with, right?"

"Right." I yawn. I'm tired but not sleepy. My muscles

ache from dancing. I want to curl up here and not get up for hours, but I have to stay awake until it's time to leave for the bus. "Wow, and on your very first night at a club."

"With an ugly guy, though. Then I look over and see *you* dancing with a hot one."

"Well, I'm pretty sure that guy was straight."

"Like it matters." Carroll pushes me over to one side of the bed and lies down next to me. "Your turn. When was *your* first kiss?"

I laugh and start thumbing through my texts. Two are from Briana, asking my advice about whether to ask out a girl she thinks is cute. "You really want to hear about that?"

"I want to hear everything about that. I'm praying it's more humiliating than mine. Was it the girlfriend?"

"Oh, no. Toni and I didn't get together until we were sixteen."

I smile. That night was magic.

It feels like a lifetime ago. I was a different person back then. We both were.

I have a bunch of texts from Toni, too. I glance down the stream. Something about the trip tomorrow.

"So, how old were you the first time?" Carroll asks.

I shift my head onto his shoulder so I won't have to meet his eyes. "Um. Eleven."

"No way! You beat me by *seven* years?"

"Well, he was almost as ugly as yours, if that helps."

"No way!" Carroll swats at my shoulder. I swat him back. "Your first kiss was a guy?"

"Yeah, but I made up for it by having eight girlfriends over the next five years."

"Ha! I knew you had an inner tramp," Carroll said. "Till the missus came along and domesticated you, obviously. But still, your first kiss was with a gross, penis-having *boy*."

"I was *eleven*. I didn't know I liked girls yet. All I knew I liked back then was unicorns."

He laughs. "I knew I was gay when I was eleven."

"Seriously?"

"Oh, yeah. Everyone else could tell, too. Fifth grade, I was already getting the crap kicked out of me every week."

Carroll always talks about how he used to get beat up all the time. I never know how to react.

"Did you ever, you know, tell anyone about that?" I ask. "Like a teacher, or your parents, or whoever?"

"No way. God, all I needed was for my parents to find out."

"So they still don't know about you?"

"They've probably heard it somewhere. They live in Arneyville, too."

We're quiet for a while. I'm getting sleepy, but I shake my head to stay awake as I click through my texts from Toni.

The first couple are about something funny Toni's friend Eli said, and a Chinese restaurant that serves punch in glasses as big as your face. The next message is something about not realizing until now how much homework had piled up for the weekend. Another text time-stamped half an hour later says maybe we should think more about our plans.

I'm still trying to understand what that means when Carroll says, "Roger Davis."

"Who?" I prop myself up on my shoulder so I can talk to him and look at my texts at the same time.

"Roger Davis. From *Rent*."

I struggle to remember. "The musical?"

"Yeah. Roger. That's who I always imagined my first kiss would be. I used to listen to the soundtrack all night and think about how everything would be all right if I could only meet someone like Roger."

I glance up from my phone. "Wait, wasn't Roger the straight guy?"

"You're missing the point." Carroll huffs. "Roger is the ideal man."

"Roger was the junkie, right?"

"Stop it!" Carroll pulls a pillow over his face. "I am never telling you anything ever again!"

"Sorry, sorry!" I lift up a corner of the pillow so he can hear me. "I'm sorry. I haven't seen that show since I was a kid. Look, we can download the movie sometime and you can tell me all about how fantastic Roger is, and I'll admit the error of my ways."

"Don't need to download it," he mumbles. "I have the DVD."

"Then let's watch it soon, okay?"

"Okay." He pushes the pillow off us.

Toni's last text, sent twenty minutes ago, says,

Don't hate me, but do you think we could do next weekend instead? I just didn't realize how much stuff had piled up. I'm so sorry.

My eyes fall closed. Suddenly all I want to do is sleep.

I should go back to my room. I don't want to have to explain this to Carroll.

It's just that I'm so, so tired.

And so…I don't know. The word *sad* doesn't seem right. Neither does *disappointed*. *Devastated*, maybe. But that doesn't quite fit, either.

When I open my eyes, it's light out. Juan still isn't back, and I haven't gotten any new texts since last night, but Carroll is sound asleep, curled up next to me.


I don't get hangovers. Mornings like this, I wish I did. If I were hungover I wouldn't have to think.

I'm wide awake by 8:00 a.m. and eager for distractions, so I sneak out of bed while Carroll's still dead to the world and go meet Briana at the gym. Briana wants to do crunches and talk about the girl she met the other night. A girl named Rosa.

"I really like her, but I think she might be kind of psycho," Briana tells me when we're on crunch number thirty. "She asked me to make a list of all my ex-girlfriends. I could see her memorizing their names. Like she was going to go online and stalk them as soon as she got a chance."

"Yeah, that's sketchy," I say.

"I mean, she's *not* sketchy, though. That's the thing. She's way saner than anyone I went out with in high school. I asked if she'd ever been arrested, and she said no."

"Why'd you ask her that?"

"The girl I went out with this summer was addicted to shoplifting. It was scary. We'd go to the mall and she'd sneak all this random stuff into my purse. I wouldn't even notice until I got out to the parking lot and suddenly I had, like, twenty different leather wristbands from Hot Topic. Hey, why'd you stop?"

I've already counted out sixty crunches and now I'm sitting up with my head resting on my knees. My mind is racing, and Briana's monologue isn't helping.

"You know what?" I say. "I really have to do some cardio. I feel like I ate an entire pizza last night."

"Yeah, me, too." Briana counts out her seventieth crunch and stands up. She leads me to the treadmills. Perfect. You can't talk on a treadmill.

We put on our headphones. I concentrate on putting one foot in front of the other. It helps a little, but my brain still won't shut up.

I think about my backpack, still sitting in my closet where Carroll nudged it aside last night. Maybe I'll leave it packed for next weekend.

Maybe next weekend won't happen, either. Maybe Toni just doesn't want to see me.

No. That's stupid. Didn't we just make a big deal about me coming to this Halloween dance?

What if Toni cancels that at the last second, too?

I never should have come here. I've ruined everything.

And Toni is clearly having a blast at Harvard with people who aren't me. Thinking about changing pronouns. Starting a whole new life and leaving me behind.

I run two miles and say goodbye to Briana, who's already on her fourth. I go back to my room and take a half-hour shower while Samantha bangs on the bathroom door for me to hurry up. Then I text Carroll and meet him at the dining hall. I wolf down a plate of pancakes and eggs while everyone around us douses themselves in coffee and moans about how hungover they are.

Across the table, Carroll is quiet, stirring sugar and honey into his tea. So I tell him about the late-night texts. About the pronouns.

"It sucks that you can't go up there," he says. "You think it's 'cause she's mad at you?"

"I don't know." I shrug. "Toni never *seems* mad. It's probably true, about T having too much work. I mean, it's Harvard. Besides, the pronoun thing has to be distracting."

Carroll raises one skeptical eyebrow. "Come on. Are pronouns really *that* big a deal?"

"Yeah, usually. I mean, everyone's different, but using male pronouns is this huge step."

"Oh," he says. "I thought you said Toni thought all pronouns were bad and that English was sexist, or whatever?"

"I don't know." I rub my forehead. Toni did say that stuff before. Did something change? Maybe I misunderstood it to begin with. Can I ask about that, or will that make me seem totally clueless?

"So, look," Carroll says. "It's okay. You can tell me the truth. Are you into that?"

I keep rubbing my forehead. "Into what?"

"You know. Are you one of those girls who's into the whole guys-wearing-panties thing, and vice versa? Like, does it turn you on?"

My head starts to ache. Maybe I'm hungover, after all. "Is this more crap from that website you found?"

"Yeah. It said some people are into guys that look like girls, or girls that look like guys. They think it's hot."

I groan. Carroll's terrible internet research skills are really getting old.

"I'm sure there are lots of people who are into all kinds of things," I say. "But I don't care about that. I only care about Toni."

"Uh-huh." He yawns. "It's weird how you talk about this stuff. Because when we hang out, you know, normally, just you and me, you come off like such a *girl* girl, but when you talk about her, you act like you totally get how she feels."

Did he just call me a girlie girl?

"I'm not one of those ultrafemme girls," I say. "I don't wear glitter nail polish and all that."

"Oh, really?" He gets this half smirk on his face that I don't like at all. "Does that mean you're kind of trans, too? Like Toni?"

"No!" I say. Then I hear how that sounds and I say, "No, but I mean, it's not like it's a big deal."

"Riiiiight." Carroll stretches the word out into another yawn. "What does it mean if your girlfriend is a guy? Do you still get to tell people you're a lesbian?"

My heart is pounding. I shouldn't think this is important. It *isn't* important.

"I don't care what other people think," I say. "That's so petty."

"Well, if you only like girls, and your girlfriend turns into a guy, then how can you like her? Or him? Doesn't that mean you're really bi?"

The back of my head throbs. I wish I'd never brought any of this up. I take a long drink of coffee. "I don't know. I don't think that's how it works."

"Well, since you're so enlightened about it all, that means you and her are, like, beyond gender, right? So it doesn't matter if your girlfriend is really your boyfriend?" He grins. "Even if that means people think you're straight?"

I can't help it. The word *straight* makes me shudder.

It's not like I have a problem with straight people or anything. I've always had tons of straight friends. It's just that being straight seems so...obvious. So conventional. It's never felt like *me*.

I don't even remember when I first thought of myself as gay. It's not like I sat down one day and decided boys were icky. I even used to get crushes on guys when I was a kid. I just never wanted to jump any of them the way I wanted to jump Toni at that Homecoming dance.

I guess maybe I could like a guy someday. Hypothetically. I'm never going to stop liking girls, though. If people started thinking of me as straight, it would really freak me out.

Carroll sees the look on my face and laughs. "Maybe you're not that enlightened, after all. Maybe you have issues like the rest of us normal people."

Now I'm mad. He's just saying all this because he knows it'll bother me. He has no idea how serious this really is.

Whenever I start to think about this stuff, I always push it out of my head. I always think I'll have time to figure it out later.

Well, what if right now *is* later? What if the stuff I've put off thinking about is actually happening right now?

Toni's friends are using male pronouns already. Soon Toni could ask everyone else to do the same thing. Come out to the whole family. After that, there could be actual physical changes. Hormone injections. Surgery.

Would Toni still be the same person after all of that?

Would Toni still want to be with me? Regular, boring me, who doesn't even know how to talk about pronouns without messing up?

I shake my head so these thoughts will go away. It only makes my headache worse. I look back up at Carroll.

"I'm not straight," I say. "It doesn't matter what pronouns Toni uses. That wouldn't make me straight."

"What's so bad about being straight?" Carroll grins. As far as he's concerned, this conversation is hysterical. "Some of my best friends are straight!"

"Oh, yeah?" I say. "Who among your many, many friends would those be?"

Carroll's grin fades, and his eyebrows crinkle. He bites his lip like he might cry.

I'm the worst person in the world.

"Crap, crap, crap, I'm sorry," I say. "Really, I am. Ugh, please just ignore me. I'm freaking out a little bit."

"Why?" Carroll lowers his mug to the table. "Are you—wait, are you mad at *her*?"

"No!" The very idea of being mad at Toni is ludicrous. "Of course not. Toni sounded really happy about this pronoun thing, so that makes me happy, too."

"No, I meant about canceling your trip," Carroll says. "You *should* be mad at her for that. Seriously."

I shake my head. "That isn't how it works. We don't get mad at each other that easily."

Carroll raises a skeptical eyebrow, but I ignore him.

"It's just that I hadn't thought about this other stuff," I say. "Like, what it means for me if Toni starts presenting as a guy. I guess it doesn't really mean anything for me, though. It's not about me."

"Sure it is," Carroll says. "Like, what do you tell your parents? 'Whoops, sorry I freaked you out, it was a false alarm, it turns out I'm into guys, after all'?"

"Oh, my parents won't care either way. They love Toni."

"For real?" Carroll frowns. "When did you come out to them?"

"Eighth grade, when I had my first girlfriend. My brother's gay, too, so they were used to it by the time I came along."

"Huh." Carroll strokes his chin. He didn't shave this morning, so there's a tiny bit of light brown stubble there. "So they'd be cool with it if you told them your girlfriend's getting a dick."

Oh, for gosh sake. "Look, Carroll, please don't talk like that. You sound like you're on Fox News."

"Sorry. I promise to behave from now on."

Carroll spends the rest of brunch telling me about the latest episode of *The Flighted Ones* while I finish two more mugs of coffee.

When I get back to my room, I'm jittery from the caffeine. My head feels like it's going to detach itself from my body and go romp around in Headache Land. There's no way I can focus on the paper I need to write. Instead, I take three aspirin and gaze at the computer screen while all the questions Carroll asked whirl around in my brain. After two hours, I know the headache isn't going away unless I talk this all the way through.

I can't talk to Toni. Not until I've done enough research

to understand all the gender stuff. Not until I can talk about it the same way Toni's new friends apparently can.

Besides, sometimes being a good girlfriend means not mentioning every single thought that passes through your head. Especially thoughts that might hurt your girlfriend's feelings.

So I text Carroll and ask him to come out for another slice of pizza.

# 5

## TONI

I think Kevin & I are going to try a nonmonogamous relationship, the text from Audrey says.

I glance around before texting back, since I'm in class, but no one seems to be paying attention to me.

What does that mean?

We want to stay together but also see other people, my sister replies.

Like having your cake and eating it too?

Whatever. Don't mock my romantic ideals.

Hey, I have the utmost respect for your romantic ideals. Who do you want to romance with besides Kevin?

No one in particular. I just want the option. Monogamy is so old-school. No offense.

None taken. I pride myself on my old-schoolness.

I bite my lip to keep from laughing out loud.

I'm sure Audrey is dead serious about the "nonmonogamous relationship" thing, but I can't imagine what it will actually mean in practice. The second Kevin hooks up with some other girl, Audrey's bound to go psychotic.

I slide my phone back into my bag and glance around the room. We're in a small basement classroom in one of the older buildings on campus. They haven't turned the heat on yet, so everyone's wrapped up in coats and scarves against the chill. Three other people are on their phones, too, which makes me feel better, but I turn to my laptop and get back to taking notes anyway. Lacey, our grad student teaching fellow, is winding down the discussion about the evolution of the two-party system.

In high school I never would've dreamed of texting in class. I was what you might call a nerd about academics. And, okay, most other things.

In college, though, everything feels more anonymous. When I was growing up, my teachers kept telling me I was supersmart, which was awesome, but here, I'm surrounded by people who heard the same thing all their lives from *their* teachers. I still want to make perfect grades, obviously, but—I mean, it's Harvard. There's no way I'm going to be at the top of my class. I don't know if there even *is* a top of the class.

Plus, I'm four weeks into my Foundations of American Government class and the main thing I've learned so far, aside from the fact that buying a semester's worth of government textbooks meant putting upward of two hundred dollars on my mom's credit card, is that there are way too many conservatives at Harvard.

Lacey dismisses the section, and I glance at my watch. I'm about to be late to meet my friends. I'm shoving my laptop into my bag when I hear my name.

"Stick around for a few minutes, will you, Antonia?" It's Lacey calling to me from the front of the room.

I grit my teeth. I hate it when people call me Antonia.

Wait. Did Lacey notice me texting? Crapola. I gear up for a lecture and meet Lacey at the front of the class.

"That was an interesting perspective," Lacey says as the rest of the class filters out. Lacey's young, maybe a year or two out of undergrad, with long, deep brown hair that's always wound into a messy braid. As though Lacey's too busy being smart to worry about anything so frivolous as hair. "Some would argue our two-party system is getting stronger as candidates move further to the left and right extremes."

Oh, right. During the first half of the discussion, before I got Audrey's text, I said I thought the Democrats only had a couple of decades left in them before the party collapsed for good. Half the room tried to shout me down.

"That's absurd," I say. "Party identification is decreasing.

How many people in the US said they considered themselves independents in the last election? More than forty percent, right?"

"Either the Democrats or the Republicans have won every presidential election since 1852," Lacey says. "It's easy to get caught up in media hype about one party or the other being up or down, but looking at the arc of history—"

"The arc of history shows that the parties have evolved," I say. "No one's trying to resurrect the Whigs anymore, but it's reductive to say all we've ever had is a party that loves abortions and a party that hates nonwhite people. We've only known it one way, but that doesn't mean it can't evolve. Or that evolution has to be a bad thing."

"You know, I think you're absolutely right," Lacey says. I blink. "Especially in a foundations class like this one, we have to be able to put aside our presumptive, twenty-first-century views and focus our analysis on the bigger picture."

That isn't what I was trying to say at all, but I don't want to argue anymore. I started the day fighting. My roommates have very strong opinions about how long my showers should take.

"So thank you for speaking up during the discussion." Lacey smiles. Not a teacher-like smile, either. More of an isn't-it-cool-how-smart-we-both-are smile.

I nod, uncertain. I don't know what to make of this conversation.

"So, I hope to hear more from you next class, Antonia," Lacey says.

"It's just Toni, actually."

"Okay, then. Toni." Lacey smiles again.

I turn to go without smiling back. I'm not sure what just happened, but something about it left me feeling vaguely anxious.

I try to shake it off as I hurry outside. It's only the beginning of October, but it's already getting cold. I'm getting sick, the way I always do when the seasons start changing. Of course, it probably doesn't help that I only slept four hours last night. The night before, too. Between reading, writing my piece for PolitiWonk, more reading, working on the transition guide, more reading, and hacking up lungs while my roommates yelled from the other room for me to be quiet, and then, yes, more reading. Sleep is a luxury I did not sufficiently appreciate in high school.

I'm crossing the street into the square, now officially late to meet the guys, when my phone rings. It's Chris. I hit Accept.

"Hey, you," I say.

"Hey back," Chris says, then pauses. "So."

Chris never calls me to say "So." Chris texts me or emails me or messages me. I haven't gotten a phone call from Chris since June.

I play dumb. "What's up?"

"So," Chris says again. "Um. I have news."

"What kind of news?"

"Um, so I. Uh. Not so much with the virginity thing anymore."

I laugh. "Congratulations. When did this happen?"

"Last night. He came for a visit."

"This is Steven, I assume? You're back together?"

"Yes. Hello. Obviously. What kind of guy do you think I am?"

"Sorry."

While Chris fills me in on more details than I'd really prefer, I check my watch. I'm fifteen minutes late. My friends are going to kill me. A bunch of us are meeting outside the Starbucks and then going to some bar they love in Jamaica Plain, and they made a big deal about everyone having to be exactly on time. We're meeting up with their friend Andy, the president and cofounder of Harvard's Student Anti-Starbucks Alliance, so we have to move fast. Being seen next to an actual Starbucks is not politically advisable for Andy.

"The problem is, I'm getting all paranoid," Chris says. "He keeps dropping these hints about guys he's friends with at school. I have this weird feeling, like maybe instead of this being about us taking the next step, it's kind of like, I don't know. A preemptive goodbye or something."

I take a long breath. Long enough to suppress the urge to say *I told you so.*

"That's absurd," I say. "No way would Steven fly all the way across the country just for a pity screw."

Chris laughs. "Thanks a lot."

"Look, Steven adores you, okay? Besides, no Stanford guy could ever be anywhere near as hot as you. Not even Elvis."

Chris laughs again. "Well, yeah. I mean, obviously."

"On that self-aggrandizing note, I have to go," I say.

"No! Wait! I have a ton more to tell you."

"Sorry, I'm already late. Can you get online later and tell me the rest?"

"Where are you going anyway?"

"Just out with some friends. I have to be exactly on time. I think it's a weird hazing ritual." I haven't told Chris about

Derek and the others. I don't want those two worlds colliding yet.

"Okay, fine. But be prepared to receive an epic email with a lot of embarrassing details in it. I have to gush somehow or other."

I concede to this plan, get off the phone and half run to Starbucks. Derek and Eli are there, along with Pete, Kartik and a couple of other guys from the UBA. I've met them before, but I don't know them very well. It's weird hanging out with such a big group when I'm really only friends with Derek and Eli. Also, no one's ever actually told me where most of the other guys are on the trans spectrum—they might be totally cisgender for all I know—and it kind of stresses me out not knowing how to categorize them.

"Where's Andy?" I ask.

"He went to hide in 7-Eleven while we waited for you," Eli tells me. "He thought he saw someone trying to take a picture of him by the Starbucks sign."

"How is 7-Eleven better than Starbucks?" I ask.

"Don't ask Andy that," Derek says. "He wrote thirty pages on it last year for his corporate social responsibility seminar."

We cut through the food court and find Andy by the Slurpee machine.

Andy glares at me. "I know you're new here, T, but punctuality is key. One picture in the *Crimson* of me by that stupid green logo and my life is over."

"I'm sorry." I hold up my hands. Andy's the only person in our friend group who not only tries to look like an aggressive, stereotypical frat boy but actually succeeds. It makes me kind of nervous. "It was an emergency."

Andy sips a Slurpee with narrowed brows. "Tell me your excuse. *I'll* judge if it was an emergency."

"It was Chris, my best friend," I say. "From high school, I mean."

"Oh, right." Kartik chuckles. "You're a freshman. You still talk to your high school friends."

"Leave him alone, dude," Derek says, even though Kartik was only joking. Derek does stuff like that. "So, Toni, what was your friend's emergency?"

"Uh." Well, Chris didn't say it was a secret. "Maybe it wasn't technically an emergency. Well. My friend just had sex for the first time."

Andy whoops and holds the Slurpee high. "Great! We've got an excuse to celebrate. Tonight, we drink in honor of Toni's high school friend's devirginification."

I cheer at that with the rest of them, but as we leave the 7-Eleven I remember I don't know how the alcohol part is supposed to work, exactly. None of us is twenty-one except for Eli, and Eli doesn't like to show ID because Eli's license still has an *F* on the "sex" line. No one seems worried, though, so I don't bring it up.

"Is Nance coming?" I ask as we take the steps down to the T.

"She's at a thing for the Dems," Derek says. "They're making phone calls to Texas about another abortion ballot measure. She'll meet us at the bar later with some of the other girls."

When we get on the train, I ignore Derek's warning and ask Andy about the 7-Eleven versus Starbucks issue. I spend most of the trip listening to Andy talk about sustainable agriculture, which actually turns out to be really interesting.

Everyone else in the group has clearly heard the speech many times before, though. They keep sighing and generally indicating dramatic boredom.

After we've transferred to the Orange Line and Andy has shown no sign of letting up in the agriculture rant, Derek barks, "Okay! He gets it! Now please let's talk about something else!"

Andy, who's sitting on the other side of the aisle from us, mutters something about geniuses never being appreciated in their own time.

I turn to Derek. There's something I've meant to tell the guys for a while.

"So, for the record, I don't actually use male pronouns," I say.

"Really?" Derek says. Pete twists around to look at us. I swallow and make myself keep talking anyway.

"Yeah," I say. "I mean, it's just that I haven't before."

Derek groans. "Sorry! We shouldn't have assumed. Damn, I should know better by now. Especially since you have that *i* in your name. What do you prefer, those gender-neutral pronouns like *ze* and *zir*?"

"I don't know," I say. "I've never used those. I get why people do, but it just seems kind of disrespectful to the English language to start making up words, you know?"

"You think so?" Derek asks. "Language is supposed to evolve. Did you know the word *sexism* wasn't invented until 1965?"

"But *sexism* makes linguistic sense," I say. "The fake pronouns just sound weird."

"Hey, now, lots of people use those," Derek says.

"Oh, yeah, yeah, I know." Crap. I try to backtrack. "That's totally cool. I'm all for people using whatever words they want. Maybe I'll decide to try them at some point."

"Do you use *they*?" Pete asks. "That's what I used to do."

Hmm. So Pete is somewhere on the trans spectrum, too. Interesting.

Well, probably. Come to think of it, Pete could've gone by *they* and still been cis. That's almost like what Gretchen does. Except Gretchen only does it for me.

Gretchen. The anxiety flares up in my chest, the way it always does when I think about my girlfriend. We only texted once today, hours ago, about a girl at the middle school where Gretchen volunteers. The girl got in trouble for munching on baby carrots too loudly during church, and she was trying to use that as her key example in a debate speech on government regulation. Gretchen told me the story over text and I sent some laughing emoticons back. We haven't actually *talked* talked since the day before yesterday.

That's my fault. Gretchen sends texts and calls on video chat way more than I do. And sometimes I don't answer right away.

I want to talk to Gretchen more. It's just that… I don't know.

This is all so overwhelming. Being up here, thinking about all this stuff, having conversations like the one I'm having right now.

I need Gretchen more than ever. But I need Gretchen *here*. With me. Not hundreds of miles away.

"I've tried using *they*," I tell Pete, "but it always makes me groan a tiny bit inside. I mean, I know there are linguistic justifications for using it as a singular pronoun, and at least *they* is an actual word, but—"

"You say *guy* and *girl*," Pete says. "I've heard you say that. You talk about your *girlfriend*, too. If you don't use *he* or *she*, why use other gendered language?"

I swallow. I can't tell if Pete is annoyed at me or just curious. Half the group is looking at me now.

"Yeah, in theory I'd like to stop saying words like *girl*, too," I say. "It's just really tough in practice, you know? Staying away from *he* and *she* is hard enough, even though I'm mostly used to it now."

"Hey, what are you guys talking about?" Across the aisle, Andy's attention is back on us. So is Eli's. All the other conversations have ended, and all eyes are on Pete and me.

"Pronouns." Pete stands up and stretches, smiling down at me in a reassuring way. "Sorry, folks. It's just yet another conversation about pronouns."

"We've been total jerks, dude," Derek tells Andy. "It turns out T doesn't use male pronouns, after all."

Andy stands up and comes toward us, gripping the pole for balance. Eli slips into the empty seat next to mine.

"Don't tell me you still use girl pronouns." Eli's voice is gentle. "You don't have to do that. You have us now."

"Stop, don't rush him—I mean, don't rush Toni," Derek says.

I don't like Derek talking about me as if I'm not here. Or, worse, as if I'm a kid. Their pet project.

Besides, I hate pronouns. Why do we even need *he* and *she*? Neither one feels right. Why can't everyone just use the same pronouns? Or if they have to be separated into categories—if our language absolutely *needs* multiple pronouns—why divide them up by gender? It's so arbitrary. We might as well have different pronouns based on how old you are, or what your favorite color is, or your astrological sign.

Mostly I hate having conversations like this one. I hate having people look at me like I'm crazy for thinking so much about this stuff. I wish I could make up my own language where everything made sense.

"I never use gendered pronouns at all," I say. "I don't want to reinforce the gender binary."

Andy snorts. "Please. Don't be one of those hypergenderqueer people who's always ragging on the rest of us for wanting to look like guys."

"That's not what Toni said at all," Derek says. "Relax, dude."

"I'm just saying, I had to go through a lot of shit to get people to call me *he*," Andy tells us. "I don't need some kid coming in here and deciding I don't get to just because binaries are evil."

I sit back in my seat, stunned.

I don't know what to say. Maybe Andy has a point. Is it disrespectful for me *not* to use gendered pronouns to talk about people like Andy? And Derek and Eli, for that matter? *I* don't like pronouns, but is it rude not to use them for people who do?

Maybe I need to rethink all of this from the beginning.

"I would never say that." I raise my voice. "I think everybody should use whatever pronouns they want to. This is just a personal thing."

"Hey, don't worry, T, it's cool." Derek looks at Andy. "It's cool, right?"

Andy shrugs and says, after a pause, "Yeah, I guess. Everybody makes up their own rules, right?"

I nod. I'm shaking, I'm so nervous.

"Look, pronouns don't have to be a huge deal if you don't want them to be," Derek says. "Toni, did you ever meet Lisa? The girl with the dreadlocks? She used to be in the UBA but she left it to start the HQSA?"

I shake my head.

"She identifies as trans, but she doesn't care about pronouns at all," Derek says. "I asked her once what pronouns she preferred, and she just said, 'I come when called.'"

"I like that way of doing it," Pete says. "Having to always tell people your preferred pronouns just puts everybody all up in your business, whether you want them there or not."

"Yeah, I can see that, sort of," I say. "I don't actually care what you call me. I just didn't want you to think I used male pronouns all the time. No one calls me by them except you guys."

"What does your girlfriend call you?" Derek asks.

"Gretchen doesn't use gendered pronouns to talk about me."

"Wow." Andy whistles. "That's a lot of effort. Must be true love."

There's that anxiety in my chest again.

We're finally at our stop, thank the lord. Andy punches

me lightly on the arm as we get off the train. I hold back, not sure what to expect.

"Listen, dude, no hard feelings, right?" Andy asks. "That came out wrong, what I said back there. I don't want you thinking I judge or anything. Are we cool?"

The expression on Andy's face is totally sincere. Nervous, even.

"We're cool," I say. "And I get what you were saying. I'm going to think about it some more. Maybe I don't give pronouns enough credit."

Andy puts out a hand to shake. I smile. We clasp hands and turn to follow the others up the steps.

The bar is smaller than I expected, but we can tell even from the outside that it's packed with people. There's a line at the door but the bouncer, an enormous drag queen in a bedazzled halter top, sees Derek and waves us to the front.

"Hey, sweetie," the drag queen says, kissing Derek on the cheek as the rest of the line grumbles. The drag queen looks at me. "Did you bring me a new boy tonight?"

"Uh. I guess." Derek motions me forward. "Barb, this is Toni."

"Hey, handsome." Barb winks at me and squeezes my shoulder. I fight to stay upright. Barb's biceps are no joke. "You a little Harvard freshman?"

"Yes," I squeak, terrified of this mammoth woman smiling down at me. I feel myself blushing and resist the urge to add "ma'am."

"You be sure to save a dance for me, okay, sugar?" Barb says.

"Oh, uh—okay."

People in line chuckle.

"Careful, Barb, you'll crush the poor kid!" someone calls out.

Barb waves us inside without asking for IDs or making us pay the cover charge. Now I know why the guys like this place so much.

Kartik and Pete fight through the throng to the bar and bring back two pitchers of beer. We find a spot on the wall and check out the crowd. It isn't what I expected at all. I've never been to a gay bar before, but I've seen them on TV, and it was always a bunch of well-dressed white guys. This place is a big mix of people, though. Men and women, all different races. Some straight couples, too. Plus a few women who I think are trans—not drag queens like Barb, but normal-looking women, wearing flowy dresses and high-heeled sandals despite the cold weather. I think there are other trans guys mixed in with the crowd, too, but they're harder to spot because they look the same as the cis guys.

"How do you know Barb?" I ask Derek.

"She's friends with Nance's ex," Derek says. "She's worked here since our freshman year."

Kartik juts a thumb in Derek's direction. "We met her when he and Nance were going out."

Derek is suddenly looking away, taking a long drink of beer.

"You went out with Nance?" I ask.

"Everybody makes mistakes freshman year." Andy laughs. "You'll see, T."

"YO! PEEEETE!" someone with an Australian accent shouts from the other end of the bar.

"YO! DOMINIC!" Pete shouts back. "GET OVER HERE, YOU USELESS ASSWIPE!"

A group of guys pushes over to us, sloshing beer onto the floor and their clothes. I can't tell if they're queer. They all have baseball caps on, but then, so do most of the guys in our group.

"YO!" the one named Dominic yells. "GUYS, THIS IS MY BOY PETE FROM CAMPUS CONSERVATIVES! AND HIS FRIENDS! PETE, WHO ARE YOUR FRIENDS?"

Pete introduces us. Dominic and the others are drunk already and in very good moods. At first I assume the "Campus Conservatives" thing is a joke, though I guess I don't actually know Pete all that well. Maybe Pete and these guys really are Republicans. The sort of Republicans who come to a mostly gay-and-trans bar anyway. We don't have those kinds of Republicans where I'm from.

"ARE YOU A FRESHMAN?" one of Pete's friends yells at me.

"Yeah," I say. "By the way, I know expressing your thoughts at the top of your lungs can be good for stress relief, but you really don't need to yell. We're not on the other side of the room anymore."

The guy laughs.

"I like this kid," one of them says.

"Dude, don't get any ideas," Andy says. "T's taken. Got a little girlfriend down at NYU."

"Like that matters, man," the guy says. "Nobody makes it through freshman year. This kid'll be hookin' up with other chicks by fall break."

"That is such an irrelevant stereotype," I say. "As if it's impossible that my relationship would be durable enough to sustain a few months apart."

"What, you gonna stay with your girl forever?" One of the other guys laughs. "You gonna get gay-married?"

"How amusing," I say as the other guys chuckle. "In fact, I find jokes about the decades-long sociopolitical movement to ensure legal and cultural equality for all simply *hilarious*."

The guys all stare at me. Huh. I used that line all the time in high school and it always got a laugh.

"Uh," Pete says. "T, we need to get you another drink."

Pete's right. Two beers later, I love everyone in the place, and they all seem to love me back. I joke around with Dominic and the other guys for half the night. It turns out they're all in the same final club. Final clubs are these exclusive all-male secret societies that have these crazy parties, but everyone on campus who *isn't* in a final club sits around mocking final clubs. When Dominic and the others get sick of hanging out with guys who want to talk only about yachts and how many BU girls they scored with that weekend, they come here to chill.

All night long, Dominic and the guys make fun of the people in their club and ask me and my friends questions about our exotic, non-final-club-centered lives. They don't even mind when we don't want to satisfy their curiosity. When one of them asks me how Gretchen and I have sex, I answer, "That is none of your damn business, you useless asswipe," and everyone just laughs harder.

It's the best night I've had since I left DC.

Nance shows up later with two cis girls I don't know

named Laura and Inez. I try to say hi, but Dominic has just finished telling a story about one of the guys in his club who'd gone snorkeling while stoned on spring break and thought a shark was attacking, and I'm laughing too hard to talk.

Nance sees me and turns to Derek. "You let him get drunk?"

"He's fine," Derek says. "Oh, wait, crap. Sorry, T. Nance, we're not supposed to say *he* anymore. Turns out Toni isn't into that."

"Whatever." Nance leaves to go to the bar.

"I'll get us some water." Derek goes after Nance.

"Did they really used to go out?" I ask Eli.

"Oh, yeah," Eli says. "For, like, a year."

"Was that before…"

"Oh, yeahhh." Eli nods vigorously. "Derek was a girl then. Our freshman year really kind of sucked, to be honest. You're doing a lot better than we were. Anyway, that's how we got stuck with Nance. Derek made us put her in our blocking group freshman year, so now we're stuck living with her till graduation."

"You don't like Nance?"

Eli shrugs. "Do *you*?"

It never occurred to me to dislike anyone in Derek's group. I assumed they were a package deal.

Derek and Nance are fighting their way back from the bar. Nance is awkwardly holding three pint glasses and Derek has four bottles of water. The music hits a low point, and we can hear them talking.

"She's such a little babydyke," Nance is telling Derek.

"She's as bad as my sister. You shouldn't bother. It's not like you need another charity case."

Nance's stories are always weird. I turn back to continue my conversation with Eli, but Eli shifts, not meeting my eyes. Then Pete says to Derek, way too loudly, "Hey, did you see the babe in the blue skirt? Hot."

Did Eli and Pete think Nance was talking about me?

*Was* Nance talking about me?

Then Nance and Derek catch my eye, and they both look down. That answers my question.

Is this because of the stupid pronouns?

Why does *everyone* always make such a huge deal about pronouns? It's as if my whole life has to be dictated by those two or three letters. I wish pronouns had never been invented.

Derek hands me one of the water bottles. Probably Derek's way of saying I've had enough to drink.

Screw that. Derek doesn't get to tell me what to do. Nance is right—I'm not anyone's charity case.

"I'm getting another drink." I push off the wall. My legs are shaky, but I propel my way forward.

"You sure you're okay?" Derek asks.

"I'm *fine*."

Then we hear someone yell across the room. Barb, the bouncer, is towering over everyone on stiletto heels.

"Who are you to disrespect my friend?" Barb screams at a guy in a Red Sox cap. "She's the prettiest girl who ever lived!"

"Leave it alone, Barb!" one of the bartenders yells.

"Yeah, well, maybe if she ate her weave she'd be pretty

on the inside, too!" the guy in the cap shouts. It sounds to me like the guy is joking, and I start to laugh, but then Barb winds back and punches the guy in the face with a loud thud. A collective shout echoes across the bar.

"We should go," Derek says.

I let Derek pull me to the door as more people start yelling. Behind us, Eli and Nance are pushing their way through. I can't see where Andy, Pete and the other guys went. I'm still shaky, so I need Derek's help, but I try not to let that be too obvious.

"DOES THIS ALWAYS HAPPEN?" I yell.

"PRETTY MUCH, YEAH." Derek laughs as we make it out into the chilly open air. "It's all part of the adventure."

The rest of our group stumbles outside. Nance and Inez light cigarettes.

"Think we can get a cab?" Laura asks.

We try for a long time. It doesn't help that everyone else who left the bar is trying to get cabs at the same time. We also aren't in the best neighborhood. None of the services we call have cars anywhere near us. After twenty minutes I'm shivering from the cold, worried about my wallet getting stolen and completely sober.

Finally an empty cab pulls up. Nance and the other two girls pile into it first.

"I can only take one more, up front," the cabdriver says in a thick, annoyed Boston accent, eyeing Derek, Eli and me.

"We can all fit," Derek says. "See how skinny we are?"

"No way," the driver says.

"We can fit one more back here, Derek," Inez, a pretty brunette, calls from the back of the cab. "We can scooch in."

"Toni, Eli, get in," Derek says. "You're skinnier than me."

"No way," I say. "You're skinnier than I am."

This is an obvious lie, but I'm still reeling from what Nance said. I don't want anyone taking pity on me. I don't want to have to squash into a cab with Nance, either.

"I can only fit one, kids," the driver calls.

"If you guys are going to be indecisive, I've got a paper due tomorrow," Eli says.

Derek and I nod. Eli climbs into the cab and it speeds off, leaving us alone in the cold with no cabs in sight.

Derek scans the empty street, then turns back to the bar. "It seems to have calmed down in there. Want to go back in? You look cold."

"Yeah. Next time I'll bring a bigger coat."

"Don't bother. You've got to get used to Massachusetts weather sooner or later."

The place is only half-full now. There's no sign of Pete and the rest of our group. Barb is at a cocktail table toasting champagne glasses with the guy in the Red Sox cap, so I guess all's well.

Derek and I find an empty booth in the back. We each order Cokes. Derek insists. "Trust me. You'll appreciate it tomorrow."

"You don't have to do that," I say. "I can take care of myself."

"I know, but you can also learn from my past mistakes." Derek laughs.

I gaze down into my drink.

"Okay, fine," Derek says. "Is this about what Nance said? Are you pissed?"

I shrug.

"You shouldn't take her seriously. She's prickly at first, but she's a great friend once she gets to know you."

I shrug again. I don't want to talk about Nance. "Who were those other two girls who were here before? Laura and Inez?"

"They were both at the last UBA meeting. You don't remember?"

"Oh, right. Laura was the one who gave the speech about making the sexual harassment policy queer inclusive. Wait, why are you grinning that way?"

Derek grins some more. "'Cause I always grin when I talk about Inez."

"Ah." Since Derek used to go out with Nance, I'd figured Derek wasn't into feminine-looking girls like Inez. Live and learn, I guess.

Inez is cute enough. Nowhere near as pretty as Gretchen, though. Definitely not my type.

If I even have a type. It's been so long, I can barely remember what it's like to be attracted to someone who isn't Gretchen.

Now I'm anxious again.

"Are you and Inez a thing?" I ask, to distract myself.

"No. At least, not yet."

"Are you going to be a thing?"

"You say that as if it's entirely up to me."

"If it *were* entirely up to you, would you and Inez be a thing?"

"Maybe. She's cute, and she's a physics concentrator. I like me some physics concentrators."

I shake my head with a smile, but I don't get how you'd ever say "maybe" about whether or not you want to go out with someone.

With Gretchen, I knew from the first night that there was something between us. Something real.

It was never only that Gretchen was pretty, either. It always felt—well, serious. Deep. There was never any "maybe" about it.

I try to explain that to Derek. It doesn't come out very well thanks to the lingering effects of all that beer, but Derek smiles at me.

"Hey, that's great for you guys. I've never been in love at first sight like that. I've always liked people the old-fashioned, boring way, where you like someone a little, and then you like them a lot, and then you like them a *lot*." Derek laughs. Derek, I've noticed, laughs more often than not. Gretchen does that, too. "You and your girlfriend must have something really special. I can't wait to meet her. When's she coming up?"

"Halloween."

"Not before that? I thought you said you guys were going to visit each other every weekend?"

"We were." I motion to the waitress for a refill. For our first couple of weeks of school, Gretchen kept trying to make plans to come up. Finally I said we were both too busy and we should just wait until Halloween and the dance.

The thing is, I *am* busy. But I'm also *aching* to see Gretchen. To touch. I never thought I'd feel so starved for physical contact.

I'm also kind of terrified of the idea, though. I'm scared

that when we're face-to-face, that ache won't be what comes through. I'm afraid it'll be the anxiety. And the anger I still can't rationalize away.

"You should ask Inez to the dance," I tell Derek. "I mean, if people ask people to dances in college."

Derek laughs even harder. "Sometimes I forget you're a freshman."

"Good. No one else does."

"Anyway, yeah, people ask people to dances sometimes. I'll probably ask her if I can get over myself in time."

I nod. "So is Inez bi or what?"

"Last I heard, she identifies as *heteroflexible*." Derek laughs again. "So she's a step up for me. My last relationship ended because it turned out his idea of bi meant 'screwing every other guy within a hundred-foot radius and then lying about it.'"

I pause with my drink halfway to my mouth. "Wait, what did you say?"

"Oh, it's nothing bad. *Heteroflexible* means she mostly likes guys, but not always. She thinks it's more accurate for her than *bi*."

"I know what *heteroflexible* means." I shake my head. "It was the stupid pronoun. Sorry, I'm dumb. I didn't know you'd dated guys. Up until now I thought you were straight."

Derek's mouth falls open.

"How have we never talked about this?" Derek says. "That's hysterical! I guess I need to come out to you, then. Toni."

Derek takes my hand and puts on a fake-serious expression.

"I have to tell you something very important about myself. I like guys sometimes, too."

We laugh some more. Derek lets go of my hand.

"Do you identify as bi?" I ask.

"Yeah, usually. What about you?"

"I don't have a label that I use for sexual orientation. I just think of myself as queer." I could go through the whole explanation for why I especially hate the word *lesbian*—it makes me think of old ladies playing pool and wearing flannel—but I don't want to get into that. I don't know who might be eavesdropping. The last thing I need is for Barb, or one of Barb's equally well-built friends, to take offense. "It doesn't seem to matter anyway since I only want to be with Gretchen."

"But what if someday you—" Derek pauses. "Never mind. When did you first identify as GQ?"

The truth is, I don't even like the word *genderqueer* that much. I especially hate abbreviating it as *GQ*. It makes me think of the dumb magazine with the half-naked girls on the cover.

I haven't heard a word I like better, though. It's like Inez with *heteroflexible*. Even though that's a stupid word, too.

"Junior year of high school," I say. "I went to this crazy private all-girl school, and we had to wear a uniform with a white shirt and a plaid skirt. It was like something out of Japanese porn. I went to the administration and asked if I could wear pants instead, and they said no. So I wound up threatening to sue the school. Eventually they changed the policy. Before that, though, I talked to these lawyers at the ACLU, and they asked me if I identified as genderqueer, because if I did, they'd put it in the argument. It would be the first time they'd had a genderqueer plaintiff in a case like mine. They were all excited about it. I didn't know much about *genderqueer* as a term, so I looked it up. In the end it turned out we didn't need to sue, after all, because the administration got scared and decided I could wear pants. Besides, if I'd let the ACLU tell people I was genderqueer, it would've gone into the news stories, and I'd have had to tell my mother, and I was nowhere near ready to do that in eleventh grade, or now for that matter. But anyway, at least I got a semiacceptable label out of the thing. So when I started coming out to people online and stuff, *genderqueer* was the word I used."

Derek stares at me. "That was *you*?"

"What was me?"

"The school uniform lawsuit! I followed your case on all the blogs. I even started a petition about you! You were my hero!"

I laugh so hard I spit Coke. "You're lying."

"No way! I can't believe this. I can't believe I didn't recognize your name when I first met you!"

"The stories probably called me Antonia," I say, making a face.

"Oh, that's right. I remember it all now. I was so jealous of you! I was completely closeted in high school, but you— you had the nerve to fight the power!"

Derek lifts a fist into the air, grinning even harder now than when we talked about Inez. I sit up straight and smile back. I never thought anyone outside my high school friends would remember that story.

"I guess it was pretty cool," I say.

"It was majorly cool! But I do have one question. This always bothered me. You had a guys' high school that was connected with yours, didn't you? So why didn't you ask to wear their uniform instead? Why did you want to wear the same uniform the girls did, only with pants? Because that's what you wound up with, right? I saw the picture—you had on some unfortunate blue-plaid pants in the end."

"It wasn't about fashion," I say.

"I know, but if it was about gender presentation, wouldn't it have made the most sense to wear the guys' uniform?"

I gnaw on my knuckle. "I didn't think about it that way at the time."

Why *did* I do that? It never occurred to me back then to want to look like the guys. Before the ACLU prompted me to start searching the internet, I'd thought of myself as butch. Now that doesn't feel right at all.

If I were doing it over again, would I want to wear the guys' uniform? I don't know. I feel more like a guy now than I did then, but I can't imagine wanting to, like, go to the guys' high school and use their locker room or whatever.

Derek probably would have. Andy, too. Maybe even Eli.

What makes me so different? Am I just in a temporary stage before I wind up the same as them? I try to imagine living full-time as a guy, wearing a suit like Brad's and joking around with guys the way Andy and Kartik do. It sounds kind of thrilling. And terrifying. When I try to picture it, I see myself dressed up like it's Halloween or like I'm acting in a movie. It doesn't seem real.

Why is this stuff so confusing? Am I really the only person in the world who thinks this stuff is complicated? As far as I know, Gretchen never thinks about this stuff at all. Gretchen's always identified as a girl without angsting about it or anything. I don't know what I'd do if I had all that spare time. I could probably train for the Olympics.

"Sorry," Derek says. "It was a long time ago anyway, but I've always been curious. Even when I was home for Thanksgiving break I used to sneak onto the library computers to see if there was any news about you."

"Why'd you have to sneak onto the computers?" I say.

"Sometimes I forgot to clear my browser history at home. My dad always checked it."

"That sucks. Are your parents better now?"

"Sort of. It's a work in progress."

"Are you out to them?"

"Yeah. I've talked to my dad and my stepmom a couple of times, but they never want to talk about it afterward. It's as if I never brought it up."

Derek has stopped laughing. It's strange having such a serious conversation after everything else that's happened tonight.

But I want to know about this. Suddenly I *need* to know.

"Do your parents call you by the right pronouns?" I ask.

"They don't call me anything. It's like they go out of the way to avoid using pronouns at all. The way you do. For different reasons, obviously."

"Do they call you the right name?"

"I don't know what they call me when I'm not there. But they don't call me anything to my face. They start out their emails with just 'Hi.' But they're better than they used to be. High school was pretty awful. I'm just lucky I made it out of there in one piece."

I nod. "What was your name before?"

Derek takes a sip of soda. "Michelle."

"How'd you pick Derek?"

"I used to be really into Derek Jeter. Look, I'm sorry, but can we please change the subject? No offense, because I understand why you want to know, but I get asked these questions all the time, and I really don't like talking about this. The past is the past, and it's better if it stays there."

"Okay," I say. Even though I desperately want to know if the Derek Jeter part was a joke. "Want to talk about Inez some more?"

"That's okay. Why don't you tell me about your parents? You said your mom is scary, right?"

Now that it's on me, I'm not sure I want to talk about this, either.

"My mom's scary," I say. "That's basically it."

That's a sufficient summary anyway.

My mother and I have gotten good at avoiding each other over the past couple of years. Over our whole lives, really.

I can count on one hand the number of significant conversations we've had. There was the time in fifth grade when I announced I was quitting piano lessons and had to listen to a speech about the tragic death of my mother's dreams of having a concert pianist in the family. The time freshman year when I came out as a "lesbian" (ick). The time junior year when I admitted that my friends and I had broken the Tiffany iced tea pitcher while we were playing Wii.

My mother and I manage to avoid most insignificant conversations, too. That became a lot easier once I got a driver's license and could spend as much time as I wanted at Gretchen's. Even before that, though, we were never the sit-around-the-dinner-table-and-talk-about-your-day kind of family. Mostly, when I had dinner at home, it consisted of me and my sister hanging off the kitchen counter eating Salvadoran food and begging our housekeeper, Consuela, to tell us stories about the crazy families Consuela worked for before ours. One was a high-ranking Republican White House official—Consuela never told me which, but I have theories—who insisted that the floor rugs be inspected every day for evidence of either bedbugs or planted recording devices.

Sometimes I wonder if my mother actually personally hates me, or if I'm just a major lifestyle inconvenience. It always seemed to bother Mom way more when I did "weird" stuff in front of other people—like when I went through my middle-school goth phase and wore a fake nose ring to school for a week—than when I just did it in the house, where none of our snooty neighbors had to know about it.

"What about your dad?" Derek asks. I blink before I remember we're still having this conversation.

"My dad would be scary, too, if my dad was ever home," I say. "But that doesn't usually happen, so."

"What particular variety of scary are your parents?"

"Oh, your basic Republican nouveau-riche Harvard-alum lawyer-for-the-overprivileged and semialcoholic housewife couple. They hate me, I hate them, et cetera. All we've talked about since I came out was my GPA."

"When you came out as gay, you mean?"

"Yeah."

"How'd they take that?"

I shrug. I'm starting to wish I hadn't asked Derek all those questions.

"I'm not sure my dad even heard," I say. "Dad was listening to a Bluetooth headset the whole time. Had it on during my valedictorian speech, too. My mom, though—she flipped out. I had to go stay with my friend Chris for a week."

"Seriously? She kicked you out of the house?"

"Not technically. It was like we were playing chicken. Mom was all, 'I won't tolerate this under my roof,' and I was all, 'So rent me an apartment,' and Mom was all, 'Don't get smart with me, Antonia,' and I was all, 'What if I did move out? Would you even care?' and Mom was all, 'Don't be absurd, I'm simply stating the facts, and the fact is, I will not have any foolishness in this family.' So I bolted."

I've told this story before. I always leave out the parts about the crying and the doors slamming and the thinking I was going to have to transfer to public school and move into foster care and never make it to Harvard. I figure people can fill in the blanks.

Even though I wind up thinking about it every time I tell the story anyway.

"Wow," Derek says. "But you went back home eventually?"

"Yeah. Chris's dad negotiated on my behalf." I take another sip. My Coke is getting warm. "Can we talk about something happier, please, before what little buzz I have left is gone?"

"Absolutely." Derek smiles. For the first time since I've

known Derek, the smile looks forced. "I think you should show me some pictures of your girlfriend and tell me the story behind every single one. It may be the closest I'll ever get to true love."

I force a smile of my own. "Fantastic idea!"

I take out my phone and we go through the pictures. Derek seems genuinely fascinated by it all. And talking about how things were between Gretchen and me in high school makes me feel a little better about us than I did before. Our relationship has the most solid foundation it possibly could. We'll see each other in a couple of weeks for Halloween, and it will be amazing. As soon as I put my arms around Gretchen again, everything is going to feel a thousand times better.

It'll be easy again. All we have to do is touch. That's the only thing I've ever needed.

# BEFORE

## GRETCHEN

I was the first one to say "I love you."

I'd been thinking it way before that night. I'd been thinking it a *lot*. But the saying-it-out-loud part seemed impossible.

I thought one of us might say it the first time we slept together, but that had already come and gone. Even without an "I love you," that night was amazing in its own right. I'd had sex before, with my last girlfriend before I left New York, but there was something completely different about being with someone you actually, seriously cared about. Someone you knew so well they were almost a part of you. Afterward, lying under the beige Pottery Barn quilt on Toni's huge brass bed, we'd laughed and whispered until I had to leave to make curfew, and then we'd written secret notes on each other's phones that we promised not to look at until later. When I got home and read Toni's note, it said,

I knew it was you. The first time I saw you, I knew it would always be you.

I clutched that phone to my chest and grinned like a doofus until I fell asleep.

It was the happiest I'd ever been. I'd probably thought *I love you* a hundred different times that night, but I'd never found the breath to say it.

When it finally happened, I didn't have to find the breath. It found me.

Toni found me first, though. It was a dark, cold Tuesday night, and I was home with my parents watching basketball. I went to the kitchen to get a glass of water, and a pair of headlights out the window caught my eye.

Toni was sitting in her Nissan out front of my house. The streetlight was on the opposite side of the road, so Toni was just a dark silhouette, her forehead tipped against the steering wheel, a hoodie pulled up over her spiked hair.

I looked at my phone to make sure I hadn't missed a text saying she was coming over. I hadn't.

I told my parents I was going for a walk. They looked at me like I was crazy—it was freezing outside—but they couldn't tell me not to. We lived in an incredibly boring suburb in Maryland where nothing bad ever happened. When I was growing up in Brooklyn, my brothers acted like they had to keep a watch out to make sure I didn't get mugged walking to the deli for a soda, but from where we lived now I could probably walk all the way into DC without running into a single wacko.

I hugged my sweatshirt around my arms as I tiptoed down the driveway, shielding my eyes against the glare from the headlights. Behind them, Toni and her car were completely still. The engine was off and she wasn't wearing a coat. She had to be freezing.

She didn't look up when I approached. I tapped lightly on the window. She turned toward me, her forehead still resting on the steering wheel.

I could tell right away something was wrong. Something had happened.

Toni smiled a faltering smile anyway.

## TONI

Lord, it was good to see her.

I unlocked the doors, and Gretchen climbed inside. She wasn't wearing a coat, and she was rubbing her hands together against the cold. "Aren't you freezing?" she asked.

"Oh. Right." I turned the key and flipped the heat on. Warm air flowed out of the vents, making my bare fingers prickle. I hadn't realized it was that cold out.

"I didn't know you were coming over." Gretchen took one of my hands and held it between hers. Her skin was warmer than mine. "Do you want to come in?"

"No."

"Do you want to drive somewhere?"

I shook my head.

When she spoke next, her voice was lower, like she already knew my answer. "Did something happen?"

I'd never told Gretchen much about my family, but that didn't mean she didn't know. Our friends had probably told her things. And she must've noticed that we only went over to my house when my parents weren't there.

I'd met Gretchen's parents the night of our first official date. It was all very old-fashioned. Well, we'd already made out a half-dozen times before our first official date, not counting the time on the dance floor at Homecoming, so it wasn't *that* old-fashioned, but the date part kind of was. I'd driven over to pick her up, knocked on the door and been greeted by her dad, Mr. Daniels. I'd gone inside and met Gretchen's mom and one of her brothers and their dog, a rescued greyhound named after the actor who played C3PO in *Star Wars*. That was the sort of family Gretchen had. Gretchen's dad was about seven feet tall, or that's what he looked like next to me anyway, but he was really nice. He and Gretchen's mom both acted like it was perfectly normal that their daughter was going on a date with another girl.

Gretchen had never met my parents. She'd hinted a couple of times that she wanted to, but she hadn't pushed. That was the thing about Gretchen. She never, ever pushed.

I'd wanted to keep her away from all of that. I'd wanted what I had with Gretchen—this perfect, precious thing we had together—to be separate. Untainted.

That wasn't up to me, though. That wasn't how life worked.

I realized it right there, sitting there in the car with her

holding my hand, both of us shivering while we waited for
the heat to fill the car. You didn't get to put all your stuff in
little boxes where nothing touched each other. You could
try, but sooner or later the boxes would start bursting at the
seams. Everything runs together in the end.

So I took a long breath, and I squeezed her hand, and I
told Gretchen what my mother had done that afternoon.

## GRETCHEN

I'd never met Toni's mom, but I'd heard enough stories
from Toni's friends to know Mrs. Fasseau was a complete
bitch. I just didn't understand exactly how complete a bitch
she was until that night in the car.

When Toni first started to tell me what had happened,
she looked calm. Her face was composed. She looked—
professional, almost. She recounted the story in the same
even tone I'd heard her use to make presentations in class.
Like she was being graded on her oratory skills.

Toni and her sister, Audrey, had gone shopping after our
Gay-Straight Alliance meeting that afternoon. Audrey had
bought two pairs of shoes for Easter even though Easter was
still a month away and no one needed two pairs of shoes for
it regardless.

The Fasseaus only went to church at Christmas and Easter,
and the whole family dressed up for it. Whenever they all
went anywhere together, there were all these rules they had
to follow—fancy clothes, no chewing gum, no looking at
phones, no slouching and other stuff that basically would've

been impossible to follow for any regular family. Which the Fasseaus, apparently, were not supposed to be.

Audrey had been in a shopping mood that day—Audrey was pretty much always in a shopping mood—and she'd begged Toni to get something for Easter, too. Toni gave in and went over to a table full of ties. She meant to just grab the first thing she saw so Audrey would get off her back, but that plan changed when she saw what she called "the most awesome tie ever created."

She showed me a picture of it on her phone. It wasn't anything supercrazy—the fabric was electric blue with cinnamon-and-gold stripes—but I could tell from the way she talked about it that Toni had developed a mild obsession with this tie. As she smiled down at the phone screen, I hoped she liked me as much as she did this blue-striped tie.

When they'd gotten home, Mrs. Fasseau had made a big deal about wanting to see what they'd bought. She did that sometimes, Toni said. Feigned interest in her children's activities. Usually when she'd been out with her friends and they were comparing notes about how impressive their respective children were.

Mrs. Fasseau hadn't been happy with Audrey's shoes, though. She'd examined both pairs, proclaimed them "cheap," and ordered Toni's sister to return them to the store.

"Buy something people will have heard of, for heaven's sake," Mrs. Fasseau said, swooping her hand over the shoe-boxes as if to banish them from her sight. Then she opened Toni's bag.

Toni had tried to not let her see. By the time she was telling this part of the story, Toni's class-presentation voice was gone. There was a glimmer in her eye as she told me how she'd tried to slide the Macy's box into her backpack. She wasn't quick enough.

When Mrs. Fasseau saw the tie, she didn't react at first. She just stared at it as if she wasn't sure it was real. Then she pulled it out of the box and dangled it from the tips of her fingers, a full arm's length away, like it was a wet painting that was going to jump onto her crisp white sweater.

"Is this supposed to be a joke?" Mrs. Fasseau asked.

Toni didn't say anything, so Audrey did. "You don't have to hold it out like that, Mom. It doesn't have rabies."

Mrs. Fasseau ignored her. She jutted her chin at Toni but wouldn't meet her eyes. She hadn't looked Toni in the eye in years. "Is it a gift for your father? Because he has better taste than to wear this, I'm afraid."

Toni shook her head. She didn't know, she told me, what made her say what she did—whether it was her mom insulting the thing she loved, or whether she just wanted to see how her mom would answer—but whatever the reason was, Toni stood straight up and told her mom, "No. It's for me. I'm wearing it for Easter."

Her mom didn't even blink. "You're planning on wearing this to church, hmm? In front of everyone we know? In front of *God*?"

The fact that Toni didn't make a snarky comeback to that—that she didn't even mention having *thought* of one—was how I knew Toni was really, really, really upset. Religion was not a topic of discussion in the Fasseaus' house. For Toni's mother to accuse Toni of doing anything in front of "God" was so hypocritical as to be automatically funny in any other

circumstances. Later, Toni would tell me she couldn't remember her mother ever uttering the word *God* before that
afternoon. She was pretty sure her mother thought of "God"
and "everyone we know" as one and the same.

Toni's mother strode across the kitchen to the junk drawer
and pulled out a pair of scissors. Toni could already see what
she was going to do, and Audrey was saying, "No, Mom,
don't," but it was too late. Mrs. Fasseau sliced the tie neatly
into two, letting the wide bottom part fall into the sink.
Then she strode out of the kitchen without looking back
while Audrey shouted after her, "Nice one, Mom! Are you
going to pay her back, at least?"

"It was just a tie," Toni kept saying that night in the car.
"Just a stupid *tie*. It didn't *mean* anything."

"I know," I said.

"My mom's reading all of this, like, I don't know—*stuff*
into it. It's so presumptive. She's acting like the tie was a
*symbol*. Like she can cut off whatever it's a *symbol* of. When
it's just a tie, you know? It's just some stupid fabric somebody stitched together in a sweatshop in, like, Bangladesh
or something. It's just that it was a *really nice* tie. I didn't actually care if I wore it to church or not, you know? I just
liked it. I didn't even use her credit card to buy it. I used my
birthday money from my grandmother. She didn't ask how
I got it, though. She didn't care."

*I care*, I wanted to say. *I care about everything about you*, I
wanted to say.

"I'm sorry," I said instead.

Then I said, "I love you."

## TONI

I couldn't believe she actually said it. Out loud.

I'd wanted to say it for months, but…what if she didn't say it back? What if she laughed at me? What if she thought I wasn't taking this relationship seriously? What if *she* wasn't taking this relationship seriously?

"I love you, too," I said.

It didn't make me want to cry any less. It didn't mean that when I fell asleep that night, I wouldn't still be thinking about my mom standing there with the scissors in her hand.

But it meant I'd have something else to think about, too. Something that made me feel like I wasn't completely worthless.

Actually, if I was being completely honest, what Gretchen just said made me feel like I was the king of the stupid planet. Not the whole planet, I mean, not, like, *Earth*, but my own personal planet. Mine and Gretchen's.

Gretchen was the beginning and end of everything. She was all I'd ever need. I'd been searching my whole life for something, but until now I didn't know what that something was.

Gretchen saying "I love you" proved that I wasn't making this all up in my head. That maybe this fantasy I'd been living in for the past five months wasn't just a fantasy. Maybe it was my actual life.

And as for my mom cutting up the stupid tie, as though she was trying to show what would happen if I crossed that invisible line, the one between girl and boy, the line that might not even actually exist—and here we were all pretending this was as simple as whether I wore a stupid tie to stupid church in front of her stupid friends (and *God*, we mustn't forget *God*, obviously)—as for that...

Today, my mom cut up a stupid tie an hour before the world's most perfect girl told me she loved me.

"I love you, too," I said again.

We kissed. It was our best kiss ever. *My* best kiss ever.

We couldn't stay in the car much longer. Gretchen's parents would be getting worried. She hadn't even brought her phone out with her. She'd just come outside to find me, shivering in her sweatshirt, tapping on the window. She'd come because she knew I needed her.

I would always need her.

As I watched her walk back to the house, I knew something between us had changed that night. Something that had been intangible had become solid. Something unspoken was now resolute.

I knew I would always love Gretchen.

What I didn't know then was that love changes. Just like everything else.

6

## GRETCHEN

"Tell me how this works," Samantha says while I'm trying to read. "Do you wear a dress and she wears a tux?"

"Nobody wears a tux," I tell her. "It isn't a wedding."

"Do you both wear a dress?" Sam asks.

"I might wear a dress if we can find one I like. I don't know what Toni will wear."

I pointedly look at my laptop. I'm rereading the instructions for Boston University's spring transfer application. The due date is November 1. Exactly one week from today. I need to decide soon if I'm going to apply.

I haven't said anything about that to Toni. But then, Toni hasn't asked me about it, either.

"Does she pick you up and buy you a corsage?" Samantha asks. "Do you dance together at the dance? Who leads?"

Samantha is very, very sweet. I have to remind myself of this often, because Samantha asks these questions all the time, and it would be annoying if she weren't so sweet.

"No," I tell her. "Toni's not picking me up. We will walk from Toni's dorm room to the other side of campus."

At least, that's what I think will happen. I haven't talked to Toni in a while. T always says it's never a good time to talk on video chat, which I understand given the horrific roommate situation. When I send a text, I always get a reply, but lately when I call Toni's phone, it's been going straight to voice mail. Then I get a text half an hour later with an apology saying Toni was out with the guys and didn't hear the phone ring.

The thing is, I know that happens. It happens to me, too. There's a lot going on for both of us. A couple of weeks ago I started going out to the middle school in Inwood with Briana to coach their debate team for our volunteer project, and I realized that holy crap, it takes a long time to prep for debate-team coaching, and it also takes a really long time to get to Inwood. Between homework and volunteering and the alternative spring break group I joined just in case I'm still here in the spring, plus all my regular life stuff—going to the gym, hanging out with Carroll, trying to read the news so I have a vague idea of what's going on outside the Village—it's really hard to find time to sign on to chat in the first place.

It's just that sometimes it feels like I'm the only one who's even trying.

Well, if Toni doesn't want to talk to me, that's my own fault. I'm the one who lied.

I shake my head. Subtly, so Samantha won't see. I don't want to think about that now. I don't want to think about that ever.

"Right, right, okay." Sam's quiet for a minute, and I think she's going to let me read. Then she asks, "How do you know how to kiss? Who starts?"

I give up and close my laptop. "Either one of us. Same as with straight people. You don't always let guys kiss you first, do you?"

"Yeah." Samantha says this like I'm really dumb. "That's how you're supposed to do it. Let them think they're the boss."

Considering that she's wearing about three pounds of black glitter eyeliner, a black leather skirt and dark green fishnets, my roommate is really very old-school.

Carroll is coming by soon. We're going shopping for the outfit I'll wear to the Halloween dance at Harvard. Samantha has been fascinated by this ever since I told her I was going. She's been fascinated since she found out I was gay in the first place.

That was Carroll's doing. When they met, the first thing he said to Samantha was, "Hey, you're from the South, right? Will your parents yank you out of school when they find out your roommate's a gay?"

Samantha thought he was joking. She played along for

a while. Then she went online and saw the photos of Toni and me.

She turned out to be totally fine with it all. I think that was partly because this way she got to ask a real, live gay person all the questions that had been building up in her head for eighteen years.

I've steered clear of mentioning the word *genderqueer*, though. I'm dreading a whole new round of interrogation. Plus, I'm still trying to avoid thinking about all that stuff that came up when Toni told me about the pronouns. I've done some research, so I feel like I have a better grip on the basics, but Toni's crew talks about all the nuances of gender day in and day out. Anything I say is bound to sound dumb. It's safest to avoid the topic altogether.

"Are you going to get a dress with rainbows on it?" Samantha asks me.

I laugh, remembering Toni's story about the girl who always makes rainbow cupcakes for their UBA meetings. "No way. Carroll wouldn't allow that. Too tacky."

"How come you're going shopping with Carroll? Is he a fashion genius? Like Tim Gunn?"

"Tim Gunn has nothing on me," Carroll says through our open door. "Except about forty years."

I bang my imaginary cymbals for his little joke. "Buh-dum-dum!"

"You ready to go?" He eyes my sweatshirt and jeans. "Is that what you're wearing?"

"What difference does it make what I wear to *buy* clothes?"

"At least put some decent shoes on. You have to wear

heels to try on dresses. Otherwise your calves won't be the right shape."

I laugh, but Carroll is totally straight-faced.

"I don't have any high heels," I say.

"Then what are you wearing to the dance?" Samantha asks. "Flip-flops?"

I've never worn high heels in my life, and I'm not starting now. When I tell Samantha and Carroll that, they look aghast.

"Trust me," Carroll says. "The missus will love you in heels."

"Toni likes me to be comfortable," I say.

Carroll makes a face at Sam. "Lesbos. So resistant to change."

Sam laughs.

I give up, say goodbye to Sam and tow Carroll out of the building. He gets over his shoe-related huff and leads me to his favorite vintage shop. We stroll down sidewalks packed with people sipping out of coffee cups and chattering into hands-free phones. I love this time of year, when it's cold enough for a sweater but not a coat, when the summer smell of sweat and fried food has faded into crisp, clean fall. The air buzzes with energy. Nothing in Maryland has ever felt like New York City in the fall.

The store Carroll brings me to is crowded and loud. It's mainly other college students, plus the occasional middle-aged hipster giving us resentful looks. Before we've made it halfway in, Carroll has handed me four dresses and is combing the racks for more.

"How many of these am I supposed to try on?" I ask.

"As many as it takes! This is tough, because it's a Hallow-een dance so it should look like a costume, but we don't want to go too far because we need to make a good impression on all the stuck-up Harvard people. We'll aim for a chic, *Mad Men* vibe but mix it up with some seventies glam."

"Uh-huh," I say. "Look, sweetie, I don't have time to try on a hundred outfits. I have to finish my Met Studies read-ing and go over my notes for the debate team, and then to-night I have an alternative spring break meeting."

Carroll throws another dress onto my pile. "Please tell me you're not dragging me to one of those again."

"Don't you want to be more involved in the planning?"

"I trust you and the rest of the activities geeks. Just let me know how much sunscreen to bring. Besides, I have my own extracurriculars to worry about."

"You do? That's great!" Except for the times he's tagged along with me, Carroll hasn't joined any student groups or signed up for any volunteer programs. I'm always bugging him about it because everyone says you have to have good extracurriculars to get into a decent grad school. "What are you doing?"

"I think his name is Victor." Carroll throws something pink and lacy at me. "Here, try this one, too."

"I refuse to wear pink." I hand the dress back. "Sorry. Anyway, seriously, what club did you join?"

"I *was* serious. Victor and I met up for the first time last night. Didn't go all the way, but maybe next weekend. Come on, let's hit the dressing room."

I follow him to the back of the store, struggling under

the weight of all the fabric. "How did you meet this guy? In class?"

"Nah. He doesn't go here."

"What, does he go to Columbia?"

"Uh-uh. Columbia's for boring people."

"So where does he go?"

"He's, uh. He's already out of school."

I stop with my hand on the dressing room curtain. "Please tell me it's not that sketchy guy from the club."

"It's not that guy." Carroll shoves me inside the room and pushes the curtain closed. "Which isn't to say Victor's not sketchy."

"You met him online, didn't you?" I call through the curtain.

"Guilty," he calls back. "I'm an internet skeezeball."

"Why can't you meet guys at school like everyone else? It's not as if NYU has a shortage of attractive gay guys."

"That may be, but I prefer to play at my own level. Okay, show me."

I pull back the curtain and pose for him in the first dress. It's blue and frumpy. Carroll shakes his head. "Next."

The next dress is red and way too short. I don't want to show him, but Carroll insists.

"I don't trust your judgment," he says. "You *chose* to put on that awful gray plaid hoodie the other day. I still have the PTSD."

I open the curtain. Carroll's eyebrows shoot sky-high when he sees the hemline.

"I see we're leaving nothing to the imagination, eh?" he

says. I yank the curtain closed, and he passes a black-and-purple dress to me through the gap.

"I told you, I don't care what I look like," I say. "Neither does Toni, usually. It's weird that T asked me to go shopping for this."

"She knows you have me in your life now. She's probably expecting me to transform you into a New York fashionista. I'm afraid I'll have to disappoint her. Sure, the raw materials are there, but if you won't even put on a pair of kitten heels, I don't know what I'm supposed to—oh, hey, that one might work."

The black-and-purple dress is okay now that I've got it on. It's not too short. But it's got way too much lace, and it's too tight.

"I can't breathe in it," I say. "See if they have it in the next size up."

"You're not supposed to breathe," he says. "Did Marilyn Monroe breathe? No. She knew how to sacrifice."

"Marilyn Monroe *died*. Give me the next dress."

"No." He comes inside the dressing room and pulls the curtain closed behind him. "We can make this one work. Here, hold your breath and I'll rehook the corset. You did it all wrong."

"Sorry. I'm not up on my vintage corset hooking techniques."

He unhooks the back of the dress and does it back up again. "You'll have to wear special underwear with this. A bustier, maybe."

"How did you learn about bustiers in rural New Jersey?"

"It's not *that* rural. We have YouTube. Hang on. I'll see if I can find one."

I do my best not to suffocate while I wait. Two minutes later Carroll is back, pulling the curtain closed behind him and clutching a purple witch's hat and a black lace wrap-around thing with bra cups. It looks like a torture implement.

"No damn way," I tell him.

"Relax," he says. "Trust me, the girlfriend will love it. Here, hold still."

I put the hat on and try not to move while he jiggles the contraption under the top half of the dress. It's kind of awkward, because we're friends, but I'm not sure we're necessarily the class of friends who can see each other naked yet. But Carroll spends the whole time muttering curse words about how the hooks aren't working, and it's about as non-sexy a moment as you can get.

"Ta-da," he finally says.

It does look good. Plus it's not as hard to breathe this way. Who'd have thought a torture contraption would lessen the pain?

"There's no way I'll ever get this on again without your help," I say.

"It's not rocket science. Get the girlfriend's roommate to do it. I'll draw her out a diagram."

I give up resisting. I even let him pick out some close-enough-to-flat shoes for me with buckles on them that look sufficiently witch-like. Only after I've spent my entire credit card allotment for the month does he allow me to leave the store.

Carroll is grinning. I am, too, actually. That was more fun than I expected.

"I'm famished," Carroll says. "You have to reward my expertise by buying me lunch."

"I don't have any money left. Your expertise has already cost me two hundred dollars."

"Well worth it," he says. "Fine, I'll treat, but we have to go somewhere cheap."

We wind up in a tiny Indian restaurant. Carroll has never had Indian food before, so I try to explain the menu and keep him from doing imitations of Apu from *The Simpsons* when the staff are in earshot.

While we're waiting for our food, Carroll unrolls one of the huge paper napkins on our table. "Do you have a pen?"

I give him one.

"Leaving your phone number for the waiter?" I ask. Our waiter is in his seventies and keeps calling me "baby doll."

"No." Carroll chews on the pen, then writes *ODE TO GRETCHEN* at the top of the napkin.

"Aww!" I laugh and clap my hands, scaring the dog sleeping by the front door.

Carroll chews on his pen for another second. Then he writes:

> *Gretchen is:*
> *Smart*
> *Pretty*
> *Wise*
> *Funny*
> *Kind*

*Fun*
*My friend.*

I stop laughing. "Aww."

Carroll ducks his head.

I turn the napkin around to read it again. "Can I keep it?"

"Sure." He's blushing.

My phone buzzes with a text. I glance at the screen long enough to see that it's from Toni, but I'm sure it isn't anything urgent. I tuck the phone away.

"Thanks for this," I say. "I really, really love it."

The waiter brings our food. Carroll starts eating too fast.

"Don't do that," I tell him. I fold the napkin into quarters and tuck it into my bag so it won't get torn. I wonder if I can tape it up on my wall later or if that would be weird. "Seriously, slow down. It's spicy."

He doesn't listen. Soon he's reaching for the water, downing a whole glass in one gulp.

"You should eat some bread," I say. "It's better for dealing with the spice."

His eyes are watering. "Thanks. I don't know why I always make a fool of myself whenever you're around." He blows his nose into another napkin.

I laugh. "Probably because I'm already a way bigger fool than you'll ever be." I pick up one of those tiny ultraspicy peppers and act like I'm going to stick it in my mouth.

"Stop! Please, I don't want anyone to suffer on my behalf." Carroll grabs the pepper out of my hand. "If you must martyr yourself, do it for someone less pathetic."

"Yeah, okay." I stir my curry. "What's with all the self-deprecating comments today, by the way? Is this about that guy you hooked up with? Victor?"

"We didn't really hook up. And, maybe." He sighs. "I don't know. I just feel like I should've gotten it over with by now."

"What?" I say. He rolls his eyes. "Sex?"

"Yeah. I mean, I've been in New York for what, two months? And what do I have to show for it?"

"A superfabulous new best friend who doesn't care if you're a virgin or not?"

"Aren't you a sweetheart," he says, but he doesn't smile. "I just want to do this right. It's been eighteen long, lonely years."

I remember feeling like that. Back when I lived in Brooklyn I was always in this huge hurry to have a ton of girlfriends. It was like I thought someone somewhere was keeping score. I wound up having sex for the first time with this girl from my old school who was so uninteresting I'm not even friends with her online anymore.

The whole episode was just really disappointing. It made me not want to try again, at anything.

Then we moved to Maryland and I met Toni and none of that stuff mattered anymore. I couldn't care less what my stats were or how they compared to anyone else's. It isn't about sticking to some made-up timeline. It's about being with someone you really care about.

I feel bad that Carroll doesn't know what that's like. He'll meet the right person sooner or later, though. Probably sooner. Like he said, this is New York.

"The thing is," I say, "hooking up with random sketchy guys who leave you feeling like crap the next day isn't doing it right. You've got to wait until you genuinely like someone and take it from there."

"I like lots of people," he says. "The problem is, they have to like me back."

"Oh." Awkward. "Maybe I can set you up with someone. Briana knows a ton of guys."

"I don't need you to set me up. I'm a drama major. I've got gay guys crawling out my ears."

"So, with all these guys around, you really think there's not a single one who might be interested?"

He stabs a piece of chicken with his fork. "New topic. Did you say one of your brothers is gay?"

All right, then. Later, I'll ask Briana if she can think of any nice, cute, age-appropriate guys for Carroll.

"Yeah," I say. "Will. He's the oldest."

"How old was he when he told your parents?"

"Hmm." I do the math. "Seventeen, I guess. I was in fourth grade."

"Were you there when he did it?"

"Yeah." I smile, remembering. "It was actually kind of funny. He was taking this fancy cooking class, and he decided to make our parents breakfast before he told them. So on a Sunday morning he got up superearly, while our other brothers were still asleep, and he made a ton of croissants with different fillings. There were chocolate and almond and ham and cheese and all these others. Back then I was obsessed with almond croissants—well, I still am, actually. Anyway, that morning I smelled them baking and I went downstairs in my pajamas and made him give me one right out of the oven. Just then my parents came to the top of the stairs. They were looking right down into the kitchen. They saw all the croissants on the table and me sitting there burning my tongue on this piping-hot almond croissant, and Will is in his apron with baking soda all over the floor, and he yells up the stairs, 'Mom, Dad, I made you breakfast! Also, I have something to tell you!' So our parents come downstairs and sit at the table, and Will sits down, too, but there's this big pile of croissants in between them, and my dad pushes the croissants out of the way so he can see Will and he says, 'Son, is this about your sexuality?'"

I burst out laughing, because it's still funny after all this time. Even though back then I'd had no idea what was happening.

Carroll doesn't laugh.

"Your dad knew already?" he asks.

"Yeah, I guess. Will had this boyfriend guy. They'd tried to keep it a secret, but they didn't try that hard. Lewis, my other brother, saw them kissing out in front of our building one night."

Carroll shakes his head. "This was here? In New York?"

"In Brooklyn, yeah."

"Figures," Carroll mutters. "New York parents are different."

"I think my parents were still a little freaked, actually."

I remember how they stayed up talking every night after that. I couldn't hear what they were saying. They'd just murmur with the door closed.

"That's nothing," Carroll says. "It's not as if they kicked him out of the house."

"No, they didn't, but I know people that's happened to. Toni had to go stay with our friend Chris for a week. And this other friend of ours back home, Kiyana, her parents tried to lock her in her house to keep her from going to see her girlfriend."

"Huh." Carroll strokes the stubble on his chin. He never shaves on weekends anymore. "That's probably about what my parents would do."

"Well, but you don't live with them anymore. They can't kick you out."

"No, but they'd freak out on that same level."

I sip my yogurt. "There's one way to know for sure."

"What? You mean telling them?"

I nod.

"No way." He spins his fork in his curry with gusto. "I'm nowhere near ready for that. I still have too much to do first."

"Like what?"

"Like, I've never even had a boyfriend. I haven't had any of the fun parts of being gay yet."

I laugh. "Taking me shopping doesn't count?"

"Not that you don't have your charms, but no." He laughs, too. I'm glad. The normal, happy Carroll is coming back. "You can't understand. Your whole life is the fun parts."

"Oh, come on. I have issues."

"Oh, sure. You have perfect parents, you get good grades without trying and you look like a badly dressed version of Jennifer Lawrence."

"Whatever." I roll my eyes at his ridiculousness.

"Oh, wait, I forgot. You do have one problem. You don't live in the same city as your beloved girlfriend. You're a whole thirty-second plane ride away. *That's* got to be the most horrifying thing in the world."

"It is, actually. Sort of."

I know he's joking, but that hit a nerve.

"We were both supposed to go to school in Boston." I don't know why I'm telling him this. Talking about it just means thinking about it more. "That was the whole plan. I was going to Tufts and Toni was going to Harvard."

Carroll slides forward in his chair. "You changed your mind?"

"No. Well, yeah. Sort of. I didn't get into Tufts. I got into Boston University, so I was going there, but then NYU let me in off the wait list, and I…" I don't want to say this. It's so embarrassing. I'm just so tired of keeping it inside. "I didn't tell Toni until the night before we left home."

Carroll whistles. "Trouble in paradise? Got to hand it to you, babe, I didn't see that coming. You totally lied to her."

"I didn't *lie*. I just didn't say anything." I shake my head. "We said we'd go visit each other every weekend, but we haven't seen each other since that night. We talked about me maybe transferring up to BU for the spring semester, but…"

Carroll doesn't say anything. He's watching me, his eyes narrow and steady.

"I kept thinking it wouldn't be hard to be apart, because we'd still visit and talk all the time," I say. "But it's not the same as it was before. We said we were going to visit every weekend, but Toni keeps canceling. Next week will be the first time all year we're going to see each other, if *that* trip actually happens. Plus…there's stuff Toni doesn't tell me now. At least, not right away. It used to be we told each other everything the second it happened."

I tear off another piece of naan.

"It doesn't feel right," I say. "It's been so long now since we've seen each other. It feels like everything's changed. Like it'll be different when we *do* see each other again. Like now that we're in different places we're turning into different people, or something."

I stare at the bread in my hand. I don't know why I just said all that.

Is that really how it feels?

Yeah. Kind of.

"That's why I'm so excited to go up there next weekend," I say in a rush, to put all that other stuff I said out of my head. "So all this weirdness can stop and we can go back to normal."

"And so you can get laid." Carroll pops a forkful of curry into his mouth.

"Yes! Exactly! So I can get laid. That's all this is really about. I'm just a total sex fiend."

"Hell, yeah, you are. Work it." He cracks a pretend whip.

I force a laugh.

"So," Carroll says after a pause. "Transferring to Boston University, hmm? Next semester? Are you serious about that?"

He's trying to sound light, but there's a hard look in his eyes.

I shrug, trying to act like I haven't thought about it much. "I don't know."

"Because you realize you'd be abandoning me to the sketchy men of New York. Without you to rein me in, I'm hopeless."

"Right, because I'm doing such a good job of reining you in now."

"Why does it have to be you who transfers? Why can't she transfer to Columbia or something?"

I shrug again. "I'm the one who lied, remember? Besides, it's Harvard. I can't expect T to give that up. It's always been Toni's dream."

"Sounds like she expects you to give up New York. Far as I can tell, you like it here an awful lot."

"Look, it's fine," I tell him. "For real. Can we talk about something else, please?"

Carroll agrees faster than I expected. "Sure."

Carroll asks which of the girls on our floor I think would be most likely to drop out of school if they got a chance to star on a reality show and/or YouTube series. We make a list on another napkin, then soak it in yogurt to hide the evidence.

I need to stop obsessing over when Toni and I will get back to normal. We're normal now.

This is the new normal, and it's fine.

I wonder if Toni knows about November 1. If Toni looked up the transfer application deadline, too.

I glance across the table at Carroll, then out the window at the city. At the leaves blowing against the restaurant windows. The taxis darting between delivery trucks while tourists cling to the windowsills of their backseats. The people hurrying by with their shopping bags, their yoga mats, their labradoodles.

Carroll is watching me with a smile. I take his napkin-poem out of my purse and press it flat to read it again. He stuffs naan into his mouth and turns away as if he's embarrassed.

Filling out the application would be a lot of work. There's only a week left until I'd have to send it in, and I have a paper due on Thursday for my Twentieth Century Hispanic-American Novels class.

I look out the window again. It's starting to get dark. I can see my reflection and Carroll's. We're both smiling. We look like a picture you'd see in an admissions catalog.

It makes me want to keep smiling forever. Sitting in this tiny restaurant, on this perfect street, in this perfect city, with my new best friend.

I don't want to give this up. Not yet.

It's just one more semester. I might as well stay. For now.

I can figure out the rest of it later.

# 7

OCTOBER
FRESHMAN YEAR OF COLLEGE
2 MONTHS APART

## TONI

I'm in downtown Boston waiting for the bus from New York to pull in, and I'm so excited I can't actually handle it. It's been two months. Two *months*.

In a few minutes I'll finally see Gretchen again. I can't believe we waited this long. What a crazy mistake.

A new bus is unloading, but I can't see the sign that says where it's from. A few minutes ago I was sure I saw Gretchen, and I jumped up and down and waved my arms so hard people looked at me funny, but it was only some blond farm-girl type getting off a bus from Albany.

When I see another flash of yellow across the station, I

try to restrain myself, but there's no way that's happening. This time it's Gretchen.

"T!" Gretchen shrieks.

My heart skitters in my chest as I push through the crowd. It's been so long since I actually saw Gretchen, since we actually *touched*, that I'd somehow convinced myself it would never happen again. That it would be another false start. We've had so many of those lately.

What a dumb way to think. Gretchen's *here*. This is *real*. That beautiful smiling face is right in front of me, laughing, brushing back tears. I hope they're happy tears.

"Oh, my God." I can't stop grinning.

"Oh, my God is right." Gretchen laughs.

We hug for a long time. I can't believe how good it feels.

"You're here!" I say when we pull apart.

"I'm here!" Gretchen's jumping now, too.

We push through the crowd again and hold hands as we get on the train. It's hard to talk on the ride back to Harvard.

I've imagined this scene so many times. I have to fix my eyes on the grimy water bottle rolling back and forth across the train floor to remind myself that this isn't another daydream.

"What do you want to do?" I ask Gretchen as we come up the steps into the sunshine at the Harvard stop. The dance is still a few hours away. I'm so excited my voice sounds shaky. Like I'm nervous.

Maybe I really am nervous.

"I have to leave my stuff somewhere," Gretchen says. "Can we go to your room first?"

"Yeah, yeah, of course."

Our common room is empty. Joanna and Felicia's bedroom door is closed, and I can't tell if anyone's inside, but my room is definitely vacant. Ebony has already left to stay over in a friend's room for the night. That's the deal we made. I'm staying at the guys' place in a couple of weeks when Ebony's boyfriend Zach comes to visit.

"Wow, you weren't kidding." Gretchen looks around the common room, taking in the couch, the rugs, the dark wood furniture that looks like it's been here for a century or more. "This is amazing. You even have a fireplace."

"Yeah. We always talk about roasting marshmallows, but you're not allowed to actually light fires. Supposedly last year some guys tried and they wound up destroying some historic bricks or something. They got, like, two thousand hours of community service. Here, you can put your bag in my room."

The bedroom is tiny—just a bunk bed and two dressers we wedged in side by side. I called tails on move-in day, so Ebony has the bottom bunk and I'm stuck with the top. I put Gretchen's bag down next to my dresser. At first we just stand there, looking at each other.

Then we kiss.

It's been *two months* since I last kissed Gretchen.

I can't believe I lasted that long. I should've shriveled up out of frustration and longing and loneliness by now.

Then we realize we have way too many clothes on, so we take care of that. And then—even though Ebony will kill me for this if she ever finds out—there's no way we're going to have the patience to climb all the way up to the top bunk.

The first time Gretchen and I had sex, I was so nervous.

It was my first time, but it wasn't Gretchen's, and that made me even *more* nervous.

Not so nervous that I didn't want to do it. I'd wanted to do it since that first night at the Homecoming dance.

Back then, I was still getting used to the idea that this person—this smart, hilarious, beautiful person, this person who could've had anyone—really and truly wanted to be with me. *Me.*

Actually, I'm not sure I ever got used to that idea. But I need it. I love it.

I love Gretchen. I love everything about Gretchen.

And if there's anything different about today compared with how it used to be between us, that isn't even worth thinking about. What matters is that we're here, together.

You don't stop feeling the way you do about someone just because you move to a new city, or make new friends, or start thinking about things differently. Love doesn't change just because *you* change.

"I love you," I say afterward. I can't say all of what I'm thinking, but I can say that much.

"I love you, too," Gretchen says. "What time do we need to leave?"

"Soon. We're meeting the guys first in their room."

"I'm so excited to meet the *guys*. They all sound like so much fun." Gretchen gets out of bed and sits on the floor, naked, rifling through a giant backpack. "Except Nance. I hate Nance."

"You don't have to hate Nance."

"Yes, I do! It's called loyalty, hello? She doesn't get to talk smack about you as long as I'm around." Gretchen pulls a wad of tissue paper out of the backpack. "My dress for tonight's in here."

"Won't it be all wrinkly?"

"Carroll packed it this way on purpose. He kept saying something about pleats. I'm gonna need your help putting it on, though. He wrote out instructions."

I laugh. "Is that guy a walking gay stereotype or what?"

"He's just trying too hard. All his gay role models growing up came from Netflix."

I get up and pull on my sweatpants. "If you say so. I'm going to get ready."

"Where, in the bathroom?" Gretchen frowns. We're used to getting dressed in front of each other. Being together for two years will do that.

"Yeah," I say. "I have a surprise. Don't worry. I'll be back soon to help with your dress."

It takes me longer to get ready than I expected. When I come back into the room, Gretchen is half in the dress, half out of it, showing lots of skin and looking more attractive than anyone in such an awkward pose has any right to be. Gretchen squirms and holds out a piece of paper. "You took forever! Hurry, I'm falling out of this thing."

I decipher Carroll's handwriting and follow the instructions. The dress is way more work to put on than any dress should be, but when we're done it looks fantastic. The black-and-purple fabric shows off every curve, but somehow it still manages to look old-fashioned and classy.

"You're so gorgeous." I wrap my arms around Gretchen's waist from behind and gaze at the two of us in the mirror. We look perfect. "This dress was an excellent choice."

"Carroll said you'd say that." Gretchen leans back and kisses me.

"You're keeping the necklace on, too?" Gretchen's still wearing the top hat charm. I have my necklace on, too, but mine's hidden under my shirt.

"Yeah. I thought it went, you know? Like, I'm an evil witch, and I draw my power from silver top hats."

"An evil, sexy, feminist witch."

"Totally!" Gretchen beams. "Now let me see this outfit that took you so long to get into."

My outfit itself isn't special. It's the same black pants and white shirt I wore to almost every high school dance after I calmed down from the craziness of Homecoming. Since it's Halloween, I also stuck a set of plastic vampire teeth in my pocket in case anyone asked what my costume was. There's something different about how I look this time, though, and it only takes a second for Gretchen to figure it out.

Gretchen's eyes widen. "Are you wearing a chest binder under that?"

"Yeah." I swallow.

"Do you, um." Gretchen bites down on a pinky nail. "Do you do that all the time now?"

"No, this'll be the first time."

Gretchen grins. "It's sexy. Here, let me see it. Pull up your shirt."

"It's kind of strange looking," I say, but I undo a few buttons so Gretchen can see the binder. My stomach flips, which is stupid. There's no reason I should be nervous.

"Cool." Gretchen runs a palm down the middle of my

ROBIN TALLEY                    177

now mostly-flat chest. The binder just looks like an undershirt, but it's supertight and not exactly comfortable.

It feels weird, having that extra layer, but not *that* weird. In some ways, it actually feels kind of awesomely normal. Especially with Gretchen touching me like that.

"You look so different," Gretchen says. "Hey, your hair's different, too."

"Yeah, I got it cut the other week. I'm not spiking it the same way anymore." I look down. Gretchen has on black flat shoes with buckles. "Are those the shoes you're wearing?"

"Yeah. I wanted to wear my Birks, but Carroll wouldn't allow it." Gretchen laughs.

I frown. I'd thought Gretchen would be totally done up, with pointy heels to match. I'd been picturing how everyone would react to me and my sex-on-legs girlfriend when we walked into the guys' room. "I'm surprised Carroll didn't force you into some superhigh heels."

"Oh, he tried, believe me." Gretchen pauses. "What, you don't like my shoes?"

"No, they're fine. Either way, the guys will definitely be impressed when they see you."

Gretchen laughs and puts on a purple witch hat. Even with the blond hair, witchy is a look that works for Gretchen. Of course, most looks work for Gretchen.

"Since when do you care what anyone thinks of how I look?" Gretchen asks.

"I've always cared. Remember in high school how I used to brag about how you were so much hotter than whoever Jess's current girlfriend was?"

"I always thought you were joking."

"I was, mostly, but..." I shrug. Come to think of it, I don't remember if I *was* joking back then.

"So you really are that superficial?" Gretchen laughs again. Gretchen's laughing a lot today. "You don't need *me* to impress your friends. They already like you."

"I know." I shake my head. "It doesn't matter. Let's just go."

"Are you really upset about my shoes?" Gretchen makes puppy-dog eyes. "Maybe I can borrow some others from your roommates. Or do we have time to go shopping? Is there a Payless in Harvard Yard?"

I laugh. "Yeah, right between Widener and Wigg."

"Really?"

"No, but it doesn't matter. I like your shoes. Very witchy."

"Good." Gretchen beams again. Just like that, we're back to normal.

We're already running late, but whatever. We still have time to make out some more.

Half an hour later, Inez, dressed as Princess Leia, opens the door to the guys' room. The common area is packed. Besides my friends, there are some people I recognize from UBA meetings and some I've never seen at all.

"Toni! You look fantastic!" Inez smiles at me, then turns to Gretchen. "Oh, my God, this must be the famous girlfriend from NYU! I love your dress! Wow, Derek said you were gorgeous, but I had no idea!"

"Yep, this is Gretchen," I say, beaming.

"You have to come in!" Inez grabs Gretchen by the hand before Gretchen can say hello. "Everyone has to see you!

Right now! Everybody, this is Toni's girlfriend, Gretchen, up from NYU!"

More than a dozen voices shout back as Inez leads Gretchen into the room. Gretchen waves. I push my way through the door after them so I can see everyone's reactions.

All the guys shout "Hi," and Nance and one or two of the others wolf-whistle. Gretchen laughs some more. Clearly I overestimated the importance of high heels.

Then, before I've even seen Derek, much less introduced them, Derek has come up to us, grabbed Gretchen by the elbow, steered my girlfriend into a corner of the room and started an in-depth conversation about Gabriel García Márquez.

Seriously. That just happened.

It's been three seconds since I entered a party with my girlfriend for the first time in my college life and I'm already on my own, just like always.

God. English majors.

I talk to Nance and Inez and their friends for a while before I run out of patience and march into Gretchen and Derek's corner. Derek is dressed as Mark Twain, in a white suit and wig with fake eyebrows and a fake white mustache. It's disturbing.

"Hey," I say. "Are you two starting your own final club back here or what?"

"No, we're just telling embarrassing stories about you," Derek says.

Gretchen squeezes my hand and kisses me on the cheek. My annoyance fades, but my chest feels tight. I can't tell if it's the binder or my nerves.

"I like Derek," Gretchen says. "It makes me feel better having you all the way up here if I know Derek's around to watch out for you."

"What am I, a puppy?" I ask.

"No, I know what she means," Derek says, smiling. "By the way, T, I like Gretchen, too."

Gretchen smiles.

"Okay, that's enough of that," I say. Not that I object to Derek and Gretchen making friends, but this is kind of weird. "You haven't met everyone officially yet. Come on."

"He really is a good guy," Gretchen whispers as we cross to the other side of the room. "I mean, I knew he would be, since you're so picky about your friends, but I trust him. He reminds me of Chris, but older and wiser."

"Derek's definitely a lot wiser," I say.

We go around the room so I can introduce Gretchen to the rest of the group. They're all in costumes or otherwise dressed up except for Eli. Eli isn't coming to the dance. Gretchen is distraught to learn this because Gretchen, unlike the rest of us, wasn't there last week to hear about the dances of Eli's past. We all dropped the subject once Eli finished the "and then they beat me up outside my *senior* prom" story.

"No, no, you *have* to come!" Gretchen tugs on Eli's arm. "It'll be fun. We can all dance together."

"Hey, Gretchen, sweetheart," Nance says, "you can dance with Eli if you want, but you have to dance with me first. I got to get in early, before Toni goes around kicking people's asses."

Gretchen laughs. "Like we'd make it through a whole song before that happened."

"Oh, yeah?" Nance says. Nance is dressed as Clark Kent, in a suit and tie with the shirt unbuttoned just enough to show the red *S* underneath. It shows off a lot of cleavage, too. I'm guessing that's not an accident. "T's that much of an ass-kicker?"

"Nah, T just gets superjealous," Gretchen says.

"Yeah, that's kind of true," I say. "One time in high school I paid someone to stop trying to flirt with Gretchen."

"You *paid* her?" Eli said. "What, actual money?"

"Well, I did her calc homework for her once."

"I was superglad you did," Gretchen says. "She was this little track-team diva brat, but she was hard to get rid of. Even though I was already hopelessly smitten with Toni by then."

"Aww," Inez and Nance say in unison.

I blush. Then I get annoyed with myself for blushing.

My chest feels tight again. My whole body feels like it's buzzing, and not in a good way. I thought people would notice I was binding tonight, but Gretchen's the only one who's said anything.

"So, should we go downstairs or what?" I ask.

The others stand up, grumbling, as if they'd just as soon hang out in the common room all night.

The dining hall on the first floor is already full. Some of the outfits people have on are really over the top. As Derek predicted, there are some straight guys in ridiculous, borderline-offensive drag, but they're definitely the minority. I see more drag *kings*, in fact. They must've come over on the Wellesley bus, because if we had practicing drag kings at Harvard, surely someone would've told me by now. It's funny to see girls dressed as Justin Bieber hanging out next to the three-hundred-year-old dark wood paneling and framed portraits of old, dead house masters.

Derek, Inez and Nance hang out with Gretchen and me for the first part of the night. Nance keeps leaning over to whisper things in Gretchen's ear, which freaks me out. I overhear words like "self-care" and "sofa support groups." Are they talking about furniture?

Derek sees me looking at them and mouths, "Don't worry about it," and I try not to. Then I overhear Nance saying, "It really makes you rethink your own sexuality, you know?" and Gretchen turns to me, looking panicked.

I take Gretchen's hand and we go to get food. For a while we avoid Nance and hang out on our own. Gretchen keeps pointing out the interesting costumes to me and whispering in my ear about how cool the dance is, but I can't relax. It didn't bother me so much in the guys' room, but now that I'm out in the open, I feel incredibly self-conscious about binding in public for the first time. No one seems to have noticed, but I can't stop thinking about it. I'm so self-conscious I'm embarrassed of my own self-consciousness.

Having Gretchen standing next to me makes me even more nervous because I know everyone's looking at us. Well, everyone's looking at Gretchen. That's what happens when your date is the hottest girl in the room and she's dressed up as a sexy feminist witch.

What the hell am I doing here? Everyone's going to know I'm faking it. I'm not serious enough about the trans thing to be wearing a binder yet. Plus, Gretchen probably doesn't even want to be here with me. Why else would my own girlfriend lie to me about something as huge as college plans?

I'm a total failure. A fraud. Anyone who takes one look at me can tell I'm just playing at everything.

"I've got to get out of here," I whisper to Gretchen.

"Why?" Gretchen looks alarmed.

"Uh." I shift from one foot to another. "I've gotta pee."

"Oh, okay." Gretchen squints toward the far end of the corner. "Is there one down here?"

"Uh," I say again. I should've realized this would be a problem. Harvard's got a few gender-neutral bathrooms around campus, so I use those most of the time, but there aren't usually gender-neutral stalls in the dorm hallways. I usually use a women's bathroom if there isn't a gender-neutral one close by, because that's never seemed like a big deal to me—I went to an all-girl school for thirteen years, after all. But I don't really want the guys seeing me go into one. And since I'm wearing a binder, it would probably be weird.

"Actually, I'll just go later," I say.

Gretchen looks quizzical. "You sure?"

"I'm sure." I shift again. My binder is starting to itch.

"Relax," Gretchen murmurs. "Are you stressed?"

"I'm not stressed," I say.

"You look stressed."

"I'm only—"

Then Pete interrupts us, yelling from the food table on the far side of the room.

"Come hang with us, T!" Pete calls. "We're having a support group meeting for the formerly genderqueer!"

All of my friends howl with laughter at this. Except Gretchen.

"Formerly genderqueer?" Gretchen whispers, smiling and waving at Pete and the others. "Is he joking?"

"Oh, uh, sort of, but not really," I say, as if I'd just forgotten to mention it. Oh, God. "I mean, you know how much I hate labels. None of them are ever exactly right. So I'm thinking about not using *genderqueer* as much anymore. It has some classist connotations, you know? I thought about other options, like *nonbinary* and *multigender*, but I think I might like *gender nonconforming* best. Well, and actually I still use *genderqueer* sometimes, since more people know what it means. My friends just like to be brats about it because they think they're funny. Basically, though, I've been, well, thinking a lot. About all of this. Yeah."

I swallow.

"Oh," Gretchen says. "Um. Okay. Is the classist stuff the only reason you're thinking about changing from *genderqueer*?"

"Well…" I'm extremely unprepared for this conversation, and I've had a few drinks. So I keep babbling. "Also, something like *gender nonconforming* seems more accurate, since *genderqueer* is so neutral, but *gender nonconforming* is more active. Like it's saying I'm actively opposed to the rigid gender binary. Plus, especially since, you know, I lean more toward the male end of the spectrum than the female end, maybe a label change sort of seems like a logical next step?"

What the hell is wrong with me? Why can't I shut up?

"What do you mean?" Gretchen's eyes are wide. "A logical next step to what?"

I gulp. This probably isn't the best time to mention that

I'm thinking about trying out using *they* pronouns, too. "I don't know."

"When did you decide this?" Gretchen's talking really fast. Sounding almost frantic. "Why didn't you tell me?"

"Um."

"Hey!" Nance comes over to us and thrusts a cup into my hand. "What's the deal, T? Your hottie shows up and now you're too cool to hang with us? Come over here, both of you. You've got to meet these Wellesley babes."

I look over warily, but Gretchen's smile is back in place.

"Let's go!" Gretchen chirps.

This time when we cross the room, we don't hold hands.

Nance introduces me to the drag kings, who did indeed come over from Wellesley, and to a punch concoction Nance invented that appears to be three-fourths vodka and one-fourth wine with a splash of fruit juice. The drag kings make less of an impression than the drinks. They both help take care of the self-consciousness, though.

Gretchen keeps smiling, laughing and joking with everyone. We stay with Nance, Derek and the group for the rest of the night. As it turns out, there's no actual dancing at this dance. Only flirting, drinking and, in the case of Derek and Gretchen, bonding over a shared love of dead white male writers.

Nance slings an arm around my shoulders as we file outside at the end of the night. Nance has taken off the Clark Kent shirt, revealing a way-too-tight Superman shirt underneath, so this is disconcerting.

"You two comin' out with us?" Nance's Southern accent is a lot stronger when enhanced by alcohol. "We're going to the Kong. Get us some General Tso's and some Scorpion Bowls. It's gonna be fierce."

Drunk Nance's grip is strong. I'm too drunk myself to shrug her off.

"Leave them be," Derek says, unwinding Nance's hand from my arm. "I'm sure they've got better things to do."

"Ohhhh, yeah," the guys chorus.

"You're all a bunch of pervs." Gretchen slurs the words, laughing. "Come on, T, let's ditch these creepazoids."

We say goodbye and cross the street back to the Yard.

"I'm sorry I got crabby before." Gretchen takes off the witch hat, wraps an arm around my waist and leans her head on my shoulder. I wonder how drunk Gretchen is. I wonder how drunk *I* am. "I get it better now that Derek explained the thing about *genderqueer* being classist. He said some people think *genderqueer* is mainly used as a label just by middle- and upper-class people, but he doesn't think that's true anymore, and he said he's trying to convince you he's right. I told him there's no way to convince you you're wrong about something like that, but he said he's going to try anyway." Gretchen laughs.

"You talked to Derek about me?" I have a feeling that will bother me tomorrow. Right now I'm more focused on the physical proximity situation. I put my arm around Gretchen's shoulders.

"A little." Gretchen isn't slurring as much now. "I like him. He really likes you, too. He says you remind him of him when he was a freshman."

"Uh-huh." That will probably bother me tomorrow, too.

"Hey, T? T! Is that you?"

"Eb?"

My roommate Ebony is waving to us from the opposite sidewalk, arm in arm with a guy who is definitely not her boyfriend from back home.

"Hey!" Ebony breaks away from the guy and jogs over to us. "Is this the famous Gretchen?"

"Hiiiii." Suddenly Gretchen's back to slurring.

Ebony laughs and turns to me. "What have you done to her?"

"No idea," I say. "She was fine three seconds ago."

Ebony turns to look at me with unfocused eyes. "Something's different about you."

"Oh, yeah. I got my hair cut."

"Yeah, and there's more, too." Ebony squints at my chest. "Ohhh."

"Ohhhhhhh," Gretchen agrees. Her eyes are closed. If we don't move soon, I'll have to drag Gretchen back to my room. I suspect that would look bad to any passing campus police officers.

"It's such a shame," Ebony says.

"Nah, she'll be okay," I say. "Gretchen has a really low tolerance. Just needs to sleep it off."

"No, I mean you," Ebony says. "It's so sad. You're so pretty as a girl."

A hand tugs on my sleeve before I can think of a response. Gretchen's eyes are open now. "Time to go home, T. 'S nice to meet you, Ebony."

Ebony waves and stumbles back over to the guy. Gretchen and I make it to the dorm without any dragging required, but the pleasant buzz that surrounded us before is gone.

"I can't believe she said that," I say for the third time. I'm trying to swipe my card to get into the entryway but my hands are fumbling. I keep missing the card reader.

"You're drunk, T. Your pronouns are slipping."

"Sorry. It's just so offensive. I thought people here were more enlightened."

"I'm sure she thought it was a compliment."

"Whatever." I stomp up the stairs to my room while Gretchen follows.

"You can't be so hard on everyone," Gretchen says. "Sometimes people make mistakes. Say the wrong thing."

"Whatever."

I open the door. Joanna and Felicia are sitting on the couch in the common room, laughing. They shut up as soon as they see us. I go straight to my room. The only reason I don't slam the door behind me is that I don't want to hit Gretchen in the face.

Gretchen says hi to the others before following me in. When we're alone with the door safely shut, I fling out my arm in the direction of the common room.

"You don't need to talk to *them*," I say. Through the wall we can hear Joanna singing one of the dumb songs from the dumb a cappella group the two of them are in. It's a Michael Jackson medley I've heard them sing a million times before. Felicia joins Joanna on the harmony. I flip them off through the closed door.

Gretchen smiles at me. "You're being such a teenager. It's cute."

"It's not cute." I sit on the bottom bunk bed and cross my arms over my chest. I hate how tiny my room is. The top of my head grazes the bottom of my bunk bed. It feels like everything is closing in on me.

"Relax," Gretchen says, whispering so Joanna and Felicia don't hear. "What's with you tonight?"

"I...don't know."

I really don't. I can't remember the last time I felt so many different things in one day.

Seeing Gretchen again was automatically supposed to translate into twenty-four-hour bliss. It wasn't supposed to be complicated.

Was it like this before? I can't remember.

Gretchen sits down next to me on the bed. For a minute, neither of us speaks. Gretchen's arms are crossed over her chest, too. Then Gretchen sighs and turns to look at me. "Why didn't you tell me?"

I sigh, too. "It really wasn't a big deal."

"You told all your other friends."

"The guys always want to talk about this stuff. It just comes up."

"I want to talk about this stuff with you, too."

"I know, but..."

"Is it because you wanted to get back at me? For keeping a secret from you, about NYU?"

"What? No! It has nothing to do with that!"

"Because I'd understand if it was." Gretchen's voice is soft. "I know you're probably still mad."

"I'm not mad! I was never mad to begin with." I reach around to scratch my back. The binder is itching like crazy. And it's hot in here. How did I never notice how hot it is in here?

I lean back on the bed, resting my head against the wall. The hard masonry digs into my scalp. I'll have to clean the smears of hair gel off it in the morning before Ebony gets back. I need it to ground me if we're going to have this conversation, though.

Gretchen's watching me, tears starting to form. Oh, God.

"Come here," I say.

Gretchen lies down and puts her head in my lap. I pull strands of Gretchen's hair between my fingers.

"You don't have to tell me anything you don't want to tell me," Gretchen says, still in that soft, sweet voice. "I don't want it to be, like, an obligation. It's just, if you're going to be not telling me stuff, especially the big stuff, then—could you maybe tell me up front that you're *not* going to tell me? I don't want any more surprises like that."

"I didn't mean to not tell you. I just—didn't tell you. I guess. Does that make sense?"

"I don't know."

I wish I could see Gretchen's face. I try to weave her hair into a braid, but my fingers are still fumbling from Nance's damn punch. I settle for stroking it instead.

"I mean," I begin, then stop. I don't know how to explain this.

Usually I think about everything for a long time before I say what I'm thinking out loud to anyone. This time I broke tradition. One night when we were studying in the guys' room, I looked up from texting with my sister about the essay she was writing for AP government and said, "I think I might like *gender nonconforming* better than *genderqueer*, actually." Derek and Eli smiled. Nance rolled her eyes, gave me a thumbs-up and went back to her reading.

It was that simple.

Except nothing about this has ever been simple, really.

"It's like this is all I think about anymore." I don't meet Gretchen's eyes as I say the words. "Even when I'm *not* thinking about it, I'm thinking about it. I spend so much time talking about it, too. It sort of comes up naturally when I'm with Derek and my friends. It's so normal, talking about it with him, that sometimes I forget what a big deal this stuff actually is. Wait, I'm messing up more pronouns, crap."

"Yeah, you are. What was *in* that punch?"

"I don't know, but you recovered from it a lot faster than I did."

"I didn't have that much. I was faking before so your friends would let us leave. Not that I don't like them, but I'm not here for very much longer, and I want to spend time with you."

"Yeah." I nod and take Gretchen's hand.

"Look, I understand what you're saying. I think it's great that this is all coming naturally to you. It's just—please, remember you can talk to me, too, okay? Derek's not the only one here who cares about you."

Gretchen is crying. I want to cry, too.

"Come up here," I whisper.

We kiss. A long, slow kiss. We aren't frantic now, the way we were this afternoon. This time we're kissing because we have something to prove to each other. To ourselves.

And because kissing is the easiest way to be close to each other.

And because we don't know what else to do.

"I love you," I say. That feels different this time, too.

"I love you, too."

We kiss some more. Then we keep going until talking isn't an option.

I've never kept anything from Gretchen before.

It isn't only about the labels, either. That's important, but it isn't as important as some of the other stuff I've been thinking about. And talking to Derek about. And writing about in the privacy-locked journal I started a few weeks back.

It doesn't mean I don't love Gretchen. I do. I always will. Gretchen is a part of me. But that doesn't mean Gretchen can understand all the *other* parts of me.

And. And. And what I said before was a lie.

I still can't forgive Gretchen for what she did. No matter how much we love each other. I know I should. I *want* to forgive Gretchen, but that isn't how this works. I can't control it.

Thinking about it makes me want to cry some more.

"I love you," I say again.

Gretchen says it, too, but I don't know what it means anymore.

I don't know what anything means right now.

# 8

## GRETCHEN

"Tell us all the gory details," Carroll says. "We want a blow-by-blow. Let those of us who don't have sex lives of our own live vicariously through yours."

It's Monday morning. November 1. I'm having breakfast in the dining hall with Carroll and Samantha. Carroll's been pestering me to tell him about all the supposedly scandalous details of my weekend since I got back from Boston last night, but I don't want to talk about it.

Besides, sex is the last thing on my mind. The sex was the one part of the weekend I know I didn't mess up.

Samantha rescues me.

"We most certainly do *not* need to hear about that," she tells Carroll. "Not all of us are flaming perverts."

Carroll clutches his chest. "That was way harsh, Tai."

Samantha doesn't get the movie reference, and I'm too glum to explain it. I stir my yogurt.

"Anyway, yeah, I don't want the *real* gore," Carroll says. "Girl parts are gross. I just want to hear about the bodice-ripping, take-me-now stuff."

"I don't think she feels like talking about it," Samantha says.

Carroll rolls his eyes.

I stir my yogurt in tighter and tighter concentric circles. When I'm about to get to the middle, Carroll grabs my wrist. "What's the matter with you?"

"Nothing."

"You're lying," he says.

"Nope," I say. "There is absolutely nothing the matter with me. I am peachy keen."

I scoop out the biggest spoonful of yogurt I can and shove it in my mouth so Carroll can't make me talk.

"She misses her girlfriend," Samantha says. "I'd be depressed, too, if I were her."

"I'm not depressed," I say through my yogurt blob.

"You mean her boyfriend," Carroll says to Samantha. "Or didn't she tell you about that?"

"What?" Samantha looks back and forth between us as if she can't tell if there's a joke here she's supposed to laugh at.

"Nothing." I swallow my yogurt. "Ignore Carroll. He's being a dick."

My phone buzzes to tell me Derek accepted my friend

request. Well, at least one good thing came out of that trip. Derek's the kind of guy I would've liked even if he wasn't Toni's new BFF. Plus he explained to me why some people thought *genderqueer* was kind of a problematic word, which was more than Toni told me.

Well, except for all that stuff Toni said really fast at the dance. I could only half follow it. I don't know if I had trouble because Toni was confused or because I'm just too dumb to understand all the intricacies.

Toni was throwing out all these words—*nonbinary* and *multigender* and others that sounded even stranger—and then, in the middle of all of it, like it was no big deal, Toni said, "I lean more toward the male end of the spectrum than the female end."

Was I supposed to know that already? Toni said it like I already knew it.

This is all my fault. If I'd just gone to school in Boston like we planned, I'd see Toni all the time. We'd tell each other everything the way we did before. I'd know what Toni was thinking before anyone else did.

Toni and I were always supposed to come first with each other.

I gave up the best thing in my life, and for what? A city? What was the point? Half the time I'm too stressed out to even enjoy this place.

"I have an idea," Carroll says. "Let's go out tonight. Get you back to being happy, bubbly Gretchen again."

"It's Monday," Samantha says. "Even *my* friends don't go out on Mondays."

"Your friends don't follow normal human patterns," Carroll says. "I know how you people feel about direct sunlight."

"We're not vampires," Sam says.

"Sorry, didn't mean to out you," Carroll says. "Come on, Gretch, your lesbo friends must be going somewhere. We can tag along."

I shrug. The only gay girls I really know at school are Briana and her friend Heidi, and I've never gone out with them. I just see them around the dorm and classes, and I go up to Inwood with Briana once a week to volunteer.

"Heidi's one of your friends, right?" Samantha asks. "On our floor? I have her cell number."

"Fab," Carroll says. "Text her."

"I can't text her," Samantha says. "What if she thinks *I* want to go hang out with a bunch of lesbians?"

"Obviously your reputation would be forever tarnished," Carroll says. "I know how judgmental goths can be. Here, I'll do it."

Samantha gives Carroll the number. I dip my spoon in and out of my yogurt. The berries are complete mush by now.

"Hey, girlfriend," Carroll says into the phone in a high-pitched voice. My head snaps up. I can't believe he really called her. "No, wait, don't hang up. Sorry, I'm not a stalker. My name's Carroll. I'm friends with your friend Gretchen. You know, the hippie chick who wears Birks with wool socks every day despite my desperate pleas?"

I kick him under the table, but I'm starting to laugh. He winks at me.

"Yeah, so," he says into the phone, "she needs cheering up. Just had a megadramatic weekend with the long-distance honey. Tears, laughter, epic reunion sex, you know how it goes. I was hoping we could hang out with you and your crew tonight. There's got to be some chic girl bar around here that we'd have to dress up and pay a twenty-dollar cover for, right? Okay, sounds fabuloso. Meet in the lobby at nine? Lovely. Ciao, *bella*."

He hangs up. I should be annoyed, but I'm still laughing.

He picks the yogurt up from where I left it on the table and chucks it into the nearest trash can, spoon and all.

"You were grossing me out with that," he says. "Are you ready to be normal Gretchen now? The one we know and love?"

I was being normal Gretchen before, too, I want to say.

"Depends," I say. "What will you make me wear?"

"We'll borrow an outfit from Tracy," he decides. "She's your size, and unlike you, she knows what the inside of a Banana Republic looks like. Hey, Sam, this is your last chance to get in on this action tonight. You never know. Maybe you'll decide muff-diving's for you."

"I'll pass," Samantha says.

"Be a loser, then." Carroll stands up and turns back to me. "No more pouting today, Gretch. I'll be at your room at seven sharp for beverages and wardrobe consultation."

Then he's off, snatching a cookie from the dessert stand and slipping it into his pocket on his way out of the hall.

"So how was your weekend, really?" Samantha asks when he's gone.

"Nothing." I shrug. "It was fun. Harvard people aren't as uptight as you'd think. Except they have no idea how awesome their dorm rooms are. These guys Toni's friends with have a bar, two couches and a big-screen TV. They download all the new movies because they say they're too busy studying to go out like normal people, but I didn't see anyone studying all weekend. I did see a bunch of drunk girls in cocktail dresses and pearls trying to get into the library at three in the morning because they wanted scones from the café, though. We're really lucky we have all-night delis."

"Pearls?" Sam said. "For real? Girls there wear pearls to parties on *campus*?"

"Parties there are like clubs here," I say. "For the good ones, your name has to be on a list or you won't get in."

"Dang." Sam shook her head. "Remind me never to transfer to Harvard. Anyway, what *really* happened? Something's wrong, I can tell. This morning was the first time since we've been here that you didn't go to the gym as soon as your alarm went off. I was afraid I was going to have to throw something on you to get you out of bed."

"I was just tired."

"Look, for real, it's okay. You can talk to me."

She's kind of right. You wouldn't know it to look at her, what with the rope-thick mascara and the black lace gloves and the fake spiderweb tattoo, but Sam's a good listener.

I could tell her the whole thing. It would be so amazing to be able to actually talk about this with someone.

I could tell her what Nance said. About how there's this whole subculture I'm supposed to join called SOFFAs. It stands for Significant Others of…something? I can't remember. It's for people whose girlfriends or boyfriends or whatever are trans.

I could tell Sam about how Nance said it's really complicated, trying to be supportive of your girlfriend and re-member to take care of yourself, too. How she kept giving me these really skeptical looks like she thought I wasn't up to the challenge.

When I looked up SOFFAs, I found a page about how partners of transgender people are often victims of hate crimes. That was information I could've done without. I felt bad for even thinking about it, though, because I know trans people get attacked way more often.

Then I felt even worse because, God, how awful to think about Toni getting hurt. Then I wondered if maybe Toni shouldn't be talking quite so openly about all this trans stuff, because what if it makes someone more likely to commit some awful hate crime?

Then I felt bad *again*, because I know it's important to be open, and being open is the only way things will get better for trans people. We learned about that in the GSA last year. It was the same with gay people. The reason more people support us getting married now is because more and more gay people came out over the past couple of decades.

The problem is, I don't care about things getting better for all those other trans people nearly as much as I care about Toni being safe.

I could tell Sam about how when Toni and I talk now, Toni never tells me anything important. I guess there's no need anymore, with all those awesome people up at Har-vard to talk to.

I could tell Sam about how I'm scared Toni isn't telling me things because Toni knows I won't understand. After all,

I'm just boring little Gretchen. I'm nowhere near as cool as all of Toni's new genius friends.

I could tell Sam I'm so scared about all this stuff I can't sleep at night.

Then I remember Sam's too embarrassed to even go to a gay bar. I bet she's never once heard the word *genderqueer*. She'd have a thousand questions before I'd even finished the story. I'm sick of explaining my life to everyone.

Besides, Carroll's almost put me back into my happy mood. I like being in my happy mood.

So I say it's nothing. That Sam was right from the beginning. That I'm freaked because I miss Toni.

I'm not even lying about that part. If Toni and I were just in the same place all the time, everything would be simpler.

Carroll's right. I need to stop thinking about this so much and focus on having fun. Distractions, that's the key.

Starting now.


"Those make your ass look cute," Carroll says nine hours later as I try on a pair of Tracy's tight gray pants. "They make you look like you *have* an ass, at least."

I laugh. "Thanks, I guess."

He passes me a plastic cup of orange juice mixed with Absolut that he stole from Juan. I take a drink and pass it back. We're supposed to meet Briana and her friends in the lobby in ten minutes. If I really want to keep up my good mood, I need to drink as much as possible tonight.

"How's the overall effect?" I ask Carroll, spinning around and nearly falling over.

"To be honest? Kinda dykey."

I laugh. "That's okay. I am kinda dykey."

"Oh? I'm disappointed. I thought you were all the way dykey."

"I am!" I say, feigning outrage. "One hundred percent dykeadelic!"

"Yeah, as if that's not obvious based on your footwear alone." Carroll points to my neon-green Crocs. I switch them out for the black witch shoes I wore to the dance. They're the only shoes I have that meet with Carroll's approval.

"Speaking of which," he says, "do I ever get to meet your partner in dykedom? Is she coming down here this semester?"

"Toni's busy," I say and take another long sip. "The classes up there are insanely demanding. It's Harvard."

"What's NYU, a safety school?" he asks. "You managed to go visit her."

I shrug.

What I don't say is that we'd been talking about Toni coming down here in the next couple of weeks, but that plan is off now.

Toni called this afternoon to tell me that a teaching fellow named Lacey had offered to set Toni up with a summer internship. At Oxford. In England.

"It's a fantastic opportunity," Toni told me. "A chance to do research with some of the top people in the field when I'll only be a sophomore! All I have to do is go over there next month for an interview."

"This came from Lacey?" I asked. "Wasn't she the one who tried to fight with you about random political stuff?"

"Oh, I was misinterpreting that. It turns out Lacey's got all these great contacts. Lacey did a program at Oxford, too, so now I've got a ton of insights into the academic culture there. It sounds incredibly stimulating. All I have to do is meet with them, and Lacey said if the lead researcher likes me, the job's mine."

"Uh-huh," I said.

"I won't be able to come to New York for that weekend we talked about, though. I'm way too behind on my work already. There's no way I can take two more trips this semester, but at least we'll see each other at Thanksgiving."

"So you'll be in England," I said. "All summer."

"Yeah. It's great, right? It's the perfect excuse not to have to go down to my parents'!"

The thing is, if Toni's not going down to Maryland, we won't get to see each other, either. Toni didn't seem terribly bothered about that part, though.

I can't help wondering if seeing me again made Toni realize that spending time with me isn't all it's cracked up to be. That we might as well spend the summer living five time zones apart.

"I'll miss you," I said.

"I know. That's the one part of this that sucks. I'll miss you, too. But we'll still see each other. You can come visit me in the UK. It'll be fun."

"Can't you get an internship in Boston or New York?" I asked. "It'd be a lot easier to visit you that way."

"No, no, listen, this internship is really competitive. It's a huge deal to be asked. I can't pass it up."

"So, what am I supposed to do all summer?" I asked. "When I'm not hanging out with you in England?"

"I don't know. Didn't you say you wanted to get a job in DC or something?"

Toni had to get off the phone after that. The guys were waiting.

"I don't see why you have this double standard," Carroll says now. "She's too busy to come see you, but you drop everything to go see her? You missed the Village Halloween parade, you know. Thanks to you, I nearly lost my virginity about thirty different times."

"Yeah, I'm sure my presence would've totally deterred you." I take another swig from the cup. "Now stop defeating the purpose of this evening for me, please."

"Oh? Remind me what that purpose is, again?"

"For me to not think about stuff that stresses me out."

"Since when does talking about your girlfriend stress you out? Used to be all you ever did was talk about your girlfriend."

"Hush." I put two fingers over his lips. "Stop harshing my buzz, man."

He pulls my hand away. "Okay, even I know that's not the right lingo. Please tell me you're not actually drunk from half a screwdriver."

"I have ultralow tolerance. You know that."

"Oh, right. How much did you have to eat today? Should we get some pizza before we go out?"

"I've eaten enough! Get off my back."

Someone knocks on the door, and I run over to answer it. It's Briana with Heidi and a girl I don't recognize. All three of them are wearing really shiny shirts.

"We heard you guys talking," Briana says. "Are you ready to go? Hey, Gretchen, you look cute."

"Thanks." I gesture back into the room, my arm waving wildly. "We are totally ready to go. This is my best friend, Carroll."

Carroll waves. The girls wave back.

"It's so cool you guys are finally coming out with us," Briana says as if it was her idea. "How come you never said yes when we asked you before?"

"Oh, um," I say.

During our trips back and forth to Inwood, Briana and I always talk about us all going out some night. She's texted me a few times asking me to meet up with them, but I was always hanging out with Carroll or talking to Toni online.

"I wanted to," I say. "I've just, you know, had so much going on."

"She means me." Carroll puts his arms around my waist from behind and nuzzles my hair. The girls laugh. "She was afraid she'd lose her lesbo street cred if you found out she was hangin' out with a stud like me."

"Keep up the *Buffy* quotes and you might earn some lesbo street cred yourself," says the girl I don't know. She smiles at Carroll.

Carroll lets go of me and smiles back at her. "Now who might you be?"

"I'm Rosa." The girl puts her hand on Briana's waist, all possessive.

I look away. I've done that to Toni before a million times.

"Shall we skedaddle?" Carroll says, and we do.

The bar they bring us to is so dim you have to squint at

people. It isn't as crowded as I expected. Everyone there looks old and bored. It's a Monday and no one except me is drunk yet.

No one cards us, so we order mojitos. We gather around a table, and Carroll tells the girls stories about the drama queens in Tisch. They laugh as if they've never heard of such things before.

By the third round of drinks, Briana and I are telling debate stories. We're talking about the time these two coaches from rival schools got into a screaming fight in the middle of a tournament. It got so bad they started slapping each other and had to be pulled apart. Briana and I are laughing like crazy, but the others are glaring at us. We leave them to their boring conversation and go off to a corner where we can hear each other better.

It's even dimmer over in the corner, so we have to lean in close to see. I remind her about the time her teammate totally ran off the stage and puked in the middle of a final match, and I'm laughing so hard I'm crying. That's when Briana puts her hand on my waist, the way Rosa did to her before, and says, "So what are we doing, here?"

And that's the funniest thing that's happened all night. I tip my head back and laugh at the ceiling. When I look back at Briana, she hasn't moved. She's got this smile that makes me nervous.

"Uh," I say. Then I turn and see Rosa. She's right behind us, looking over Briana's shoulder, her face drawn. "Uh, so, your girlfriend's, like, right there."

Briana drops her hand and turns around. Rosa is backing away.

"Baby!" Briana says, reaching out to give Rosa a hug.

Rosa runs to the door.

"Baby!" Briana calls out again and runs outside after her.

I finish the rest of my mojito and giggle to myself.

Heidi comes over. "Was that what it looked like?"

"I have no idea," I tell her. I motion to Carroll, who's hanging out by our old table, looking bored, and signal for him to get me another drink. He nods and goes to the bar.

"Aren't you going after them?" Heidi asks.

"What for?"

"You're involved now."

"I didn't do anything."

"That's not what it looked like to me."

"What does that matter?"

Heidi shakes her head and follows the others outside.

I want to stay where I am, but after a minute I get lonely, so I go join Carroll at the bar. He puts his arm around my waist, and I sag against him. The bartender glares at us and takes someone else's order.

I'm very, very drunk. I turn around to hug Carroll full-on and rest my head on his shoulder.

"Please deliver me from lesbian drama," I say.

He hugs me back.

"Want to go?" he asks.

"Yeah, but I'm scared the girls will see me and draw their claws."

"Don't worry. I'll protect you."

I let him pull me out of the bar. I sway on the sidewalk, looking around for Briana and the others, but the whole world is blurry. Carroll holds me upright, flags down a cab, and pushes me inside.

"You're not about to puke, are you?" Carroll asks.

"Shoot, girl!" the driver says. "If you're going to throw up, get out of my cab!"

"Don't worry," I mumble. "I never puke." I slide down to lay my head in Carroll's lap.

The next thing I know, Carroll's shaking me awake. We're out front of the dorm.

How did that happen? How much time did I lose?

This is awful. I hate this. I hate everything.

"I don't know what's happening," I say as Carroll half drags me into the lobby. "I thought it was okay, but instead it's all different. Toni's different, and I don't know if it's bad different, but I know it's not good different. I mean, *things* are different. Does that make sense? Now Toni's leaving me here all summer and it's like she doesn't even care, won't even miss me. It's like I don't matter anymore, and it makes me want to, like, die inside, and it's all my fault."

I'm crying, getting his shirt all wet.

Carroll hauls me into the elevator. There are people in there with us, looking at me, but I don't care. Carroll keeps his eyes fixed straight ahead.

When we get to our floor, he pushes me down the hall-way. I'm stumbling, but he keeps pushing me faster.

Samantha is there when we get to my room. When I see her, I start crying all over again.

"It's November 1," I tell her, but my words come out all wrong. "Toni didn't even ask if I applied."

"What the—" Samantha takes me away from Carroll and leads me to my bed. "What happened to her?"

"I don't know," Carroll says. "Some girl hit on her and she flipped out. I'll get her some water."

He leaves. Samantha closes the door behind him and drags the trash can over to my bed.

"I never puke," I say, pushing the trash can away.

Samantha pushes my sweaty hair out of my face. "Do you want me to get your girlfriend on the phone?"

"No!"

"Okay, okay, sorry. What do you want me to do?"

"Will you…I don't know. Will you just sit with me?"

She nods. Carroll never comes back with the water, so Samantha gets me some from the bathroom.

I tell her everything. Every word I can choke out in between the sobs that won't stop coming. Samantha listens, and she tells me she understands, and she tells me it's going to be okay.

I'm probably just still drunk, but whatever the reason, I fall asleep believing her.

BEFORE

SEPTEMBER
SENIOR YEAR OF HIGH SCHOOL
11 MONTHS TOGETHER

## TONI

I had to tell Gretchen. I'd already waited too long. At this point, *not* telling felt like lying, and lying to Gretchen was the worst thing I could possibly do.

The hard part was finding the words. I'd never said them out loud. I'd never even typed them. I'd been lurking on sites and forums, and I was starting to learn the vocabulary, but I'd never posted myself. That would make it too real.

Talking to Gretchen would make it realer still, but I had to do it. We'd promised we'd always be honest with each other.

I'd tried to practice in advance but I always gave up half-way through. It was too scary. Besides, I didn't need to practice. This was Gretchen. Maybe I'd have trouble thinking of the words to use, but Gretchen always understood me. Gretchen understood everything.

## GRETCHEN

Something was wrong.

When Toni texted me to come meet her after tennis practice, she sounded way too serious. "We have to talk," she'd said. Nothing good in the history of ever has started with the words *We have to talk.*

"What's the matter?" I asked as soon as I saw her. She was sitting on top of a picnic table by the courts, still in her practice clothes, frowning down at her phone screen. Her hair had wilted during practice. Now, instead of its usual spikes, Toni's hair hung down over her forehead, making her look younger than she was.

"Nothing," she said quickly. "Hi. Come sit down."

She smiled at me and scooted over on the table to make room. I climbed up next to her, brushing off some loose leaves that had blown onto the table's surface. Toni put her phone down and clasped her hands together. Her eyes darted to me and then away again.

The only other time I'd seen her look this nervous was when she showed me her Harvard application essay. It was about how in middle school she'd been obsessed with the news coverage of the Arab Spring, and that was what had made her want to become a professional political scientist so she'd have an excuse to study every nuance of social justice movements.

The essay was brilliant. Naturally.

"So what's up?" I asked.

Toni didn't look at me. Her smile had faded. "We should talk about something. It's important."

Oh, *God*. I knew it.

She was breaking up with me.

*Why?* I tried to think. There had been that party when I talked to Renee off in the corner for an hour. Toni got jealous sometimes about things like that, but she never got *angry*.

I must've done something else. What? How could I explain it so Toni would change her mind? Oh, God, oh, God.

"I think I'm genderqueer," Toni said.

Oh. Was that all?

I breathed out. I was so relieved I just nodded. This wasn't a big deal. All that mattered was that she still wanted to be with me.

"Okay," I said.

## TONI

"Okay," Gretchen said, nodding.

I waited for the freak-out, but Gretchen just looked at me with raised eyebrows, waiting for me to go on.

All the sites said when you came out to someone as trans, you should explain what that meant in a lot of detail. Some of them said it was better to explain it in a letter or an email, because then the person you were coming out to could react in private and do research on their own before they tried to talk to you about it. I couldn't write Gretchen an email about this, though. That would feel so fake.

"*Genderqueer* is, like, when you think you have both masculine and feminine qualities, and you don't fit into either end of the so-called gender binary," I said. "It's like a philosophical disagreement with the idea that everyone has to live in either the *male* box or the *female* box."

"Oh, right. I remember." Gretchen smiled. "We did that whole big thing on it in the GSA, didn't we?"

"Oh, yeah." In junior year we'd read a collection of essays by transgender and genderqueer writers called *Beyond the Binary*. It was my idea. I'd already read it, and I wanted to have people to talk to about it. It was hard, though, because I pretended all my opinions about it were totally objective reading comprehension–focused thoughts, when actually I kept wanting to jump up and down yelling, "It all makes so much *sense* now!"

"I knew you were really into that book," Gretchen said. "I wondered if maybe you identified with it some."

"Yeah, I did. Like, a lot." I nodded. This was going great so far. I took Gretchen's hand and smiled. I hadn't expected Gretchen to run for the hills at the news or anything, but I'd expected some surprise, at least. Maybe some shock. The sites said sometimes significant others didn't take the news well because they were worried it made them gay. Or straight, as the case may be.

"So…" Gretchen said.

I waited for the questions to start.

## GRETCHEN

Was I allowed to ask questions?

I was trying to be respectful. Well, I was also trying to

remember everything we'd read in that book about what *genderqueer* meant, and everything Toni had ever said about it during all those long discussions. She'd said a lot.

That was last year, though. I hadn't known there was going to be this incredibly major quiz on it today.

I wanted to ask what *genderqueer* actually meant in the real world. Toni had said something about the "binary" being bad, but did that mean she thought the binary was bad for everyone, or just her? Was she different now than how she was before, or was she still my same Toni?

Wait, was I even supposed to call her *she* anymore? The book said some genderqueer people like to use other pro- nouns, like *sie* and *hir*.

Was Toni still a girl? Was Toni *ever* a girl?

Wait. If Toni wasn't a girl, did this mean she wasn't my girlfriend anymore? What did that make her? Just my friend? I couldn't call Toni my friend. It felt like saying she wasn't as important as she was.

Wait. Maybe Toni really *was* breaking up with me. Maybe she thought she couldn't have a girlfriend anymore if she was genderqueer.

No, that couldn't be it. She was holding my hand. You didn't hold hands with someone while you dumped them. Did you?

Wait. If Toni was able to see beyond gender and I wasn't, did that mean I wasn't as smart as she was? Because, well, the gender binary had never especially bothered me. I mean, I didn't think it was fair that some people felt oppressed by it, but as for me, I'd always just felt like a girl. I had breasts and a vagina and I was perfectly content with them. I'd never really thought about my gender very much.

What if Toni didn't like my body anymore, though? What if she didn't like *her* body? Was *I* still allowed to like it?

Would we still get to have sex? If we did, would it be different now?

Had Toni been not liking the sex all along? She sure seemed like she liked it.

What did any of this *mean*?

I swallowed all my questions and fought to keep a smile on my face.

If I asked, I was guaranteed to say the wrong thing. I'd sound just as dumb as I actually was when it came to this stuff. Then what would Toni think?

Better to stay quiet. Then Toni would know I was totally fine with it all and we could go back to normal. Whatever normal was.

## TONI

It freaked me out how Gretchen wasn't saying anything. I babbled to fill up the silence.

"I'm actually not really sure about *genderqueer* as a label," I said. "It isn't perfect, but the thing is, no label feels perfect. I hate that our society is so focused on labels, but I guess that's how things are. Pronouns, too. I've already stopped using gendered pronouns. It took some getting used to, but it's really freeing. You don't realize how sexist our language patterns are until you really look at how you use language yourself, you know?"

"Gendered pronouns," Gretchen repeated. "Like…okay. So you aren't saying *he* or *she* anymore?"

"Nope."

"How long have you been doing that for?"

"I started trying to do it in my head two weeks ago. It was really hard at first. I've only been doing it out loud since Monday."

"Wow." Gretchen looked down at where our hands were clasped. "I'm sorry. I didn't even notice."

"That's okay. That must mean I don't sound totally awkward, at least."

Gretchen didn't answer. I babbled on.

"It's not that I'm, like, completely opposed to the idea of gender," I said. "It's just that I want to challenge what society views as 'normal' gender. Like, it doesn't bother me that much if someone calls me *she*—I mean, okay, it bothers me a little bit—but it bothers me way more if someone calls me a girl. Like when teachers are talking to a class and they say 'Girls, settle down.' You know?"

Gretchen nodded. She got it. Of course she got it.

But I wished she wasn't being so quiet.

"I just know—" My voice hitched. My cheeks felt beet red. "I just know I'm not female. And, so, well, I don't know what that makes me. Can you wait while I figure it out? Would you?"

Gretchen nodded but didn't meet my eyes.

"So do you still, like." I laughed to show what a stupid question I thought this was. "I mean. Even with all of this. Do you, you know. Do you still love me?"

## GRETCHEN

It bothered Toni when someone called her *she*?

*I* called her *she*. I was doing it right now, in my own head.

Oh, my God. How was I going to stop using pronouns for Toni inside my own head?

I didn't know, but I'd have to do it somehow. Toni stopped using pronouns in two weeks. I could do it for her.

Oh, crap. Crap crap crap. I couldn't even not use *her* for one *sentence.*

It bothered Toni that people thought of her as a girl.

I'd been thinking of Toni as a girl from the day I *met* her.

She *was* a girl. She was my *girlfriend*. We were lesbians. Together.

Not anymore.

Okay. Okay. It was all right. I'd get used to this. I had to.

I loved Toni. Love conquered all.

Besides, this wasn't that big a deal. We read a whole book about it. I knew the basics. I'd even wondered what it would be like to be transgender. Or what it would be like if Toni was. But that had been so hypothetical, and this was so...not.

Toni was giving me this sharp look. There were tears in her eyes. Oh, *crap*. I didn't even have to speak for her to know I was totally screwing up the pronoun thing in my own head.

Then I thought back a few seconds and realized what she'd just asked me.

"Yes!" I laughed, a little bit of the tension draining out of me. Maybe it really was this simple. "Yes, of course! I'll always love you. And of course I'll wait while you figure it all out. You really thought I wouldn't? Over something like *this*?"

"No. I don't know." Toni laughed, too, and wiped at the corner of her eye. "Sorry. No, I didn't think that. It's just— you're the first person I've told, that's all."

We were both laughing. God, it felt so good to laugh. I squeezed her hand. Toni's hand.

"I mean, there's no reason anything would be different with you and me, right?" I meant it as a statement, but it sounded like a question. I wanted Toni to say she'd always love me, too. No, that *Toni* would always love me, too.

"Right." Toni leaned her head on my shoulder. The weight of it felt so good. So important. We had to stay as connected as we could. I didn't know how big this thing was, but I knew it wouldn't come between us. "I don't want that to be different at all."

"So just tell me what you need," I said. "I want to help. If you want to talk stuff through, or if you just need me to hold your hand, or, you know, anything. I'm here. I'll always be here."

"I love you," Toni said.

"I love you, too."

We kissed. It was the first time we'd kissed after I knew, but it didn't feel any different. It didn't feel like I wasn't kissing a girl. It just felt like I was kissing Toni. My Toni.

This would be all right. I didn't understand all the details of this gender stuff, but I didn't need to. I understood Toni, and that was enough.

For now.

9

NOVEMBER
FRESHMAN YEAR OF COLLEGE
1 WEEK APART

## TONI

"Mine started last Monday," Joanna says. "When did yours?"

"Monday, too," Felicia says. "Wait, are we all in sync now? We should ask Ebony."

"We could ask—" Joanna says, then stops. They both turn toward me, then turn back again just as fast.

Good. I'm trying to read, and I can't focus with them yammering.

All four of us set up our desks in the common room since our bedrooms are so tiny. Which means I have to listen to Felicia and Joanna's boring-as-hell conversations all the time.

I can't deal with it. Not tonight.

I have two papers due in the next forty-eight hours, and I'm dangerously behind on the reading for my Supreme Court seminar. Last night I was on video chat with Chris until three in the morning, nodding along to a story about Steven's latest episode of borderline infidelity. I haven't slept more than five hours in one night since October. I've had the same sinus infection for the past three weeks. I started using *they* as a gender-neutral pronoun, but it's harder than I thought it would be. My girlfriend is pissed at me.

And now I have to listen to my roommates talk about their stupid *periods*.

"Do you think she even still gets hers?" Felicia whispers.

"I can hear you," I say. "I'm five feet away."

Joanna and Felicia giggle behind their hands.

"Why are you still here anyway?" Felicia asks. "Aren't you supposed to be at that thing?"

I rub my temples. "What thing?"

"For your friend," Joanna says. "The Korean girl. Or guy, or whatever."

"Oh, *hell*." I forgot about Eli's party. I slam my laptop closed and run to the bathroom to fix my hair.

"What is it?" Joanna calls from the common room. "Is it her birthday?"

"No, it's not *his* birthday," I call back, breaking my pronoun rule in Eli's honor. "It's just a party."

Actually, the party is what the guys call a "secular-slash-Buddhist bar mitzvah." Today Eli started on testosterone. According to Nance, it's time for Eli to "get down with his bad manself."

Which is great and all. It's just that I'll probably be looking at an all-nighter after I get back. Well, Eli won't hold it against me if I only put in a quick appearance.

I ignore Joanna and Felicia's cackles on my way out and pull my hood up against the wind. I trudge across the Yard, dodging a hyper-Japanese tour group by the John Harvard statue, and stepping carefully over slush puddles.

I can't believe it's already this cold in November. Massachusetts sucks.

I grumble to myself the whole way to the guys' house, but I manage to smile when I knock on their common room door. Low voices and laughter drift out from the other side.

Nance opens the door. "Hey. We wondered if you were ever going to show."

"Sorry. I fail."

"Whatever," they say. "Come in. We're playing I Never."

The last thing I need is alcohol. "Can I play with Diet Coke?"

"If you put a big load of rum in it."

"Guess I'll just watch, then."

Nance shrugs and points me to an empty couch. Everyone else is sitting on the floor, laughing with heavy-lidded eyes. The game must have been underway for a while. The room looks the same as usual except that there's a banner with a stork on it that reads It's a Boy! strung up over the bar and a brown statue of Buddha with a balloon tied around its neck next to the chips bowl.

"Hey, man," everyone choruses as I pass. Derek, who seems more sober than the others, looks up and nods at me. I nod back.

Eli is lying faceup on the floor, eyes half-closed, head lolling.

"Congrats, dude," I say as I step over Eli's spread-eagled form.

"Is that T?" they say groggily. "Where you been, T? I missed youuuuuu."

"Sorry I'm late. Roommate issues."

"Yeah, yeah, yeah," Eli gurgles. "Sure. Totally."

"Yo, Eli," says Andy, poking them in the side. "It's your turn, man. Think of something you've never done."

"This game sucks," Eli moans. "I've never done *anything.*"

"Then how are you already so drunk?" I ask.

"I'm cheating."

"He is," Pete says. "You missed it, T. Nance says she's never streaked in the Yard, and Eli drinks. Lacey says she's never had a threesome with two guys, and Eli drinks. Derek tells some long-ass story about masturbating to Madonna or some bull, and Eli—just guess."

"Drinks?" I say. "Seriously, you guys?"

"I wasn't talking about masturbating to Madonna," Derek says. "I was saying I didn't understand her interpretation of sexual empowerment philosophy until the *Hard Candy* album and—"

"Whatever, man. It doesn't matter," Nance says. "The point is, you could come in and say you'd never grown a mustache and bungee-jumped off the Golden Gate Bridge, and Eli would up and drink."

"I tried to grow a mustache last year," Andy says. "My mom wanted me to. She kept talking about how 'hand-some' I'd look with facial hair. I finally had to break it to her. 'Mom,' I said, 'I know you're psyched about me taking T because I can finally start to look like the son you always wanted, but mustaches make me look pervy.'"

Everyone laughs.

Hold up. I try to think backward in the conversation. Did someone say something about Lacey?

I glance from face to face. There are a few people from outside our usual crowd—some guys in the UBA I don't know very well, a girl I don't recognize at all…and Lacey Colfer, my Foundations of Government teaching fellow. The one who set me up with my internship interview at Oxford. The one who's expecting me to hand in a not-yet-written paper on the separation of powers tomorrow.

Derek sees me looking.

"T, this is Lacey," Derek says. "She was UBA president the year before last."

"Hi, Toni." Lacey waves at me sheepishly. "Don't tell Dr. Morris about this, okay?"

"Deal." I smile at them. I wonder if this will get me a break on my paper's due date.

"Never have I ever," Eli moans. "Um. Never have I ever used a strap-on?"

I'm too astonished to hear the words coming out of Eli's mouth to pay attention to who drinks and who doesn't. Maybe I should've gone for the rum, after all, if this game is already on to sex toys.

"Am I next?" Inez asks.

"No, it's my turn," Derek says. "Never have I ever. Uh. Hooked up with a bio-guy who wasn't circumcised."

"Ew," Nance and some of the others say. Then Nance takes a quick drink. Ha!

"I told you, stop cheating, man," Andy says to Eli, who's finishing off a drink.

"I'm not this time!" Eli says. "I've done that. It was disturbing."

"Yeah? Well, don't worry, man. Those days are way behind you," Nance says. "I'm setting you up with some of my Wellesley friends. You'll be fighting off the ladies before you know it."

"Don't need to fight 'em off," Eli says. "Just one girl. That's all I need."

"You sure?" asks Kartik. "There's lots of girls out there, man."

"I'm sure," Eli says. "Just need one perfect girl. Like Toni's girl."

"Yeah, Toni's got that part all set," Andy says. "And T's not even on T yet. Ha, ha! Get it?"

"I didn't know you had a girlfriend, Toni," Lacey says.

Too. Many. Worlds. Colliding.

I wait until one of the others takes a turn ("Never have I ever gone down a girl who lived in Dunster, 'cause Dunster girls are hella gross, y'all!"). While everyone is laughing and drinking, I slide off the couch and tap Derek's shoulder. "Can I talk to you?"

Derek smiles, gets up without a word and leads me into one of the tiny bedrooms. From the number of baseball caps hanging off the dresser, I suspect it's Eli's. We close the door and sit down across from each other on the creaky hardwood floors.

"What's up?" Derek asks. "Oh, and before I forget, you should call Gretchen back."

"The hell? How do you know about that?"

"She messaged me. I think she thinks you're mad at her."

Wow. I do *not* need those two teaming up against me. I can't talk to Derek about Gretchen if they're always going to take Gretchen's side.

"Stop looking at me like that," Derek says. "What's the matter? Is it what Andy said?"

"No, there's something I've been thinking about, and I wanted to ask you—wait, which thing Andy said?"

"Oh, you know what I mean. His little pun. With the 'yet' at the end." Derek takes a drink and smirks at me. "By the way, I've heard him say that sober, too."

Oh. Sure, that bothered me. I don't want to admit that, though.

"No," I say. "I'm just crabby. Plus, I'm sick. Plus, I have too much work to do. Plus, it feels like my universe is collapsing in on itself more and more every day."

Derek grins. "Welcome to Harvard."

"It isn't funny."

"Never said it was."

"I don't want to call Gretchen back."

Derek stops grinning. "Why?"

I shrug. "Every time we talk now, it's—tense."

"Since when? Halloween?"

"Yeah." I pull a stuffed lion off Eli's bed and hold it in my lap, looking into its furry face so I won't have to meet Derek's eyes. "It's weird. It never used to be like that. We didn't fight once in high school."

"Then that was what was weird."

Derek was supposed to reassure me. Not make this harder.

"What do you mean?" I ask.

"Everyone fights sometimes. It doesn't matter how great your relationship is. There's never perfect harmony because there are always differences of opinion."

That doesn't make any sense. Maybe Derek doesn't really know that much about relationships. I mean, Derek's never been with anyone for more than six months. Except Nance, but that doesn't count because Nance is…Nance.

"Gretchen and I've had differences of opinion before," I explain. "We just don't fight about them. Back in high school, if we disagreed about something, we'd talk about it and then laugh it off and not talk about it again. Now we're still doing that. We're just skipping the laughing part."

"So maybe you and Gretchen are finally starting to be normal now," they say. "Not the other way around."

"It doesn't feel that way at all. It feels like what's happening now is…" I don't know how to explain it. There's just this weird feeling that crops up every time Gretchen and I talk. It's like the tickle I always get in my throat right before a really bad cold comes on. "Like it's not a good thing. At all."

"Oh." Derek frowns. "Well. That sucks. Anyway, you'll figure it out. You guys are perfect together. Avoiding her isn't going to help, though."

I sigh. "Avoiding them is my only option."

"*Them?*" Derek frowns. "Wait. Are you using *they* pronouns now?"

"I'm trying it out." I shrug. "It's hard to get used to."

"Yeah, I tried it once and hated it. I think the new pronouns people have come up with, like *ze* and *hir*, are easier. Then it's as if you're just speaking a different language. Like you're permanently in French class."

"Yeah, maybe." I shift. Talking about pronouns feels a little too…close. I still haven't mentioned what I really wanted to ask Derek about. I'm not quite ready to go there. "So, how's it going with Inez?"

Derek grins. "She's awesome. Last night we went to see that musical theater version of *The Bourne Identity* they're doing at the Agassiz, and we stayed up talking for four hours about whether it was ethical to sleep with a guy who had amnesia and didn't remember what his type was."

"It took you four hours to decide that?"

"Well, we hooked up, too."

I laugh. "Are you two officially together now?"

Derek shrugs. "We're taking it slow, you know? We'll stay casual until we decide for sure if we definitely like each other enough to make it an actual commitment. We've got plenty of time."

"Casual" is a foreign concept to me. I've only ever been in one relationship, and it's been many things, but casual was never one of them.

Maybe you're supposed to plan everything in advance with relationships, like Derek and Inez are doing. Maybe that's why it's been so strange lately between Gretchen and me. We didn't do any planning. We met, we liked each other, we fell in love. Boom, boom, boom. Not a single bump along the way.

"I've been thinking," I say. Suddenly my original topic seems much less scary than the route my mind just took.

"You know how I'm doing that internship at Oxford this summer? I thought maybe while I'm there, I'll try getting people to use male pronouns for me, just so I can see what that's like. Do you think that's, um, a good idea?"

Derek's whole face changes, their grin spreading wide. "You mean you want to present as male for the whole summer?"

I fiddle with Eli's stuffed lion. "Maybe?"

"That's awesome!" Derek applauds, and I laugh. Then they abruptly stop clapping. "I mean. If that's what you want to do."

"Why? Do you think it would be weird?"

"Well, it's always kind of weird, but it's good weird. It's, like, freeing. Like you get to stop living alone in your head all the time, because everybody else sees you the same way you see yourself." Derek coughs. "I mean. If that's what you want to do."

It sounds incredible, the way Derek describes it. Except…

"Why do you keep saying that?" I ask. "About it being what I want to do?"

"Uh," they say. "Well. I've been accused, in the past, of being *too* supportive when people are thinking about transitioning."

"Accused?" I laugh again. "By whom?"

Derek nods toward the common room. "Some theorists who will remain nameless have suggested that Eli would've started taking T last year if I hadn't scared him away with my overt enthusiasm. But to those theorists I say, why tiptoe into the water when a flaming cannonball is perfectly effective?"

"Right," I say. Even though I'm not completely sure what Derek means with the cannonball metaphor.

"There are also those who would say I should've waited longer before scheduling top surgery," Derek goes on. "Some might argue that just because I've been positive I wanted it since the first time I read about it, which was *eight damn years ago*, when I was in *middle* school, that I should still keep on waiting, just to make *extra*, *extra* sure."

I shake my head. "Those people are lame."

"*Those people* include certain individuals whom I'd trust with my life."

I'm dying to ask who they mean, but I don't. I'm positive it's Nance.

Derek first told me about the surgery plans a few weeks into the semester. Now that it's officially scheduled for this summer, we've been talking about it more and more. I'm actually pretty impressed Derek doesn't talk about it every second of every day. That's what I'd do.

I can't imagine it, though. Top surgery is basically a double mastectomy. Afterward they reconstruct your chest to look like a guy's. A cis guy's.

It sounds so freeing. Not having to deal with binders. Not having all this extra stuff you don't need hanging around on your chest.

Sometimes when I think about it, though, the idea freaks me out. Surgery. Getting cut open. Getting part of you cut *off*. Gone, forever.

There's no turning back. No in-between. You get that done and you're a guy. Poof.

Maybe that would be wonderful. Or maybe…

"Er, T?" Derek says. "You look kind of freaked."

"Sorry." I shake my head. "Just, you know. Thinking."

Derek nods. "Being at a party like this will do that to you."

I shrug.

Derek's been certain about wanting surgery from day one. Since they were way younger than I am now.

Does that mean I'm not really trans, if I don't have that same certainty? I want to try male pronouns. I think I do anyway. Maybe I shouldn't, though. Not if I'm not 100 percent positive I really want to live as a guy forever and always.

The thing is, I know for certain that I don't want people to see me as a girl. Shouldn't I want to fix my body to match that? *Shouldn't* I be sure?

Derek's sure. Eli's sure. Everyone but me seems to have everything figured out.

"So, do you want to go on testosterone, too?" Derek asks.

I knew that question was coming, but it's still scary to hear it. I hate getting shots, but I guess it would be worth it if I really wanted hormones. If I was positive I wanted to do what Eli's doing.

I give Derek my previously prepared nonanswer. "My parents pay for my health insurance. They see my doctor bills."

"So do mine, but that doesn't have to be a problem if you know how to work the system," Derek says. "I can get you in to see my doctor. He's a great therapist—he gave me T, plus he put me on some SSRIs that are way better than what I was taking before—you know, if you need those, which, hey, maybe you don't. But the best part is, his office will help with the billing. That's how I'm getting the top surgery this summer. I'm using the inheritance my great-grandfather left me. My doctor's office will make sure my parents never see a single bill."

This conversation is moving way too fast. Drugs. Surgery. It's all so…official.

"I don't know if I want to—um. Do anything. Physically, I mean," I say. "For now, at least. I just had this idea for next summer, about the pronouns."

"Like a test run." Derek grins.

"Yeah." Maybe I shouldn't have brought this up. Derek seems awfully excited. "Maybe."

"Uh-huh." Derek coughs again. "You know, you don't have to wait until summer to use the pronouns if you don't want to. You could start by telling some people here in the States to start using them."

Yeah, right.

"I think it'll be easier to deal with in a different setting," I say.

"Maybe. Also, this way you get out of having to discuss it with anyone close to you in your regular life." Derek quirks an eyebrow.

"Stop analyzing," I say. "I still haven't completely made up my mind I want to do this at all. Besides, everyone close to me in my regular life already knows I'm trans. I mean, gender nonconforming. On the trans spectrum."

"Really? Everyone?" They raise an eyebrow.

"Yeah." I hate it when Derek doesn't believe me. I've never once lied about any of this. "I'm just not that close to many people. Besides you guys, it's only Gretchen. Oh, and my friend Chris at Yale. I haven't told Chris yet, but I will. Soon."

"You didn't tell your other high school friends?" Derek asks.

I shake my head. "There was no one else I really wanted to tell."

"It must've been weird, being trans and going to an all-girl school," Derek says. "Being surrounded by hugely reinforced feminine gender norms."

I shrug. "It didn't really bother me. I mean, I'd never gone to a coed school at all until I came here, so I didn't know any different. Maybe it, like, affected me subconsciously."

Derek grins. "A subconscious devotion to blue plaid."

"God, save me." I grin back.

Derek nods, looking serious again. "I guess it goes without saying that no one in your family knows?"

"Oh, hell no. I'd be perfectly happy if my mother went to the grave without finding out, and now that I'm out of the house, I'm sure my dad's forgotten I exist. Until it's time to sign the next tuition check."

"What about your sister? How old is she, again?"

Hmm. What *about* my sister?

Audrey and I have never talked about this. My sister has no problem with the gay stuff, of course—Audrey always came to the Youth Pride festivals and Queer Proms I organized in high school, usually with a boyfriend in tow—but we've never sat down and discussed any of it.

I could think about it, though. I wouldn't need to worry about Audrey telling my parents. My sister doesn't get along with Mom any better than I do. I feel a familiar pang of guilt at leaving Audrey alone in that house, but at least Mom is basically never there.

"Sixteen," I say. "Hmm. Maybe I should try talking to my sister about it when I go home for Thanksgiving. See what happens."

Derek whistles. "You *are* serious about this, aren't you?"

That hurts. I cross my arms and tuck my hands into my armpits. "You thought I wasn't?"

"No. I'm impressed, that's all. Maybe you're more of a flaming cannonball than I thought. Oh, and speaking of Thanksgiving, are you coming with us to the game?"

"Yeah, definitely." The Harvard-Yale game is the week-end before Thanksgiving. It's at Harvard this year, which is good, because Nance is the only one of us who has a car, and I'd rather not listen to Nance moon about hot Wellesley girls for a full three-hour drive to New Haven. "Chris is coming up and staying with me. You guys don't mind hanging out with a Yalie, do you?"

"Nah, we're used to it by now. Nance's girlfriend is coming up, too."

My mouth drops open. "Nance has a girlfriend? At Yale?"

Derek laughs. "Don't act so shocked. She's always been a hit with the ladyfolk."

I *am* kind of shocked, but I don't want to insult Derek by saying so. "Hey, that reminds me. Can I ask you something?"

"We have proven that in fact you can and do. Often."

"Very funny. How well do you know Lacey Colfer?"

"Uh. Why?"

I shrug. "I just didn't know you guys were friends. Lacey's the TF who set me up with my internship."

"Oh!" Derek nods slowly. "So that's why she was asking about you."

"Uh. I guess."

I'm dying to know what Lacey said about me, but if I ask it will seem like I'm interested, which I'm not. Obviously. I barely know Lacey. More importantly, *way* more importantly, I'm in love with Gretchen. Derek knows all that, so it's dumb of me to worry about them thinking anything else. Except…I just kind of have this sense that I shouldn't say anything more.

"Yeah, she just asked if I knew you," Derek says. "I ran into her this morning in Lamont. I told her you'd be coming here tonight, and she said she wanted to come, too. She and I, uh, we went out for a while."

Of course.

"Derek," I say. "How many people currently sitting in that common room have you hooked up with at one point or another?"

Derek smirks. "Look, the whole Harvard queer community is really incestuous. You get used to it after a while."

"Uh-huh."

I shake my head. So what if Derek and Lacey were together once upon a time? It's funny, that's all. One more funny thing in my completely hilarious life.

I try to laugh, but no sound comes out.

A door opens behind me. I turn around, squinting at the sudden influx of light from the common area and the indistinguishable silhouette standing in the doorway. I hadn't realized how dark it was in here.

"Sorry, E." Derek stands up quickly. "We didn't mean to invade your territory."

"It's okay." Eli turns on the light and closes the door. As my eyes adjust to the brightness, I can see the bags under Eli's eyes. "Uh, can I talk to you about something?"

"Yeah, I can head out." I stand up, too.

"Actually, maybe I could talk to both of you?" Eli says. "If you don't mind, T?"

"Yeah, yeah, sure." I sit back down. So does Derek. Eli's tone sounds pretty intense. I don't remember any of these guys ever wanting to talk to me about something serious before.

Eli sits in the desk chair, towering over us for once. On the desk I can see a pharmacy package. The first dose of testosterone must've come in that. I wonder if it hurts, giving yourself a shot. I can't imagine doing that every single week.

Derek's looking at the package, too. "How you feeling, E? Any achiness yet?"

Eli reaches around and rubs their back. I guess that must've been where the shot went in. "A little, yeah. Is it supposed to be making me moody yet?"

Derek laughs. "I don't know, man. It's probably pretty soon for that."

Eli nods. "I figured. So, yeah, I'm still stressing out about tomorrow. Like, a lot."

"Tomorrow?" I ask.

Derek looks at Eli. "Do you want me to fill T in?"

Eli nods.

"He's going to tell his parents tomorrow," Derek says. "They're getting on video chat at eight in the morning."

"Jeez, why so early?" I ask.

"That's ten p.m. where they are, in Korea," Eli explains. "Every time I talk to them, we're all in pajamas."

"Do you know what you're going to say?" I ask. Eli nods, their eyes fixed on the carpet.

I can't imagine telling my parents. Just like that. I wouldn't even know what words to use. It wouldn't be anything like telling Gretchen. I knew Gretchen would accept me the way I was, no matter what.

My parents barely even accept me as it is. I close my eyes for a second, and all I can see is the determined grimace on my mom's face as that striped tie fell into the sink.

It was just a stupid tie. But to look at my mom's face, you'd think its destruction was essential to preserving life as we knew it.

"You're going to be great, man," Derek says to Eli. "You've got your talking points all lined up. When you practiced for us yesterday you were awesome."

"You don't even know what I said," Eli says. "You don't speak Korean."

"Your tone was great," Derek says. "You sounded really confident."

"I just think it's awesome that you're doing this at all," I say. Eli looks up from the carpet and meets my eyes. "Seriously. I'm incredibly impressed. I'd be way too scared."

"I *am* scared, though," Eli says.

"Well, yeah," I say. "Anyone would be. But that's part of it, right? You know it's going to be hard. That's why making up your mind to do it is such a big deal. I bet that's the hardest part, though. Now all you've got to do is follow through. It'll be a piece of cake from here."

"Really?" Eli looks hopeful.

"Really," I say. "I mean, you already took down a whole needle full of hormones, right? *And* you're coming out to your parents. You're basically a superhero at this point."

Eli laughs. Derek grins and reaches onto the bookshelf toward Eli's row of X-Men action figures. Derek grabs Mystique and tosses it to Eli, who laughs again and holds it up overhead.

"T's coming out, too," Derek adds. "To his sister. I mean, their sister. Right, T?"

"Right," I echo, the laughter dying in my throat.

"That's awesome, T!" Eli claps their hands, beaming. They look so excited for me I'm feeling even more anxious than I did before.

"So tonight, you guys both need to relax," Derek says. "Let's go back out there. The game's winding down. T, you can play a couple of rounds without getting smashed."

I sigh. "I still have two papers to write."

"Everyone always has two papers to write. That excuse for not doing stuff stops working around three months into your freshman year. Whoops, you're there now."

I groan again, but I follow Derek and Eli back into the common room. Everyone smiles and looks genuinely happy to see us. I smile back, and I don't even have to force it.

Nance offers me a beer. I take it.

Derek is right. I need to relax.

There's no rush. I have plenty of time to figure everything out.

Except that I just said I'd come out to my sister at Thanks-giving. And Thanksgiving is only two weeks away.

Holy crap. Holy, holy, holy crap.

NOVEMBER

FRESHMAN YEAR OF COLLEGE

3 WEEKS APART

## GRETCHEN

"Okay, Gretchen, you be Mom," Carroll says. "Sam, you're Dad."

"Why do I have to be your dad?" Samantha whines.

"Because my dad won't say anything, so your Southern accent won't distract me."

"I don't know how to act like your dad," Sam says.

"I don't know how to act like his mom, either," I say.

"It's easy," Carroll says. "Both of you just be hick-like and judgmental."

"Shouldn't some of your acting-class friends do this?" I

ask. "I don't think Sam and I will really be able to make this, you know, authentic."

"Remember, hick-like and judgmental," he says again. "Okay, I'm going to start."

It's the middle of the night. We're in the dorm basement because it has a couch and no one else ever hangs out there, and because Carroll says the basement's perpetual reek from the trash compactor reminds him of his hometown.

He's decided to come out to his parents over Thanksgiving, and he wants to practice. I agreed to help because I owe him. Carroll's been really patient at listening to me lately. He even came with me to see the new Angelina Jolie movie last weekend. I'd thought it would take my mind off how stressed I was about whatever's going on with Toni (which it didn't). Samantha agreed to help him practice, too, because—actually, I don't know why Sam is helping.

Carroll goes over to hide behind a pillar. "Are you ready?" he calls.

Samantha slumps over in her chair and grabs her crotch, flipping her light brown braids over her shoulders. She sticks her other hand out in front of her face like she's holding a cigarette.

"Is that how you think dads act when their kids are about to come out to them?" I ask her.

"How am I supposed to know?" She takes a drag off her imaginary cigarette.

I don't have an answer for that, so I just call, "We're ready."

Carroll comes out from behind the pillar with his head down. His hands are clasped behind his back like he's hiding something. I wonder if his real plan is to shoot his parents. Maybe he'd prefer that.

"Son, it looks as though you want to talk to us," I say to start him off.

"Yes, Mom, I do." He looks at Samantha, takes in her crotch-grab and purple fishnets, and manages to stay in the scene. "You, too, Dad."

Samantha takes another drag.

"Go ahead, Carroll," I say. "You know you can always tell us anything."

Carroll frowns at me, then turns to look at his hands.

Samantha and I wait. And wait. I wonder if he expects us to give him another prompt, and I try to think of what else I could say, but he says, "Forget it. I can't."

He stomps back to the pillar.

"Carroll!" I jump up and go after him. "Yes, you can. It's just us. Just practice."

"You threw me off," he says. "With that part about how I can tell them anything. They've *never* said that. They would *never*."

"I'm sorry," I say. "I didn't know."

"Yeah, well." He runs his hand through his hair. "I'm all off track now."

"Can we try again?"

"I don't think so. I'm too freaked."

"How about we take a break and then come back to it?" I say. "Let's go out. We can get some candy at the deli."

"The novelty of that has worn off, my dear."

I can't tell if he means for that to hurt my feelings, but it does.

"I'm really sorry," I say.

"It's okay. I'm tired anyway. Let's just go upstairs."

We go. Samantha keeps up the dirty-old-man act in the elevator, still smoking her imaginary cigarette, not noticing Carroll's disdainful expression. My phone buzzes with a text from Toni.

Dead from work. Cannot write anymore. Cannot read anymore. Going 2 fail, get expelled, etc. Send help.

"What's the missus want this time?" Carroll asks.

"Nothing," I tell him.

I text back.

You're such a liar. You just finished your last paper didn't u.

Toni replies:

Whatever. I'm dead from work all the same.

I smile down at the phone. It's nice to have a normal exchange with Toni. Lately we've been having all these tense conversations that seem an awful lot like fights. We always pull back before we actually start to argue, but I can still feel the anger there, bubbling below the surface.

The elevator gets to our floor, and now I'm exhausted, too. Samantha has dropped her cigarette act. She yawns.

As she opens the door to our room, Carroll pulls me back. His eyes are shiny.

"It's going to go okay, right?" he asks once Sam's closed the door behind her.

I can't remember the last time I saw him this earnest. No joking around, no over-the-top gestures.

"Yeah," I say. "It'll be fine. Just remember to relax. It won't work if you go in there all wound up."

He nods superfast, turns on his heel and takes off down the hall. I go into my room. Samantha has already fallen into bed, still in her fishnets.

"Hey," I say, nudging her foot. "You're going to rip those if you sleep in them."

"No, I won't." Her eyes are closed but she sounds wide-awake. "I've been falling asleep in fishnets for years. There's an art to it. You bend your legs just so before you fall asleep so you won't be tempted to kick all night."

"Or you could just take your fishnets off," I say.

Sam opens her eyes and glares at me. Then she sits up, pulls up her skirt, pulls down her fishnets and collapses back into bed.

"Sorry," I say. "I wasn't trying to be annoying."

"I know," she says. "You never actually manage to be annoying. By the way, that is, itself, annoying."

I don't know what to say to that.

It's still late, but I'm not tired anymore. I change into my sleep T-shirt and shorts, and think about doing my Met Studies reading. Instead I stare at my phone, wondering if I'll hear from Toni again or if that complaint about homework was all we had to say to each other today.

"If you want to really succeed in not being annoying," Sam says, "you could turn out the light."

I flick the switch. "Hey, can I ask you something, or are you sleeping?"

"I am obviously not sleeping."

"How did you decide to be goth?" I've been wondering since September. I know it's not the music, because all Sam listens to is Katy Perry. "Was it because you liked the clothes, or was it something your friends were already into?"

"None of my friends at home were goth," she says. "Ridge Spring, South Carolina, does not have a goth scene."

"Oh. So was it, like—did you really like *Vampire Diaries*? Or—"

"Look, not all of us are gorgeous blond lesbians, okay?" She yawns. "Some people have to work to get noticed."

The first part of what she said makes me squirmy, so I only answer the second part.

"Maybe that's how it was back home, but it doesn't have to be that way here," I say. "This is New York. Nobody stands out here anyway."

That might be my favorite thing about New York. The anonymity. In this city you can be whoever you want. No one knows any different.

"I guess," Sam says. "It did pretty much suck back home. No one there got it. I was worried that when I met real goths they'd turn out to be obsessed with blood and animal sacrifice and Ouija boards, but now that I'm up here it's actually pretty fun. None of my goth friends ever really wants to talk about the scary stuff. We just hang out and wear cool clothes. Plus goth guys are cute, when they remember to wash their hair."

I laugh. "Okay. Forget I said anything. Go to sleep."

She fake-snores. I laugh again.

My phone buzzes. I take it out to tell Toni I'm going to bed, but Toni's text says:

Btw think I'm not going to dc 4 tgiving. Might volunteer at a food drive here. So I won't have 2c the scary mother.

I jump up, grab my keys and my computer, go out into the deserted hallway, sit down on the floor and open video chat.

Toni doesn't answer my call. Instead I get another text.

Sorry, I can't get online right now. Battery almost out and outlets all taken.

I roll my eyes to the ceiling and press the Call button on my phone. Toni answers on the third ring.

"I can't talk, either," T says. "Ebony's sleeping and the demon twins are in the common room."

"So go out in the hall. That's where I am."

There's rustling. Doors opening and closing. Then Toni sighs. "Hey."

"Hey."

"What's up?"

"What do you mean, what's up?" I ask. "Tell me you're not serious about Thanksgiving."

There's a long pause. It's strange, not being able to see Toni's face. I'm used to video chat. It's still not the same as being together, but at least online I can see what's going on. Get some sort of clue from Toni's face.

Finally Toni says, "It's just…the closer it gets, the worse it seems."

I suck in a breath. "I've only seen you *once* since the beginning of the semester."

"I know. I'm sorry. I want to see you, I just…really, really don't want to go down to Thanksgiving. I hate being around my mother. You know that."

I want to cry. Instead I chew on my lip and look straight ahead. There's a stain on the carpet in the shape of Idaho. I focus on that so I can keep my voice steady.

"You already canceled your trip here so you can go to England for your interview," I say. "If you don't come home for Thanksgiving, we won't see each other until Christmas. That's another five weeks from now."

I'm angry, but I feel guilty at the same time. If I'd gone to school in Boston, we wouldn't be having this problem.

Toni sighs into the phone again. "I'm so tired. Can we talk about this later?"

"*When?*" The anger in my voice masks the guilt. "You know Thanksgiving is *next week*, right?"

"Please don't be mad at me."

Oh, God. I suck. That was such an un-Toni-like thing to say. We *never* get mad at each other. "T, what's really going on?"

"Nothing. I'm just tired, and it's cold here, and I have so much work to do still, and I've had a sinus infection for three months, and I hate my roommates, and I'm having a really tough time adjusting to using *they* pronouns and I think I need to try using *ze* instead but I'm afraid that's going to be even harder, and I told Derek I'd come out to my sister over Thanksgiving but now I think I'm too scared, and also I really, really, really, *really* cannot possibly emphasize how much I do *not* want to see my mother next week or, really, ever again."

Whoa. "You're coming out to Audrey? As trans? I mean— as gender nonconforming?"

Toni sighs into the phone, long and heavy. "I don't know. I was going to, but I don't know."

Well, that explains it. This isn't really about me or even Toni's mom. Toni's just nervous about coming out. I soften my voice.

"You don't need to be scared," I say. "Audrey will be okay with it."

Toni breathes out so long I can't tell if it's a sigh or a groan. "It's *so easy* for you to say that."

I close my eyes. Toni's right, obviously. I'm not the one taking the risk.

The thing is, I'm right, too. Audrey adores Toni. Toni could come out to her as a secretly evil warlord of some country we've never heard of and Audrey would be cool with it.

"I know, but seriously," I say. "I promise you, Audrey will be completely fine with you being...you know. Look, to be honest, I think she already suspects."

"Why would Audrey suspect? They have no frame of reference. They're only a kid."

It takes me a second to figure out who Toni means. I hope Toni's serious about switching pronouns again, because the *they* stuff is hard to follow.

"Audrey's sixteen," I say. "When you were sixteen, you'd already founded the GSA. Of which, by the way, Audrey's an active member. She'll get this. Trust me."

Toni mumbles something.

"What?" I ask.

"I said, would you come with me?"

"Come with you?"

"When I tell my sister. Audrey likes you. It won't be weird if you're there."

It might be kind of weird, actually, but if it will make it easier for Toni, then of course I'll be there. It's one thing I can actually do to help.

"I absolutely will," I say.

"I think I can do it if you're there."

"You can do it. I know you can."

"I'm glad you called me."

"Same here," I say. "Toni?"

"Yeah?"

"I love you."

"I know. Me, too."

We get off the phone, but I don't go back to my room. I check my email. I check my friends' latest updates. Then I play one of those gem-drop games on my phone until my battery is almost dead.

I'm so absorbed I don't see Carroll coming until he sits down next to me. I let my last game die and look over at him.

"I can't sleep," he says.

"Tell me about it."

"Why are you out here?"

"I was talking to Toni. Didn't want to keep Sam awake."

He laughs. "You are such the übergirlfriend. Always at her beck and call."

"*I* called *Toni*."

"Yeah, yeah. I bet you still wound up the selfless comfort-giver while she sobbed in your ear."

Sometimes Carroll irritates me.

"You should go ahead and get married," he says. "You're such a little fifties wife already. Hey, if she becomes a guy it'll be legal even in, like, Russia, right?"

I know I should tell him not to say that kind of stuff, but I don't have the energy. I lay my head on his shoulder instead. He puts his arm around my waist.

"Mind if I practice my monologue, as long as we're not talking?" he asks after a minute.

"Sure."

He drones on, something from Shakespeare about the air and the glorious sun and an elephant. I tune him out and close my eyes and think that maybe everything will be okay, after all.

That's when I realize what's been bothering me this whole time. Why I've been sitting in the hall playing games instead of lying in my nice warm bed listening to the "Ocean Waves" audio track Sam plays to get to sleep every night.

That phone call was the only time I've ever said "I love you" to Toni and not had Toni say it back.

# 11

## TONI

"Harvard's a *disgrace*!" Chris screams into the crowd. "I bite my thumb at *all* y'all!"

"Yo, your friend is a dork, T!" Nance howls.

Nance is the only one enjoying this. The rest of the crowd is booing Chris, who's balanced precariously on the John Harvard statue.

The game was this afternoon. The only football game of the season that anyone pays attention to—Harvard versus Yale. Yale won, thirty-five to three. So Chris has a point about us failing. Screaming Shakespearean insults about it in the Yard in front of hundreds of drunk Harvard students while wearing a bright purple Yale sweatshirt still isn't a great idea, though.

Ironically, Chris is one of the few people in the Yard who *isn't* drunk. Chris is on a so-called "detox diet" and has turned down every single offer of alcohol, even though the offers have been coming in since before we woke up this morning. Ebony's new boyfriend, Paul, showed up in our common room with three bottles of champagne at 8:00 a.m. and nearly poured it all over Chris's head at the sight of that purple sweatshirt.

Chris decided this trip would serve as a "post-dumping pick-me-up weekend." That's right—Chris and Steven have officially broken up. I heard the story on the bleachers this afternoon, Chris shouting over everyone else's cheers so I could hear. "Steven decided he needed to explore some new horizons. I believe their names were Brandon, Justin, Cameron and Travis."

I know getting dumped is rough, but if I'd known Chris intended to climb the statue, I wouldn't have agreed to come back to the Yard. My friends all planned to go straight to their house after the game, but Chris spotted the crowd and ran right for it. The rest of us had no choice but to follow. Me because I felt obligated, and Nance and the others because they think Chris is hilarious. I keep explaining that ze's normally much better behaved, but no one believes me. I think it's partly because they all keep laughing whenever I try to pronounce one of the gender-neutral pronouns I've started using. Apparently whenever I try to say *ze* or *hir* out loud, I take a long pause first, and when I finally say it my voice gets really high and hoity-toity. The whole effect is, I'm told, quite entertaining.

"You got your asses kicked today!" Chris screams to the crowd. "And guess who's number one in the new *U.S. News & World Report*? Huh? Huh?"

"Stanford, you loser!" someone shouts back. Chris gives hir the finger.

"You've got to get him down from there," Derek says. "They're turning vicious."

"I'll help," Eli says.

Eli and I shove our way toward the statue, where a few people are waving their beer bottles menacingly at Chris. It's slow going since Eli and I are both five-foot-one on a good day, but people take pity and let us pass. I doubt Chris is in any actual danger—Harvard isn't a beer-bottle-throwing kind of school, game or no game—but it isn't a good scene either way.

"Hey," I say to Chris when we're close enough to be heard over the jeers. "Time's up, dude. Let's get out of here."

"Okay, but first!" Chris holds up a stern hand. "Repeat after me, T. 'Yale rules, Harvard drools.'"

"I absolutely will not say that," I say.

Eli reaches up to help Chris down. "They'll kill you, man."

"Okay, okay." Chris takes Eli's hands and carefully jumps down from the statue. The crowd cheers. Two freshmen immediately climb up to take Chris's place, holding their Harvard beer cozies over their heads in triumph. I wonder if they're drunk enough to think we actually won.

"Glad to see you all survived," Derek says when we get back.

"It was *thisclose*." Chris holds up a thumb and forefinger.

"Can we go home now?" Eli asks. "You two are coming with us, right?"

Chris throws an arm around my shoulders. "Can T and I meet up with you guys later? I need to whine to my girl some more."

Derek and Eli both do double takes at the "girl" thing. I shake my head and they let it go.

Nance hands me a Bud Light from a cooler. Chris and I say goodbye to the guys and go stand on the front steps of my dorm. People are celebrating all around us—it's very Ivy League to celebrate losing a football game—which means we can talk without being overheard.

"So, what's happening in your life, Toni, my love?" Chris asks. "Clearly it's better than mine, since you don't appear to be a miserable wreck. Of course, you've always been good at faking it."

I hate that Chris hasn't been drinking. I've had two beers already. It makes me feel vulnerable. I pass my beer can to Chris, and ze tries to pry off the tab without actually opening it.

"I'm okay," I say. "I like my friends a lot."

"I like them, too," Chris says. "Very friendly. As friends should be."

"Yeah, they're good guys."

"That they are. Guys, I mean. Is there anything you want to tell me, Toni, my love?"

"Uh, yeah." This is as good a time as any. At least we aren't making eye contact. I take a deep breath and start to say, *I identify as genderqueer. Or gender nonconforming. Or—something.*

*I don't know yet. I'm still figuring it out. Is that okay? That I'm still figuring it out?*

Instead I say, "I think I have to break up with Gretchen."

Chris drops the beer. It lands on hir foot. "Ow!"

"That's what you get when you drop a full can of beer," I say. I'm trying to sound light, but my heart is pounding. I'm as shocked as Chris that I just said that.

I've been trying to figure out what to do for weeks now, but I've never actually thought about *breaking up*. Breaking up has always been the last thing I'd ever want to do.

Now that I've said it out loud, though, everything feels different.

Chris hops on one foot. "I can't believe you said that."

"Sorry."

I lead us to another section of steps, where it's a little quieter, and sit down.

"There will be no more of this talk." Chris sits down next to me and waves a finger in my face. "You and Gretchen are getting married and having little pink-haired babies and that's the end of it."

"Chris."

"You guys have been the relationship model that I've aspired to for as long as I've known I was supposed to aspire to relationship models, okay? It didn't work out with Steven and me, yeah, but that's because Steven sucks. Literally, and often. It's not because my entire understanding of romance is flawed due to *your* shortcomings."

"Chris." I sigh. "I'm pretty sure this isn't actually about you."

"You like someone else, right?" Chris pulls away and looks at me, hard. "It's that Derek."

"Chris! No! God!" I can't believe this. Maybe Chris doesn't know me as well as I thought. Or maybe neither of us knows each other that well now that we're off in our own separate college universes. "It's nothing like that. Derek's a guy, for starters."

"Well, I didn't know if maybe you were into guys now. Those kinds of guys at least."

"'Those kinds of guys'? What, like they're alien creatures? Do you not have trans people at Yale?"

"Oh, uh." Chris frowns. "I guess we do. I bet I'd know some if I'd joined one of the gay groups. Everyone in those groups are just so full of themselves, though. Besides, I meet plenty of guys on the crew team as it is."

I laugh. My heart has slowed down to a flutter. "There's more to joining organizations than meeting potential hookup partners."

"If you say so. Anyway, look, I don't want to get off track, because this part is important."

"Which part?"

"The part where you're crazy."

"Chris, listen to me—"

"No, *you* listen."

Chris gives me that look again. I shrink back. I don't remember Chris being so intimidating in high school. Maybe it's those new, even bigger crew-team muscles. They make my friend look slightly like a blond, gay Superman.

"Seriously," Chris says. "You think you'll ever find someone like Gretchen again? Someone gorgeous and smart who'll put up with all your BS and think it's cute? Because I hate to break it to you, but you won't."

"What?" I can't tell how much of that was a joke. "You're saying Gretchen's too good for me?"

Only *I* get to think that.

"I'm saying she's one in a million," Chris says. "And you're an idiot. If I met a guy version of Gretchen, I'd hang on for dear life."

"I've *been* hanging on for dear life." My heart is beating fast again. The words are coming fast, too. Faster than I can think them. "I don't think it's working. I think Gretchen would be a lot better off without me, and I think she—I mean, ze—knows that, too. Gretchen's just too nice to say so."

Wow. I can't believe those words even entered my brain.

I don't want to take them back, though. Even though they hurt.

"You're crazy," Chris says. "She worships you."

"Gretchen doesn't really know me."

"So, what, all your awesome new friends do?"

I shrug. "Maybe."

Chris is still giving me that look. Probably thinking about what Steven did. Thinking I'm just as bad.

It isn't like that, though. I'm not talking about abandoning Gretchen on some sort of stupid whim. I'm taking this seriously. I'm trying to be mature.

"Not to knock your Harvard friends, because they're great and all," Chris says. "But you're still getting to know them, and they're all older than you. What are you going to do when they graduate? Do you have any friends in your own year? I mean, seriously, do you really want to cut things off with your *real* best friend right now?"

"It'll be a long time before the guys graduate." Besides, I prefer not to think about what will happen after that.

"Well, either way, you're crazy." Chris sighs. "I don't know if you're aware of this, but breaking up *sucks*. Just look at me."

Yes. I'm extremely aware that breaking up sucks.

I'm really worried about it, actually. All these awful scenarios keep running through my head.

Gretchen gets, well. Kind of emotional sometimes. What if I do something and it makes Gretchen, like—*really, really* upset? So upset I need to—I don't know—be worried?

No. It's ridiculously arrogant of me to think I'm that important. That a couple of words from me could be enough to set off something like that. I've got to stay rational here.

"I know you feel wretched, but that's because your breakup only just happened," I tell Chris. "The wretchedness will fade."

"Toni. He first cheated on me a month ago."

This is new information. "Seriously?"

"Seriously. He told me right after it happened. I cried, he cried, he said he was sorry and promised he'd never do it again, and I took him back and tried to act like nothing had happened. Then, a couple of days ago, he changed his mind and dumped me, after all. Once he got over the initial wave of guilt, I guess, he realized he wanted to be free to pursue his herpes agenda more than he wanted me. He was too nice to cheat on me again while we were still together, I'll give him that, but he wasn't too nice to break my heart."

"Jeez, Chris. I'm sorry."

"So." Ze coughs. "You can see why I'm not thrilled at the idea of you doing the same thing to a good friend of mine."

I look down at the crumbling step. "It wouldn't be like that. I'd never cheat on Gretchen. If we broke up, it wouldn't be for some petty reason. Plus, I haven't decided for sure. I'd only do it if I thought there was no other choice."

"T, I'm sorry, but there's always a choice."

"It doesn't make sense anymore!" I don't know why Chris can't see this. It's all so clear in my head. "Me and Gretchen! We never made sense. Gretchen's always been way out of my league. We make even less sense now than we did before."

"Why don't you make sense?" Chris asks.

"All I do anymore is drag everything down."

I can't tell how much of what I'm saying is the beer and how much is real. Every word *feels* real, but this can't possibly all be true, can it?

"Gretchen's always stuck trying to cheer me up," I say. "Trying to get me to talk about stuff I don't know how to talk about. Trying to understand stuff ze can't understand."

"Have you explained it? Maybe she *can* understand."

"No, Gretchen can't. And, no offense, neither can you."

I stop. I don't have to look at Chris's face to know I've gone too far.

"I'm sorry," I say, even faster now. "I didn't mean that you aren't—"

"I get it, T. Please don't fall all over yourself trying to apologize. It's embarrassing."

Chris exhales and slings an arm across my shoulders. We look out across the Yard at everyone else having the time of their lives. My roommates, Joanna and Felicia, are across from us, messing around with their friends from their a cappella group. They look happier than I've ever seen them. Probably because they don't know I'm in such close proximity.

I heard them talking about me yesterday. I was in my room and they were in the common room, watching *The Flighted Ones* and getting ready for some party you can't get into unless your name's on a list. Once they turned the TV off, I could hear every word they said. They still haven't figured out how thin the walls are. I have no clue how either of them got into Harvard.

"It's like, why can't she just be a lesbian and be done with it?" Felicia asked.

"She's too cool for that," Joanna said. "Being a lesbian is boring. Being—whatever she is, that's the new trendy thing."

"It's antifeminist." Felicia went to one session from a Women, Gender and Sexuality class before she switched to Social Studies. We've all been suffering for it ever since. "It's saying women can't be strong, so if you want to be strong you have to be a guy."

"Yeah," Joanna said. "I can totally see that. Do you think we should tell her or something?"

"Like she'd listen. She's so full of herself."

After that I put on my headphones and stayed in my room, working on a paper that wasn't due until Wednesday for my Expos class. I didn't even come out to pee until I heard them bang the door closed on their way out.

Usually I just laughed them off, but that conversation stuck with me. Even though obviously everything they said was bull. None of what I've been doing has anything to do with trends or being cool. And I'm not full of myself.

Besides, who the hell are they to talk? Joanna gets up at six in the morning to start a ninety-minute hair-care regimen, and Felicia wears designer high heels every day even though they always get caught in the sidewalks. Joanna and Felicia are the ultimate gender conformists. Neither of them has the right to talk about feminism until they stop posting pictures of themselves in bikinis.

"So, here's the thing, T," Chris finally says. We've been sitting quietly for a long time, but I look back up, glad to have something to focus on other than my roommates. "It sounds to me as if you're making excuses."

"Excuses for what?"

"I don't know. It's just that your train of thought on this is, to put it mildly, extremely hard to follow, and that's always a giveaway. Mind if I smoke, by the way?"

"If you *what*?" Chris pulls out a cigarette while I watch in horror. "You *smoke* now?"

"Only when I'm stressed." Chris lights up, inhales and blows out a long string of smoke. I cough. "Like when my friend tells me something completely crazy out of nowhere."

"You really think I'm that far off base?"

"Maybe…but I think you have to do what you think you have to do."

"I love Gretchen." I wish I still had that beer. "I don't want Gretchen to be with anyone but me."

"Well, that tells you what you should do, then."

"I don't know if it does." I tug on the back of my hair. Gel comes off on my fingers. I wipe it on the step. "I don't know if loving someone and not wanting them to be with someone else is enough of a reason to stay. Not when there are other complicating factors."

"If you love someone, isn't *that* the complicating factor?"

"Love doesn't exist in a vacuum." I take a breath, forcing myself to go slowly. "Chris, honestly, you should see how awful I've been lately. I'm so self-absorbed and bratty. I've even lied a couple of times. I used to *never, ever* lie to Gretchen. I planned this summer internship in England without even asking what ze thought, like a total asshole. It's as if all I care about anymore is me."

Chris nods.

"I need to narrow my life down," I say. "It's not fair of me to string us both along this way. Gretchen's bound to meet someone else who will actually be a decent girlfriend."

And if I end things now, I get to spare myself the trauma of seeing that happen up close.

Chris takes another puff. "Look. Just be straight with me. You're absolutely sure there isn't somebody else in the picture on your end?"

"Yes!" I can't believe Chris is still obsessed with this. "God, there's no one else. I wouldn't even have *time* for anyone else."

"I only ask because, in my experience, ninety-nine point nine percent of the time when someone decides they need to break up out of thin air, and they have this long laundry list of reasons why, the real reason is they want to go out with someone else. Or multiple someone elses."

"Well, trust me, I'm in the other point one percent."

"Okay, okay, if you insist."

I shake my head. "I don't want to talk about this anymore."

"You brought it up," Chris says. "I thought you were just going to tell me the reason you started talking all funny is because you're a dude now."

I throw up my hands. Suddenly I feel like laughing. Of course. Chris has probably known all along. Chris probably knew before *I* knew. "I can't get anything by you, can I?"

"Relax, T. It's all good. Hey, do you still not do hugs?"

I think about it. "Maybe it's time I reconsidered that policy."

We hug. It's been so long since I hugged someone who wasn't Gretchen, I'm not entirely sure I'm doing it right.

"It's good to see you again," Chris says. "Especially the new, dude you."

I swallow. It's so weird to hear hir say that. "I know what you mean."

"I missed this."

"Me, too."

We pull back. I can't look at Chris after what we just said. I know Chris is a good guy, but even good guys start looking at you differently after they find out something like that.

"I'll see you again in a few days anyway, right?" Chris says. "For Thanksgiving."

"Ugh. I guess."

"Not looking forward to the trip?"

"That is a gross understatement."

"I know. Me neither. I'm so not ready to see Steven."

"I'm not ready to see anyone."

"Anyone meaning your mom?"

I don't answer. I mean my mother, yes, but for once, there

are things I'm dreading even more about this particular holi-
day. Like talking to Audrey.

And talking to Gretchen.

We get up, stepping carefully to avoid the alcohol puddles,
and cross the Yard. Chris's Yale sweatshirt gets more angry
looks, but there's no yelling this time.

"You've got a good thing going here," Chris says. "Maybe
I should transfer next year."

"Like you'd ever."

"Yeah, okay, call my bluff. You should come down for the
Race, though. It'll be fun. The crew team leaders might let
me in the freshman race."

"Doesn't Harvard always kick Yale's ass at the Race?"

"Yeah. So you'll have a good time."

"Okay, then, it's a plan."

Chris holds up a hand. "High five."

We high-five and laugh as we walked up the steps to the
guys' house.

Maybe it will all be okay.

Thanksgiving break is a few days away. I still have time
to think about how to handle this.

I still have time to make up my mind.

Even though my palms are already sweating.

12

## GRETCHEN

"I can't believe they're together again," Toni says.

"I can," I say. "They love each other. They're a good couple, deep down."

"Steven cheated on him."

"Chris said he forgave him. Besides, you see how they are when they're together. They make each other happy."

"I'm just saying, three days ago Chris was totally heart-broken, and now they're both acting like everything's fine. It's great that they like being together, but that doesn't make them a good couple. I like diet soda, but it's still full of all those chemicals that give you cancer and stuff, you know?"

It's the night before Thanksgiving. We're home in DC, in the car coming back from a party at Renee's house with our high school friends. Chris and Steven spent the first half of the night making catty comments about each other from across the room. Then they started making out on the love seat.

We're driving to Toni's house now. When we get there, Toni's going to come out to Audrey.

Neither of us mentions that.

It's been a tense visit already, between Toni getting all annoyed about Chris and what happened when we first arrived at Toni's house this afternoon. Instead of saying hello, Mrs. Fasseau, who hadn't seen Toni since August, walked into the kitchen, took one look at Toni and me standing by the counter and asked, "Can anyone tell me why my daughter is walking around this city dressed like a vagrant?"

Besides being mean, what she said didn't even make any sense. Toni isn't wearing a binder this weekend, and aside from the now permanently affixed Red Sox baseball cap, T really doesn't look any different than before.

Toni said, "I'm hoping the neighbors will think you've taken in a stray," and it went downhill from there. Toni and Mrs. Fasseau will look for any excuse to get in an argument. Soon they were both yelling so loud, Consuela had to go into the dining room to roll the pie crusts.

It'll be okay after tonight, though. Sometime in the next hour, Toni will talk to Audrey. Audrey will be cool about everything, and then Toni will calm down.

It's going to be an awesome weekend. Toni and I will

spend as much time together as we possibly can. Things will get back to normal for both of us. And for *us*, us.

"Cheating is basically the worst thing ever," Toni says.

"I know," I say. "I totally, completely agree with you on that. Steven is a total jerkface for cheating. It's just—maybe I'm a crazy romantic, but I also think that forgiveness is basically the *best* thing ever."

"I know," Toni says, sighing. "You're right. You're always right about this stuff."

I sit back in my seat, surprised. I don't remember the last time Toni said I was right about something.

"Maybe when we come back for Christmas we can try to hang out with them together a little bit," I say. "Maybe see if you can forgive Steven, too."

"I won't have to," Toni says. "They'll be broken up again by then."

Toni's worked up. It's only natural. I should try to do something about it, though. It won't be good if Toni's still in this mood when we talk to Audrey.

"Oh, come on," I say. "That's what people told us when we started college, remember? That we'd be broken up by Thanksgiving?"

"People are stupid," Toni says with a grunt.

We're at a stoplight. There's got to be another way to put Toni in a better mood.

"What did you think of that outfit Renee had on?" I try to sound light, teasing. "Her top was more of a bra than a shirt. Do you think I could pull off that look?"

"Your light's green," Toni says.

Wow. Okay. I pull through the intersection and pretend that didn't faze me.

"Are you nervous?" I finally ask.

"I don't want to talk about it."

"Okay." I try to think of something else to say. Talking to Toni isn't supposed to be this hard. "Can you believe how tan Marie got? I mean, I know she goes to college in Florida, but what does she do, spend every day on the beach? Do you think classes are optional there or something?"

"Can you pull over?"

"What? Oh, uh, sure."

We've just turned into Toni's McMansion neighborhood. There's a grove of trees inside the front gates. I pull the car in under them, away from the streetlights. I don't know if Toni just wants to take a breather or is about to have a full-on meltdown, but either way, privacy will be good.

"What's going on?" I ask.

"I'm sorry," Toni says.

"For what?"

Toni shrugs. "Nothing. It doesn't matter now. I just have really stupid ideas sometimes."

"No, you don't. Telling Audrey's a good idea. I know it's scary, but—"

"That's not what I mean." Toni pinches the bridge of T's nose. "Chris was right. I was being an idiot. I don't know what I was thinking."

"Chris? About what? I didn't even see you talk to him tonight. Was there something—"

"Can you come over here?"

I unbuckle my seat belt and climb over until I'm perched

on the edge of Toni's seat. We're in my mom's ancient SUV, and it doesn't have the easiest setup for cuddling, but I put my arms around Toni anyway.

"What's wrong?" I ask. I smooth Toni's hair back and kiss T's earlobe.

Toni kisses me, hard, and I forget about the rest of it.

We move into the backseat, because the front doesn't have tinted windows, and Toni always thinks about these things. I don't. I can't. I'm too caught up in the way this feels. Toni's hands on me, our lips moving together. Our bodies that know every rhythm of each other.

"I love you," I say.

Toni doesn't answer. I wish I hadn't said it in the first place.

I close my eyes and move in for another kiss and stop thinking altogether.

Toni's parents go to bed early, so when we get to the house, most of the lights are out. Toni has managed to be back in town for twelve hours without seeing Mr. and Mrs. Fasseau for more than five minutes at a time. I don't know how they can keep this up all weekend, especially with Thanksgiving tomorrow, but if any family can pull it off it's this one.

I knock on Audrey's bedroom door a couple of minutes later. She's got an Amy Winehouse song playing, which makes me smile. I haven't seen Audrey since August, so when she opens the door, for a second I forget why we're there and I give her a happy hug. Then Toni coughs behind me, and I remember I promised to kick off this conversation.

"Hey, Audrey," I say. "I know it's late, but can we come in and talk about something important?"

"As long as you aren't here to tell me you're taking the car back to Boston with you," Audrey says, looking at Toni. We come in and sit down on these faux-fur butterfly chairs Audrey has, with cheap fabric stretched over thin aluminum tubes. I'm always sure I'll fall out of them. Audrey sits on the bed. "Dad said if you do he won't let me get another Nissan. I'll be stuck driving Mom's old Range Rover to school and honestly, it's so embarrassing."

"I don't want the car," Toni says. "No one drives at Harvard."

"Good," Audrey says. "Can I have your room, too?"

"No," Toni says.

Audrey laughs. Toni doesn't. I want to tell Toni to relax, but I've already done my job. My only responsibility from this point on is to sit here and be silently supportive.

"So, what did you want to talk to me about?" Audrey looks back and forth between us. She's still smiling, but I can tell she's getting nervous.

After a long pause, so long I start to get worried, Toni looks down and says, "Um. So. Look. Do you know what *transgender* means?"

"Yeah, duh," Audrey says. "I'm in the GSA, remember? I read that same book you guys did. Hey, is this about your friend Nance?"

Toni's head shoots back up. "What?"

"That girl Nance. I saw where she posted on your page, and I looked at her profile. She was talking about working on a guide to gender transitioning at Harvard. Is she trans-gender?"

"No. Nance isn't trans." Toni cracks a tiny smile. "At least, not as far as I know."

"Oh." Audrey looks even more confused.

"I am."

"Oh. Oh!"

Audrey stands up, then sits back down. She looks at me with wide eyes. I give Audrey a tiny nod so she knows she heard right. She grabs a throw pillow with a pink peace sign on it and hugs it to her chest. I wait for Toni to explain that actually, the best word to use for T is *genderqueer* or *gender nonconforming*, not *transgender*, but Toni doesn't say that.

"Are you freaked?" Toni asks instead.

"No," Audrey says. I wonder if she's telling the truth. "I mean, I kind of had a feeling. Even before you left. It's just weird to hear it for real."

God, I know what she means. It's one thing to have an inkling, but knowing that it's your life now…

"You had a feeling before?" Toni asks. "Really?"

"Yeah," Audrey says. "Mainly because of the lawsuit thing. I mean, I get not liking skirts, but you seemed like you *really, really* hated them."

"Oh."

"So." Audrey smiles really big. She's talking faster than usual. "Does this mean you're a full-time guy now, or what?"

"No," Toni says. "Not yet."

Wow. I've never heard Toni use the word *yet* for that be-fore. Does that mean Toni's definitely decided to transition? Or is this just how Toni's explaining it to Audrey?

I close my eyes and bite my lip to keep from asking questions.

"When?" Audrey asks. I open my eyes to watch Toni's reaction.

"I'm not sure," Toni says. "I'm still figuring it all out."

"How do you know you're transgender if you're still figuring it out?" Audrey asks.

"Because I know I don't consider myself female," Toni says. "I never have. But it's only been since I started school this year that I've thought about it in these exact terms."

That much I knew. Toni told me that the first time we talked about this stuff. *I just know I'm not female*, Toni said then. *I don't know what that makes me. Can you wait while I figure it out? Would you?*

"I thought you said you didn't believe in the binary gender system," Audrey says. "You said it at that one GSA meeting last year."

"I don't," Toni says.

"So if you don't believe there's a binary system, why would you want to be a guy?"

I never would've dreamed of asking Toni that question myself.

"Uh." Toni falters. "I don't know. For real, though, I'm still thinking it through. Maybe I don't want to go all the way to becoming a guy. I'm not sure. All I know is, I definitely don't see myself as a girl."

Oh. Okay.

At first I'm relieved. Then I feel guilty about feeling relieved.

"Oh," Audrey says. "I thought you were supposed to *feel*

trans? That video we watched said trans people felt like they were born in the wrong body."

"Yeah, I don't get that," Toni says. "I wasn't born in the wrong body. This *is* my body."

"But you just said you don't see yourself as a girl. You just said!"

Audrey's frustrated, and I am, too. I'm so glad she's saying all this stuff. I've never asked these questions. I've been so scared of saying the wrong thing.

"I don't see myself as female," Toni says. "But I don't think I'm in the wrong body, either. That seems way too extreme. I don't want to switch bodies with someone else. I'm just not positive I like my body exactly the way it is right now."

*I* like Toni's body exactly the way it is right now.

What does that mean for me? Or for Toni?

Also, the way Toni is explaining it to Audrey sounds much simpler than the way Toni's always explained it to me. Is that because Toni is trying to make this easier for Audrey? Or have I just been overcomplicating things in my head?

"All right." Audrey nods. "So for you it would be like getting regular plastic surgery. Changing your outsides, not your insides."

"Yeah." Toni looks confused. "I guess."

"Like a boob job," Audrey goes on. "Only, I mean, in reverse."

That makes me laugh. Neither of them does, though.

"Is it because of all your new friends up at college?" Audrey says. "Are they, you know, peer-pressuring you to be more trans than you are normally?"

I've wondered that, too. I'm glad I never said it out loud, though, because Toni looks pissed.

"No one's pressuring me to do anything," Toni says. "If they were, it wouldn't make a difference. I know who I am."

Audrey bites her lip. "Sorry. I'm just trying to understand."

Toni softens right away. "I know."

"So you're going to be my brother," Audrey says. It's so strange to hear her say that. "Someday. Maybe. Probably."

"Yeah," Toni says.

What?

Okay, seriously. What the hell happened to *gender non-conforming*?

What happened to *I'm still figuring it out*?

All of a sudden, Toni is going to be a guy? Someday? Maybe? Probably?

What the hell does this mean for *me*?

"So, are you straight now?" Audrey asks.

"No!" I say before Toni can reply.

I expect Toni to agree with me. Instead Toni laughs. "There's nothing wrong with being straight, Gretch."

"I know that," I say. "*You're* certainly not straight, though. You're queer, same as me."

"Well, yeah, but I don't like guys," Toni says. "I like girls. So if I wind up being a guy, then yeah, I guess technically I'd be straight."

Oh, my God. This is really real, isn't it? This is really going to happen.

Jesus. Toni is going to be a guy.

"That's not how it works," I say.

"It's not?" Toni and Audrey ask at the same time. Then they laugh at their overlap.

I want to cover my ears and go "La la la." Instead I say, "I don't know. I guess it's different for different people."

They aren't listening to me anymore. They're still giggling.

"If you're going to be a straight guy, you need to get a new haircut," Audrey says. "Only a gay guy would wear that much gel."

"Lay off my hair!" Toni says. Audrey flicks Toni with her finger, and Toni flicks her back.

This whole awkward scene has brought them closer. That's so weird.

The weirdest part is that I can't remember the last time I saw Toni this happy.

I try to smile, too, but my bottom lip is quivering. They don't notice, though. They're still laughing.

I tell them I have to go to the bathroom. Then I sit on the toilet seat and cry.


I don't have a curfew anymore, since I reminded my parents I get to stay out all night anyway at school. I can stay at Toni's as long as I want to.

I dry my eyes and wash my face. When I get back to Audrey's room, neither of them seems to have noticed I was gone so long. Toni is giddy that Audrey's taking the news so well. The three of us hang out talking for another hour. Audrey's dying to get away from their parents, so Toni invites her to come along to London next month for the internship interview. (Assuming their parents say yes, which they will.

The Fasseaus will take any opportunity to get their children out of the house, including shipping them overseas.)

This annoys me because I'm still not thrilled about Toni going so far away for the summer, but I stay quiet. Finally Audrey yawns and talks about how she had a long day at school, so Toni and I go back down the hall.

We lie on Toni's bed. It's late, and Toni's staring at the ceiling with an unreadable expression. I'm still freaked out from earlier, but I can't show it.

"So, that happened," Toni says.

"Yes, it did," I say, neutral.

"It was better than I thought it would be."

"Yeah. Your sister is awesome. I knew she'd be cool about it."

Toni rolls over onto an elbow, looking at me for the first time since we left Audrey's room. There's a softness in Toni's eyes. I haven't seen that expression there since last August.

"Thank you," Toni says. "So much."

"Oh." I don't know what to say. Those words mean so much. "I didn't…"

"You did. You were there. You being there with me meant so much."

Toni's head drops onto my shoulder. I lie there, feeling Toni's soft weight on my chest, my heart exploding.

"I love you," I say after another long moment has passed. Because it's true, and because I want to say it. And because I want to see what will happen.

Toni doesn't answer.

Maybe Toni's asleep. I shake T's shoulder gently. "T?"

"Hmm?" Toni says.

"I love you," I say again.

"Mmm-hmm." Toni's awake now.

"What's going on?" I ask.

"Nothing."

"Whatever it is, you can tell me. You know that, right? It's always been that way." I pull at a corner of Toni's bed-spread and twist the fabric around my fingers. "Am I doing something wrong?"

"It's nothing," Toni says again.

We aren't looking at each other. I'm lying on my back, studying the cracks in Toni's ceiling. Toni's head is still on my shoulder, facing away from me.

"I can help," I say. "I want to help."

I mean it. I will do anything in the world to make us go back to the way we used to be.

I don't know what changed. All I know for sure is, there's something Toni's not telling me. Three months ago I wouldn't have thought that was possible.

"I know you want to help," Toni says and sighs.

"So tell me what you need. What you said to Audrey, I—I didn't know it was like that, but, I mean, it's great. Are you—did you change your mind about labels? You told her you were just trans. Did you decide not to use *gender non-conforming* anymore?"

Toni shrugs. "I'm mostly using *genderqueer* again. It's simpler. Since it's all under the *trans* umbrella, though, I figured that would be easier for Audrey to understand."

"Oh." I try to smile. "That makes sense. So, what you said, about maybe being a guy someday. Is that—like, do you really think that? Like, what do you think is the—I mean, if you had to put, say, a percentage on it. Do you think there's a ninety percent chance you'll be a guy? Or, you know, a fifty percent chance, or a thirty percent chance—"

Toni's staring at me. "Why are you asking this?"

"Because I want to—I don't know." Crap. I'm doing what I swore I wouldn't. I'm asking questions, and I'm saying the wrong thing because I don't know what I'm talking about. "Never mind. Ignore me. Look, just tell me what I should do, and I'll help however I can."

"You can't help," Toni says.

"Why not?"

"Because it doesn't—it isn't—"

Toni jumps off the bed. The movement comes so fast, it scares me.

"It's just better if—" Toni paces across the room. "It isn't fair—"

"What isn't fair? What are you talking about?"

"I was right, before. Chris didn't understand—"

"What? What does this have to do with Chris?"

Toni flips on a light switch. I hold my hand in front of my eyes to block out the glare.

"We have to get out of here," Toni says, not looking at me.

I've never seen Toni act like this. It's scaring me.

"Okay." I'm woozy from lying down for so long, but I hunt around for my car keys.

It turns out Toni doesn't want to take the car, so we walk down the long driveway of the Fasseaus' house. We follow the subdivision's wide, curving road to the tiny fake park where no one ever goes. It has a bench, some brown shrubs and a fountain with a cement pool around it where little kids throw pennies in the summer. It's November, though, so the fountain is drained and silent, the pool just a gray stone hole.

I have my big coat on but I'm cold anyway. Toni doesn't even have a coat, but Toni isn't shivering. Just pacing.

"You're freaking me out, T." I sit on the bench. I'd rather keep moving, but Toni's pacing is making me anxious. "Is this about your mom? Do you want to tell her this weekend, too? Because I know it'll be hard, but once it's done it'll be like ripping off a Band-Aid. You won't even—"

"Stop," Toni says. "You have no idea what it'll be like. You can't possibly imagine."

I know Toni's right, but still. That hurts. A lot.

"Okay," I say, "but I can help. I can—"

"Wait." Toni sits down next to me and takes both my hands. "Never mind. I'm sorry I said that. That's not what— can we pretend I didn't say that?"

"Okay." This sudden calm is freaking me out even more.

We don't talk for a long time. Toni keeps holding my hands, looking down at them as if they might break.

"You're scaring me," I say after it feels as though hours have passed.

"I'm sorry." Toni looks up at me. "We have to stop."

"We have to stop what?" I ask.

"This." Toni swallows. "We have to break up."

No.

What?

*We have to break—*

"No. No. No!"

I'm on my feet, but I don't remember getting up. I blink down at Toni until Toni looks away. Then I run to the fountain. I step over the side and into the dry, empty basin. I need to move. To do something. Something that isn't listening to this.

"Gretchen," Toni says from behind me. "Look, don't."

"Don't do what?" The fountain has a ten-foot cherub statue in the middle, holding a stone torch. That's where the water's supposed to spout from. I stride across the basin and climb up onto the base of the statue.

Toni's stepped over the side and is sitting on the fountain's edge, watching me. I try not to meet Toni's eyes.

"Someone's going to see." Toni looks from side to side into the darkened neighbors' houses, at the expensive cars lined up in each driveway, the neat piles of leaves raked up by gardeners and standing along the curbs so the county can come vacuum them up.

"I don't give a f—"

"Shh!" Toni stands up. I guess I must be shouting pretty loud. "Be quiet! Seriously!"

"Don't tell me what to do." I lower my voice and wrap my hands around the statue. "You've said enough already."

"Believe me, this isn't what I want," Toni says.

"Oh, yeah?" The stone is freezing. I wrap my sleeves around my hands and try to get a better grip around the cherub's shoulders. "Here's a thought, then. Don't do it."

"It's not that simple."

"Then explain it to me."

I can't see it, but I hear Toni's shrug. We've been together for two years. By now I can hear Toni's every gesture no matter how far away I am.

I knew this was coming. I just didn't want to know.

"I can't be in a relationship right now," Toni says. "I need to figure myself out first. I can't expect you to wait around in the meantime."

"You're not *expecting* me to do anything." I finally get a good grip and swing around to look back at Toni, the statue safely between us. "It's my decision what I want to do with my time. I *want* to be there while you figure yourself out."

"I'm a terrible partner right now. All I ever think about is myself."

"I don't care! Anyway, you're not a terrible partner. This is all my fault for not going up to Boston. I'm sorry, okay?"

I expect Toni to argue with me. Instead Toni just stands there.

I swallow. "That's what this is about, isn't it?"

"No." Toni doesn't sound very convincing. Or convinced.

"It was a stupid thing to do anyway." I swallow again. "I don't know why I even wanted to."

"So, why did you?"

I don't know how to answer that.

"I love you," I say instead.

I come back around from the other side of the statue. That's the last time I'm saying it. My last try.

"I love you, too," Toni says.

Something breaks inside me.

"Then what the hell is the *problem*?" I'm yelling again, but there's still no movement in the dim, lonely street. This is why Toni made us come outside. Toni knew I'd yell. That thought makes me angrier. "It's a damn good thing I never filled out that transfer application for BU for next semester, since apparently you don't want me up there anyway. Did you even remember that? The application was due November 1. I never sent it in. You don't even know, because you never even asked me anything about it!"

"Wait, what?" Toni just stares at me.

I can't handle this. Toni doesn't even *think* about me anymore. I'm so far down on Toni's list of priorities it's embarrassing.

It isn't just because of what I did, either. I don't think it's even mainly because of that anymore.

It's the trans stuff. That's become Toni's whole life. I don't fit anymore.

"This is about your new thing, isn't it?" I say. "God, don't you get it? I don't care what gender you are or you aren't! It couldn't possibly matter less to me!"

Toni doesn't answer right away, so what I just said hangs out in the air, the words uncoiling, like a spider slowly dropping from its web.

"Well, it matters to me," Toni finally says. "A lot."

I shake my head. I should take back what I said—*"your new thing,"* God, how insensitive can I possibly be—but I can't. All of this is coming from somewhere outside me. The real Gretchen is hovering over us, watching this play out, powerless to change it.

Toni and I never fight. *Never.*

We don't get mad at each other. We smile and pretend like nothing's wrong.

We've been doing it for years. We're really, really good at it.

If we hadn't started fighting, we'd be fine. If I hadn't gone to NYU, we'd be fine. If Toni would just stop thinking about trans stuff for five seconds, we would be *totally fine*.

"I'm sorry, okay?" I can't even tell if I'm yelling anymore. "I'm sorry I went to New York. I'm sorry I ruined everything."

"It's just—" Toni's voice is strained. Like it's hard to form words. "I just don't get why you lied to me. What was the point of hiding it?"

"I don't know!" I climb up higher on the statue. "I don't know anything, okay? Is that why you want to get rid of me? Because I'm so dumb compared to everyone else you know? Am I holding you back?"

Toni doesn't answer.

I punch the cherub in the face. It doesn't flinch. My hand hurts a lot, though. Toni jumps over the railing into the basin and grabs for my arm. "Christ, Gretchen! Did you break anything?"

I slide down from the statue and pull my arm away before Toni can touch me. The pain is bringing me back to myself, just a little. "What do you care?"

"Look." Toni takes off the baseball cap, revealing a mess of matted red hair. I don't like Toni's new hair. "I realized something. Derek and Inez, they just started going out, and they're taking it slow, making sure it's what they want. I re-alized, you and me, we never did that. We just jumped right in. That's not how it's supposed to go."

"What the hell are you *talking* about?" I shout. "That's all total *bull crap*! Who cares what works for somebody *else*? I don't care about stupid *Derek*. I care about *you*!"

"I care about you, too," Toni says. "That isn't the only

thing that matters, though, don't you see? There has to be more."

"No." My chest is rising and falling like I've just run a marathon. "I don't see. I think you're full of crap."

"Do you really mean that?" Toni's eyebrows crinkle.

Somehow, in the middle of all this, Toni has managed to make *me* feel like the guilty one.

I reach back to punch the cherub with my other hand. Toni grabs my arm before I can swing.

"Let go of me!"

I'm crying. I pull my arm free, but I don't go for the statue again. Instead I reach back with shaking hands and untie the leather cord with the top hat charm from around my neck. When it comes free, I throw it as far as I can. It lands in someone's backyard.

"I'm sorry," Toni says, looking down at the cement. "I think deep down this is what we both need. You deserve better than me."

"Yeah, well, you're a shitty mind reader," I say. "You don't get to decide what *I* need. Only *I* get to decide what's best for *me*."

Toni reaches for my other hand, the sore one. This time I don't pull away. Toni holds my hand carefully, turning it to look at my knuckles.

"You're bleeding." Toni reaches into a jeans pocket and pulls out a tissue.

I sit down on the cement floor of the fountain, my back against the statue. The cold seeps through my jeans, making me shiver. Toni sits down next to me and presses the tissue onto my fingers. Pieces of it come off onto my bloody skin.

ROBIN TALLEY                                    283

I'm still crying, but I'm calmer now. I don't bother to wipe my face.

"Is that why you're going to England this summer?" I ask. "Are you trying to get away from me?"

"No," Toni says. "God, no. I meant what I told you about visiting."

"It's not the same and you know it." I lean my head on Toni's shoulder.

"I know."

"What is it? Why is coming back here so horrible? Is it your mom?"

"It's my mom, but it's also…all of it. Being down here… it's like I never left. Like I'm still the same person I was when I lived here."

"You want to be somebody else instead."

"Sort of, yeah."

I turn my hand over and lace our fingers together. "I want you to be whoever you want to be."

"I know."

"I don't want to hold you back. I wouldn't."

Toni doesn't say anything.

"I'm serious," I say. "Tell me what you want me to do, and I'll do it."

Toni nods, slowly.

"Just please don't leave me." My voice breaks.

Toni picks up my hand and kisses my fingers. The bleeding has stopped.

"This isn't really what you want," I say. "I know you think you do, but trust me. I know you. You don't want to do this without me."

"I love you," Toni says.

It takes all my powers of restraint to keep me from getting up and dancing.

"Here, I know what we should do," I say. "Let's just take a break. Until the end of the semester. Then you can see if this is what you still want."

"That's only a few weeks," Toni says.

"It should be long enough to decide."

When it comes to the big decisions, Toni either acts totally on impulse or agonizes forever. Most of the time, it's the agony route. Toni waffles back and forth, makes a decision, then decides that decision was wrong and starts all over again.

It can last days, weeks, months. Toni thinks through every aspect, makes mental flow charts, considers every possible outcome until it's been beaten into the dirt.

It's something I've always liked about Toni. Most of the time, T takes things very, very seriously.

This time, Toni's indecision will work in my favor. I'm certain of it. Tonight was obviously one of those impulse decisions. Soon Toni will realize this was a huge mistake. Soon I'll get a phone call begging me to let Toni take it all back. Pretend this never happened. Maybe it'll even happen before the end of Thanksgiving weekend.

I can't believe I didn't think of this sooner.

"How does it work?" Toni asks. "Taking a break? Do we just not talk until after finals? Or even text?"

We've never gone more than a day without talking. Even in high school when Toni was at Sanskrit immersion camp and wasn't supposed to have any English communication, we texted back and forth in secret all day.

I can handle it, though. I can handle anything if that's what it takes to be with Toni. Besides, once Toni realizes what a mistake this was, we'll be right back to talking all the time.

"Yeah, I guess," I say.

"Do we…go out with other people?"

"Sure." I have to force myself not to laugh. I can't imagine ever wanting to go out with anyone else. "Then at Christmas, we'll see how it went."

Toni nods slowly.

I slide over until I'm sitting in Toni's lap. I wrap my arms around T's waist. T hugs me back.

We sit like that for a long, long time. Then I get up and go over to Toni's neighbor's fence. Toni watches me but doesn't say anything.

I climb the fence and find my necklace hanging from a dogwood tree. I pick it up and climb back over to the other side, but I don't put it on.

Instead I stand there, knowing Toni's watching me. I stare down at the charm as if I've never seen it before. Then I slide it into my pocket.

I'm never letting go of this again.

BEFORE

## GRETCHEN

I put down my phone and picked up the letter again.

I could've recited it with my eyes closed by that point. Instead I went over every word on the page one more time.

I wanted to make sure I hadn't missed anything. That this wasn't some mistake.

Maybe it would turn out I'd misunderstood. Maybe my life could go on just as I'd planned before I ripped open that purple envelope.

Nope. I wasn't getting off that easy. The letter still said the same thing it had the first time I read it.

NYU was delighted to offer me a place in its incoming

freshman class if I was still interested. Sorry about the wait-list thing.

If I wanted to come, I had to send back the reply form and a deposit check. Postmarked today.

I'd already talked to the Boston University people on the phone. Just dialing the number felt like a betrayal.

They'd been so nice, though. They just said I should let them know what I decided. Their niceness only made me feel worse.

My parents had been way too nice about it, too. They'd lose the deposit they'd already made to BU if I switched, but they said that was all right. The important thing, they said, was that I think, hard, and decide where I really wanted to spend the next four years.

The one person I hadn't talked to was Toni.

For almost two years, being part of Toni-and-Gretchen was what I did.

I played volleyball. I did homework. I read books and watched movies and hung out with my friends.

I did it all as one half of a whole. I couldn't imagine being anything else.

I still didn't know how I'd gotten this lucky. I wasn't any-where near as special, as interesting, as Toni. But Toni had stuck with me anyway.

If I put this form in the mail, the shaky grasp I had on happiness would get that much weaker. Would I still be able to hold on?

I needed Toni like I needed to keep breathing. If I was smart, I'd pretend this letter never came.

It was just New York. Just a city. Cities didn't love you back.

Except. God, I loved New York.

I loved the rhythm of it. The energy. The sense of possibility you got just by stepping outside your door.

I loved NYU, too. I loved the crisp way downtown smelled in the fall. I loved the way the students walked with a certainty in their step. Like there was no question in their minds. They were all exactly where they wanted to be.

Sometimes, when I was walking through the Village, it felt like New York *did* love me back. It felt like those streets lined with bustling coffee shops and gleaming office buildings and knockoff clothing stores—it felt like they were wrapping their arms around me. Telling me I belonged.

I lay on my bed, staring at the ceiling, crushing the letter to my chest. I'd had it for two days now. Every time I'd seen Toni in those two days, I'd laughed and talked and joked around the same as always. I hadn't said a word about what the letter said.

If that wasn't a betrayal, I didn't know what was.

I uncrumpled the letter and read it again.

*We are delighted to offer you a place in the freshman class...*

Toni wasn't the only one who wanted me.

I didn't always have to be one half of a whole. I could be whole all on my own. Maybe.

I'd never know for sure, though. Not if I went to Boston. Not if I followed Toni's dream instead of my own.

I felt awful for thinking that. But the thought wouldn't go away.

I wanted to see Toni every day. Every hour. The need to be with Toni lived deep in my stomach, a knot that kept unfurling and retying.

I knew what would happen if I went to Boston. I'd see Toni every week. We'd hang out at Harvard. I'd become friends with Toni's friends, just like I did when I moved to Maryland. Toni and I would go out together as a couple. Everyone would know me as Toni's girlfriend.

Every time I looked at Toni, I'd know exactly who I was. Exactly where I belonged. Every day would be just as wonderful as every day had been since Toni and I first met.

I didn't know what would happen if I went to New York.

Not knowing was terrifying. Anything could happen. I could wind up miserable. I could regret my decision the second I set foot in my dorm room at NYU.

I'd have no one to depend on but myself.

It was the not knowing that made me reach for my pen. It was the not knowing that made me fill out that form, sign my name at the bottom with my fingers trembling, slip the sheet into the prestamped envelope and carry it outside and down the driveway.

I closed my eyes when I opened the mailbox and dropped the envelope inside.

There was no way to know what would happen next. The idea, the uncertainty of it all, made me want to throw up.

And it made me want to dance.

13

## TONI

"A break?" Derek asks. "Are you serious?"

"I guess so," I say.

"What does that mean?"

"It means I chickened out."

"Or you didn't really want to do it in the first place," Derek says.

"Or both."

"Can I interest you in Bible study? Through fellowship with other Christians, even the greatest stress can be overcome."

Derek and I are sitting on the steps of the Lamont library

while Eli tries—and, mostly, fails—to hand out flyers for the Bible study the Harvard Christian League is hosting tomorrow night.

Eli is in the Harvard Christian League. Somehow, I've known him for three months without picking up on that.

"I feel worse than if I hadn't said anything to begin with," I tell Derek as a girl in pigtails flips Eli the bird. "Everything's all uncertain now. I hate not knowing exactly where I stand. It's like we're in this sketchy in-between place and it's awful. It's *awful*."

"Breaking up sucks, dude," Derek says.

"I feel like the worst person in the world."

"I bet she thinks she's got you beat."

I drop my head into my hands.

Someone taps on my glove. I don't move.

"Well, if you don't want it, I'll just dump it out," Nance says.

I look up. Nance is standing over me, holding out a cup of coffee from the Lamont café. I take it.

"Oh. Thanks." I take a sip. "Wow, pumpkin latte. Thanks, Nance."

"You like those, right?" Nance passes a cup to Derek and takes one down the steps to Eli, then jogs back up to where we're sitting. "Everyone else drinks cappuccinos, but you got a pumpkin one that other time we were here."

"Yeah, I like them a lot. Thanks." I can't believe Nance remembered that.

Nance sits down next to Derek and me. We watch Eli try to convince a group of guys wearing wrestling team sweatshirts to come to Bible study. They listen politely, but two of them are biting back laughs. I hope Eli doesn't notice.

Eli's been pretty depressed ever since his party. At first I thought it was a side effect of starting T, but Derek told me it's because his parents canceled their call at the last minute. Eli was all set to come out to them, but never got the chance. I wonder what that would feel like. Being ready to let something loose, only to find out you have to keep it inside, after all. It's hard to imagine what could be worse.

"Derek, can you talk to Gretchen online and see if she's all right?" I ask.

"Sure," Derek says. "Also, not sure if you want me to point this out, but you said *she* instead of *ze*, there."

"Don't bother," I say. "I've given up trying to subvert the English language. There's no point trying to make broad philosophical statements when I've completely lost my grip on all sense of self."

"That's profound, T," Nance says.

Eli takes a break from passing out flyers and sits next to us on the steps, sipping the coffee Nance brought him. Nance brushes Eli's scarf to the side and tips her head onto his shoulder. Eli's a lot shorter than Nance, so her head is tilted at a painful-looking angle. He laughs.

*He. Her.* It just doesn't sound right.

None of it sounds right. Not *they*. Not *ze*. And *definitely* not *she*. It's all so arbitrary.

But *not* using pronouns feels arbitrary, too. I'm never going to convince the entire *world* not to use them, and that's the only way I'd stop feeling weird about it.

"This might be the first time I've ever just sat here and watched people like this," Derek says.

"Yeah," Eli says. "It's strange. I feel like I'm supposed to be in this state of constant motion. Like, if I'm not actively writing a paper at this moment I'm a failure at life."

"Exactly," Nance says. "Not to mention, it always freaks me out whenever I'm forced to actually look at the Harvard population and see just how many white people there are at this school."

Really? There are a lot fewer white people at Harvard, percentagewise, than there were at my high school. I'm the only one of my roommates who's white. Ebony and Felicia are both black, and Joanna is Vietnamese. I felt a little weird at first, like I was boring next to them. Then I remembered that I bring in the LGBTQIA diversity angle, so I was still contributing.

It's true that the UBA seems to be mostly white, but my friends are kind of a mix. Derek's black and Eli's Korean, so Nance and I are the only white people in our immediate group. Hmm, maybe Nance was actually just complaining about *me*.

"So, Toni," Derek says, "what with you being in a state of existential despair and all, I guess this isn't a good time to mention that we're supposed to have the transition guide finished before finals."

I gulp down my latte.

"No," I say. "It's not. I don't have time for anything. I did no work at all over Thanksgiving because I was too freaked. I seriously cannot believe how far behind I am."

"That's how it goes your first semester until you get used to the pace," Eli says. "You always feel behind."

"Is that information supposed to be helpful?" I ask.

"Hey, T, watch out," Nance says. "I know your whole thing with the hottie sucks, but you don't need to get snippy."

"I know, I know," I say. "Sorry, Eli."

"No problem, man." Eli claps me on the shoulder. "You've got lady problems. I get it."

I'm lucky Eli's a forgiving guy, because Nance speaks the truth. At the rate I'm going I won't have any friends left by the end of the semester.

Eli gets up to pass out more flyers. One guy actually takes one. Based on the guy's blank look, map and flip-flops, though, I have a feeling the guy is a non-English-speaking tourist, not a potential Christian Leaguer.

"Why are we sitting out here anyway?" I ask. "It's cold. Let's go into the café."

"That's too far away," Derek says.

"From what?".

Nance sighs with exaggerated exasperation and leans in to talk quietly to me. "Look, when Eli was on flyering duty last year, some freshmen hassled him."

"What? Why would anyone want to hassle Eli?" Eli is even smaller than me. He usually wears a custom-made suit jacket with suspenders plus the occasional snappy bow tie. I can't imagine anyone less threatening.

"I don't know," Nance says. "People are assholes. Anyway, we try to watch out for him now when he does this stuff, but we can't let him know. He thinks we're just out here enjoying coffee on the Lamont steps on a frigid late November afternoon, and he's going to keep on thinking that. Right?"

"Right. Sorry." Now *I* feel like an asshole. How much else am I going to mess up today?

At least I'm not as bad as the freshmen last year who did whatever they'd done to Eli, just for looking different.

Nance is right. People really are assholes.

"By the way," Nance says, speaking louder now so the others can hear, "can I just say that I feel a lot worse for Gretchen than I do for you? I mean, I know you're upset, but trust me, it's a lot harder to get dumped than to be the one doing the dumping."

"I didn't dump Gretchen."

"Only because you let her talk you out of it," Derek says.

Even Derek won't take my side. I need to explain this better.

"I didn't let her talk me out of it." I catch my own pronoun this time. "Gretchen. I didn't let Gretchen talk me out of it. I mean, yeah, Gretchen made a good point, about me not having the right to decide what's best for both of us. It's like, how arrogant am I, really? Before I did it, I'd been going back and forth all night anyway about whether it was really what I wanted. It's all just so confusing. I don't know how anyone ever knows for sure what they want."

"I see what you're saying," Derek tells me. "The thing is, though, she's got a point, but that doesn't mean she has final say over what happens to you guys, either. You have to do what *you* have to do."

Chris said that the night of the football game. *You have to do what you think you have to do.*

"Everything hurts," I say.

Nance pats me on the shoulder a little too hard.

"It was your decision," Derek says. "You can still change your mind."

"Is that what you would do?" That question sounds pathetic even to my own ears.

"Well, I wouldn't have broken up with her in the first place," Derek says.

"What?" I almost choke on my latte. "Why didn't you tell me that before?"

"What difference does it make? You're the one living your life, not me."

"But—"

But I might not have done it if I'd known that.

Derek always seems to have it all figured out. Derek's life is the one I want.

"You two were way happier than almost any other couple I've known," Derek says. "She's on board with the trans stuff. Not to mention she's gorgeous and funny and smart. I'd have hung on to her as long as I could. But everybody's got their own thing going on, so if you need space, you need space."

"What if I don't need space?" I ask.

"You've only had space for two days," Nance says. "Try it out."

"Bible study! Tomorrow night!" Eli's yelling now. They can probably hear it on the second floor of Wigg. "Wherever you are in your spiritual journey, there's room in your heart for the Lord!"

"Did I tell you what she said?" I ask the others, charging ahead without regard for pronouns. I still don't like how they sound, but I don't have time to think through my linguistic choices anymore. "She asked me to give her *percentage odds* on whether I was going to transition. She said figuring out if I'm trans was my *'new thing.'* Then she said, 'I don't *care* what gender you are. It couldn't matter *less* to me.'"

Nance nods. "So?"

*"So?"* I say. "So she shouldn't have said all that stuff!"

"Why?" Derek asks. "It sounds to me like she's just trying to understand. I'm sure she only meant she'd be supportive no matter what."

I can't believe them. Aren't they listening to me? "Did you hear the part where she called it my 'new *thing*'?"

"Yeah, that part's lame," Nance says. "She shouldn't have said that. It's like she's implying that you're going through a little phase or something."

Derek shakes his head, but I nod vigorously.

"What really gets me," I add, "is that she's acting as if it isn't even important. When this is the most important thing in my life right now. She doesn't get that."

"T, look, I see what you're saying, but you're dramatically overanalyzing," Nance says.

"Yeah," Derek says. "You've got to cut the girl some slack."

"She doesn't get it," I say. "She's barely even thought about any of this stuff. She doesn't know anything about what it's like being trans."

"What, do you only want to date trans people from now on?" Nance asks. "Or would anyone with a PhD in queer studies work for you? God, do you ever even listen to yourself? You're as bad as—you know what, never mind. I'm

going inside to get a damn brownie. Derek, you talk some
sense into this kid."

We watch Nance storm up the steps to the library. Derek
lets out a low whistle after the door swings closed behind
Nance. "Nice going. I've never been that good at getting
rid of her."

"Should I go say something?" I clearly crossed a line.

"Nah, you'll just piss her off," Derek says. "Don't worry
too much, though. I don't think that was entirely about you."

Eli comes over and gazes up the steps after Nance, then
pats Derek on the shoulder. "Dude, I know she's your best
friend and all, but when Nance starts screeching like that, I
can't handle it. One of these days I'm going to lose an ear-
drum."

"Give her time," Derek says. "She'll calm down. Uh,
probably."

Wait. Best friend? *Nance* is Derek's best friend? What does
that make me?

The door behind us bursts open so loud we all turn to
look. Nance is back already. Eli makes a beeline for the bottom of the steps and starts yelling about Bible study again.

"Okay, look." Nance doesn't sit back down, so I stand up.
It's clear Nance has something to tell me. "I decided I should
explain this to you, because I think you aren't intentionally
being a jerk. I think you really just don't know any better."

I look to Derek for help, but Derek is still sitting down,
deliberately looking away from us.

"Uh, thanks?" I say to Nance.

"Shut up and listen," Nance says. "You know that thing
you do where you try to figure out everybody's story the

second you meet them? Whether they're trans or cis or queer or straight, so you can decide whether you like them?"

The hell? "I don't do that!"

"You totally do that. I saw you doing it the first day you met us. You couldn't tell about Eli, so you were checking him out hard-core for, like, ten minutes. It was embarrassing."

I turn around to make sure Eli didn't hear that, but Eli's yelling at another batch of tourists. "Nance, I've got no clue what you're talking about."

"Don't play dumb. You do it with everyone. You try to put people in boxes so you know where you stand next to them. That's why you latched on to Derek like a sycophant."

"I did not!"

"Please, guys, leave me out of this." Derek's still looking straight ahead.

"Look, it's all right," Nance says. "I'm not saying any of this is bad. Everybody does it when they're new. It's part of figuring out who you are. Like how you're trying out every label in the gender-identity handbook."

"There's a gender-identity handbook?" Derek asks. "Wish I'd known. Can you order that on Amazon?"

"Quiet, you." Nance nudges the back of Derek's coat with the heel of a cowboy boot. Derek laughs. "The point is, you can't decide your girlfriend sucks just because she doesn't know all the details of how this works. She doesn't know any trans people except you, and us. *Most people don't.* That doesn't mean she isn't worth your time."

"I never said Gretchen wasn't worth my time." I can't believe Nance is lecturing me about this. "Gretchen's amazing!"

"Yes, we are totally not tired at all of hearing how amazing Gretchen is," Nance says. Derek laughs again. "I'm just asking you to check your labeling. Okay? You can pick your own labels all you want, but don't try to put them on everybody else for them. You know how complicated this is for you? Well it's exactly that complicated for everybody else, so stop shortchanging us."

At the bottom of the steps, Eli's voice is getting shriller, the pamphlets waving in the air.

"It's six-thirty!" Eli yells. "Do you know where your soul is? How long will you wait to experience the abundant life God has planned for you?"

"It's six-thirty? Crap!" I almost spill what's left of my coffee.

"What now?" Derek asks.

"I'm late. I was supposed to meet my project group for Race and Politics at the Science Center at six-fifteen. *Crap.*"

"Damn," Derek says. "You better get yourself together, man."

Nance raises an eyebrow at me. "Think about it."

I nod even though I want desperately to roll my eyes. I wave goodbye to the guys and hurry away.

The Science Center is past the Yard, about as far from Lamont as you can get. I have to forge my way through banks of dirty gray snow, elbow past Japanese tourists trying to take my picture, and shout "Excuse me!" three times at a bunch of freshmen throwing a Frisbee in the twenty-mile-an-hour wind. Plus I have to pee thanks to that latte, but there's no gender-neutral bathroom out this way, and now that I'm binding every day I feel weird about using the women's bathroom. I have no choice but to hold it until I get back to my room.

What the hell was that about? What gives Nance the right to analyze me? Nance barely knows me.

I don't really do any of that. Put people in boxes. I'm *opposed* to putting people in boxes. It's why I hate labels and pronouns so much.

Okay, sure, I do spend a lot of time thinking about labels and pronouns. And yeah, I did try to figure out Eli's gender presentation right away on that first day—and Nance's and Derek's, too—but anyone would've done that. It doesn't mean I did something wrong. Eli didn't seem to notice. Besides, Eli likes me way more than Nance does.

I can't believe Nance called me a sycophant. I'm not going around kissing up to Derek. We're *friends*. Nance is probably just jealous. Anyway, why didn't Derek tell Nance to shut up?

Unless…surely Derek doesn't think Nance is *right*.

By the time I get to the lobby of the Science Center and see the rest of my project group already gathered around a table, I'm in a worse mood than ever. Then two of them glare at me and I forget about feeling grumpy. I'm late, and they're probably right to think I'm a tool. Even my friends seem to think that.

"Finally, you're here," one guy says. "Did you bring the Katrina outlines?"

"Yes," I say, taking the only empty seat left. "But, um. I didn't completely finish them."

The guy, who I'm pretty sure is named Mike, groans.

"I know, I know, I'm sorry," I say. "Look, I really tried. I did as much research as I could, I flew Delta just so I could get the fastest Wi-Fi, but—"

Then the girl next to me interrupts.

"I didn't finish, either," the girl says. "I got through the first two sets of readings, but then I had to go to my grand-mother's, and—"

"Me, neither," says a guy across the table. "I really thought I could do it, but there was too much going on."

"We were all busy over Thanksgiving!" Mike says. "We agreed we were going to divide up the research and the out-lines, and then today we'd put it together and come up with our presentation themes, and—"

The girl next to me bursts into tears. Mike looks like he's ready to murder someone. People start grumbling to each other, shooting angry looks around the table. Soon it will be chaos and we'll never get this project done.

"Look," I say, trying to sound diplomatic. "We can still get an A even if we're behind right now. I bet the other groups are behind, too."

"I saw Tina Nguyen's group already working on their PowerPoint last night in Lamont," Mike says.

"Shut up, Mike," I say. The girl next to me sniffs, then giggles. "How about we all go home, finish our outlines to-night and meet back here tomorrow at lunch?"

Everyone nods except Mike, but we're all ignoring Mike now anyway.

Now I'll have to spend all night reading about Hurricane Katrina. Because my life didn't have enough downers in it already.

But when I get back to my room, my plan is derailed before I'm even through the door. Joanna and Felicia are sitting side by side on the couch in the common room, and as soon as they see me they stop talking. I can tell right away they're up to something.

"What?" I ask when I get sick of the silence. I dump my coat and bag, and turn to face them, kicking the snow off my shoes.

"We need to have a meeting." Joanna's wearing a black cashmere sweater and pumps, and holding the same purse my mother bought in Tysons Corner for upwards of six hundred dollars. Felicia's in a white lace top that looks more like a sundress than something you wear in Boston in November. I wonder if they're going to a party after this or if they just got dressed up to ambush me.

Why do they always have to dress that way? Gretchen doesn't. Neither does Ebony. It's like Joanna and Felicia are trying to be as girlie as humanly possible. They might as well be wearing signs that say We're Cisgender, and Don't You Forget It.

Hang on. Is this what Nance meant? About me always trying to put people in boxes?

I remember taking one look at Joanna and Felicia on move-in day and deciding that they weren't worth my time. Maybe Nance had a point about me and the instant judging.

On this one, though, I'm pretty sure I was right.

"Oh?" I say. "A meeting? Should I go print off some agendas?"

"We should talk," Joanna says. "So that we're all up front and there's no awkwardness."

"Is there awkwardness now?" I ask.

"Yes," Felicia says. It's the first time Felicia has spoken since I got here.

They're both eyeing me closely. I'm wearing a button-down shirt from the men's section at J. Crew that makes my flat chest slightly more noticeable than usual. My roommates have never said anything about me binding before, though.

I cross my arms and sit in my desk chair. Joanna and Felicia have to turn around to look at me. If they want to talk, I'll talk, but I'll do it on my own terms.

"I'm not clear on what the problem is," I say.

"You look different than you did before," Felicia says. "You act different, too. It makes the rest of us feel awkward."

"By 'the rest of us,' I take it you're referring to yourself?"

"Joanna doesn't like it, either," Felicia says.

I look at Joanna, but Joanna doesn't say anything.

"By 'different,'" I say, "I take it you're referring to the increased masculinity of my gender expression?"

Felicia blinks. "Yeah, if that's what you want to call it. Plus, there's your friends—"

"My friends never come here," I say. "Even if they did, what do you care?"

"The thing is," Felicia says, "you can't get offended about this. I'm not prejudiced or anything. It's none of my business what you do. Plus, I have gay friends, and if you ask they'll tell you I'm totally cool with all of them."

I do not have the patience for this.

"*What* exactly is your problem?" I ask.

"There's a box on the housing form you're supposed to check," Joanna says. "For if you're, you know, like you are. So they can pick your roommates out specially."

That's true. The freshman housing application included a check box for *transgender*.

The problem was, I knew my mother would read my housing application.

"We barely see each other as it is," I say instead of explaining that to Joanna. "I don't see how my existence is making your life more difficult."

"I didn't sign on to live with a guy, and neither did Jo," Felicia says. "I don't like being uncomfortable in my own room."

"No one bothered to ask if *I* was comfortable," I say.

"Are you even still a girl?" Felicia asks. "Do you have—you know—the right parts?"

I sit back in my chair.

"Do I have *what*?" My anger spins into embarrassment, then shame. I want to go grab the quilt off my bed and hold it up in front of me.

No. I'm right, and Felicia's wrong. I cling to that knowledge.

"Why the *hell* do you think that's an acceptable question?" I ask. "Do I go around asking you about your—your *body* parts?"

"Look, my parents won't feel safe with me living here if you've got a you-know-what," Felicia says, chin lifted, hands folded demurely. As though this is a perfectly legitimate conversational topic and not a hugely invasive interrogation.

I knew people said stuff like this. I've seen it on TV.

I never thought anyone would say something like that to me, though. I didn't think I'd know anyone stupid enough.

Felicia's not stupid, though. That's just the thing. You don't get into Harvard by accident.

I stare at my roommates. Joanna fidgets, but Felicia just stares right back at me. It feels like I'm naked under a microscope. Like I might actually cry.

Compared with my roommates, Gretchen really does have a PhD in queer studies. Felicia doesn't care if I'm gender nonconforming with a leaning toward the male end of the spectrum or if I'm all-out transsexual. To Felicia, I'm just a freak.

"Okay, um." I don't know what to say. That doesn't happen often. I run a hand through my hair and blink a few times, fast, just in case I might actually be tearing up. "Look, all I'm trying to do is get through the school year. I know you guys don't like me, and, granted, the feeling is mutual, but we don't have to be friends. You leave me alone and I'll leave you alone, just like we've been doing since August. After this year we never have to see each other again."

"The end of this school year is six months away," Felicia said. "And you still haven't answered my question."

"Because *my* body is none of your damn business!" I'm nearly shouting. "Christ, Felicia, try to be a human being, here!"

"Look," Joanna says, "we're not saying you have to move out—"

"Uh, yeah, I should hope not, because I'm not going to." I'm sputtering now. I feel like I'm going to explode.

"Who's moving out?" Ebony asks from the door. "What's going on?"

Joanna shifts. Felicia doesn't move.

"Aren't you supposed to be at practice?" Joanna looks at the clock over the fireplace.

"What the hell is this?" Ebony asks. "Don't tell me you went ahead with that dumb-ass meeting."

"You knew about this?" I ask.

That hurts more than anything Felicia and Joanna said.

"They told me this morning they wanted to do it, and I told them they could suck it." Ebony dumps a bag of workout gear on the floor. I loosen my grip on the back of my chair a little. "What a load of horse hooey. Felicia, you're in college now, so put on your big-girl panties and learn to deal. Next year you can go off and live with all your little tight-ass prep school friends and not have to put up with anyone who isn't exactly like you ever again. Come on, T, let's go to Annenberg. I'm starving."

I'm supposed to be spending the next six hours looking up stuff about Hurricane Katrina, but all I want to do is get out of this room. I shove my laptop in my bag and put my coat back on.

"You know I went to a prep school, too, right?" I say to Ebony when we're free and clear of the psycho twins. My hands are shaking. I shove them in my pockets.

"Oh, right," Ebony says. "Uh, sorry. No offense."

"It's okay."

"Look, I'm sorry I didn't warn you about that. I didn't think they'd go through with it."

"It's okay." I'm grateful for what Ebony did back in the common room, but I don't want a bodyguard, either. "It's impossible to take them seriously."

"That's right. Don't let them get to you." Ebony punches me in the arm.

"Ow."

"Sorry. Hey, listen, I meant to ask you. I know most of your friends are upperclassmen. Do you have a blocking group yet? Some of us on the team are talking about going in together, but we want to get another person."

Blocking groups are how housing is assigned starting in sophomore year. You get together with a group of other freshmen and you put all your names in together. Then your whole group gets assigned to one of the upperclass houses and you stay there until graduation. That's how Derek, Nance and Eli wound up together.

"Are you sure?" Suddenly I'm self-conscious. "The others in your group are cool with it?"

*I didn't sign on to live with a guy.*

"Of course I'm sure," Ebony says. "Some of them are probably in Annenberg now. You can come meet them and see if you're up for it. I already told them about you."

"What did you say?"

"Oh, I warned them you're a big dorky Government concentrator, but they don't mind. They're weird that way."

For the first time since Thanksgiving, I smile. I can't believe everything that just happened.

Ebony starts typing a text to someone, and automatically I reach for my own phone. I'm about to tell Gretchen the whole story when I remember.

I slide my phone back into my pocket, my smile fading.

I bet it'll be a long time before I feel like smiling again.

# 14

DECEMBER
FRESHMAN YEAR OF COLLEGE
2 WEEKS APART

## GRETCHEN

The days move slowly now.

I'm waiting for Toni to call and take it all back. While I wait, I try to pass the time.

I leave a lot of voice mails. I start with Chris.

"Hey," I say to his recording. "I guess you heard what happened. Um. I know you're probably on Toni's side and that's fine, but I want to talk sometime just to, you know, talk. Can you call me if you have a second?"

Chris doesn't call back for four days. Finally I get a text.

Sorry, I can't get involved. Luv u tho.

I leave a message for Derek. "Hey, it's, um, Gretchen. You know, Gretchen Daniels, from NYU, T's—um anyway, I just wanted to call to… I don't know. I…never mind."

I hang up. Derek sends me a message the next day asking if I'm all right and if I want to talk. I don't reply.

I don't call Toni. I don't text Toni. I don't email Toni.

Those are the rules. They seemed so easy when we came up with them. Much better than the alternative.

All of this sucks. It sucks more every day.

At first I blocked Toni's updates from my feed. Then I wound up going to Toni's profile every half hour to see if there was anything new. Finally I gave up and undid the block.

For a week and a half, Toni's updates about having too much work and needing more coffee and hanging out with fabulous Harvard people have been my only proof that Toni still exists.

I've become obsessed with my phone charger. I bought an extra one and I carry it with me everywhere. I plug it in every time I see an outlet, even if it's just for a couple of seconds.

I never take the subway if I can help it since I don't get service down there. I sleep with my phone next to my pillow so it'll wake me up if a text buzzes.

Still there's no call. No apology. No *I made a huge mistake. Let's pretend it never happened.*

I thought this part would be over by now. I thought it would be over a long time ago.

I did everything wrong. I've been doing everything wrong ever since I decided to mail that stupid form back to NYU.

I thought I was being bold. Taking a risk. When really I was signing away everything that was good in my life.

"You're taking a break," Carroll tells me over breakfast Wednesday morning. "It's time to get over yourself, my dear. Some of us have real problems."

I hug Carroll. He's right.

He came out to his parents over the break. It didn't go well. He hasn't told me the details, but I got the gist of it from his expression when we first came back into town.

Hugging Carroll reminds me that it doesn't matter if all my old friends—who are really Toni's friends anyway—don't want to talk to me.

Carroll's *my* friend. I don't need anyone else. Having fun together is what Carroll and I do best.

Enough moping around. Enough desperate waiting. It's time for a distraction.

"You know what we should do?" I say. "We should go out to that club again. The one we went to at the beginning of the year. We'll get wasted and dance with the sketchiest people we can find."

"You're absolutely right," Carroll says, yawning. "Let's go *right now*."

It's nine in the morning. We're in the dining hall, having coffee and edamame. We have class in twenty minutes. I look up the club on my phone.

"They don't open until ten p.m.," I say. "Oh, and tonight they're closed for a private event. We could go tomorrow."

"I can't last until tomorrow. I'll have to find some sketchy guy to hook up with online tonight. It'll be your fault because you put the idea in my head."

"Oh, don't act like I'm your enabler."

"Blow me."

Samantha sits down next to Carroll with a tray full of eggs and bacon. The sight makes me want to gag.

"Gretchen? Are you okay?" Samantha asks. "You look green."

"She's fine," Carroll says. "Give her a carrot or something."

"She looks sick," Samantha says.

"I'm not sick." I sit up straight again. "Carroll and I are going dancing tomorrow. Want to come?"

Carroll glares at me, but I don't care. It's not as if Sam will come anyway.

"Don't you have your paper due for Met Studies?" Sam asks.

"I'll do it, don't worry," I say. "Come on, we'll get dressed up. You can wear your new silver fishnets."

"I'll pass," she says.

"What's the matter?" I ask. "Don't you like fun?"

"Not as much as you two do, apparently."

"You're right," Carroll says, rubbing his eyes. "Gretchen and me, we are the party-down duo."

Sam and I have our first class in the same building, so we walk over together after breakfast.

"Hey," I say as we pass under some scaffolding. "I just had the best idea. Can you dye my hair black? I'll pick up the stuff at Ricky's and we can do it tonight. It'll go great with this outfit I want to wear to the club tomorrow."

"Since when do you care about hair?" Samantha asks. "Or outfits?"

"Since…I don't know, whenever."

"Do you think you'll look good with black hair? You're so pale."

"Hey, you're into the vampire look, right?" I laugh. "Please just say you'll do it."

"I'll do it if you want me to, but you're making me nervous with this stuff. Look, I know it's got to be hard. You and your girlfriend were together for so long, and—"

"Are," I correct her. "We're still together. We're just on a break for a couple of weeks."

That's what I keep saying. To myself. To my friends. To anyone who will listen.

I don't even know what it means, though. What's a break, really? How is not talking to each other and agreeing to go out with other people any different from regular old breaking up?

Toni still hasn't called me to take it all back. I was so positive that would happen first thing. I guess I don't know Toni as well as I thought I did.

Maybe I should've just let Toni go through with it that night instead of making things worse. I acted like a little kid throwing a tantrum because I wasn't getting what I wanted.

Thinking about what might've happened if I hadn't fought back makes me nauseated. I stop walking and grab on to the scaffolding to steady myself.

"Right, I know." Samantha stops with me, not noticing that I'm about to fall over. "It's got to be hard when you've been with someone for so long and then all of a sudden—"

"Hey, now!" I laugh. I let go of the scaffolding and take a step. Then another. Then we're walking again.

I can do this. I'm not going to throw up at nine in the morning when I'm not even hungover.

"No analyzing!" I say. "This is only about hair, okay?"

"Okay, okay. It's just that you've been acting strange ever since Thanksgiving. Sorry, but I couldn't help noticing."

I forgive her, since it's fine as long as she doesn't talk about it. We make it the rest of the way to class without further gastrointestinal distress.

After class I go to Ricky's and pick up some Jet Black Hair Goo. That night Samantha applies said goo to my hair in our bathroom sink. It comes out looking gooier than I had in mind, but I look totally different than I did before, and that was the whole idea.

"You look like Morticia Addams," Carroll says the next night when he shows up at my room. Samantha took off a long time ago. She said she was meeting up with a guy and might not be back until late.

"I know, right?" I say to Carroll. "Don't you love it?"

"Not in the slightest, but I love *you*, dollface."

Carroll kisses me on the nose with a loud smack. I can tell from his breath that he's already well on his way to being drunk.

"Did you bring some to share?" I ask.

"Naturally!" He holds up a brown paper bag. "We have to drink out of the bottle unless you have cups."

I don't have cups, but that's fine with me. Carroll's bag holds a half-empty bottle of cheap white wine, a parting gift from last night's sketchy hookup.

"What do you do with these guys?" I ask him once we're nearly done with the bottle. I check my phone. It says it's at full power but I plug it in again just in case. "Are you being safe, at least?"

"That's the least of my concerns," Carroll says. "And for your information, Miss Nosy, we don't go all the way. Alas, I still have yet to lose the big *V*."

"Waiting for Mr. Right?"

"Just Mr. Not Repulsive."

We finish the bottle—Carroll makes me down the last few chugs on my own, since he had a head start—and leave for the club.

They don't card us this time, I guess because it's a weeknight, so we head for the bar as soon as we get inside. The music isn't as good as I remember, and the place isn't as crowded as it was last time, but after a couple of shots, I don't care. I put my phone's vibrator on High so I'll know if it rings even if I can't hear it.

We're dancing to a remix of some terrible boy band song when Carroll grabs my shoulder and shouts in my ear. "LOOK NINETY DEGREES CLOCKWISE!"

"What?" I'm very, very drunk. Just staying upright requires a lot of effort. I remember what ninety degrees means, but I'm stumped by the clockwise part.

Carroll turns me around. There's a Latina girl in a black dress looking at us.

"GO DANCE WITH HER!" Carroll shouts.

I shake my head. The movement almost makes me fall over. "I don't want to dance with her."

"YOU'RE ON A BREAK! YOU'RE SUPPOSED TO HOOK UP WITH OTHER PEOPLE! THAT GIRL'S HOT!"

"THEN *YOU* GO DANCE WITH HER!"

So he does.

He leaves me alone on the dance floor and goes up to this girl, who's with a group of friends, and says something in her ear. The girl laughs. Then Carroll puts his arm around her waist and they're grinding.

I can't believe it. I push toward them and yell "HEY! WHAT THE HELL IS THIS?" in Carroll's ear.

Carroll reaches out and pulls me in until the three of us are smashed up against each other. The girl smiles at me. I want to cry.

"THIS IS MY FRIEND!" Carroll yells to the girl. "SHE AND HER BAT-CRAZY TRANNY GIRLFRIEND ARE ON A BREAK AND SHE'S ALL DEPRESSED ABOUT IT! I NEED YOU TO HELP ME CHEER HER UP!"

"I'M NOT DEPRESSED!" I shout.

"THAT SUCKS!" the girl shouts to me. "YOUR GIRL-FRIEND, SHE'S CRAZY!"

"NO, SHE'S NOT! SHE'S GREAT!" Damn, I broke the pronoun rule. "I mean—"

"FORGET IT AND DANCE, GRETCH!" Carroll shouts.

So I do. I close my eyes and go with it.

And it's the best I've felt since break.

We're all three fantastic dancers, or else I'm still just re-ally, really drunk. We stay in a tight pack for song after song, grinding our hips and then our entire bodies.

At some point, there is also kissing involved.

That wasn't part of the plan, but there's nothing stopping

me now from doing whatever the hell I want. If what I want to do is to kiss some random girl, and to watch some random girl kiss Carroll (wait, is that really what's happening? That's what it looks like, but that can't be right, can it?), then that's what I'll do.

Maybe I'll do it even if it *isn't* what I want to do. Who the hell is going to stop me?

This goes on for a long time. So long I almost start to feel sober. That's bad, because when I'm sober I'll just freak out again.

The girl's friends tell her it's time to leave, and she's gone with a wave. I still don't know who she was. I don't want to know. Somewhere in the back of my brain a little voice buzzes, telling me it's the first time in two years I've kissed someone who wasn't Toni. That little voice makes me want to throw up again.

Carroll pulls me toward the exit, but I make him stop at the bar first so I can have another shot. Then I have one more. I buy shots for Carroll, too, so I don't have to do them alone.

Now that the little voice in my head is quiet again, the buzzing alcohol is much more pleasant. All I want is for it to get louder and louder until it erases everything else.

I give Carroll my wallet to deal with the cabdriver since he never has any money. I check my phone to see if any calls came in. Nothing.

The next thing I know we're stumbling into my room. Samantha is still out. Carroll and I collapse onto my bed, and I am suddenly aware that I cannot fall asleep. If I fall asleep

I will have awful, torturous dreams, the kind you can't really wake up from.

Carroll is lamenting the lack of cute boys at the club tonight. I make sympathetic noises and pet his hair. It has almost as much gel in it as Toni used to put in. That makes me sad.

I tell him I miss Toni. I tell him I think this isn't just a break. I think this is for real. I think I'm never, ever getting Toni back.

I'm crying. Carroll hugs me, and I cry all over his new shirt, which always makes him mad. He must be incredibly drunk, too, because he doesn't make me turn my face away.

While I cry, he talks. He tells me that his dad said he was ashamed of him. That he said he wished Carroll was just a criminal instead of being gay, because then when his dad's friends heard about it, they'd feel sorry for him. He said no one felt sorry for the guy whose son was a fag. Carroll says he wishes he hadn't told him, that it was a terrible mistake, that his dad made him feel weak and useless and like he was nothing, nothing, no one.

I'm still crying. Carroll is, too. I hug him harder. Then we're kissing.

The music from the club pounds in my ears. I close my eyes and remember the girl in the black dress. The girl I kissed who wasn't Toni.

The kisses are getting deeper now, and then our clothes are coming off.

I think, *Whatever.*

I think, *I can do whatever the hell I want.*

I think, *Toni's trying new things. I can, too.*

I think, *Toni doesn't care. Toni doesn't need me anymore. I've served my purpose and now Toni can get on with her real life with people who are better and smarter and cooler than me.*

I open my eyes, and this is actually happening. I am actually doing this. It isn't all in my head.

I think, *This is fine, this is fine, this is fine.*

I close my eyes again, and I keep them closed. All I want is to feel good, and I do, sort of.

It's like the hair, and the dancing, and the drinks, and the girl in the black dress. It's what I need.

I need to be feeling something.

I wake up alone with a massive headache. I stretch, groan, look up at the ceiling.

Then I notice the smell.

It takes me a second to place it. Then I lean over, and I see.

Someone has puked over the side of my bed. Multiple times.

It wasn't me. I never puke. And Samantha's bed is empty. It looks like she never came home last night.

I get out of bed groggily, stepping around the puke. The room is spinning. Normally I don't get hungover, but normally I don't drink my body weight in vodka shots.

I make it halfway to the bathroom before I remember what happened.

Oh. *Oh.*

I sit down on top of a stack of papers on the floor. Then I close my eyes and count to a hundred.

When I open my eyes again, the room is still spinning and the memory hasn't gone away.

I look at the clock. It's six-thirty in the morning. At eight I'm supposed to be in my Writing the Essay class for a discussion on the ethics of citing internet sources.

Where the hell is he?

I force down two Advil, find my room key in the trash can next to the condom wrapper and walk down the hall in my ratty sweats. I bang on his door for three minutes. Juan finally swings it open and blinks at me. "You know what time it is?"

"Sorry," I say. "Is he here?"

Juan trudges back to his bed, lies down and throws his arm over his face.

I look to the other side of the room. Carroll is sitting at his desk with his laptop open. I can't see what's on the screen.

"Hey," I say. "Can we talk?"

"About what?" He doesn't look up.

"I don't care what you talk about," Juan mumbles. "Just don't do it in here."

Carroll rolls his eyes and comes to stand in the doorway. He leaves the door open. "I'm kind of in the middle of something. What do you want?"

I don't know what I want. I didn't come here with an agenda. I just wanted to see my friend. To make sure everything's all right.

Because I have this feeling. Even before I got here, even before I saw the way he's looking at me, I had this feeling.

"Can we go somewhere and talk?" I ask.

"What for?"

"What do you mean, what for?"

"I don't want to talk to you," he says.

"I know last night was weird, but you don't have to—"

"We're not friends anymore," he says.

Why do other people get to make these unilateral decisions about my life?

"Why?" I ask, because I need to hear it.

"I don't like being used," he says.

"Used?"

"Please shut up, both of you," Juan groans. Carroll ignores him.

"I know you have issues, but that doesn't mean you get to do whatever the hell you want all the time," Carroll says. "Get a damn therapist."

"What? I can't believe this. You're one to talk!" Then I lower my voice. "I know you're upset about what happened with your dad, but—"

"That doesn't have anything to do with this. Yeah, I have issues, but my issues are *normal*. You and your screwed-up shemale ex are in a league all your own."

Okay. Wow. I take a step back.

"Look," I say. "Let's just pretend last night never happened. It was just some random thing anyway."

"Yeah, right. Like I could. From now on every time I see you, it's going to be all I think about." He shudders. I want to die, just a little bit. "I never would've done anything like that if you hadn't started it."

"What?" I sputter. "We *both* started it. At the same time. Remember?"

"What I remember is *you* dancing like a maniac in that club, hitting on everything that moved, like some bi nympho or something."

"Well, I remember it wasn't *me* who pulled a damn condom out of my pocket. I don't even *have* condoms in my pocket."

For a second we just stare at each other. My heart is pounding so hard. This feels so much like that night by the fountain.

"I've been trying so hard to do everything right here," Carroll says, quieter than before. "I was going to leave all the crap back at home. I'm supposed to finally be away from all that. This is supposed to be my chance to do what I always wanted. Then you butt in and mess it up. You're acting all psychotic just because some loser dumped you. What, you figured she's growing a dick so you might as well try one out for yourself? Well, do what you've gotta do, but leave me out of it."

I close my eyes.

I deserve this. I deserve to be completely and utterly alone.

"Hey, Carroll. Hey, Gretchen." A girl's voice. I open my eyes. It's Tracy, Carroll's friend from Tisch. "Why are you guys standing here with the door open? Gretchen, are you coming to breakfast with us?"

"No," Carroll says. "Gretchen's got someplace else to be."

I leave without speaking. I find my way back to my room, crawl into bed and pull the blankets over my head.

I never want to come back out.

# 15

## TONY

"I've decided I like the term *gender variant*," I say.

"Any particular reason?" Nance asks. "Or is this just your new flavor of the week?"

Nance and I have never talked about what she said to me on the library steps that day, but we have a cautious truce of sorts going on, so I'm pretty sure she's just teasing me now.

"It's more all-encompassing," I explain. "It's broad enough to get around those tiny boxes that labels put you in."

"Okay, sure," Nance says. "Except *gender variant* is a label, too."

I sigh. "It's an alternative label. It's flexible. It allows space to define yourself within it without being constricted by the limits of the terminology itself."

Half the people at the table roll their eyes. By now I've learned not to take that personally.

We're studying in a coffee shop a couple of blocks from the Yard. It's a Thursday night, and the place is so full we had to sit at the counter for an hour before Nance noticed this spot was free. Now six of us are gathered around a table meant for four in the corner next to the handicapped entrance. Eli's laptop doesn't fit on the table, so he's balancing it on his knees.

"Have you thought about just using *nonbinary*?" Inez asks. "My friend Luis uses it. They say it's really freeing to get away from people's expectations of defining yourself as just one of two genders."

"Yeah, sure," I say. "That's a contender, too. Lately I've been giving more thought to labels, and I think I might've been underestimating their importance. I've been focusing on pronouns, but I think the labels people choose for gender identity matter more. I can't believe I only just thought of this, but you know, at my high school, I founded our Gay-Straight Alliance. That's what it was called, the GSA. I left everyone else out of the name—bi people, asexual people, intersex people. I even left out trans people. I mean, come on, I put in *straight* people but I left out *myself*. If that doesn't show labels have power, I don't know what does."

"Every high school calls it the Gay-Straight Alliance," Derek says. "That's the default. You calling your group that is unlikely to have any deep hidden meaning."

"Besides, all those group names leave someone out," Andy

says. "The UBA does it, too. It's got gay and trans people in the name, and even intersex and asexual people, but it leaves out aromantic, questioning and pansexual."

"And *hijra* and two-spirit," Inez says.

"And genderqueer and genderfluid," Derek says. "And a ton of others."

"Acronyms always fail," Nance says. "Because it doesn't matter how many letters you include. It only matters who you actually *represent*. That's why GSAs don't bother me, because they use *gay* as an all-inclusive term. But the GSA at the school I volunteer at does way more work with different kinds of people than the UBA does here."

"For real," Derek says. "I can't remember the last time the UBA ever did anything remotely helpful for bi people."

"They barely do anything for trans people, for that matter," Andy says.

I expect one or both of the trans outreach cochairs currently sitting at the table to argue with him, but nobody does.

"Well, I'm just going to say, I agree with Tony," Inez says. "Labels matter more than they probably should. If someone told me they were *gender variant* all I'd know is that they defined themselves somewhere outside the traditional boundaries. I wouldn't have any set expectations for their gender identity or expression."

"See!" I say. "*She* gets it."

"By the way, way to work that terminology, my cis-het chica," Andy says, tipping his hat to Inez.

Derek grins at me. He and I haven't talked about what Nance said, either. If he thinks I'm a sycophant, he seems okay with that.

WHAT WE LEFT BEHIND

I decided to try using gendered pronouns full-time as an experiment. I thought it would be hard to get used to, like saying *they* and *hir* was. So far, it's actually been way easier. I don't have to stop halfway through a sentence and figure out what word to use. You forget how much simpler life is when you can just talk without thinking about it.

I'm leaving tomorrow for my interview at Oxford, and I've decided to spend the whole weekend presenting as male. I'm spelling my name with a *y* instead of an *i*. That's what I asked my friends to do anyway. I haven't changed my name online or anything extreme like that.

I have a ton of work to finish before the weekend, though. So does everyone. That's why we're here. We aren't actually supposed to be talking. Everyone's probably annoyed at me for getting us into yet another group debate on labels and queer theory. Pretty much everyone's smiling, though, so I don't think they mind too much.

"Hey, you guys," a familiar female voice says behind us.

I feel a hand on my shoulder and turn around. It's Lacey, my teaching fellow.

"Hey, Lacey," the others chorus. Nance snickers.

"Join us," Derek says to Lacey. "We can fit one more chair."

"I will, but only for a second," she says. "I'm supposed to meet someone."

Lacey pulls an empty chair into the narrow space between me and Eli. Eli moves over to make room until he's basically sitting in the aisle. Everyone smiles except Andy, who's typing furiously on his laptop, muttering, "Hang on, hang on."

"Hey, Tony," Lacey says. She's speaking so low the others

wouldn't be able to hear unless they try hard. Which they all seem to be doing. "I heard about you and your girlfriend. I wanted to say I'm sorry. I know it's got to be rough."

"Yeah," I say.

How could she possibly have heard that?

Well, in any case, I absolutely do not want to talk to her about Gretchen. I start to turn back to my computer.

"Your interview's this weekend, right?" Lacey asks.

I look back up. "Yeah. I'm flying out tomorrow."

"Tell Dr. Raavi I said hi, and that he's going to love you."

"Could you tell him that second part yourself?" I ask.

Lacey laughs. "I already did. This weekend is mostly a formality. By the way, when he offers you tea, make sure you say yes or he'll get offended. The man's obsessed with his tea."

"Will do," I say. "Thanks again for setting this up. I can't tell you how much I appreciate it."

"It's nothing," she says. "So many people used to help me out when I was an undergrad. It's nice to be able to do it now myself. Dr. Raavi asked me to pick the best kid in my section and send over the name. So really I'm doing *him* the favor."

I bristle at being called *kid*, but I don't let Lacey see. "Well, thanks, again."

"Sure. But there was something else I wanted to talk to you about."

"Shoot."

"I also wanted to say…" Lacey drops her voice lower. No one at the table is typing now, not even Andy. "I thought you might want someone to talk to. I know how hard it is after a breakup. If you wanted to maybe grab some coffee sometime. Next semester, I mean, when I'm not your TF anymore."

Nance kicks me under the table. Derek makes a high-pitched sound, then covers his grin with his hand.

Once upon a time I might've been ever-so-slightly flattered by this turn of events. Not after everything that's happened, though. So I give Lacey the most polite response I can think of. "Listen, thanks, but I can't really think about dating anyone right now. My girlfriend and I are still trying to work things out."

"Oh! Oh, I'm sorry." Lacey's eyes flick from side to side. She's finally noticed the others can hear us. "My mistake. Listen, please don't think this has anything to do with the internship, or that A on your midterm or anything else. It was a total coincidence."

"Okay," I say. I hadn't thought of that before, but now that she brought it up...

"Good luck with your girlfriend," Lacey says. "I'm sure she's great. And have a great trip. Oh, and hey, it's time for me to meet my friend. See you guys later."

With that Lacey's gone, her kitten heels clicking rapidly on the tile floor as she hurries away from us.

As soon as she's outside, everyone except Derek and me bursts out laughing.

"I can't believe Lacey's going after freshmen," Nance says. "She's always into the newest transboy on the block."

"No, she's not," Derek says. "Shut up, Nance. Look, T, Lacey's cool. I'm sure she was telling the truth about it not affecting your grades and stuff."

"Maybe I should ask her out," Eli says, scratching his chin. "If she's into trans guys."

"Yeah, you should go for it, man," Nance says. "She's hot. Plus, you don't have a whole big pile of baggage like T here, so that's got to work in your favor."

"Oh, come on," I say.

"Ignore Nance," Derek says. "T, you're just a freshman. Believe me, you have way less baggage than the rest of us. Nance has no right to talk given that she's currently sitting with her back to the door just in case one of the three girls she's got mad at her right now walks in. Anyway, Eli, you should totally ask Lacey out. See if she wants to go to the party the Harvard Texas Society is having on Sunday. You can learn how to line dance and you won't have to talk that much."

"I'll look stupid line dancing," Eli says.

"Everyone looks stupid line-dancing," Derek says. "That's the whole point. It's an equalizer."

Eli still looks dubious. Or maybe the testosterone is just making him moody.

"Tony, why did you say Gretchen's still your girlfriend?" Inez asks. "I thought you were breaking up. Do you really think Lacey's that hideous?"

Lacey is far from hideous, but I don't want to go out with her. I don't want to go out with anyone who isn't Gretchen.

I want *Gretchen* to go out with other people, though. To get on with her life without me getting in the way.

Except—well, if I'm being totally honest, I kind of don't want *that*, either.

I wonder what Gretchen's doing now. If she's okay. It's so strange not talking to her every day.

"No." I stand up. "I mean, I wasn't lying. I don't know. I have to figure it out. But first I have to pee."

There are a few chuckles as I make my way past the cash registers toward the bathrooms. I have a moment of panic when I realize I'm about to go into an off-campus bathroom—do I use the men's or the women's?—but then I see the unisex symbol on the door. I try to open it, but it's locked, so I'm standing in the hallway, waiting, when Eli sidles up next to me.

"Someone's in there," I say, nodding toward the door.

Eli nods. He doesn't look at the bathroom or at me. His eyes stay fixed on the floor.

"I talked to them," he says, so softly it takes me a second to understand.

"Really?" I ask. He looks up, his eyes meeting mine. "Your parents?"

Eli nods.

"How did it go?"

He shakes his head and drops his eyes. His lower lip quivers.

"Oh, God. I'm sorry, Eli."

He shakes his head again. "My mom didn't say very much, but my dad—well, it wasn't good. I don't know what's going to happen. I don't know if they'll let me stay here, and I don't know if they'll let me come home."

I let out a low string of swears. "Have you talked to the others? Derek?"

He shakes his head again. "I'm too embarrassed."

"Don't be. They'll totally understand. They'll want to help."

"There's no way to help." Eli meets my eyes again. "I don't want anyone else getting involved. I'm not ready to talk about it with my roommates. I don't want them looking at me with sad eyes every single minute of my life. Promise you won't tell anyone?"

I feel completely lost. If I can't ask Derek how to deal with this, what am I supposed to do? What am I supposed to *tell him*?

"I promise," I say, since it seems so important to him. "And, look, your parents were probably just shocked. I bet they'll calm down and start to see things rationally after some time has gone by."

Eli's staring at the floor again. "Maybe."

"Whatever they say, you're still awesome," I say. "*We* know how awesome you are. Who cares what they think?"

A tiny ghost of a smile flickers over Eli's face. It's gone again just as fast.

"And I wanted to tell you before, but I think it's incredibly brave of you to decide to start taking T, especially when you're living so far from home," I say. "I don't know if I'd ever have the nerve."

"You will," Eli says. Behind us, the bathroom door opens and a blond girl comes out. I force down the thought of Gretchen. "Trust me. You will."

I motion for Eli to go into the bathroom ahead of me. I didn't even need to go in the first place.

But I stay there in that hallway by myself, staring at the blank space on the wall that Eli just left.

My life feels like a giant stack of 5000-piece jigsaw puzzles. I can't imagine how I'll ever solve even one, let alone all the others.

Eli's only two years older than me. He's already started T *and* come out to his parents. I can't imagine doing even one of those. I can't even imagine how I'm going to make it through one weekend of being a guy.

But I'm desperate to find out.

I have to sit in the London airport for two hours, waiting for Audrey's plane to arrive. Something about a suspicious package at Dulles.

I try to study while I wait, but it takes most of my concentration just to stay away from the Starbucks cart. I desperately need caffeine. If I had coffee, though, I'd have to pee, and I can't go into a public bathroom at the airport. I doubt there are gender-neutral bathrooms here. If I went into the women's bathroom, I'd look out of place. If I went into the men's, I'd *feel* out of place.

Consciously making an effort to present as male is way more work than I expected. I had to examine all my clothes as I packed, making sure my pants (trousers, they call them trousers here) fastened the right way, that nothing had any tiny lace accents or flowers on the hems (I couldn't believe I hadn't already expurgated all that stuff from my wardrobe, but I'm bad at throwing things away), and that there are no pleats on the fronts of my button-down shirts. Most of my clothes already look generically male, or at least androgynous, but you have to be extra careful if you really want to pass. I also ordered a couple of new binders two weeks ago from a store Derek told me about. They cost ninety dollars each, but they were worth it, and hey, it was all going on Mom's credit card.

Audrey's flight is delayed yet again. I give in and buy a mocha. When I finally meet my sister outside customs, I'm already getting fidgety.

"That took forever!" Audrey says. "The customs dude was flirting with me, which I figure has to be a good thing, right? Except, oh, my God, he made me tell him my whole life story. Anyway, hi! It's good to see you. Or am I even supposed to see you? Are you like a stealth agent?"

Audrey knows I'm a guy for the weekend. I sent her a long message about it. She replied with one line: S'cool. Laters.

"You can see me," I tell her. "I'm not invisible."

"Okay, good. Where's the bathroom? I have to pee so bad!" Audrey looks around the customs area. "Hey, what about you? Are you going in the men's bathroom?"

"No," I whisper, because Audrey's practically shouting. "I'll wait and go at the hotel."

"What, you're just going to hold it?"

"Yup." I throw the rest of my mocha into the trash.

"Oh. Okay. So, by the way, am I supposed to act differently with you now? So people don't find out you're a girl?"

"Well, not announcing it in the middle of a crowd would be a good start."

"Oh. Sorry."

"It's okay."

Audrey's irritated me ever since my parents brought her home from the hospital. (I can't actually remember that, but it's a safe assumption.) I can never stay mad at her for more than a second or two, though. No one can. There's something about Audrey that makes you incapable of sustaining negative feelings toward her. She's a lot like Gretchen that way, actually.

We take out some cash at an ATM, then get tickets to take the train into the city. The train is delayed and I can't hold it any longer, so I bite the bullet and use the women's restroom, darting in and out, and keeping my head down, even though no one looks at me twice. Finally we get on the train, make it downtown and get a taxi to our hotel.

Neither of us has been to London since our parents brought us here on a sightseeing trip when I was twelve. All I can remember about that trip is wanting to kill myself from being in such close proximity to my mother for so long. Audrey remembers it well, though. She talked for years afterward about how much she loved the tour guides at the Tower of London. She's going on the tour again this weekend with one of her online friends while I'm at my interview.

Wow. *She, she, she, she, she.* Now that I'm used to it, it's funny how even *thinking* in gendered pronouns makes life easier.

Dad's travel agent made all the reservations for us, which means we're in a nice hotel. It's late when we get in, so we order room service. Audrey wants to go out, since our jet-lagged brains are wide-awake. I've got my interview in the morning, though, and I make her stay in with me. She pouts, but she gets over it fast. We watch old movies until we fall asleep.

The next morning, Audrey goes to meet her friend and

I take a train to Oxford. At first I can't find the building where I'm supposed to meet Dr. Raavi, and I have to ask for directions. The people I ask look at me funny. I can't tell if it's because of my accent, or because of how I look in my binder, or because they're just British and therefore rude. It makes me jittery and self-conscious, but I find the right building with ten minutes to spare.

There's a little old man sitting at the reception desk. A *porter*, that's what they call them.

"I have a meeting with Dr. Raavi," I tell him.

The porter looks bored. "Your name, please?"

I hesitate. Lacey's the one who sent my name over. What did she tell them? Will Dr. Raavi be expecting me to walk in looking like someone named Antonia?

The appointment book is open on the desk in front of us. I glance down at it and see an hour blocked off with the words *Mr. Tony Fasseau*.

Lacey told them I was a guy.

Why did she do that? I only told my inner circle I was presenting as male for this trip. Did Lacey just assume? Or did Derek tell her?

I wanted to be in control of how this information gets out. Maybe that isn't a choice I get to make, though.

"Fasseau," I tell the porter, who's looking at me with some suspicion. I can only pray he won't ask to see ID.

He doesn't. He simply points me to the third door on the left and goes back to slumping over his desk.

My interview is easy after that. I accept the offer of tea, as Lacey instructed, and I don't complain when Dr. Raavi pours milk into it, even though milk in tea grosses me out.

"Is Tony short for Anthony or Antonio?" Dr. Raavi asks me after I compliment his disgusting milky tea. I want to hug him for asking, but I suspect that wouldn't help my chances.

"Antonio." It's close enough. If he somehow found out the truth, I could always claim he'd misunderstood me.

"Italian?"

"No, my family's French, but my mother's into names from that era."

"What era would that be? Ancient Greece?"

"No, the, uh, 1920s."

"Ah," Dr. Raavi says. It's clear from the vacant look in his eyes he never cared in the first place. He was only making small talk. Oh.

He changes the subject to political philosophy, and I try to keep up. After forty-five minutes and two more cups of gross tea, Dr. Raavi stands up and shakes my hand.

"Lacey Colfer was one of the best assistants I ever had," he says. "Her recommendation is worth more than any curriculum vitae. If you'd like to come here and work for me this summer, young man, I'd be pleased to have you."

My head is spinning from the tea and the job offer and most of all from the "young man."

"Yes, sir, I'd like that," I say.

"It's settled, then. You'll start the first of June."

I get back to London, still on my high, hours before I'm supposed to meet up with Audrey and her friend. So I buy lunch at McDonald's in Covent Garden. Then I walk up and down the street, going into all the clothing stores. I go straight to the men's sections and browse through shirts and pants (trousers). No one looks at me oddly, although one store employee does try to up-sell me some Burberry stuff.

After an hour I get bold enough to take some shirts into the men's dressing room at Diesel. I'm hyperparanoid, looking around for the British equivalent of Marjorie, the angry-at-life sales associate at the Target back home who once kicked me out of the men's room there the one time I dared to sneak in, but no one stops me. No one even looks at me.

I buy two shirts and go down the street to Next. There I buy two more.

I'm addicted. I buy so many men's clothes I can't carry them all. I have to take a taxi back to the hotel and leave my bags with the front desk. Then I put on one of my new outfits with a brand-new binder underneath and go to a pub I spotted that morning.

I don't even have to pee, but I go into the men's bathroom anyway. I stand at the tap with a smile on my face, letting the water run over my hands until my fingertips turn pink. Then I go back into the pub, sit at the bar and order a Guinness, because that seems appropriately British.

I text Audrey and ask her to meet me there. I feel better than I have in a long time. Definitely the best I've felt since Thanksgiving. But I don't want to think about Thanksgiving. So I sip my Guinness and drum my fingers on the bar like I'm impatient. As though there is anywhere else I'd rather be than where I am right now.

I stand up to stretch. A guy bumps into me from behind, sloshing beer on my hand.

"Sorry, there, love," he says.

"Love." Great. "Love" is what people say to girls here.

Dr. Raavi can call me "young man" all he wants, but I still haven't fooled Random British Pub Dude.

I order a second pint.

Audrey shows up at the same time as my beer. With her is a girl carrying the same purse Joanna bought last month at Neiman Marcus for five hundred dollars. I wonder how much it costs in British pounds.

"This is Emily," Audrey says. "Emily, this is my brother, Tony."

I can't tell if Audrey's joking. Didn't she tell Emily the truth?

Audrey's grinning, but Emily looks completely serious. She holds out her hand.

"Pleased to meet you, Tony," she says, in an accent that people here would probably describe as "posh."

"Hi." I shake her hand.

"Emily goes to the London School of Economics," Audrey says.

I wince. It sounds very uncool to spell out the full name of LSE. I wouldn't have cared a year ago, but Harvard's made me a snob about these things.

"Emily's friends are having a Christmas party tonight," Audrey goes on, oblivious. "Can we please go?"

"Absolutely," I say.

The girls find us a table and we order food. I ask them about their day. Audrey's positive the cute French guy who was on the tour with them is in love with her, but Emily looks dubious.

"Are you in an accelerated course at university?" Emily asks me as our food arrives.

"Accelerated?" I ask. "No. I don't think there are any accelerated programs at Harvard. I'm just a regular freshman."

"Oh. Did you leave school early, then?"

"No." Where's she going with this?

"I think Emily's just saying you look kind of young," Audrey says.

Oh. Right. If I'm going to keep this up, I'm going to have to get used to people noticing that I'm short for a guy.

"Oh, I didn't mean to suggest—" Emily starts to say.

"It's okay." I interrupt her before she can make a bigger deal about it. "I know I'm short. I figure if I put enough product in my hair that adds a couple of inches, right?"

Emily doesn't smile.

To change the subject, I tell them about my interview. Emily finds it hilarious that Oxford is taking on an American freshman as a research assistant. I find Emily annoying.

When we finish eating, Audrey and I go back to our hotel so she can change before the party.

"Did you tell her about me?" I ask Audrey once we're alone.

"What? You mean about your secret identity?" Audrey laughs. "I told her I was in town with my brother, and that was it. That's what you wanted me to say, right?"

I give Audrey a hug. She laughs and hugs me back.

"I like the new you," she says. "The one who gives hugs and talks like a normal person instead of saying everyone's names over and over."

Audrey doesn't know what's going on with Gretchen and me. If she did, she'd probably like the new me a lot less.

She worships Gretchen. I guess it runs in the family.

We take our time getting ready. I decide to change again, so I iron another of the new shirts I bought today. It's a little too big, so I roll up the sleeves. Audrey's mascara was confiscated by airport security, so she spends twenty minutes with the hotel concierge trying to determine the British equivalent of her brand. She goes to two different drugstores until she finds it. I'd have accused her of acting especially girlie to cancel me out, except Audrey's always been this way. Besides, if security had confiscated my binders, I'd have threatened another lawsuit.

We meet Emily at the Angel tube station and walk to her friends' house. It's a smaller party than I expected—only about fifteen people, hanging out on the first floor of a group house, wearing droopy reindeer antlers and paper hats. Emily introduces Audrey and me as "my new American brother and sister friends," and no one seems to think anything of it.

Everyone's pretty mellow and relatively friendly considering they're British. They're especially interested when they find out I go to Harvard. They all want to ask me if I know their friends at Harvard, and talk to me about their plans to go to Harvard for business school, and ask if I saw Reese Witherspoon on campus when they filmed *Legally Blonde*?

That's the first icebreaker of the night. The second comes when Audrey starts making out with a British guy named Harvey.

I probably should be keeping a better eye on my sister. Make sure she isn't invalidating any treaties or picking up any STDs.

I can't focus on Audrey, though. Because for the first time

in my life, I'm surrounded by people I've never met before, and they all think my name is Tony.

The guys ask me about football, by which I'm pretty sure they mean soccer. Sadly, I know nothing about sports. The guys mostly ignore me after they figure that out.

The girls, though. The girls smile at me the same way they smile at the guys. They bat their eyelashes the way my high school friends used to do at the guys on the lacrosse team. Two of the girls even invite me to visit them in London while I'm here for the summer. It's like nothing I've ever experienced.

These people think I'm a guy. A *real* guy.

When the girls start yawning, I pry Audrey away from her new friend Harvey. We have to be at the airport early tomorrow, and it's hard enough getting Audrey out of bed in her own time zone.

In the taxi back to the hotel, Audrey slumps onto my shoulder and closes her eyes. I wonder if she's drunk. I didn't see her drink after we left the pub, though. She wakes up when we get to the hotel, but she looks gloomy.

"Are you feeling guilty about Kevin?" I ask as I sort through the rest of my bags in our room.

"Kevin won't care." Audrey flops onto the couch and turns on the TV. "We have an open relationship."

"Oh, right. How's that working out?"

"It's okay. I think it was the right call. No offense, but I think it's too limiting to be a hundred percent monogamous all the time. I mean, what's the point, right? Look at Mom and Dad. They're in the most stable monogamous re-

lationship ever, but it only works because they never speak
to each other."

Wow. I try to meet Audrey's eyes, but she's staring at some
terrible Adam Sandler movie. "Is everything going okay at
home?" I ask her.

She shrugs, her gaze still fixed on the screen. "Same as
ever, I guess. Just quieter with you gone."

I swallow. I don't know what to say. So I sit on the couch
and watch the movie with her in silence. Before long, though,
the jet lag catches up with me, and I fall asleep.

I don't know if Audrey sleeps, too, but I know she's awake
at 3:18 a.m. That's what time the clock says when I wake up
to the sound of my sister crying on the couch next to me.

My glasses are bent against the couch cushion. I straighten
them out, put them on and blink hard until I wake up all
the way.

"Hey," I say. "What's wrong?"

Audrey shakes her head at me. Then she gets up, goes into
the bathroom and closes the door behind her. I can still hear
her crying as the knob clicks into place.

"Hey." I sit down on the floor on the other side of the
closed door. "You don't have to hide in there. Just tell me.
What's going on?"

"Nothing." Her voice is so clear through the thin, cheap
hotel wood, we might as well be in the same room.

"Please?" I say.

"You'll get mad."

"Why? Did you break something of mine?"

She laughs, then sniffles loudly. "No."

"Then I won't get mad."

"It's dumb."

"Just tell me."

I hear her sliding down to sit on the floor. We're right next to each other now, with only the door between us.

"It's harder than I thought it would be," she says.

"What is?"

"This thing with you. The new you."

Oh. I should've known.

"I thought you liked the new me," I say.

"I do." She sniffs again. "It's still hard. It's fun having a brother, I guess, but I miss my sister, you know?"

Oh, God.

"Say something," Audrey says. "Or I'll think you're mad."

"I'm not mad," I say slowly.

Am I really Audrey's *brother*?

Today was amazing. Having people call me *he*. Shopping in the guys' sections without anyone looking at me funny. Having straight girls flirt with me.

Maybe I'm not gender variant. Maybe I'm, well. A guy.

It's just—does it have to be an either/or thing? Having people look at me for a weekend and think I'm a guy is awesome, but these are people I'm never going to see again. Do I really want my own sister to think of me as a guy all the time? For the rest of our *lives*?

Am I still going to want to be a guy when I'm thirty? When I'm *ninety*? How the hell am I supposed to know?

Derek knows. He's getting surgery this summer. He's positive he's never going to look back.

God, I envy that.

I can try out pronouns and labels as much as I want, but it's not going to make me any more certain.

What if I never figure this out? What if I spend the rest of my life going back and forth? Is there a test I can take that will just tell me the answer? Like the personality test that told me I'm introverted and judgmental? (Not that I needed to take a test for that one.)

I guess it all goes back to what Nance said. Trying out labels, putting everyone I meet into little boxes—the way I did with all my Harvard friends, the way I did with all the British people I met today—it's all a part of figuring myself out. Trying new ways to define myself. As a Harvard student. As gender variant, or gender nonconforming, or whatever else feels right on any given day. As part of my awesome group of friends.

For two years, I defined myself through my relationship with Gretchen. Now that that's on hold, I'm adrift, wandering freely. Too freely.

It feels more important than ever that I come up with the right label to plaster on myself. A way for people to see me. People who aren't Gretchen.

Because when Gretchen looks at me, she just sees me. It's like she said—she really doesn't care about all my gender stuff. She likes me for me. Loves me, I guess.

God, that's true. She really loves me.

God, I'm an asshole.

I climb to my feet and rest my palm on the door handle. "Can I come in?"

Audrey sniffs, and for a second I think she's going to say no. Then I hear her sliding back from the door. "I guess."

I push open the door. The bathroom is tiny compared to the rest of the suite—just a toilet, a sink, a shower and a few square feet of cold floor tile. When I sit down next to Audrey, my not-very-long legs fold against the door awkwardly, my feet planted flat on the wall next to hers. She's turned away, facing the shower curtain. I can't see if she's still crying.

*I miss my sister, you know?*

I want to be the sister Audrey wants me to be. No, not the sister. The sibling.

I need to stop defining myself according to other people's expectations. I need to figure out who I am. Not just whether I'm a guy, either.

What do I actually want for myself? Outside what my friends see, or my girlfriend sees, or my family sees?

Maybe things will never be the way they were before between me and Audrey. Because *I'm* not the same.

Maybe that's okay.

"Can I, uh, hug you?" I'm still not really sure how to initiate hugs.

"I thought you don't do hugs," Audrey says with a sniff.

"I'm trying to start."

Audrey turns, and I get a glimpse of her red eyes before she tips her head onto my shoulder. Wow, hugging feels nice, especially when you're upset. I don't know why I stayed away from it for so long.

"Anyway, I'll deal." Audrey pulls back and sniffs again. "Seriously, I'm happy for you. You can be a boy or a girl or a dolphin or anything you want and I'll be happy for you."

I smile. "A dolphin?"

"I saw it on *South Park*."

"Thanks for being happy for me. I'm sorry I made you cry."

"It's not like you did it on purpose." Her voice sounds more normal now. "I know it's really uncool of me to be upset about this. Sorry."

"Uncool?" I laugh again. "Where'd you get that from?"

"I just mean, if I were more hip and modern and in college and stuff, I'd just go with it and not start crying randomly or whatever. The way Gretchen is."

"Gretchen?" I swallow.

"Yeah. I mean, when you told her she was just, like, 'That's cool,' right?"

"Oh. Yeah, I guess." Gretchen never cried or anything. At least, as far as I know.

"So listen, don't be offended, but I just want to sit by myself for a while." Audrey taps my bare foot with her own. "I just need to, you know, think."

"All right." I stand up again. "How about you take the bed and I'll sleep on the sofa in the other room?"

"Okay." I hold out my hand to pull Audrey up. She climbs to her feet, smiling. "Wow, you seem stronger than before. Is this being-a-guy thing making you more buff?"

I laugh. "No. You have to take hormones for that. Or just go to the gym and not eat cheeseburgers for every meal. None of which I've been doing this semester."

"Better watch out or you'll gain the freshman fifteen." Audrey chuckles and goes into the bedroom, closing the door behind her.

"Don't forget," I say through the door, "our flight's at—"

"Yeah, yeah, yeah, I know. Hey, now that you're getting a sex change, could you also be less anal?"

"No chance. Night."

"Night."

I change and climb onto the couch, pulling a pillow behind my head. I'm exhausted, but I can't stop thinking.

Do I really want to leave behind *everything* from my life before?

This weekend was fun. It's such a rush, having everyone think I'm a guy.

Roller coasters are a rush, too, but I don't want to ride one every day until I die.

This is a big deal. Everyone keeps telling me it's the biggest decision I'll ever make.

If I really do it, I'll have to tell my mother someday.

No way. I'm not ready for that. I won't ever be ready for that.

Then what the hell am I doing? What was this weekend even about? Why am I torturing my little sister? Why did I lie to my new boss about my name? Why do I keep switching my labels around? Why didn't I correct Chris when he assumed I was transitioning?

When will I figure this all out? Why does it have to take so long? Why can't it be over and done with?

I need to talk this through with someone.

I pick up my phone. It's 7:00 p.m. in New York. I could call. I could—

*No.* I stop myself before I push the button.

I can't. Gretchen hates me after what I did at Thanksgiving. The last thing she wants is for me to call her out of the blue to whine about my new *thing*. I've got to figure this out on my own.

I can do this. I want to—

Oh, who am I kidding? I don't know what the hell I want.

I fall asleep just as my alarm goes off.

# 16

DECEMBER
FRESHMAN YEAR OF COLLEGE
2 WEEKS APART

## GRETCHEN

I check my phone again.

It's on. It's charged.

No one's called me. No one's texted.

This sucks. Everything sucks.

I go back to sleep.

I can't sleep.

I've been lying in bed, thinking, for hours. There's nothing I hate more than thinking about myself.

Well, no. Getting dumped and left alone to deal with the dumb stuff I do is a lot worse, actually.

Dumb stuff, for example, that may or may not have messed up the one good thing I had here. And just generally demonstrated my vast stupidity.

With every minute I lie in bed, it seems more and more likely that it's all over now. That everything that once worked in my life has been erased from it. That I have nothing left. At all.

See? Thinking about myself leads to bad, bad places.

Someone's knocking on the door. Crap.

I haven't seen anyone since I left Carroll's room hours and hours ago. I don't know where Samantha's been since yesterday, but it's just as well. I can't face the sight of another human being.

My phone buzzes with a text.

I jump up so fast I knock my phone to the floor. I scramble to pick it up, but my hands are asleep from where I was lying on them and my fingers are trembling. I try as hard as I can to not think about what I want the text to say.

I want the text to say:

Don't worry, Gretchen, it was all a dream. Toni will call you in a few minutes to whine about homework and find out what you want for Christmas. Carroll will stop by later and ask you to come out for pizza. Your life will go back to being exactly the way it's supposed to be.

I pick up the phone and click Read Message.

The text says:

r u in your room? We're out here knocking.

It's from Briana. I flop back into bed.

"Come in," I say, not caring if I'm loud enough for them to hear.

I must be, though, because the door opens. Briana comes in with Rosa and Heidi behind her. I guess their drama from that night at the bar, whatever it was, is over.

"Jesus," Rosa says. "What did you do to your hair?"

"It's a metaphor for my life in general," I say.

"Are you sick?" Briana asks. "It, um, kind of smells in here."

"Yeah, I'm sick," I say.

The girls hover by the foot of my bed.

"Sorry," Briana says. "We were just going down to get some food and wanted to see if you ate yet."

"No," I say.

"No, you didn't eat?" Rosa asks. "Or no, you don't want to come eat with us?"

"No, I don't want to ever get out of bed again." I close my eyes.

I turn off my phone and throw it across the room. It lands on a pile of my dirty clothes. It can stay there forever as far as I'm concerned.

"Uh," Briana says. "Okay. We'll see you around, Gretch. Hope you feel better."

They're gone.

I roll back over to face the wall.


There's another noise at the door. I look at the clock. It's 8:16. I don't know if it's a.m. or p.m.

Someone's shaking my shoulder. I swat their hand away.

"Leave me alone," I say.

"Just tell me if you're alive, at least," Samantha says.

I roll over and squint at her. "You're back."

"Yeah. What on earth did you do while I was gone? It smells awful in here. Wait—did you *puke*?"

I forgot about that.

"No," I say.

"You're lucky I have two little brothers." Samantha's got a squirt bottle and some paper towels now and is on her hands and knees next to the bed. "I've cleaned up more puke in my lifetime than anyone should ever have to."

"Thanks," I mumble and turn back toward the wall.

"Are you sick?" she asks.

"Kind of."

"Are you hungry? I have bananas and trail mix."

I am kind of hungry, now that the puke smell is mostly gone. "Okay."

Samantha gives me a bag of food and starts cleaning up my side of the room. She puts the dirty clothes in a pile and plugs my phone into the wall charger, but to my relief she doesn't turn the phone back on.

While she works, she tells me it's Friday night. That means it's only been fourteen hours since I talked to Carroll in the hall. It feels like at least a year has passed.

Samantha tells me where she's been. Apparently some guy, Draven, invited her to a concert in New Haven, but then he turned out to be a prick. Only when she's finished telling me all about how Draven used a fake ID to rent a car and then lied about it to the cop who pulled them over does she ask me.

"So, what happened? Is this about Toni again?"

I start to tell her about last night. Instead I say, "Yeah. It's about Toni."

Then I'm crying. Because it is about Toni. It's always been about Toni.

I haven't cried all day. It feels sort of good, the coolness on my cheeks.

Samantha gives me a tissue from the box on her desk. Then she goes over to the minifridge and hands me a bottle of orange juice.

"What's this for?" I ask, wiping snot off my face.

"Orange juice always makes me feel better," she says.

I take a gulp. Then I tell her about last night. She watches me talk, nodding the whole time.

"I knew it would happen sooner or later," she says when I'm done.

"You did?" I hiccup.

"Even Draven predicted it. I was telling him about you and Carroll, and he said if you guys hadn't already slept together, you would before finals were over."

"Go, Draven." I take another sip. The orange juice is making me feel a tiny bit better.

"I'm sorry Carroll was such a jerk to you," she says. "To be honest, I've always thought he was a jerk."

At first I think she's just trying to comfort me. All I can remember is months of Sam giggling at Carroll's jokes in the dining hall.

"You have?" I ask.

"Oh, yeah. He's incredibly rude and selfish to everyone except you, since you were the cute girl he got to carry around like a nice handbag. Now I guess he's too embarrassed to be around you, so he's moving on to a new accessory."

I can't process all this at once.

Samantha's wrong. I know Carroll a lot better than she does. He isn't like that.

And I get why he's upset. It's like he said—he had this ideal life he was trying to live here, where he got to have all the gay fun he'd dreamed of back in rural New Jersey. Back home he used to get beaten up just for existing. Now he's finally somewhere he doesn't have to pretend to be someone he's not.

Until I came along and messed it all up.

"It's not like that," I tell Samantha. "I think he's just ashamed. He hates himself for letting it happen."

"He's not some helpless victim here. These things take two, last I checked."

That makes me smile, just a little. I stop before Samantha notices.

"If you hate him so much, why have you been hanging out with us all semester?" I ask her.

"Because I wanted to hang out with *you*, and you never go anywhere without him. I know how that is, when your entire world is centered around one person. You think they can do no wrong. It was that way with me and my boyfriend all last year before that bitch Stephanie started prowling around." She sighs. "Sorry. I'm still bitter."

"It wasn't like that with Carroll and me," I say. "We're just friends."

"Seriously," Samantha says. "Was it really that different? You spent all your time together. I mean, when's the last time you had a *normal* friend? Do you even remember how it works?"

Hmm. Carroll's the only real friend I've had in years who wasn't Toni's friend first. Except Briana and her crew.

And Samantha. I've never really thought of Sam as a friend, though. I don't know why.

Isn't that why I came here, though? To do my own thing, without Toni? Make friends who were all mine?

Instead I've spent all year obsessing about Toni, and... I'm pretty sure Toni hasn't been obsessing about me back. At least, not as much as Toni's been obsessing about Toni.

And I get it. For real. The gender stuff is a big deal. I promised I'd wait while Toni figured it all out, but in the meantime I forgot I was supposed to be figuring myself out, too. Maybe *that's* what college is for.

"Anyway, if Carroll was really your friend, he wouldn't have said that to you this morning," Sam says. "No matter how awkward it was."

"Maybe he was having a psychotic break," I say. "It would be freaky, being gay and then randomly hooking up with a girl."

"Well, you did it. Was it that freaky for you?"

I think about it. "Nah. I mean, it was weird, and I don't think I want to do it again, but I'm not, you know, suicidal over it. Sex isn't that big a deal to me."

"So you didn't suddenly turn straight last night? Or bi, or whatever?"

I almost smile. I forget how Sam is about this stuff. She's like the exchange student my brother hosted in middle school who thought it was absolutely fascinating that our family went to church once a week. He kept asking questions about which saints were our favorites and whether the Virgin Mary put candy in our shoes at Christmas.

"No," I say. "Why would I do that?"

"I don't know. Maybe if you liked it?"

I smile for real at that. "Well, it was okay. But not, you know. Stellar."

"Not as good as with girls?"

"Not even close."

"Well, that's not his fault. He didn't know what he was doing."

"Is there that much to it? It seemed straightforward enough."

Samantha laughs.

I don't think she gets what I'm trying to say, though. The thing is, your sexual orientation is only this tiny part of your actual sex life. I mostly like girls, but I've been attracted to guys before, and it really isn't a big deal.

But there is one thing I figured out last night. Sex needs to be tied to something else. Something bigger. You can't just stick it in the middle of any relationship and expect it to work. At least, not if you're me.

"Anyway," Sam says, still laughing, "Carroll's the one who has issues. Don't let him get to you."

I finish the juice. "I have issues, too."

"I know. Speaking of which, how come when I first asked you what was wrong, you said it was about Toni?"

The tears are back.

"Sorry," she says. "Want more juice?"

"No, it's okay."

I said it was about Toni. Everything's about Toni. My whole life is about Toni. It has been ever since we met.

Maybe that's not how it's supposed to work. I don't know. I've always loved it, though. When everything is about Toni, I know what I'm supposed to do. Who I'm supposed to be. I don't have to worry about being happy because I *am* happy. Being one half of Toni-and-Gretchen felt a million times better than just being Gretchen ever did.

Except now I can barely even remember how just being Gretchen really felt.

"Do you think Toni will be mad when she finds out what happened?" Sam asks. "Will she throw a big hissy fit?"

"Toni doesn't throw hissy fits," I say, even though that's not entirely true. "Besides, we're on a break. It's okay for me to do whatever."

"Even with guys?"

"I don't see what difference that would make."

"Uh. Okay, if you say so."

"Seriously. Trust me, *that's* not the problem. Toni isn't petty like that. It's just—" I rub my eyes. "Well. To be totally honest…all along, I kept thinking Toni was going to call me and take it back. You know, what happened at Thanksgiving. Every day I thought it would happen, but it hasn't. Yet. So now I kind of think maybe it's not going to, and I don't know what to do next."

Sam sits down on the foot of the bed. "I'm sorry."

"Plus, I used to—" I can't say it. "Ugh, it sounds so stupid."

"I spent the past two days listening to Draven argue with himself about which girl in *Black Swan* was the hottest. You'll sound fine."

That makes me laugh. I hiccup again and force the words out. "I— Wow. I really, honestly thought Toni and I would get married someday. You know?"

Samantha smiles. "That doesn't sound stupid at all. I thought I was going to stay with my ex-boyfriend forever, too."

I fix my eyes on the ceiling. "How did you deal when you broke up?"

"Oh, I'm still pissed. Just not as much as I used to be." She shrugs. "I was really, really mad for a long time. Then I came to New York, and I realized there are a lot of guys out there. Sure, a lot of them are jerks, but some are okay. I'm glad I don't have to stay with some guy I knew in high school for the rest of my life. I can get to know other people without feeling guilty about it."

I can see what she's saying. It almost makes sense.

It's just that I don't *want* to get to know other people. I want to be with Toni.

Being with Toni was the best thing about my life. I don't want that to change.

Maybe it's supposed to, though.

Maybe I should have listened to what Toni said that night by the fountain. Maybe if I hadn't been so angry it would've made more sense.

"I don't know what to do now," I say.

"You don't have to do anything," Sam says. "Except your work. Let me guess. You haven't studied since Thanksgiving."

"Um. I did some reading the other day."

"Right. So, my advice is to get out of bed, wash your sheets, do your homework and pray you don't fail the whole semester." Samantha stands and throws away the orange juice bottle. "Oh, and I would also advise against having sex with any more gay guys. At least until after finals."

I smile at her. "You're very wise."

She pulls a Pixy Stix out of her purse and tears off the end. "At least one good thing came out of all this. With Carroll gone, we won't have to watch *The Flighted Ones* ever again. God, I hate that show."

"Me, too. Hey, can I have one of those?"

She gives me a Pixy Stix and we toast. The fake sugar burns my throat, then hits my brain with a pleasant hum. I have a new friend.

Maybe everything really will be okay now.

Maybe I can actually handle this.

17

## TONY

"No, no, *no!*" I shout.

The bright, empty white screen of my laptop shines back at me, the tiny, unintelligible error message that had popped up fading into nothing. Mocking me.

The computer doesn't care how much I curse. It doesn't care that I have a twenty-page paper due in ten minutes. It doesn't care that my world is in a constant state of upheaval, with only one constant—the never-ending stream of work I'm still behind on.

"Chill, T," says Ebony's boyfriend, Paul, as he pokes at the keyboard. "Going all loco won't help."

"Well, I don't see how it can possibly hurt!" I yell.

"It hurts me," Ebony says. She's sitting on the common room couch, typing on her own laptop. "There's nothing you can do. Sit down and let Paul do his thing."

I sit, but it takes all my energy to make my voice sound normal as I say, "Paul, please, please, please, please, if there is a God in heaven, please, tell me you can fix my computer. I will totally owe you forever. I'll buy you, like, a car or something."

"Whether there's a God in heaven is open to debate," Paul says. "You shouldn't say that kind of thing to a Philosophy concentrator. If you'll leave me alone for five seconds, though, then yeah, I can probably fix your computer. I'll take that car, too."

I grab Paul's hand and kiss it. "You're literally saving my life."

"No, I'm *literally* not. You shouldn't say things like that, either. It's just bad grammar."

"You also shouldn't go around kissing other people's boyfriends," Ebony says. "You're single now, remember?"

As if I could forget.

Paul pushes some buttons on my keyboard, restarts my laptop and hands it back to me. It's working! My paper's still here! I want to hug him, but I restrain myself.

I save my file, back it up in a hundred different ways and send it to my Expository Writing instructor.

Then I look at my watch. I'm already late. Again.

"See you guys later!" I say. "Thanks again Paul! Remind me to buy you a present!"

"I'll be waiting on that car!" Paul says.

"I was thinking maybe some gummy bears," I say as I grab my coat.

"Don't forget, the crazy girls will be here tonight!" Ebony calls after me as I run out the door. "Wear a helmet when you get back!"

I couldn't care less about Joanna and Felicia now. We've been avoiding each other successfully ever since their little "meeting," but I have bigger problems than the two of them.

The guys and I are going out to lunch at a restaurant Brad recommended. Nance is treating us all because she got a summer internship at an investment bank in New York and she wants to lord it over us.

It's Monday, the first day of Reading Period, the week before exams. Classes are over, so you're free to obsess over how much work you have to do without all those lectures getting in the way.

Usually no one leaves Cambridge during Reading Period. There's too much anxiety to be had. My friends are going out regardless, though, because my friends are insane, and because the lobster at this place is supposed to be incredible.

I'm the last one to get to the train, like always, and the guys give me crap about it, like always, and then we go downtown.

I love my friends. I really, really do.

We have a big table at the restaurant since there are six of us—me, Derek, Eli, Nance, Inez and Andy. Nance instructs us all to order lobster or steak, the most expensive items on the menu, which we do. Except for Eli and Inez, who are vegetarians, but they promise to eat extra dessert to make up for it. We talk and laugh and forget, for a couple of hours, how much work is waiting for us at home.

Even Eli is smiling, which is awesome to see. He told me last night that he talked to his mom again. Just her this time, without his dad. She told Eli that it was going to be hard for them for a while, but she thought his dad would come around before too long. Eli said he hopes his dad will have changed his mind by summer break.

"If he hasn't," Eli said to me in a low voice while we huddled on the front steps of the guys' house, "I guess I'll just go back as Elizabeth. I've done it every other year."

Eli said it like it was no big deal, but I could hear the quiver in his voice. By summer he'll have been on testosterone long enough to look really different. He'll have facial hair, like Derek.

Eli's a guy. Through and through. To have to put on a dress and pretend to be someone he's not…hell, I can't even imagine. It makes me want to fly to Korea and grab his dad by the shoulders and shake him until his teeth rattle.

But Eli's sitting across from me at the table now with a grin bright enough to blind someone. So I grin back at him. If he's happy, I'll be happy for him.

Today everybody's grinning. Finals still feel far away, but friends are close.

We're almost done eating, and Derek's in the middle of a story about how Shari, the hyper blond from the UBA, once tried to recruit people to volunteer at a "postfeminist sex-positive antiharassment bikini carwash, for charity," and everybody's howling with laughter, when our waitress comes over and calls out to the table at large, "Can I get you ladies any coffee?"

The laughter cuts out all at once.

Derek opens his mouth, then closes it. Andy blinks up at the waitress as if he isn't sure he understood her. Eli just stares down at his empty plate.

The waitress knows she did something wrong. She's backing away, an apology on her lips, when Nance speaks up.

"My friends are *guys*," she says. "Get it? Not *ladies*."

"Oh, I'm so sorry," the waitress stammers. "I didn't mean anything, I was only—"

"I know you didn't mean to," Nance says. "Just be more careful from now on. You can't go around making assumptions like that. It's not up to you to decide who people are."

The waitress leaves without waiting to hear if we want coffee.

None of us does anyway. Not after that. Nance pays the check (the waitress gave us the dessert for free, thanks to Nance's guilt trip) and we walk toward the train to go home. Ahead of me, I can see Derek's shoulders slouching. Eli hasn't said a word since the waitress left.

No one suggests we go anywhere else. We've already wasted too much precious studying time, and none of us feels like trying to have fun anymore.

Next to me, Eli takes halting, shuffling steps. I think about clapping him on the back, but if it were me, that would only make me feel worse.

Wait. *Is* it me?

How the hell should I know?

I remember what Nance told the waitress. *It's not up to you to decide who people are.*

I stop walking.

"Hey, I have to go, actually," I say. I hold out my hand for a cab.

"Uh, yeah, we know," Nance says. "We're all going. That's why we're getting on the train."

"No, I have to go to DC. I have to talk to my mom. I have to tell her something."

Everyone stops walking. They stare at me.

"Your mom?" Derek says. "What, right now? Um, maybe you should stop and think about this."

"I don't need to," I say. "I've got to do this now."

"Do *what*?" Derek asks. "T, this is insane. You can't make this decision just like that."

"It's Reading Period," Nance says. "You have too much work to go to DC. Besides, you'll be back there in a week. You can talk to your mom then."

"I'll be fine," I say. A cab pulls up. I tell the driver, "I'm going to Logan."

The driver nods, and I open the back door.

"You're going straight to the airport?" Inez asks. "Shouldn't you at least go to the dorm first and get some stuff?"

"Yeah, and on the way, we can talk this through," Derek says. "Trust me, this isn't something you want to decide on a whim."

"I don't need anything from the dorm," I say. "I already have my wallet and my phone. I'll see you guys later."

"Tony, look, I'm begging you. This is a huge thing you're doing. What are you even going to *tell* her, exactly? You're still figuring yourself out. Please, just think about this, because you really don't want to—"

The cab pulls away before I can hear what Derek thinks I really don't want to do.

It doesn't matter what Derek thinks. It isn't up to anyone else to decide who I'm going to be.


My plan was to take a cab from the airport to my parents' house. But I called Audrey while I was waiting for my flight to board, and Audrey called Dad, and Dad called his secretary, and his secretary called a car service. So when I come through airport security at BWI, the first thing I see is a bored guy holding a white sign that says Miss Antonia Fasseau.

I don't like car service drivers. Cabdrivers don't give a crap about you and will do what you ask as long as you pay them, but car service drivers have a schedule. You can't ask them to drive around the block twenty times while you make up your mind about whether you really want to go inside.

So when the car stops outside my parents' house, I have no choice but to step out onto the curb and gaze at the house I grew up in. It doesn't feel like home anymore. If it ever did.

It's the middle of the afternoon. No one will be home except Consuela and my mother. Mom is home most days unless she's out doing her "volunteer" work. Or shopping. Mainly the latter.

Consuela opens the front door when I knock. I can tell from the look on her face that Audrey called the house, too.

"It's wonderful to see you!" Consuela says. "Such a surprise. I already made up your bed."

"Thanks! It's great to see you, too." She hugs me, and I hug her back. I'm still getting used to how hugging feels. "I'm not sleeping over, though. I'm flying back tonight. Where's Mom?"

Consuela steps back and points wordlessly toward the kitchen. I shed my coat on the bench in the entryway as I go. It's so strange how different the house looks now that I'm not used to seeing it every single day. It was like this at Thanksgiving, too. The place is still huge, like always, but somehow it looks smaller than before. The kitchen counter-tops look like they're slightly askew. The stainless steel appliances are so shiny they look fake.

I don't see Mom. I reach into the fridge for a soda and wander to the sink so I can gaze out the window. I'm unscrewing the bottle cap when I hear her voice. It sounds as though she's in the den just down the hall.

"No, I don't know why she's coming here," Mom is saying. "You know no one tells me anything. That girl won't say two words to me if I don't pry them out of her. Neither of them will."

She's talking about me. And Audrey, too. This is so weird.

"No, I don't know if she's all right." Mom sighs. It sounds like she's on the phone. "I hope she is. I don't know how to—no, no, please don't speak to me that way." She pauses. "Robert, I have asked you before not to speak to me that way."

She's talking to Dad.

I don't want to be hearing this. I back away toward the opposite end of the kitchen, moving slowly, trying to stay silent.

My sneaker squeaks on the tile. Crap crap crap. My heart is pounding.

Seconds later, my mother appears in the doorway, the phone hanging silently in her hand. She stares at me without speaking for a moment.

"Did that idiot driver leave your bags in the trunk?" she finally asks. "Consuela, call Mr. Fasseau's office and have the car sent back."

I hadn't realized Consuela was in here, but when I turn, she's just ten feet back, reaching for the kitchen phone.

"No, don't call." I take a gulp of soda. It goes down the wrong way, making me grimace. "I didn't bring any bags."

"I was afraid of that." Mom glances at Consuela, who hurries out of the room. "When I heard you were coming I knew it had to be the sort of rash, impulsive decision you've made before. Did you drop out of school?"

"No!" And she wonders why I don't want to talk to her. "Of course not."

"Then why show up here out of the blue? Are you failing?"

"Failing? No. Why would I be failing?"

"Maybe if you hadn't studied for your exams enough."

"We haven't had exams yet. And all I ever do is study."

"When you were here at Thanksgiving, you made it sound like all you did was sit around talking to your new friends."

"Believe it or not, I'm capable of multitasking."

This is how it always is with my mother and me. She makes accusations. I give rude answers.

But I spent the flight down thinking about how I wanted to handle this, and I resolved not to get caught up in our usual sniping. So I bite my lip before I can say any more. I have to talk to my mother like a normal person.

I put my soda down on the counter, walk past her into the formal living room and sit on the couch. It's the good couch. The one you aren't allowed to sit back on because you might mess up the fabric draping.

When we were kids, Audrey and I weren't allowed in this room at all. Every single piece of furniture in here—this couch, the chaise longue, the armchairs, even the tiny "accent tables" that are scattered everywhere—is white. This room was always reserved strictly for cocktail parties and afternoon teas.

While I'm sitting on this couch, there's no risk I'll let my guard down, no matter how far my mother gets under my skin.

"I need to talk to you," I say. "It's important."

Mom sits down on the chaise, as far away from me as she can get.

"I suppose it must be." She looks me up and down, assessing, the way she always does. I arch my back ramrod straight. "Since you appear to have bought a last-minute plane ticket on my credit card to tell me about it."

I doubt Mom has ever looked at her credit card bill in her life. She went with her friends to some spa in Bethesda and paid twelve hundred dollars for a microderm facial the day after Thanksgiving because she needed to "decompress" after the trauma of watching Consuela cook our meal.

"Yes, it is." It would be so easy to snap at her. Instead I launch into the speech I memorized on the plane. "So. I'm sure you've noticed some unusual things about me. The way I used to repeat people's names instead of using pronouns, for example."

"Of course I've noticed the way you talk," she says. "So has everyone else. You sound like a foreign exchange student. I've always told people it's part of your general obstinacy."

*Why do you hate me?*

I don't ask it out loud, but I want to. I've wanted to for years.

Once last year, I asked Gretchen what she thought about it. We were in her basement watching TV. Gretchen was lying with her head on my chest. I was playing with her hair.

"Your mother doesn't hate you," Gretchen said. "She doesn't know how to relate to you. That's all."

"My mother doesn't know how to relate to my sister, either, but Mom doesn't accuse Audrey of being worthless all the time."

"She's never said you're worthless," Gretchen said. "Honestly, I think she just finds you intimidating."

I didn't believe Gretchen at the time. I still don't. The idea is really attractive, though.

My mother doesn't hate me. She just finds me intimidating.

"Well, I talked that way for a reason," I tell her now. "I didn't want to use gendered pronouns because I didn't want to reinforce the binary concept of gender."

"That's absurd."

I've got to say, my mother certainly doesn't sound intimidated.

I shake it off. I close my eyes, throwing out the rest of my speech.

"I'm transgender, Mom." I swallow. "I'm a guy."

The words hang in the air between us.

I take a long, uneven breath. There's no turning back from this.

I open my eyes in time to see Mom jump up off the chaise.

She stands up, staring down at me. She doesn't blink. I can see the whites around her irises.

For a second I honestly think she's going to hit me.

Instead she turns around and walks into the kitchen, her footsteps steady, as if she's going to retrieve a plate of appetizers.

Am I supposed to follow her? I don't know the rules here. I didn't get a chance to brush up on any suggested coming-out guidelines. My phone battery died while I was waiting to leave the airport in Boston. Soon after the twentieth text from Derek came in, begging me not to do what I was doing.

So I sit on the couch, growing stiffer and more frantic by the second.

Did I seriously just tell my mother what I think I did?

The clock over the fireplace says three minutes have passed when Mom comes back into the room. Her hand is shaking.

She's holding a cigarette. I never knew she smoked.

I start to say something, but she holds up her other hand, palm facing out. That was how she used to order Audrey and me to be quiet when we were little. It works now, too.

"You are eighteen years old," she finally says, after a couple of puffs of smoke. "You don't know what it means to be a woman yet. You have no idea what it means to be a man."

"I know how I feel," I say. "I've felt this way for as long as I can remember. The best word to describe me is *genderqueer*, I think. I've tried a few others, but none of them feel quite—"

Mom interrupts me.

"You're confused," she says. "This is the sort of phase teenagers go through. It'll pass as you mature."

Right.

My mother has honed this skill over the years. She tries to think of the one thing she can say that will hurt me the most. I usually try not to give her the satisfaction of reacting, but I usually fail.

"Oh," I say. "Okay, then. Thanks. How silly of me to mistake my little phase for a set of complex emotions I've been sorting through for my entire life. Now that you put it that way, I see that you're absolutely right. I'm just 'confused.'"

So much for being civilized about this.

It's that word. *Phase*. Is there a crueler word in the English language?

Why do words have so much damn power over me? Over all of us?

"That's enough," she says. "I'm sick of the way you always get smart with me."

I hate that expression, too. *Get smart*. As if she'd prefer I were stupid.

Maybe she would. A stupid child over a deviant one.

"I'm not the only one who's this way," I say. "There are thousands and thousands of people in the world who identify as a gender other than the one they were assigned at birth."

"You weren't *assigned* any gender at birth," Mom says. "It's not as though we picked it out of a hat, for heaven's sake. You were a girl when you were born and you're a girl now. Thousands of other people may be freaks, but that doesn't mean you need to be one, too."

Wow. Maybe there's a harsher word than *phase*.

My first instinct is to walk out the front door, find a cab and go back to the airport. Instead I grip the arm of the couch, the Italian silk upholstery wrinkling between my fingers.

"It wasn't easy for me to come here and tell you this," I say. "I knew you'd react this way."

"Believe it or not, I'm trying to cope with this without flying off the handle," Mom says.

She's right. I don't believe it.

"What you have to realize, Antonia," she continues, "is that no mother dreams her little girl will grow up and decide she wants to be a little boy."

"It isn't a decision. It's—"

"I know, I know, it's not a choice, et cetera, et cetera. We went through all this back when you were just becoming a lesbian."

Ah, the good old days.

"The fact is," she says, "I didn't see it that way then, and I don't see it that way now."

"Then I won't try to argue with you," I say. "Look, you don't have to be happy about this, but you could at least take me seriously. This isn't a phase. I'm eighteen years old. I'm an adult now, and this is my life."

She puts out her cigarette and draws another from the pack in her pocket. Her hands are still shaking.

"All right, then. Since you're such an independent adult now, what is it you want to do, exactly? Have a sex-change operation?" She says the last part with a laugh, as if she's saying "fly to Neptune."

"The first step is taking hormones," I say. "That's as far as I want to go for now."

Wait. Where did that come from? When did I decide that?

Well, where did it come from when I told her I was a straight-up *guy*? When did I figure *that* out?

Jesus Christ, am I making this all up as I go along?

"Well," my mother says, "if you expect your father and me to pay for you to take drugs to support this ludicrous idea, you're—"

"I don't *expect* you to do anything," I say. "You asked me a question, and I answered you."

"All right. Then give me your credit card."

"What?" This had definitely not factored into my re-hearsals.

She holds out her hand. Oh, my God.

I fumble in my wallet and pull out my Visa card.

"Your ATM card, too," she says.

"What? How am I supposed to buy food and books and stuff?"

"You have a meal plan. We'll have your books shipped to you."

My throat closes. "You're not serious."

"It's time you learned your decisions have consequences. If you're so determined to do this, we won't subsidize it. You'll have to find a way to pay for it yourself."

She's giving me an ultimatum.

It isn't too late to change my mind. I'm still not entirely sure I even made it up yet.

No. Screw this. Screw her. I can borrow money from my friends for a while. Then I'll…get a job, or something.

But how am I going to get to Oxford this summer? What part-time job will pay my rent and airfare and work around my class schedule and—

I'll deal with it later. I'll figure everything out later.

I hand her my ATM card. Blood pulses in my veins. I'm hyperalert of the heat pumping through the ceiling vents, whooshing past my face. It's hard to breathe. How will I even get back to Boston tonight?

Never mind.

"All right." I stand up. "I've said what I came here for. I'm going home."

Mom stands up, too. She folds her arms across her chest and turns to stare at the clock over the fireplace. It's huge, three feet across, with a white-and-gold frame and giant black hands. It's supposed to look like it's hundreds of years old, but actually, Mom ordered it from some website when I was in fourth grade.

She stares at the clock, drumming her fingers against her elbows. The cigarette is burning down to nothing in her hand, but she doesn't put it down. There are no ashtrays in this perfectly manufactured room.

"Toni," she says, still looking at the clock. Huh. She usually calls me *Antonia*. "Listen. It doesn't have to be this way."

She slowly bends down and lays my two cards on the coffee table. Like an offering.

"You're the one making it this way," I say. I watch her carefully.

"I don't see why you can't just keep being like this." She doesn't meet my eye, but she nods toward my ambiguous button-down shirt and jeans. I traded my binder for a sports

bra from a shop in the airport. I thought that might make
her freak out a little less. I stuffed the binder in the airport
gift bag and hoped she wouldn't notice the way it bulged
out of my back pocket, but my mother notices everything.

"There's no reason for you to tell people you're a boy," she
says. "If you really think you feel that way, I don't see why
you can't keep it to yourself."

Ah. I didn't say a word about telling anyone else, but I
should've known that's exactly where her mind would go.

"Who are you worried about me telling?" I ask. "You
don't even know anyone at Harvard anymore."

"Your father has contacts in the alumni associations. Word
spreads fast about this sort of thing."

Right. She's worried about the neighbors.

And Dad's coworkers. And the people at the snooty Catholic church we go to every Christmas and Easter. And the
Republican congressmen who come to our catered May Day
barbecue every year.

"The way you are now, everyone thinks—well, they used
to see you as a tomboy." My mother runs a hand over her
perfectly waved hair. "When you were younger, it was cute.
Even your father and I thought so. That's how you got your
nickname, you know. We'd meant to call you Annie, but
when you were three, you insisted on going to church in
slacks. Your father was the one who started calling you Toni."

I don't answer. I'm too stunned. I'd never known any of
this before.

"You're too old now to be a tomboy," she goes on. Her
cigarette is trembling where it dangles from the tips of her
fingers. "I don't like the way you dress or the way you talk,

but at least our circle here is used to it. For you to take this farther because your new friends have planted some ideas in your head, however, is selfish and shortsighted. Even if you won't think of how your behavior reflects on your father and I, you should at least care about what the community thinks of you. You're getting a good education. You're interested in politics. You could do well someday. Do you want to be known as a laughingstock in this city for the rest of your life?"

I swallow. I wish I thought what she was saying was completely ludicrous. I wish I couldn't see her point.

I *do* want to work in politics someday. But you don't see a lot of trans people on MSNBC.

"I don't care what people think," I say, shaking that off. "I need to tell the truth about who I am."

She sighs. "When, exactly, did you decide this?"

Does she know? Can she sense, somehow, that I'm still deciding it right now, as I stand here?

No. That isn't what she's asking. She doesn't want the details of when I went from cisgender to genderqueer to gender variant to wherever the hell I am right now.

She just wants to know when I started to hate wearing dresses.

"I told you," I say. "I've always known."

She nods slowly and looks back at the clock. "Is it because of something I did?"

I want to say yes. To say she raised me wrong. To hurt her back like she hurt me.

"No," I say. "I've always been like this. When I was a kid

I used to lie in bed at night and pray that when I woke up in the morning, I'd be a boy."

I have to swallow more stale, heated air before I can keep going.

I'd forgotten all about that, but it happened. Oh, my God, that really happened. I never understood what it meant until now.

"When I got old enough to look it up, I found out it's more common than you'd think," I tell her. "I can send you some books—"

"No. Please don't. I do not need *those* kinds of books in this house."

She gets quiet after that.

My credit and ATM cards are still sitting on the coffee table. My mother pointedly looks down at the cards, then back up at the clock.

I pick them up off the table and hesitate, waiting for her to snatch them out of my hand. She doesn't.

I don't want her money. Not after what she said. But the five dollars in my wallet isn't even enough to get me back to Boston for finals.

"Goodbye," I say.

She still doesn't say anything. So I leave.

I bang open the front door and take deep, long gulps of fresh air, my heart slamming in my chest as I walk as fast as I can down the sidewalk. There's a cab stand by the convenience store three blocks away.

*When, exactly, did you decide this?*

I decided it five minutes ago, perched in my mother's stark-white living room.

I decided it when I was twelve years old, the first time I saw myself in the mirror with my hair cut short.

I decided it this afternoon, on the street, outside the restaurant. Because some waitress called my friends and me "ladies."

I don't want anyone to ever call me a "lady" again. That's the only thing I know for sure.

Oh, my God.

This isn't theoretical anymore. This is happening. I can't turn it back.

Is this what I even want? Did I just make a huge mistake?

Yes. I did.

I just told my mother I was a man.

Since when? Three weeks ago I wasn't even using gendered pronouns.

No. Wait. Maybe what I just did wasn't a mistake. Maybe it was the best decision I've ever made.

How the hell am I supposed to know for sure? How does anyone ever know *anything* for sure?

I told my mom I wanted to start hormones. Where did that come from? Sure, I've been thinking about taking testosterone, especially since Eli's T party. Did I at some point subconsciously decide I definitely wanted to do it? Or did I just say that to freak out my mom?

Why is it so hard to understand what's happening inside my own damn *brain*?

I don't know what I want. I don't know how to figure this out. I'm not ready. I'm not ready.

I stop walking. I can hardly breathe. I sit down on the sidewalk and put my head between my knees.

Oh, my God.

Oh, my God.

What the hell did I just do?

Did I just *lie*? And if I did, what am I supposed to do now? Go back in the house and tell my mom, "Whoops, I changed my mind, I'm an idiot, please ignore me?"

*WHAT THE HELL DID I JUST DO?*

I can't do this on my own.

I can't go from point A to point B. I couldn't find either on a map.

I need help. I need someone who knows me better than I know me.

Telling my mother might have been a mistake. I don't know yet.

But I already made another huge mistake this year. I can fix *that*, at least.

I go to the convenience store and get in a cab. When I get to the airport, I go straight to the US Airways counter and change my flight.

Then I get on the next shuttle to New York.

# 18

## GRETCHEN

My phone buzzes.

I don't look up. I'm in the groove.

It's ten-thirty on a Monday night. My middle school debate team has their final competition this week, so I'll be spending all day tomorrow in Inwood helping them get ready. I'm going over the kids' speeches now. They're actually really good—for a bunch of seventh graders who rolled their eyes at me when I first said the word *research* to them back in September, they've done a ton of work and put together some really cool arguments—but they still need help. I'm trying to figure out how to explain gently that they shouldn't make references to Disney movies in a speech about climate change, no matter how well they think the movie plot works as a metaphor for international environmental policy, when my phone buzzes again.

At first I ignore it, but then Samantha yells from across the room, "Gretchen, if you don't check your daggone phone, I'll throw my daggone computer at your daggone head!" So I check my phone.

At first I think I'm reading it wrong. The From line says Schnookums. That was how I programmed Toni's name into my phone more than two years ago.

I haven't gotten a text from Toni since Thanksgiving. Even if Toni did text me, there's no reason Toni would say:

I'm downstairs, come get me?

But that's what this text says.

I show it to Samantha to make sure.

"Yes, that's what it says," she snaps. Sam is writing a paper, but she isn't enjoying her work as much as I am. "Your girl-friend is downstairs. Go get her before she texts again."

"My girlfriend can't be downstairs. I don't have a girl-friend."

"Okay, well, unless someone stole her phone and is play-ing an incredibly lame joke, you'd better go down. Just don't bring her back up here. I don't have time for lesbian drama."

I'm on the elevator, still looking down at the text to make sure I didn't imagine it, when someone shouts, "Could you hold it?"

I stick my hand out. The door bounces back open.

Carroll's standing on the other side.

For a split second I start to smile. I want to tell him what's going on. He'd appreciate the oddity of this moment.

It would be so easy. He'd sidle in next to me in the elevator as if we were going to grab a snack. I'd tell him about Toni, he'd chuckle and things would be normal, just for a second.

Except they can't be. "Normal" between Carroll and me means something else now. Because he can't deal with what happened. And that's his problem, not mine.

No one can be perfect all the time. I deserve friends who don't expect the impossible from me.

Carroll's still standing outside the elevator doors, staring. His face has gone completely white.

Then he backs up until he's against the wall. "Never mind. I'll take the next one."

I let the door close.

I don't regret it, either, as I drop the fourteen floors to the lobby. Maybe by senior year, Carroll will have grown up enough to forgive me. I'm not going to wait around, though. I have more important things to do.

By the time I get to the lobby, all I can think about is Toni's text. I still halfway think it has to be a mistake. Then I spot the Red Sox baseball cap sticking out like a beacon in the sea of black North Face coats.

Tons of people are moving around. Talking, laughing. Coming in, going out. In the middle of it all, there's Toni, absolutely motionless.

I blink about twenty times. I shake my head and look again. Toni's still there.

Then Toni's walking over. It's like we're in slow motion.

The security desk is between us. Toni can't come any farther without being signed in as a visitor. I don't know if I'm supposed to do that or not. I blink some more.

Toni blinks back at me. "What did you do to your hair?"

The spell breaks.

"Oh, right." My fingers twitch as I tug on a few black strands. I don't know if it's from nervousness or the three bottles of Diet Coke I've had tonight. "That. I was in a mood. Don't worry, I'll get it fixed when we go home for break. Sam says they'll have to use some serious industrial-strength bleach, but whatever."

Toni nods. "Can I come in?"

For a second I almost say no. Then I come back to myself. "Yeah, yeah, of course."

We sign in at the desk and Toni comes through to my side. We don't kiss. We don't hug. We don't touch at all. It's so, so strange. It's like Toni's someone I used to know from camp instead of the great love of my life.

I take Toni to the basement where we rehearsed Carroll's coming-out scene a million years ago. I can't think of anywhere else we could talk alone.

And I can tell Toni wants to talk. That's a good thing, because I want to talk, too.

"So, uh." I gaze around the basement, but there's no one else here except the trash-compactor smells. My fingers itch to touch Toni. I clasp my hands behind my back. "I didn't know you were coming to New York."

"Yeah, me, neither."

Toni sits down on the ratty couch. I lean against the wall opposite. Toni's hands are shaking.

This whole scene feels way too much like that night by the fountain. There's no way Toni came here to break up with me *again*, is there?

"I made a huge mistake at Thanksgiving," Toni says. I stop breathing. "I'm so sorry. I can't believe I ever thought those things, let alone said them. It must've been temporary insanity. I wish I could take it all back, but I know I can't, so can we please just pretend it never happened?"

I close my eyes and savor this feeling.

I can smell the dank basement scent. I can feel the cinder block wall digging into my back. I can hear the hum of the industrial radiator. That's how I know this isn't a dream.

Toni's really here. Toni's really saying this.

I open my eyes and sit next to Toni on the couch. My arms slide around Toni's shoulders. Toni's hands move to my back, my waist. Finally. *Finally.*

"Yeah," I say. "We definitely can."

We kiss. Oh, oh, we kiss.

Ten minutes ago I was upstairs thinking about climate change while Samantha banged on her computer keys behind me. Now I'm here. Kissing Toni.

I can pretend Thanksgiving didn't happen. Pretend the past few weeks didn't feel the way they felt. We can move on with our lives, together, the way I always wanted us to.

I hadn't wanted to let myself hope this moment would come. But it did.

"I came out to my mom," Toni says when we stop kissing.

I feel it like a jolt. The spell has broken a second time.

"Are you serious?" I ask. "When?"

"This afternoon."

"Wow." I'm not sure what to think about that, but I guess it doesn't matter. I'm back to being the supportive girlfriend. I squeeze Toni's shoulder. "What, on the phone?"

"No, I went to DC."

"Wow," I say again. This doesn't even sound real, but I can tell it is from Toni's face. "What happened?"

"She smoked a cigarette in front of me. I never knew she smoked."

"What did she say?"

"She threatened to take my credit card away, but then she didn't really do it. She was extremely pissed, though. I'm sure the real explosion is coming at winter break."

"Wow." I shake my head. This seems impossible. I didn't even know this was happening until it was over. "Congratulations. I can't believe you really did it."

"Me, neither. I just decided to do it at lunch today, actually."

"Lunch…in Boston?"

Toni nods.

"Wow." I look at my watch. "It's eleven p.m. You've had a busy day."

"Yeah. Doing a lot of stuff I should've done a long time ago."

I smile and kiss Toni on the cheek, just because I can. "Um, can I ask you a question?"

"Of course."

"Do you know you've said the words *she* and *her* about twenty times so far?"

"Yeah, that." Toni nods. "I decided I'm tired of letting language have so much power over me. I'm sick of worrying about labels. I started using gendered pronouns when I went to London and then I sort of never stopped. I presented as male over there, too. I've even started spelling my name with a *y*. And using *he* and *him* pronouns full-time."

"Oh." The jolts are coming faster and faster. I can't believe all this has happened, and Toni—Tony—never told me. I know we were on our stupid break, but it still doesn't feel right. "What was that like?"

"It was amazing, actually. Audrey had a little minimeltdown while we were there, though."

"Oh, poor Audrey."

"Yeah. She's okay now. Just needed some time to adjust."

I'll have to call Audrey soon. Make sure she really is okay.

"What exactly did you tell your mom?" I ask.

Tony's smile falters. "Well. Actually, that's the problem. I kind of told her I'm going to transition. Start on testosterone sometime soon."

Another jolt. "Oh. I didn't know you'd decided that."

Toni shakes Toni's head. No, *Tony* shakes *his* head.

"I kind of didn't actually decide that," he says. "But I told her I did. It just sort of came out."

"*What?*" I don't see how that's possible. "What happened?"

"I don't know." Tony bites his lip. I sit back and take a closer look at him. He actually looks kind of miserable.

God, it's so hard to think of Toni as Tony. As *him*.

"I'm actually kind of incredibly freaked out about it," Tony says. "I don't know what I'm supposed to do now. I need your help."

"Sure, of course," I say.

I don't know how I can help with this, though.

I can handle the name change. I can handle the pronouns. Tony seems to be handling those things just fine, too.

But he flew down to Maryland and told his mom he's going to transition to male—just on a crazy whim, apparently—and somehow *I'm* supposed to fix this problem?

"Why did you say that if you didn't mean it?" I ask.

"I don't know." Tony slumps down on the couch. "Maybe on some level I *did* mean it? I don't know for sure. That's the whole problem."

Holy crap.

"Um," I say. "I'm not sure I can actually help with that. It sounds like you just need to think this through. Maybe, with. Um. A therapist?"

Tony's eyes flash with something that doesn't look like affection, but it fades as quickly as it appeared. So quickly I probably imagined it. "I don't want to talk to a therapist. I want to talk to my girlfriend."

Three weeks ago I wanted nothing more than to hear Toni use that word for me.

No, not Toni. Tony.

I replay that word in my head. *Girlfriend.* I'm somebody's girlfriend again. God, it feels so good.

"Anyway, we can talk about this later," he says. "How have *you* been? It's so weird that we haven't talked in so long. I've missed you so much. Even though your hair is still freaking me out."

I smile and lean my head on Tony's shoulder. He squeezes my hand. For a second it's like we're back the way we used to be. Like we're in high school again. Like I can tell Tony what's bothering me, and Tony will make me feel better.

Him. I can tell *him* what's bothering me.

That's going to be so hard to get used to.

"I've been okay," I say. "Except Carroll and I aren't friends anymore. That's been hard."

I choke up on the last part. Tony runs his fingers over the inside of my wrist. It feels so nice. "What happened?"

"Well." I hesitate, but there's no point holding this back. I don't want to keep secrets from Tony now that we're finally talking again. "We actually got drunk and wound up having sex last week, and he's having, you know, issues."

Tony lets go of my hand and jumps up.

I fall back on the couch. My heart flutters.

"You did *what*?" Tony asks.

"It was after Thanksgiving," I say because Tony looks furious. "Believe me, I know it was a dumb thing to do."

"You had *sex*?"

"Yeah." I can feel my face turning red. I don't want it to. I don't want to feel ashamed.

"Carroll's a *guy*," Tony says.

"So?"

"*So?*" Tony's pacing now. "That's not—it isn't—he's so *pathetic*—"

I stand up, too. My calm from before is gone. "You broke up with *me*, remember? You don't get to be angry about this."

"I'm not angry." Tony's fists are clenching the way they do whenever Mrs. Fasseau is in the room. "I'm just shocked. He's a *guy*. You're *gay*, remember?"

"I thought you were sick of labels. Whatever happened to revolting against the gender binary?"

Maybe that was mean of me, but I'm not going to feel bad for saying it. Tony's being mean, too.

Tony sits back down, breathing heavily.

"Fine," he says. "Fine. It's fine. Whatever."

I watch Tony's chest rise and fall—under a binder, of course—and suddenly this all feels so familiar.

It feels like it did that day back in August. When I took Tony to the swing set near my house and told the truth about going to NYU.

Tony sat down, breathing just as hard as he is now, saying, "Fine, fine, it's fine." The same way he just said it.

Tony was lying then. And he's lying now.

"You don't think it's fine," I say. "Don't lie to me."

"Oh, because you've never lied to me." Tony's breaths are coming faster now.

"You're mad at me," I say. "Just say it."

Tony shakes his head. "It doesn't matter. Whatever this thing was, I'll pretend it never happened. The past is the past and it can stay there."

I was ready to agree to that plan a few minutes ago. Now I'm not so sure.

"What's the point of pretending?" I ask.

Tony glares at me. "The alternative is for me to keep being pissed about this. Is that what you want?"

"I'm not allowed to have an opinion about what you do," I say. "How come it doesn't work the other way around?"

Tony jumps up again. I stay where I am.

"What do you mean, 'what I do'?" Tony asks. "Are you talking about what I *think* you're talking about? I'm going through something huge and life-changing, not experimenting like a little kid."

"Oh, so *I'm* acting like a little kid? I'm not the one flying all over the East Coast, coming out to people when I'm not even sure I mean what I'm saying!"

Tony stares at me. I stare right back.

"I'm not—" Tony swallows. "Look, I know you can't understand what I'm dealing with, but this is the person I am."

"I *want* to understand," I say. "But you hardly even talk to me about it. You only want to talk to your other friends."

Tony drops his head. I can't tell if he's angry at me or if he's about to cry.

"My other friends understand already." His voice is quieter. "That's why I want to talk to them about this stuff. They just *get* it, and…"

And I don't.

"I know," I murmur. I try to slow down. To think about every word before I say it. "I've been trying to understand, when you let me. The thing is, *I'm* a person, too. I have friends and a life apart from you. That's why I came to this school. To start making decisions for myself. That means sometimes I'm going to do stuff you're not going to like."

Our eyes are locked. We've never talked like this before. It's kind of scary.

But I have to keep going.

"I used to think I'd done something wrong," I say. "It turns out all I was doing was being me. Sorry, but that's how it is. Who I am."

Tony sits back down. "You're not really sorry."

"I'm not sorry I'm not your perfect girlfriend who always says the right thing and who you can show off to your friends, if that's what you mean."

"You are my perfect girlfriend." Tony's voice is soft. "You were anyway."

"Maybe in your head," I say. "Being perfect in real life is way too hard."

Tony stares down at his feet. "I thought you could help me."

"You thought I was going to make everything better?" I shake my head. "I can't make everything better for *me*. I don't have the first clue how to do it for you. The thing is, though, you don't need me to. You can do this on your own. You *have* to. No one can figure this out but you."

There's something glistening in Tony's eyes. I can't tell if it's tears or anger. Maybe both.

"I'm not going to apologize for what happened with Carroll, either," I say. "It was stupid, yeah, but I didn't do anything wrong. We said we were going to see other people."

Tony looks at the floor. All I can see now is the back of his head.

"I just can't believe it," he says. "I get what you're saying about it not being officially against the rules or anything, but it just feels like this huge gut punch. It's not even that he's a

guy. It never crossed my mind that you actually would've—
I thought you'd—"

Tony trails off. That's when I figure it out.

Tony said that stuff about how we should go out with
other people, but it never crossed Tony's mind that I might
actually do it.

He thought I'd just sit around, waiting, while he figured
everything out for the both of us. Like Penelope in the stupid *Odyssey*, weaving her damn tapestry and waiting for her
hero to save the day.

Maybe that's sort of what I *was* doing. With the freaking
out and getting drunk and making a fool of myself. I was
keeping myself busy while I…waited.

Tony even said that, back at Thanksgiving. That he didn't
want me to be stuck waiting around. I should've listened.

I don't want to be Penelope.

I thought we knew everything about each other. Maybe
that was true once, but something's changed. I've changed,
and so has Toni. Tony.

I don't want to go back. I don't want Tony to go back,
either.

"Do you know why I came here instead of Boston?" I ask.

Tony stares at the wall behind me. "I think so, but I want
to hear it from you."

"Okay." I look down at my hands. "It was because I
wanted to see what it was like to just be me. You know?
Not half of me-and-you. We'd been together for so long,
I'd forgotten."

Tony blinks. His eyes are definitely wet. "I never wanted
that. To see what it was like without you."

"You were always you, though." This is so hard to explain, but it seems so important that I try. So essential that he understands this. "You never seemed like you lost yourself. Even back home, in high school, everyone always saw you as just Toni. You knew who you were. You have this confidence about yourself that I've always been jealous of. I needed to figure out who I was, too."

Tony dabs at his eye. "So, what did you figure out?"

"I don't know." I shake my head. Tears dribble down my chin. "I've still got a long way to go. I just think it's important that I keep doing it."

Tony nods slowly. "Okay."

"I love you," I say. For the last time.

Tony leans back on the couch, staring up at the ceiling. "I love you, too."

I sit down. Tony squeezes my fingers. I bring Tony's hand up to my face and kiss it.

I'll miss this. So much.

"Did I tell you about when Chris came to visit me for the football game?" Tony asks.

"A little."

"We talked about you."

"Yeah?"

"I told him I loved you, and I didn't want you to ever be with anyone but me."

I smile. "Yeah?"

"I said I didn't know if loving someone and not wanting them to be with anyone else was enough of a reason to stay together, when I was too obsessed with my own issues to even be honest with you. Or to listen to you the way I should."

"That sounds very…mature, actually."

"Chris called me an idiot."

"Yeah, well. I'm not saying he's wrong."

Tony smiles. "He also said I'd never find anyone else like you."

"That's not true at all."

"You think? I'm pretty sure it is, actually. You've always been way too good for me."

"Tony. Be serious."

"I am serious."

I look down at our intertwined fingers.

It isn't like that night at the fountain. That night I felt as though I was sinking into an abyss. This time it feels like, even if I'm drowning right now, I'll still be alive tomorrow. Part of me is going away, but there are other parts that will keep going.

"So this is it," I say.

Tony squeezes my hand. "It doesn't have to be."

"Are you saying it's up to me?"

"I think I am, yeah. I think I trust you with this decision more than I trust myself."

I smile, but I'm not happy.

I reach in my pocket and pull out the top hat charm I've been carrying since Thanksgiving. I look at it for the last time. It's been worn down over the months. It's not shiny anymore.

"I still love this," I say. I smile and slide it into Tony's palm.

"Then keep it." Tony puts it back in mine and folds my hand closed. The metal is warm against my skin.

We sit there for another hour, not talking. At midnight, Tony stands up, leans over, and kisses me silently on the forehead.

We don't say goodbye.

AUGUST
SUMMER BEFORE SOPHOMORE YEAR OF COLLEGE
8 MONTHS APART

## TONY

She's not going to know it's me.

The phone rings once, twice, three times. She doesn't pick up.

Of course not. She wouldn't recognize this number.

This isn't going to work. It was a stupid idea.

The phone clicks.

Oh, God. Oh, God. Maybe I should hang up. What if *she* hangs up once she hears it's me?

"Hi?" she says.

It's her. It's Gretchen. I haven't heard her voice since— oh, God.

She sounds just the same. She sounds happy. She sounds beautiful. You wouldn't think you could hear *beautiful* over the phone, but you can.

"Hi," I say. It comes out as a squeak.

"Stacey?" she says. "Is that you?"

Who the hell is Stacey?

"Who the hell is Stacey?" Crap. I didn't mean to say that out loud.

Gretchen sucks in a breath. Oh, hell. Calling her was the worst idea I've ever had.

"Tony?" Her voice is low. Almost a whisper. "Is it—hi. Is it you?"

"It's me." I swallow. "Do you—should I hang up? It's okay. I'm sorry. I should've texted first. I—I'm sorry."

"Don't be sorry!" She laughs. God, I've missed her laugh. The sound always makes me think of that first night at Homecoming. Her blue-painted toes dancing over the polished wooden floor. "It's so amazing to hear your voice. I've—I mean. I missed you. That's okay to say, right?"

I laugh, too. "I hope so. I've missed you so much."

"All summer, it's been so hard, you know?" Her voice still sounds light and happy, but there are pauses between her words, as if she's thinking hard about what to say. "Being around all our old friends and everything in DC, and you not being here. I've seen Audrey, like, twenty times, but not you."

I know Gretchen isn't trying to make me feel guilty, but I do. Only kind of, though. Going to Oxford was the best thing I could've done. My job was amazing, and being in a different country was even better. No one knew me. No one expected me to be anything except who I felt like being. "Was it a good summer, though?"

"Well." I might be imagining it, but it sounds like Gretchen feels a little guilty, too. "Actually, yeah. I joined this pickup volleyball team that plays on the mall after work. The people are really cool. Plus Heidi's in town, so I've been hanging out with her, and one of my professors helped me get this great internship at the Folger."

"Yeah, I heard about that."

"Oh, yeah? You been keeping tabs on me?"

"Er, maybe?"

We both laugh.

"So, who's Stacey?" I ask.

"Oh, nobody. How's Derek and the rest of the crew?"

She's trying to change the subject. I let her. "Derek's great. His surgery went really well. He said he feels fantastic and he bought all new shirts for the fall. He got one with a picture of Dorothy Parker on it that he's really excited about."

She laughs again. "That's great. Did you know Nance and I have been emailing?"

"Yeah. She mentioned."

"She's actually turned out to be pretty cool. She pointed me to some online groups that have really great information."

"Yeah, she told me she was going to do that."

"She also said something about Eli staying in the US over the summer. What's up with that?"

I sigh. "I guess Eli's dad is still having a hard time with things. His mom said he needed more time, so Eli stayed in Boston for the break. It worked out because Andy's mom got him an internship at the last minute, but it's been rough for him."

Gretchen sighs, too. "I bet."

"It could be worse, I guess. At least he didn't have to de-transition to a girl and go back to Korea."

"Yeah. God."

We're both silent for a second. Then Gretchen clears her throat.

"By the way, did Nance also tell you she's trying to set you up with some girl she knows at Wellesley?" she asks. "Because she told me that. I think she was trying to make me jealous."

There's a new strain in Gretchen's voice. I don't answer her. I don't know what to say.

"Also, I guess you heard Chris and Steven are officially done," she goes on, rambling now.

"Oh, yeah," I say. "Thank God. Chris told me he's psyched to go back to school. Apparently there are three different guys on his crew team he can't wait to ask out."

"Really? That's awesome. Good for him. Also, did you hear Renee and Liz got back together? They posted all these pictures of them making goo-goo eyes at each other out at Great Falls."

"Yeah. Renee told me it was supposed to just be a sum-mer fling, but I don't buy that. She sounded way too lovey-dovey."

"Wow," Gretchen says. "Sounds like you've kept up with everything."

I don't respond. There's no way to answer her without bringing up what we're not saying. That we've both spent the summer talking to everyone except each other. That this is the first time Gretchen and I have spoken since December, and it's so hard to say anything that really matters.

There's an awkward silence. "Can I ask you something?"

"Of course," I say.

"Did you ever talk to your mom again? I mean, did you ever tell her…you know."

Did I ever tell my mother the truth, is what Gretchen means.

"Not yet," I say. "I might, at some point, but there's no rush."

"Have you seen her at all?"

"Not since that day. I stayed at Derek's for winter break, and then for the summer I flew straight from Boston to the UK. I just don't have the energy to deal with family stuff. I've got enough to think about without worrying what *she* thinks."

For a moment we're both silent. I can hear Gretchen pulling in a breath. Finally she says, "So, what do *you* think?"

We both know what she's asking.

"Pretty much the same stuff I thought before," I say. "I keep cycling through all the options without ever actually finding answers. I thought for sure I'd have it all figured out by the time this summer started, but now the summer's ending and I'm not any closer than I was the last time I saw you."

"That's all right." Gretchen's voice is soft. "You don't have to have it all figured out yet. You've got your whole life to make sense of it all."

"Yeah, I guess." I feel a dull but familiar twinge of sadness. Gretchen doesn't know what this is like. It's so easy for her to tell me to take my time. She doesn't understand how badly I need to know. How it feels like nothing I do counts until I have it all pinned down. How it's as though everything is on hold until the day I wake up and realize I have all the answers, and I know who I'm supposed to be. I'm a guy, or I'm not. I'm A or I'm B.

Or both. Or…maybe neither.

I hate the idea that we're all controlled by some arbitrary binary system, and yet I'm desperate to find out where I belong in it. Even if my place is somewhere outside the system entirely.

The one thing I have figured out is that labels and pronouns and all of that don't matter. Not unless I let them. As much as I love words and language, they're just human constructs. A word can't define me. Only I can.

And I can't fix all the problems with the English language single-handedly. The one thing I can decide is what I want people to call me.

*He. Him.* That's what I'm using. It doesn't feel perfect. It doesn't mean I definitely think I'm a guy. But out of the options I've got, *he* is the one that feels right. For now, at least.

There's so much behind all of this. So much. But I swallow down my thoughts and smile into the phone. It isn't Gretchen's job to understand everything about me when I can't even do it myself. I've been trying so hard to rely on other people—Gretchen, my friends at school, even my mom—to tell me who they think I should be, but in the end I'm the one who's got to figure it out.

"When I get back to campus, I've got an appointment set up with Derek's therapist." My fingers twitch as I say the words. I know this shouldn't be embarrassing—nearly everyone I know is in some kind of therapy or other—but it still feels like I'm revealing something dark and secret. "Just, you know. So I can talk to someone other than the inside of my own head."

"T, that's fantastic." She sounds so happy, I start to wonder if she thinks there's really something wrong with me. Then I remember that's not how Gretchen works. She sounds happy because she's genuinely happy for me. "I'm so glad you changed your mind. That'll be great."

"Yeah, well, it's a start." I swallow. I'll never forgive myself if I don't say it. "Gretchen, I—I'm sorry. About everything. I was horrible to you."

"What? No, you weren't."

"Yeah, I was. I look back on it and I feel so awful. I was so self-centered that first semester. All year, really. Probably in high school, too. I've always made everything about me and my issues. I never ever even asked you about yours."

"Well, I never asked you much about your stuff, either. I was always scared I'd say the wrong thing and you'd hate me."

I laugh. "Like I could ever hate you. You're perfection embodied in the form of a blond Birkenstock-wearing Brooklynite."

Her laugh is softer. "No, I'm not. You know that, right?"

Yeah, I guess. I put Gretchen up on a shiny pedestal from the first moment I saw her. I'd convinced myself she was the ideal girl for me before I'd even heard her speak.

The funny thing is, I was right. People—even Gretchen—are too complicated to be perfect.

At that moment, though, she was perfect for me. Maybe we were even perfect for each other.

It's so weird, how you can love someone long enough for that love to change. I didn't know love *could* change, but it can. Just like people.

"I think I do," I say.

"Hey, T!" Chris's voice booms in from the kitchen. I swear he's gotten louder since high school. "Are you going to make me eat all these hot dogs by myself? Because I can, but it's not gonna be pretty."

"Who is that?" Gretchen asks. "That sounds like Chris."

"Er. Yeah. It's Chris."

"Wait. Where are you?"

"I'm here." I smile. My shoulders are starting to relax. The tension is flowing out of my body. Gretchen forgave me. "I'm at Chris's house."

"Wait, here? In Maryland?"

"Yeah. I flew in this morning. I'll go back up to Boston tomorrow so I'm staying with Chris tonight."

"Wait." Gretchen's stumbling over her words. "You're *here*?"

"I'm here." I let out a tiny laugh.

Gretchen's laughing, too. "Wait. So I can—can I come over? Can I come see you?"

"That would basically be the most amazing thing ever, yeah. If you want to. I would've told you sooner, but I didn't know if you were still, you know. Mad, or anything."

I hear a jingle of keys on the other end of the phone. "I'm coming right now. I'm getting in the car."

"That's the best news I've heard all summer." I'm not even exaggerating. My grin is so wide, my face hurts.

"Okay, good." I hear a car door open and close. "I have to get off the phone now because I don't have my hands-free thingy. Stay at Chris's house. Do not go *anywhere*, do you hear me?"

I laugh. I'm actually going to see Gretchen again. To be in the same physical space as her. "Wouldn't dream of it."

"Okay, I've got to go. I'll see you soon, though. Bye!"

"Bye," I echo. The phone clicks off.

I stare down at the blank screen. The phone is warm in my hand. I feel more awake than usual. More alive.

I need to go tell Chris she's coming over, but I stay where I am for now, letting my eyes fall closed. It's too much to take in.

This is really happening. Gretchen will be here soon.

I don't know what's going to happen when she gets here. But not knowing is okay.

Actually, the not knowing might be the best part.

★ ★ ★ ★ ★

# ACKNOWLEDGMENTS

Sometimes there are characters you know so well you forget they're fictional, even if you're the one who made them up. That's how I feel about *What We Left Behind*. Toni and Gretchen have been living in a corner of my brain since I first decided I wanted to be a writer. Their story changed and evolved over the years, and so did I. But I never stopped loving them, just as they never stopped loving each other.

I can't quite believe it's time for these two to climb outside my head and live on a printed page, but here we are. And we all had a lot of help getting to this point.

Thank you to Jim McCarthy, agent extraordinaire, who gives wise advice at every turn, and who simply *got* this book and these characters in a way that meant so much.

I'm so grateful to my amazing editor, T. S. Ferguson, who always asks the right questions, from the big ones ("Is there enough closure on this plot thread?") to the little ones ("Are you spelling this *Clueless* reference correctly?") and knows how much every question matters. Thanks, too, to the whole Harlequin team that made this book a reality—Natashya Wilson, Lauren Smulski, Emma Alpern, Emily Krupin, Jennifer Abbots, Lisa Wray, Jennifer Stimson and so many more, plus the UK folks—Anna Baggaley, Elise Windmill and the rest of the fabulous Mira Ink crew.

Thank you to all my amazing writer friends who offered beta-reader notes, moral support and wine-drinking assistance while I worked on this book. Anna-Marie McLemore, aside from being the best Lambda Literary Writers Retreat roommate ever, you were one of the very first people to read this manuscript, and your notes on it helped to make it what it is. Thanks to the DC/environs writer crew—Lindsay Smith (thank you so much for thinking up the awesome title!), Jessica Spotswood, Caroline Richmond, Miranda Kenneally, Andrea Colt, Kathleen Foucart, Tiffany Schmidt and many, many other awesome people—for your notes, your advice, your friendship and your tips on staying sane. And thank you to the Fourteenery and the DC MafYA, aka the coolest kids on the block.

Thanks to Erica George for showing me around and letting me sleep on her futon when I came up for my Harvard research trip, and to Georgiana Konesky, my Harvard beta reader, who told me no one calls it *Wigglesworth* (it's just *Wigg*, you guys). Thanks to Sarah Schrag for letting me steal the croissants story, and to Nadine Heyman and Jennifer Brody for the NYU and Harvard inspiration, and the olden-days fun.

Thanks to my family—Mom, Dad, Mary, Steve, Matthew,

Josh, Aaron and the whole extended clan—for supporting me through this crazy writerly life.

And thank you most of all to Julia, for all of the things. I <3 you.

# Book 1 in the brand-new
## *Well of Souls* series

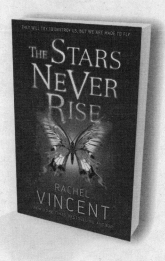

Sixteen-year-old Nina Kane should be worrying about her immortal soul, but she's too busy trying to actually survive. Her town's population has been decimated by soul-consuming demons, and souls are in short supply.

Wanted by the Church and hunted by dark forces, Nina knows she can't survive on her own. She has to put her trust in Finn, a fugitive who just might be an exorcist of the Church…

www.miraink.co.uk

# Book 1 in the brand-new
# THUNDER ROAD SERIES

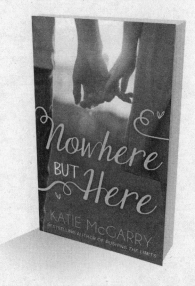

Recently out of high school, Oz is consumed with
the fact that a recent screw-up might cost him
everything. He has one shot at redemption: ensuring
that Emily, daughter of notorious Reign of Terror
motorcycle club member, is kept safe.

But, as forbidden feelings spark to life, Oz and Emily
will face an adversary that threatens not only
their relationship, but their lives…

www.miraink.co.uk

# THE LONG-AWAITED AND FINAL INSTALMENT IN THE WHITE RABBIT CHRONICLES

Ashton 'Frosty' Martin is both elated and despondent when his dead girlfriend Kat comes back as a Witness, with a task for him – to help fellow slayer, Milla – who also happens to be the girl who betrayed them all to Anima Industries, causing Kat's death.

Milla is the last person on Earth Frosty wants to help. But as he learns that Anima have more tricks up their sleeves, he knows that they are all about to be collateral damage again – unless they can find a way to work together and rebuild their trust.

**www.miraink.co.uk**

M426_AMZP

# 'An absolute page-turner.'
## —Cat Clark

Trapped by a raging blizzard, Nash is forced to spend Christmas in the confines of the prestigious Bathory boarding school where she dreams of becoming head girl. But strange things are afoot in the school's hallways and legends of the Beast of Bathory begin to run wild. When the girls' matron goes missing, it's clear that something altogether darker is to blame—and that they'll have to stick together if they hope to survive.

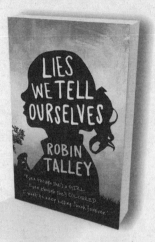